MW01128114

Lacybourne MANOR

GHOSTS AND REINCARNATION SERIES

KRISTEN
NEW YORK TIMES BESTSELLING AUTHOR
ASHLEY

Lacybourne Manor
Kristen Ashley
Published by Kristen Ashley

Interior Design & Formatting by:
Christine Borgford, Type A Formatting
www.typeAformatting.com

Cover Art by:
Pixel Mischief Design

ISBN-13: 978-1540457189
ISBN-10: 1540457184

First ebook edition: August 5, 2011
Latest ebook edition: December, 2016
First print edition: December, 2016

Discover other titles by
KRISTEN ASHLEY

GHOSTS AND REINCARNATION SERIES

Sommersgate House

Lacybourne Manor

Penmort Castle

Fairytale Come Alive

Lucky Stars

DISCOVER ALL OF KRISTEN'S TITLES ON HER WEBSITE AT:

www.kristenashley.net

This book is dedicated to all my good friends at the now, sadly, demolished *Bournville Community Centre* on the Bournville Council Estate in Weston-super-Mare, North Somerset, UK.

Thank you for introducing me to that beautiful country and the wonderful people in it by being so welcoming, so kind, so hilarious and sharing so much with me.

Wish I had a rich hot guy who would have helped us keep the old girl afloat.

I miss you all.

But boy, we had some good times, didn't we?

PROLOGUE

People try to explain magic in a variety of different ways.

They use the excuse of science, miracle, divine intervention, luck, fate and coincidence.

It's all just magic in one form or another.

AND THE PUREST magic is love.

And the purest, *purest* magic is *true* love.

EVERYONE HAS MAGICAL powers.

Some know they do.

Some would never believe.

Some are greater than others.

Some are good and kind and true.

Some are evil and wicked and violent.

And sometimes they all get tangled together.

THIS IS THE story of the purest, *purest* form of magic, *true love.*

It is a story about all kinds of magic, mixed up in a crazy, mystical mess.

ESMERALDA CRANE WAS there when Royce Morgan first laid eyes on Beatrice Godwin.

It was the Year of our Lord, 1522, and even though Esmeralda had already lived a goodly number of years in two centuries, she had never been blessed to witness true love.

He was handsome, a rich, land-owning knight wearing shining spurs. He had thick hair the unusual color of sunshine mixed with honey and eyes the color of the richest, most fertile clay.

She was dark of hair and fair of skin, her hair so dark it was only a shade lighter than black, and her skin so fair it was without blemish except for the freckles that danced across her nose. She had extraordinary hazel eyes. Eyes that could be more green then brown on occasion (with ire, which was a good deal of the time, considering her fiery nature), more brown than green on other occasions (with love or happiness, which was also a good deal of the time, considering her kind heart).

Esmeralda watched their stormy courtship with fascination.

There were times that his personality (which was mostly autocratic, reserved and often cynical) would grate roughly against her personality (which was buoyant, free-spirited and often explosive).

Esmeralda feared both these stubborn souls would never see the magnificent stars in each other's eyes and understand what kind of precious gift they had been given.

As ever, the magic of true love was victorious. Esmeralda should never have doubted it.

Even though Esmeralda wasn't invited, she created a glamor for herself so she could attend Royce and Beatrice's wedding.

One rarely had the honor of witnessing true love in the giddy hours right before its consummation.

But she felt the black soul there that day, dark as midnight. The soul was sitting in the church, as bold as can be, even though lightning should have struck it dead the minute its foot crossed the sacred threshold.

As Royce and Beatrice stood in the front of the church, Esmeralda saw the stars in the lovers' eyes.

Alas, Esmeralda knew those stars were now crossed with darkness.

She hurried from the church before the ceremony was finished, jumped on her sweet-spirited, but not very swift, nag so she could quickly get to her larder. There, she pulled out herbs, incense and oils, all the while muttering to herself. She put all of her efforts, all of her energy, all of her (considerable) power and all of her (even more considerable) magic into a protection charm that would keep the lovers safe.

Once done, exhausted with her efforts, she shrugged off her fatigue and scurried to Lacybourne Manor, frightened that she would be too late.

Nearly to the doors of the grand house, Esmeralda found that she *was* too late.

She came upon the newly-wedded pair outside the house, lying entwined under a copse of trees, the blood from their slit throats now fertilizing the soil around them.

Esmeralda wanted to cry, to scream, to keen into the night all of her despair that their love had not been consummated. The glorious consummation of true love, the like of the love between Royce and Beatrice Morgan, would have protected them like a powerful shield.

The old witch, no matter how tired, was not yet done with magic that night.

She picked up the delicate hand of the fallen Beatrice and saw the flesh and blood beneath the girl's fingernails. The same could be found under the nails of the once mighty knight.

Taking her dagger, she gouged the human particles from beneath the lovers' nails and also collected a dagger blade full of the soil that had absorbed the couple's mingled life blood. Lastly, she pierced the point of the dagger into her finger and squeezed her own blood into her powerful brew.

Working swiftly, the witch mixed the protection charm with a fierce shake. More of her conjuring was muttered, she opened her charm and sprinkled her potion around them.

Forever linking them.

Forever, through eternity, binding them together.

Until one day, many, many years in the future, the stars in the lovers' eyes would uncross.

Esmeralda knew the black soul would hunt them but she prayed that her protection charm and the added power of violence, death and true love would protect them.

The witch knew one day, they would find each other again.

And that day, they would need her.

Chapter ONE

Reincarnated

Marian Byrne stood at the door of Lacybourne Manor smiling at the last tourists that left through the grand entry.

At seventy years old, she'd been a volunteer for The National Trust working at Lacybourne for seven years. She had no idea how long she would be able to continue, her feet were killing her.

Marian was tall, straight, thin as a rail and had the energy of a fifty-year-old (or at the most, a fifty-five-year-old). Her hair was cut short, its curls dyed a peachy red that was *not* old lady peach but a color she, personally, found very becoming.

She was under strict instructions to have all the tourists and their cars and the other flotsam and jetsam cleared from the area before the man of the house came home.

Colin Morgan had inherited Lacybourne just over a year before. His aunt and uncle left no heirs, so upon their untimely death (he of cancer, she of a broken heart, the latter Marian believed although the doctors said differently) the man from London became owner of the grand house with its medieval core.

The old owners were not nearly as demanding as Mr. Colin Morgan. They would often mingle with the tourists and even open some of the private chambers.

Not Colin.

He closed the house all days except Mondays and Tuesdays and allowed it open only one Saturday a month. It was available solely from February through June, which was quite a muddle for The National Trust as that cut out the height of the tourist season and school holidays. And he expected all of the tourists and The National Trust pamphlets and laminated leaflets that lay about the rooms to be locked out of sight by the time he came home.

This would have vastly annoyed Marian, if she hadn't met Colin Morgan.

He was near as the spitting image of the man in the portrait that hung in the Great Hall.

For that reason alone, Marian knew she'd do whatever he required.

The day had turned gusty, the sky already dark with encroaching night. The clouds, long since rolled in, had begun to leak rain.

Marian began to push the heavy front doors closed when she heard a feminine voice in an American accent call, "Oh no! Am I too late?"

Marian peeked out the door just as thunder rent the air and lightning lit the sky, illuminating the woman who stood on the threshold.

Marian couldn't stop herself. She gasped at the sight.

The woman was wearing a scarlet trench coat belted at the waist and her long, thick hair, the color of sunshine liberally dosed with honey, was whipping about her face. She had lifted a hand to hold the tresses back but she wasn't succeeding. The tendrils flew around her face wildly.

"It's so hard to find time to fit Lacybourne in the schedule, it's rarely open," the woman continued as she smiled at Marian.

It was then that Marian realized she'd been holding her breath and she let it out in a gush.

The woman standing before her was the image of the *other* portrait that hung in the Great Hall.

She was not, however, dark-haired, like the lady in the portrait, but rather blonde.

Marian thought that interesting, considering Colin Morgan had the exact visage of the long since murdered owner of this house, except Colin's hair was dark, nearly black, rather than fair.

"I'm afraid you are late, my dear. We close at four thirty, on the dot," Marian informed her lamentably.

The disappointment was evident on her face, Marian could see it by the light shining from the entry. She was pleased at this. She hadn't been volunteering at Lacybourne for seven years without having some pride in the house. It was nice to know this woman on the threshold so desperately wanted inside.

There were other reasons as well that Marian was pleased the woman wanted desperately to be inside.

"Why don't you come back tomorrow?" Marian asked, her voice kind, her face smiling but her mind working.

She was wondering how she could finagle a meeting between the American woman and the man of the house.

For she *had* to find a way to arrange a meeting.

It was, quite simply, Marian Byrne's destiny.

"I can't, I'm working. I couldn't be here until well after it closes. I've been trying to find time to get here since last year."

"What time could you arrive? I know the owner of this house, perhaps, if I explain—"

"No . . . no, please, don't do that. I'll just try to get here next Monday," she offered politely then lifted her hand in a gesture of farewell.

Giving one last, longing look at the house, she started to leave.

Marian rushed her next words in an effort to stall the woman and then she fibbed (for, she knew, a *very* good cause), "He's a lovely man, he won't mind. I'll stay personally to give you a private tour. Or he might like to do so himself, considering how much you wish to see the house."

She'd turned back, hesitating. "I couldn't."

"Oh, you could," Marian moved forward and encouragingly placed her hand on the woman's forearm. "Truly, he won't mind."

That was an outright lie, Colin Morgan would very much mind. But what could she do? She could see the indecision on the other woman's face, Marian *had* to do something.

She forged ahead. "We'll set it at six o'clock, shall we? You can give me your telephone number and I'll phone you if there's a problem. What's your name, my dear?"

"Sibyl," she said, smiling her gratitude so sensationally Marian felt her heart seize at the sight. "Sibyl Godwin."

It was with that announcement that Marian's hand clutched the woman's arm with vigor far beyond her seventy years.

"I'm sorry, what did you say your surname was again?"

The woman was studying her with curiosity and Marian watched the spectacular sight as the hazel in the other woman's eyes melted to the color of sherry as curiosity became concern. Her hand, Marian noted distractedly, had moved to cover the older woman's hand protectively.

"Godwin."

At her single word, Marian couldn't help herself.

She whispered, "Oh my."

"TELL HER, NO," Colin Morgan said into the phone, his rich, deep, baritone voice showing his obvious irritation.

"Mr. Morgan, she's been wanting to see the house for over a year. She's a very busy lady "

"I said no."

"She'll be very disappointed."

Colin attempted to conjure an image of the woman to whom he was speaking. He assumed he'd met her at some point but he couldn't remember. Her voice was strong but it betrayed her age. If it hadn't, he would have told her exactly how little he cared that an unknown American would be disappointed at not having a private evening tour of his home. The very idea was ridiculous.

Instead, he said, "If you would, please remind this woman of the opening hours of the house and request that she visit *during* them."

There was a sigh and if he wasn't mistaken it was a vaguely reprimanding sigh. "Very well, Mr. Morgan."

"Thank you, Mrs. Byrne."

For the life of him, he had no idea why he was thanking the older woman for annoying him, but the impeccable manners his mother had drilled into him would not allow him to do otherwise.

When he replaced the handset in the phone he dragged frustrated fingers through his dark hair and looked up at the two portraits in front of him without seeing them.

Tomorrow, Tamara would be at Lacybourne. He had far more interest in entertaining Tamara (or more to the point, allowing her to entertain *him*) than avoiding some American wandering around his house proclaiming everything "quaint" and exclaiming, "Oh, if these walls could talk!"

The will of his Uncle Edward and Aunt Felicity was clear; he inherited the house *only* if he continued to open it to The National Trust.

Colin did so but under his terms.

He had no idea why he moved into the house in the first place. He vastly preferred London to this sleepy seaside town and the enormous house was far too big for only one man to be in residence.

If he was honest with himself, it was, he knew, those bloody portraits.

His eyes focused on them but he didn't have to look at them to know what they portrayed. He'd long since memorized them.

Since he was young and his parents would bring their children to this house during holidays to visit their childless aunt and uncle, he and his brother and sister were always fascinated by the portraits and the famous, romantic, yet grisly history of their subjects.

For obvious reasons, as Colin grew older, the portraits became all the more captivating.

Throughout his life everyone said he resembled the long dead Royce Morgan, but as he grew from a child to a man that resemblance became stunningly clear.

It was that, Colin knew, that drew him to this damned house.

That and the portrait of Beatrice Morgan, of course.

She had been Beatrice Godwin when the portrait was painted. She'd only been Beatrice Morgan for scant hours of her short life. She stood in the portrait holding a fluffy, black cat in one arm with the hand of her other arm resting lovingly on the head of a great mastiff. She was surrounded by the black shadows of trees with the blue-black backdrop of night and the sky behind her was dark and, strangely, rent with a bolt of lightning.

It was unusual for these old portraits to depict their subjects smiling, but regardless of the dire, nightly setting, Beatrice Godwin was most definitely smiling, magnificently. In fact, it looked like she was close to laughing. Her face was not painted white, her neck was not bound in some hideous ruff, her hair was not tamed but its dark curls were flying wild about her face.

The portrait of Royce Morgan, on the other hand, did not depict him as smiling. He stood wearing armor in front of a mighty black steed that Colin knew, from the many books on the subject of Royce and Beatrice in the library at Lacybourne, was named Mallory. In the painting, Royce looked fierce and battle worn and Colin had little doubt why the lovely, smiling Beatrice Godwin had caught the warrior's eye.

Colin's mother and younger sister had always believed in the romantic notion that Colin would find the reincarnated Beatrice, marry her and live happily ever after with dozens of children flitting around Lacybourne. Local legend said that the unconsummated love of Royce and Beatrice would one day, with magical help, be fulfilled when their tormented souls rested in new bodies.

Colin grew up believing it too. Since he could remember, he knew somewhere in the depths of some hidden place in his soul that he was meant to play a vital part in the Royce and Beatrice Saga.

Because of that, since he was a young boy, he had always been in love with Beatrice Godwin or, at least, the idea of her.

Now, Colin was thirty-six years old and he had no interest in falling in love. He'd done it once and he'd never do it again.

Furthermore, he didn't believe in love or magic or destiny. He believed you made your own destiny or bought it, sold it, stole it or wrested it away from anyone who wanted to keep it from you.

Instead, he was considering asking Tamara Adams to marry him. She, unlike all of the other women in his vast experience (and most of the men), made absolutely no bones about the end to which she used her many, talented means. She blatantly and with purpose used scheming, lies, tears, guilt, begging and sex to get exactly what she wanted.

Tamara had done it since he knew her, which had been most of her life as their parents had been friends for as long as he could remember.

Colin Morgan did not love Tamara. He wasn't certain he even liked her. Then again, Colin didn't like most people, and he specifically did not like women.

Indeed, it could be said that he disliked women with a ruthless passion.

He had reason.

Colin came from money. His father and mother were both members of the upper, *upper* middle class. Michael and Phoebe Morgan had both been (if somewhat distantly, in the case of his father, but *not* in the case of his mother) doting to their three children: Colin, Claire and Anthony.

Colin had gone to Harrow then Cambridge then he took a job on the Exchange. Within two years of graduating from Cambridge, Colin started his own brokerage firm. Then, shortly after, he stopped buying and selling stocks and started buying and selling companies. Or, more to the point, wresting companies away from their mismanagement, cleaning them up and selling them off, sometimes in pieces, for a vast profit.

He was known as ruthless but he didn't care in the slightest.

He *was* ruthless.

Since he was a young boy, he'd never cared what people thought of him. Colin always exceled, always triumphed, no matter what. It was simply his nature. Part of his success was natural ability and extreme intelligence, both of which Colin had in abundance. Nevertheless, Colin was driven to succeed, pushed himself to be the best and settled for nothing less in himself or the people around him.

His father didn't need to encourage his son or make demands of him. Michael Morgan often found himself concerned about his son's single-minded pursuit of anything he wanted.

Phoebe Morgan's feelings went well beyond concerned catapulting directly to outright worry.

As Colin grew older and matured, their son's seemingly easy accomplishments, his determination and aggressive competitive streak set him up as a target. It didn't help matters that he was unbelievably handsome, fabulously sexy, unusually tall, mentally and physically strong and inordinately rich.

Colin had it all and what he didn't have, he obtained.

Many people didn't like that.

Colin was a target to those who wanted to best him or those who Colin bested and who wanted vengeance.

These were mostly men.

Colin was also a target for those who wanted to tame him, trap him or wished to bask in the blazing spotlight of his glory.

These were *always* women.

Therefore Colin Morgan understood innately that nearly everyone was capable of betrayal, anyone could be (and was) devious and no one lived their lives without ulterior motives.

He cared for his family, had close friends, but anyone not in his private circle mattered nothing to him.

Colin rarely trusted. He knew from a wealth of experience that people did not deserve to be trusted.

And the majority of those "people" were women.

It had started with a girl who became besotted with him when he was still a young man. She'd written him long, lovesick letters and posted them to Harrow. He had little interest in her but didn't have the desire to tell her to stop writing. Yet when he came home for a holiday, he found her kissing another boy at the tennis courts at their club. Upon seeing his knowing face, she assured Colin she did, indeed, love him, but she certainly wasn't going to be bored and lonely on Saturday nights while he was away at school.

Then there was the first woman he actually felt some emotion for, a bright woman at Cambridge, a woman with raven hair who reminded him, somewhat, of the portrait of Beatrice.

They had been seeing each other for some months when he'd come across her at a pub when they were out separately one night—she with her girlfriends, he with his friends. Colin had been pleased to see her and approached while her back was to him.

"I cannot *believe* you're dating Colin Morgan. He's gorgeous!" He heard her friend say.

"Yes," his girlfriend replied, "*and* he's got a *huge* trust fund."

All the girls had laughed. Colin had walked away and the next day when she phoned, he hung up on her. He completely cut her out of his life, turned away from her if he met her on the pavement and put the phone down on her the dozens of times she called. He never told her what he heard, he never gave her the chance to explain herself, indeed, he never spoke a word to her again.

Then there was Portia.

Colin had met Portia in London shortly after starting his own brokerage. Slowly, over time, she'd broken down the barriers that seemed, for no reason at all (and yet every reason), to have been around his heart since he was born. Eventually, after a great deal of effort on her part, he'd fallen in love with the passionate, chestnut-haired beauty.

On the verge of asking her to marry him, he'd come home far earlier than normal and found her naked on the floor in the living room of his flat. She'd been on all fours, his best friend, Kevin, on his knees behind her.

He could still remember when her face, looking strangely bored and definitely resigned, turned to him. He could still remember how her expression melted to horror at being caught.

Colin had never been so furious in his life. He'd nearly torn Kevin limb from limb, and he could have easily struck Portia and not regretted it.

Instead, he'd walked out of the room, moved out of the flat they shared and remorselessly turned his back on the both of them, never seeing either one of them again.

Though, she had phoned. He could also still remember the pleading in her voice when she tried to win him back.

"Colin, I've been with you for months and you didn't ask me to marry you. I need to get married, I *have* to. Don't you understand? That's what girls like me do," she explained as if it was the most natural thing in the world.

She was hedging her bets, pursuing Colin with Kevin waiting in the wings.

Kevin married her. They divorced after a year with Portia in possession of a good deal of Kevin's trust fund *and* personal earnings.

That had been over a decade ago. Since then many different women drifted in and out of Colin's life. At six foot two, he had a lean, muscular body that he kept fit with relentless determination. He had thick, waving hair, only a shade lighter than black, light-brown eyes the color of clay, strong, prominent cheekbones, a hard jaw and, incongruously, an immensely sensual, generous lower lip.

What he didn't have was any problem attracting women. His family name, the quantity of his money, his good looks, his arrogance and cold heart (that many women felt they could melt) made him an object of great attraction.

He considered himself lucky. Women were a banquet before him and he had a lusty appetite. Colin took what he wanted, devoured it mercilessly and then left the remains without a backward glance.

However, his mother was complaining. Both his sister, Claire, and brother, Tony, had made good marriages. Claire, nearly immediately after being wed, had two children one after the other. Tony's wife was now pregnant.

Colin's mother wanted her eldest son settled. She wanted him to provide her more grandchildren to spoil, more opportunities for her to meddle and dote, and lastly, she was simply just too tired after thirty-six years of worrying after Colin. She didn't understand his heartlessness and she was deeply concerned about his antipathy towards women. She wanted proof that his heart was mended (from whatever had rendered it broken) so that she could live out her old (ish) age knowing he was happy.

Enter Tamara Adams.

Colin knew that Phoebe Morgan didn't much care for Tamara but then again, his mother didn't have to sleep with her.

Colin liked sleeping with Tamara even if she wasn't the best he'd had. What she lacked in imagination or even sometimes passion, she made up for in sheer will, which worked very well to Colin's benefit.

Shaking off these thoughts, he moved through the house to his study, uncovered the sandwiches Mrs. Manning left for him on his desk and smiled a small smile to himself.

His housekeeper was perfect. She was industrious, thorough and mostly unseen.

He settled behind his desk and made several business calls while he ate then made several more after he finished. Finally, late at night, he phoned Tamara, finalizing plans with her to spend the rest of the week and weekend at Lacybourne.

"I can't wait to see you, darling," she purred and he had to control his annoyance at the endearment that didn't even begin to sound genuine. He disliked it when she slipped into the usual feminine tactics and made them obvious. She was far more talented than that. "Are you in bed?" she continued suggestively.

"No," he replied tersely and she immediately read his tone, not a stupid girl (which was one of her attractions) and quickly rang off.

While preparing for bed, he was unable to assuage his unease and wondered if he should scrape off Tamara and find someone else. Although who that would be, he did not know. After thirty-six years, he had long since given up on the idea that Beatrice Godwin's reincarnated soul would enter his life, smiling magnificently at him and melting his modern day warrior's heart.

Tamara knew she was entering the straightaway, heading for the checkered flag, and the more she seemed sure of her position, the more irritating she became.

Colin lay in bed, crossed his hands behind his head and listened to the rain.

He did not relish the idea of finding a replacement for Tamara, though it didn't really matter who it was. Although it did matter how she looked. Colin had a definite type and Tamara was that type.

Tamara had jet-black hair, ice-blue eyes and never allowed the sun to touch her alabaster skin. She was petite and watched her diet like a hawk so that she would not put an ounce of extra flesh on her slim body. She dressed impeccably and had her own trust fund. Her parents were friends with his parents and were also, most assuredly, upper, *upper* middle class.

She was, for all intents and purposes, perfect, or at least as perfect as a woman could get in Colin's dire estimation.

The rain still falling, his tired thoughts turned from Tamara to Beatrice Godwin.

He had no way of knowing if Beatrice Godwin was petite, except she was suddenly there, right beside him and she was not petite. She was long limbed and her body was lush with curves.

And there she was, lying in bed with him, completely naked, her skin glowing, her eyes heated with passion.

His mouth was on her, his hands were everywhere. She felt so damn good, she tasted so good, he couldn't get enough of her. He felt the blood singing through his veins, burning through him with lust and . . . something else.

Colin was a man of many passions and refined tastes. Only the best suited him and he only accepted the best. He knew passion and desire. He liked sex, enjoyed it immensely but it was always just that, sex—an experience, a release. The act of intercourse was another skill to acquire, hone and use with ruthless determination to meet his own ends.

But he'd never felt a desire so strong it was a need before, desire that was so insistent it was nearly violent.

But he felt that with Beatrice.

Colin lifted his mouth from her nipple and looked at her face. He was surprised to see her lustrous dark locks had turned gold. Her hazel eyes were warm, melting to a liquid brown and when she opened her mouth and whispered, "Colin," her voice was husky with her own need.

He had to have her, immediately, he could not, *would* not, wait a moment longer. He pulled himself over her, opened her legs and her hands glided into his hair.

He opened his mouth to say her name but somehow "Beatrice" wasn't right.

But he had no time to sort his confusion because he was ripped viciously from her arms as they were both hauled out of the bed.

At the side of the bed, strong hands holding him back as he struggled, he watched as the faceless, dark entities that kept him hostage tore her out of the bed the other way.

He roared his fury, brutal feelings he didn't quite understand surging through him as he watched her battle across the room. Colin came to the instant realization that she was life to him, she was breath. The world, the entire world, his whole being, heart and soul, was wrapped up in her.

He struggled fiercely but in vain. He watched, his gut wrenching in despair, as the sharp, shining blade swiftly, without delay, slid across her throat causing hideous blood to splatter everywhere from the gaping wound at her neck.

He woke, somehow, even though it couldn't be possible, to a high-pitched, blood-chilling, woman's scream.

Chapter TWO

Dream Man

Sibyl Godwin woke to the thunderous, rage-filled roar of a man.

Her eyes flew open and Bran, her cat, flew off the bed with an angry mew while Mallory, her dog (who had been taking up most of her wide mattress) jumped awkwardly off the other side and began barking.

The roar could not have come from the throat of the man of her dream.

That throat, in her dream, had just been slit.

She realized she was panting and absolutely, utterly terrified.

The shutters were closed on the windows and she threw back the heavy covers of her bed, running to the windows and throwing them open to let in the moonlight.

There was no moonlight.

She ran back to the bed and switched on her bedside lamp, wondering distractedly why she hadn't thought of that first.

"Be quiet, Mallory!" she ordered and her mastiff immediately sat, his large tongue rolled out and a glob of drool slid off the side of his lip and landed with a plop on the carpet.

"That's disgusting," Sibyl told the dog affectionately as she shakily sat at the edge of the bed.

Her dog came forward, his whole body moving in opposite tandem with his fiercely wagging tail. He nudged her trembling hand and she sat there, petting her pup and trying to get control of her panic.

Something, she knew from years of experience with this type of thing, was terribly, horribly wrong.

"I need to call Mom," she announced to Mallory and he just looked at her, all of his earlier mood gone, currently in blissful dog world as she scratched behind his ears.

She opened the drawer to her bedside table, took out the calling card that was her lifeline to home and grabbed the phone. She carefully dialed the numbers on the card and then added the memorized numbers that she knew would ring the phone in her parents' house in Boulder, Colorado.

"Mom?" Her voice was just as shaky as Sibyl felt, and even though thousands of miles separated mother and daughter, Marguerite Godwin heard the tremulous tone.

"My goddess, Sibyl, what's wrong?"

"Oh Mom, I just had the most terrible dream."

And then, Sibyl started crying.

SIBYL GODWIN HAD led a charmed life.

She was born to Albert Godwin, an Englishman, a professor of Medieval History and an amateur archaeologist, and Marguerite Den, a hippie, a follower of Wicca and a hopeless romantic. Her parents loved each other with a love that just made your toes curl with happy delight at the sight of it.

Bertie and Mags had two daughters, Sibyl and Scarlett. Sibyl, named thus because Mags thought it was appropriately witch-sounding. Scarlett, after Mags's idol and the best romantic heroine in the history of woman (which, at worst, was only a few short days after the beginning of the history of man, if one believed that sort of thing), Scarlett O'Hara.

Mags and Bertie loved their daughters with a love that was a shining testimony to all that was good and right about parenthood.

Even if they were just a tad bit weird and a much larger bit eccentric.

Mags, Sibyl and Scarlett happily followed after Bertie from teaching post to teaching post, at the University of Arizona, UNLV, UCLA, UC Berkeley (which Mags *adored*) and, finally, he gained tenure at the University of Colorado in Boulder.

Mags spent a lot of time communing with Native Americans, opening sacred circles in the mountains or the desert depending on where they lived (often she would simply resort to their backyard, which frightened (or annoyed) the neighbors because she would do this skyclad, or utterly naked), doting on her small family and fretting after her two daughters.

Not that there was a great deal to fret over, Sibyl and Scarlett were both bright, vivacious, thoughtful and had wonderful senses of humor.

Sibyl did have a bit of a temper (or more than a bit on occasion and an explosive bit on other occasions).

And Scarlett had a penchant for collecting and discarding men (*not* on occasion but all the time).

Sibyl, Mags was convinced, was a clairvoyant, often having strange, vivid dreams of events that came true. Mags was certain these were premonitions if only her daughter would just learn to read them. Mags tried to help Sibyl channel this extraordinary power but Sibyl didn't have any interest (much to Mags's everlasting chagrin).

Further concerning Mags and Bertie was that Sibyl, from a very early age, had the deep belief that she would one day meet her one and only true love. A knight in shining armor—kind, loyal and strong—her soulmate, heartmate and helpmate. Sibyl knew to the depths of her very soul that one day she would meet this man who would turn her world golden and provide her with all the joy and happiness she could endure.

Scarlett was, luckily (in Bertie and Mags's opinion), a lot more down-to-earth.

Nevertheless, there were two more worries for the Godwins.

Both of their girls' hearts were way too open (and easily broken).

Then there was the way the girls looked.

And that was all Marguerite's fault.

There was a reason stodgy, bookish Bertie Godwin fell for flamboyant Marguerite Den.

He'd told her straight out one day.

"You're sex on legs, woman."

If Mags had been any other kind of woman, that might have been offensive. But considering the fact that she adored her red-haired (then), tall, straight-backed, thin, balding (now), brilliant, adorable husband, she found it the highest of compliments.

Easy to feel complimented by your very own husband, much harder to deal with when all the men who looked at your daughters obviously felt the same way.

If Bertie had hair, he would have lost it after years of tearing it out worrying about his girls. Even though he was a pacifist (he couldn't have married his hippie wife if he was not) and found all firearms distasteful, that didn't mean he didn't eventually resort to resting a shotgun by the side of his front door whenever one of his daughters was picked up for a date (desperate times, desperate measures, as it were).

Both girls were elegantly tall but they were not slender.

They were curvy.

Very curvy.

Sibyl had a tumble of shining, golden, thick, waving hair, warm hazel eyes and peaches and cream skin with freckles dancing across her nose. Scarlett had a mass of curly, equally thick, auburn hair, flashing blue eyes and freckles dancing *everywhere*.

Scarlett had poured her big heart into medical school.

Sibyl had poured her big heart into everything.

Bertie worried fiercely about his firstborn. She seemed not to be able to find her calling and the longer she waited for her true love, the more restless she became.

She'd graduated from university with a degree in languages, speaking three. She took this knowledge and went straight to work for Customs and Immigration, trying to help struggling, poverty-stricken foreigners in their efforts to get into the country. Red tape, small minds and politics frustrated her out of that job.

She'd gone back to school to become a social worker and quickly threw herself into a job helping victims of domestic violence. That job nearly tore her apart, literally, when she became personally involved in her caseload. She parted ways with the charity, able to see that she was incapable of establishing appropriate boundaries considering she wanted to fight everyone's battles.

Bertie didn't even want to remember what happened with the people at the animal shelter.

This carried on for years, until Sibyl finally walked into their home in Boulder and asked Bertie and Mags if she could move to Brightrose Cottage.

Brightrose Cottage was where the Godwins would spend a goodly amount of their school holidays. The cottage was located in a small clearing of a dense wood that seemed somehow removed but was still very close to the small seaside town of Clevedon in the beautiful English county of North Somerset. Bertie had bought the house run down and derelict. Even though surrounded by trees, the clearing allowed cheerful shafts of sunlight to penetrate and warm the nearly ancient ruin. Even in disrepair, Bertie had fallen in love with the place and its location and happily anticipated the work ahead of him in restoring it.

While Scarlett and Mags trundled off to Glastonbury, Bristol or other hippie hot spots, Bertie, with Sibyl a constant at his side, got down to the business of bringing Brightrose back to its original charm.

Under the creaking, warped stairwell they'd uncovered the arched remains of a window that dated back to the early 1400s, and together they designed the stained glass that would be refit. They'd painstakingly refinished the wide-planked floors and Jacobean doors. They'd run the thick, coarse ropes up the stairs to act as period-fitting banisters. They'd fitted the heavy wrought iron sconces to the walls and chandelier over the huge, gleaming, round dining-room table. They'd scrubbed years of dust, grime and soot off the stones of the inglenook fireplaces in the living room and the dining room and the vast hearth in the kitchen. In all the rooms they'd patched, primed and painted the plaster. On occasion, they uncovered and exposed secret alcoves, embedded beams and Somerset brick.

They'd scoured the local antique stores and dragged back heavy pieces of furniture, carefully bringing them back to their former glory and positioning them perfectly around the house. They'd refitted the awkward kitchen to be a cook's (or, Bertie's, to be precise) dream and built a lovely summer house in the garden for Mags's potions and witch paraphernalia.

In the end, Brightrose Cottage was lovingly, beautifully and meticulously restored and it showed in every inch of the home. It was cozy, quaint, warm and inviting.

You didn't live at Brightrose. You didn't visit Brightrose.

You *experienced* Brightrose.

At Sibyl's announcement that she wanted to move to England, Bertie demanded, "What on earth are you going to do there?"

Unfortunately, no matter how much he loved her, there were limits to his patience when it came to his daughter's flightiness. She was thirty-one years old, she had to find an anchor.

This, Bertie felt, should come in the form of a man (although he would never *dream* of uttering this notion in front of his feminist wife).

But Sibyl didn't allow herself to get close to men. Bertie found himself having the most unusual wish that his elder daughter could treat his sex the way his younger daughter did, taking them (quite terrifyingly frequently in Bertie's opinion) and then leaving them with nary a thought.

Sibyl seemed, as with most anything, to find the most damaged men she could collect (quite terrifying infrequently in Mags's opinion). Then she bent over backwards, turned herself inside and out and twisted herself in knots to sort out all their troubles. And in the end, even though most of them would have probably laid down their lives for her, she scooted them on their way so some other woman could sort out their *new* problems of having lost the glory that was Sibyl.

"I've no idea, Daddy," she'd answered his irate question, her voice small, so small he kicked himself for his sharp tone. "But I feel I need to be there. It's the only place I've ever been truly happy and at peace."

Now, how could a father argue with that?

Especially when that peace had been found mostly in his company, and he knew exactly what she was talking about when it came to Brightrose Cottage.

They'd then argued about how, since there was no mortgage on the property, she could live there without paying. They'd won her over by explaining that Scarlett's medical school would cost more than the house was even worth and they'd signed the deeds over to her.

Mags and Bertie were thrilled when Sibyl had found a part-time job in a local community centre working with old people and children (how much trouble could old people and children get her into?).

She supplemented this with a small but soon lucrative business selling handmade bath oils, salts, lotions, shampoos, conditioners and divinely scented candles to exclusive shops and boutiques around Somerset (oils, salts and lotions didn't live and breathe or have angry ex-husbands, which they felt was a good thing).

It seemed Sibyl was more at peace in England, but neither Bertie nor Mags could shake the feeling that their daughter still seemed restless.

And they knew exactly why.

For, as the weeks, months and years passed, it became more and more clear that Sibyl's abiding belief that her one true love would walk in and shine his light on her life was not going to happen.

THROUGHOUT THE TELLING of the dream, Marguerite muttered, "Oh my," and a couple of times the stronger, "Oh my goddess."

Sibyl, as usual with her mother, didn't leave anything out, including an abbreviated version of the very passionate activities that preceded her dream lover's grisly murder.

Nor the belief that this lover was *her* lover, the man of her dreams, the man who would change her life forever.

Which, of course, led to the distressing fact that at the end he'd been killed.

"What do you think it means, Mom?"

Sibyl knew her mother read tarot cards, runes, tea leaves and palms as well as dreams. She wasn't really good at doing any of this but she tried very hard.

"You say this man was vivid in your dream?" Mags asked.

"I could draw you a picture, that is if I could draw," Sibyl answered.

"Describe him," Mags demanded.

Sibyl did, in great detail, leaving nothing out.

"Oh my," Mags whispered.

"Will you stop saying, 'oh my' and tell me what you think this means?" Sibyl was at her wit's end.

Mags sighed hugely. "Honey, it means you need a man."

Sibyl rolled her eyes. Even being a militant feminist, her mother often solved many serious issues with the words "you need a man." Mags was very into the healing power of sex.

Then again, Sibyl's mother had been lucky enough to marry the love of her life, had a completely faithful marriage and an active sex life that continued to this very day (a fact that Sibyl unfortunately knew all too well).

In order to get her emotion in check, Sibyl counted to ten. Bertie had taught her this tactic years ago when it seemed clear that Sibyl would never learn to control her fiery temper.

Sometimes it worked, sometimes it, spectacularly, did not.

After she finished her count, Sibyl said, "I need to get some sleep, I've got to be at the Centre tomorrow."

"Where's the cat?" Mags asked.

Sibyl had no idea why her mother would want to know where Bran was. "He's wandered back in the room somewhere, why?"

"Because that damned dog of yours would probably make any murderous scoundrel a cup of tea if he had opposable thumbs. The cat would scratch his eyes out."

Sibyl couldn't help but laugh because this was true.

"I love you, Mom."

"I love you too, baby. Get some sleep, go out on the prowl this weekend and find yourself a blessed man, for goddess's sake. No woman should endure a year-long dry spell."

"Thanks for the advice, Mom," Sibyl uttered the expression of gratitude but her tone said very clearly she didn't mean it.

Mags, as usual, ignored her daughter's tone. "I'm serious, Sibyl.

Even if it is only sex, or companionship, everyone needs it." Sibyl remained silent at Mags's tender urging. Mags sighed and then said, "See you soon, my darling girl. It'll be April before you know it."

Finally.

The thought of seeing her parents in April *did* make Sibyl feel happy and relaxed.

"I hope so." Again, Sibyl's tone said exactly how she felt.

After hanging up the phone, she left the shutters open. She lay in bed thinking of the dream, or more to the point, the man in the dream.

He was immensely handsome, dark and . . . well, *hot*. His touch set her on fire, it was fevered and insistent and nearly worshipful. Until she was ripped from the bed, his presence seemed the only thing in the universe. There was nothing else but him, his hands, his mouth, his body. He was her very essence (except a male), her other part, her completion.

Mallory broke into her thoughts by lumbering onto the high bed and settling in, squeezing poor Bran and Sibyl to the edge leaving them hanging on for dear life. Somehow, even in this awkward but familiar position, she was finally able to allow her mind to calm enough to go to sleep.

Even if she did do so with the image of the handsome, hard-jawed, dark-haired man burned on the backs of her eyelids.

Chapter THREE

Reunion

"Oh, for the love of the goddess, get out of the car, will you?"

Sibyl was addressing her dog *and* cat, who both somehow managed to fit themselves into her old, red MG convertible.

Sibyl didn't know how she'd managed to get herself in this terrible snag nor did she know how she managed consistently to find herself in a variety of terrible snags, something that happened with disturbing frequency.

Her day had not gone well. It was a busy day that included bingo afternoon at the Pensioners' Club of the Day Centre and tryouts for the kids' annual talent show in the Community Hall.

Sibyl was responsible for running all the myriad community programs put on in the Centre and Hall. The Day Centre and Community Hall comprised (along with a vast kitchen, several small offices, some storage rooms, a stage and narrow backstage area) an enormous, but dilapidated old building on a council estate in a deprived area of Weston-super-Mare, a small, seaside city in the West Country.

Early afternoon, after a two-course lunch had been served to the pensioners and many of them had gone home on the minibus the council provided the estate, Sibyl had pulled back the sliding doors and exited the smoky Day Centre.

She heard the bingo call, "One, one, eleven, legs eleven," sounding behind her coming from Marianne, the bingo caller's, hoarse, cigarette-clogged throat.

Sibyl entered the vast Community Hall, sliding the doors shut behind her to see Jemma, her dearest friend in England, sitting in an old, beat-up plastic chair and staring in horrified fascination at the stage. Sibyl glanced toward the stage to see what held Jemma's attention only to witness four very young girls dressed in alarmingly alluring outfits far older than their tender years, gyrating their hips and lip-syncing to a popular song.

Sibyl dragged a chair over to her friend and sat down to watch as the children carried out their inappropriately suggestive performance.

The song ended and both Jemma and Sibyl sat in stunned silence.

"Hey, Miss Sibyl," one of the girls called.

"Hi, Flower," Sibyl called back, her voice sounding strained.

"How'm I going to handle this?" Jemma muttered, *sotto voce*. "This is a family show."

Sibyl felt for her friend and tried not to grin in amusement at her predicament. Jemma ran a small youth project out of a side office of the Community Hall. Sibyl volunteered for the project and coordinated its efforts in the Community Centre.

The girls were going to have to be told that they should do something more age appropriate, and considering the fact that age ten was the new eighteen that was not going to be an easy task.

In an effort to help her friend, Sibyl called, "Girls, can you come down here for a word?"

The girls clattered eagerly off the stage. They did this because Jemma Rashid and Sibyl Godwin were the shining lights of these young girls' often unhappy, promiseless lives.

Jemma, petite, dark-haired and chocolate-eyed, was a local girl who was devoted to her community and even more devoted to her family. This kind of devotion was not experienced by many of the children on the council estate where they lived and where the Community Centre was located. Many had well-meaning but hard-working parents. Others had thoughtless or even abusive, lazy, wastrel parents. Devotion to family and community was a rare concept and one to be savored whenever it became available.

Sibyl, on the other hand, was American, a fact in and of itself that made the girls think she was the coolest of the cool. However they loved her accent—they loved her style, her spirit and her incredible beauty more. She was nice to them, always, and she had the best smile—a smile that could warm you from the very top of your head straight down to the tips of your toes.

The girls arrived to stand before their two idols and they shifted on their feet, twisting their ankles awkwardly, waiting for the opinion that meant everything in their small worlds.

Jemma looked at Sibyl and Sibyl returned her friend's look. Both were at a loss.

Then Sibyl had an idea, it was a lame idea but it was, at least, an idea.

"I *love* that song!" she exclaimed. "Who chose that song?"

"It was me!" Flower cried.

Even raised by a hippie, Sibyl felt for the girl who had such a terrible name, a name she knew (because she heard) other children used to make fun of her. Flower's mother was even flakier than Sibyl's and had four children by four different fathers and another one on the way. Flower's mother was always out partying and never home. The care of the entire family rested on Flower's ten-year-old shoulders, evidenced by the fact that her three brothers were, at that very moment, fighting in the back corner of the hall.

"Good call, Flower," Sibyl enthused, lying through her teeth.

Jemma turned to her friend, her eyes round and her brows raised.

"Though, I hear it all the time on the radio. *All* the time," Sibyl continued.

"I know, it's *very* popular," Katie, another of the girls announced, thinking this was a selling point.

Sibyl particularly liked Katie, a bright girl with a head on her shoulders. She had both parents at home, her mother owned a small cleaning business and her father was currently redundant, trying to find a job and was a recovering gambler. Sibyl knew this because Katie's father ran the local Gamblers Anonymous meetings on Tuesday nights in the Day Centre (but, of course, Sibyl would never tell a soul this information).

Sibyl went on, but gently, "By the time of the talent show, do you think people might have heard it a bit too much? Even you girls might be tired of it by then."

The girls looked at each other, not at all convinced since it was their most favorite song of all time. How could they *ever* be tired of it? Not in a *million* years.

"I know!" Jemma exclaimed as if a thought just occurred to her. "Why don't you let Sibyl find a song for you? Something American."

This caught the girls' attention and four pairs of enthusiastic eyes collectively swung to Sibyl.

It was Sibyl's turn to stare at her friend, her eyes round, her eyebrows raised.

"And," Jemma dug Sibyl's hole deeper, "she'll help you with outfits and dance steps and *everything*."

Sibyl made a choking noise but swiftly hid it and smiled warmly at the girls.

She was going to kill Jem, or maim her for life, or, at least, never speak to her again.

Jemma was very artistic, knew all the latest songs and was a natural at choreography. Sibyl loved music, loved to dance, but had always done it to the beat of her own drummer and wouldn't know how to create a choreographed dance if someone was forcing her to do it by shooting at her feet with pistols.

Nevertheless, the girls excitedly agreed to this new development, happy to spend more time with their American goddess.

"What have you done to me?" Sibyl hissed at her friend as the girls scattered and Jemma motioned for the next act to come to the stage.

"Relax, I'll pick the song, I'll choreograph the dance moves, you just have to teach them," Jem assured her then finished. "I'll help, of course."

"You better or I'll make those girls a laughingstock."

"I'm already thinking of something."

This, Sibyl could believe. Jemma was sharp as a tack and nothing got by her.

As the next act prepared to begin, Sibyl got up.

"Off for your afternoon chat with Meg?" Jemma inquired, sorting through CDs to put the next act's in the player.

Sibyl spent bingo afternoons with her favorite pensioner, Meg. Meg was her most favorite oldie (an affectionate term everyone at the Centre had for the members of the Pensioners' Club of the Day Centre).

Meg had paper-thin, soft skin, was diabetic but ate with gusto and was at least five stone overweight. Her eyes, nose and mouth collapsed happily into each other whenever she smiled, which was a lot.

Meg was the first oldie to give Sibyl a welcoming, encouraging smile on her first day on the job. Sibyl hadn't even known she needed that smile, but she'd been so homesick Meg's smile had touched her heart and Sibyl had never forgotten it. She found herself often ensconced in corners with the old lady after their luncheon was done, shooting the breeze in happy companionship. Even though they'd get together often, Meg and Sibyl always set aside bingo afternoon to have a chat before Meg took the minibus's second trip round the estate to her lonely home at the end of the day.

Bertie's parents had both died before he left England. Mags's parents had lived long enough to meet and love their grandchildren but not long enough to see them grow and mature into beautiful, young women.

This meant Meg was the closest thing to a grandmother Sibyl had. Every time Meg looked at the younger girl, Sibyl felt awash with her love and this wasn't surprising. When she was younger, Meg told Sibyl she used to take in orphaned babies and children while they were being placed into other homes, raising them from days to months, and on a few occasions years, before they found a permanent placement.

Sibyl had no problem believing this. Meg had a lot of love to go around.

"I just wish, Sibyl, my love, that one of them would come to see me now that I'm in my old age. Just one of them," Meg had said to Sibyl some days before. "So I'll know they're all right."

Without anything to say to make her feel better, Sibyl had just patted Meg's hand and knew from experience that the babies likely didn't even know that Meg was a part of their lives. The older ones, Sibyl had no excuses for.

Now, Sibyl smiled at Jemma.

"Yeah, Jem, can't miss my dose of Meg," Sibyl told her friend. "See you later."

Jemma nodded and shouted to the group of boys on stage, "Ready?"

At their affirmative nods, Jemma flipped a switch and rap music filled the air.

Sibyl opened the doors to hear Marianne yelling, "Unlucky for some, number thirteen."

She found Meg in her corner and watched her older friend's face collapse in a smile at the sight of Sibyl. The smile stayed where it was as Sibyl recounted Flower, Katie and their friends' antics in the Hall.

The minibus came shortly after and took the bingo club home. After they were all safely away, Sibyl wandered the Hall and Centre, getting prepared to put it to bed until Kyle, the Centre's volunteer caretaker and resident handyman (not to mention Jemma's father), opened it up that evening after supper for the recovering Gamblers.

Jemma met her in the Day Centre. They were going to lock up together, as they usually did on a Tuesday night. They were about to leave when Jemma stopped and cocked her head, listening with mother's ears, then rushed to the restrooms at the back of the Centre.

Annie, another member of the Pensioners' Club, was locked in one of the stalls. She'd been stuck there for hours and missed the minibus ride back to her home. For some bizarre reason, Annie didn't pull the emergency cord in the bathroom and couldn't explain to Sibyl or Jemma why she'd not done so. This was likely because Annie, at the best of times, was a tad bit confused.

Thanking all the goddesses that Jemma had heard Annie (and cursing the minibus driver to perdition for not checking his load, which he was supposed to do), rather than leaving her locked in the bathroom for the night, Jem and Sibyl located the keys to the door and released the old lady.

Then Sibyl drove her home.

As Annie was blind, Sibyl helped her into her council house. Once she opened the door to Annie's house, though, she was struck by a rancid smell and immobilized with shock when she saw the utterly hideous state the old woman's home was in.

"Oh, Annie," she whispered under her breath, for once happy that Annie was not only blind but mostly deaf as well.

The house smelled terrible and was absolutely filthy.

"My children take care of me," Annie said defensively, obviously cottoning on to what Sibyl was seeing (and *smelling*) and telling the lie she'd been mouthing at the Day Centre for what appeared to be months.

"I know, Annie, but it's been a bit since they've been around. Let me just tidy up. It won't take a minute."

It had taken over an hour *and* Sibyl had to call Jem.

Jemma had turned up on Annie's doorstep with her two children, her twelve-year-old boy, Shazzie and fourteen-year-old girl, Zara. Jemma's big, kind, chocolate-brown eyes had rounded at the sight of the squalor that was Annie's abode and that was *after* Sibyl had already carried three bags of rubbish out to the bins.

In Annie's foul kitchen while the children were watching television with the old woman, shouting at her to tell her what was happening on a screen she could not see, Jemma stared into the refrigerator.

"She hasn't a bite of food in here," Jemma pulled out a carton of milk and gave it a cautious sniff before yanking her head back in horror. "Oh my Lord."

"Give it to me," Sibyl told her friend and poured (or, more to the point, *shook*) the offending milk in the food-encrusted sink. Sibyl watched as Jemma twisted her long, dark-brown hair and fastened it more firmly in her ever-present, huge hair clip, ready to engage in war against the vile kitchen. "We've got to keep a closer eye on Annie. Do you know if she even has children?" Sibyl asked.

Jemma was pulling on yellow, plastic gloves. "No idea. I'll call Dad."

Jemma's dad and mum knew everything about everyone on the

council estate. Both of Jemma's parents worked at the Community Centre with Sibyl. Jemma, her parents and her brothers and sisters all lived on or around the council estate where the Community Centre was located. Jemma's parents were both young but Kyle had arthritis and her mum, Tina, endured terrible troubles with her feet, thus they couldn't work "normal" jobs so they volunteered at the Centre. This caused them to do more than full-time jobs anyway but they could do them in their time, at their pace.

Jem phoned Kyle and then she and Sibyl cleaned, then scrubbed, then vacuumed Annie's little house while the children entertained the old woman. They left, politely declining Annie's offer of a chocolate from a box since thrown out. While they were leaving, Kyle shouldered his burly body through the door, his hands filled with bags of groceries.

"Get the kids home," he ordered his daughter gruffly, as only a father would do to a daughter who spent her afternoon cleaning the home of an old lady she barely knew. "Sibyl, luv, you go home too. Tina and I have this covered," Sibyl turned her head and caught Tina waving from the passenger seat of Kyle's beat-up Ford Fiesta.

Sibyl waved back as the kids ran to greet their grandmother.

"Thanks, Jem," Sibyl said to her friend, not knowing how to express her gratitude at sharing their awful task.

"We must take care of our own," Jemma muttered, clearly disturbed by what she had seen.

She called her kids, blew a kiss to her mum, gave Sibyl a wave and they walked off in the opposite direction while Sibyl stood for a moment to watch the clouds forming.

Another storm was coming. It was late February and spring rains had come to Somerset.

Mentally making plans to talk to Social Services the next day about Annie and give a piece of her mind to the minibus driver, Sibyl drove to Brightrose to let Mallory out for his comfort break.

She'd wanted to change out of her work clothes to something more comfortable, but she no longer had time. She could wear jeans to the Centre but she took her work seriously and wanted her oldies and the kids to know that she did. Therefore, she dressed for work, not in a suit but well enough that they knew she gave her job her respect.

She was wearing a long, cocoa-colored corduroy skirt, a pair of red cowboy boots, a long sleeved, fitted, V-neck, red T-shirt and a deep magenta, twill, tailored jacket. She had a strap of brown leather tied as a choker around her throat and from it hung a small silver disc with the tiny word "Peace" placed subtly and artfully on it in bits of battered bronze (this, a beloved gift from her mother). And she had heavy, dangling, ornate earrings of garnets and silver dripping from her ears. Her long, heavy hair hung in a mess about her shoulders.

She only had time to pull a brush through her hair and spray herself with a perfume of her own styling scented with bergamot, musk and lilies of the valley.

She allowed Mallory into the garden when Bran, unusually, darted out the front door.

She had a cat door in the bottom half of the split farm door that led from the kitchen to the back garden where Bran liked to hang about and spend his hours in the sun. Bran rarely ventured out front, for some bizarre cat reason, always keeping close to the house in the back.

But off he went through the front though, quickly becoming a shadow in the dark night.

There was nothing for it, she was already late. Bran would have to brave the unknown wilds of the front garden and wood until she came home and Sibyl had to trust that her clever cat would survive (though she had little doubt he would). Sibyl trudged back to the car, Mallory, as ever, loping hot on her heels. She opened the car door to retrieve Mallory's treats that she'd bought that morning (he always received a treat if he did well on his comfort breaks and got himself a little exercise, or, because of her soft heart, even when he didn't which was far more often). But, upon opening the door to the car, Mallory shifted his enormous bulk into the passenger seat and sat, staring forward, obviously thinking it was time to take a joyride.

She was about to order him out, when, to her astonishment, Bran, who *hated* the car and anywhere Sibyl might take him in it, darted into the car and curled up on the driver's side floor.

Any effort she made to pull out the recalcitrant dog met with loud, angry "woofs" and the cat sunk his claws into the carpet and would simply not let go.

"Okay!" she gave up with ill grace after what she considered a valiant struggle. "You'll come with me, but you have to be good. I'm already outside of visiting hours as it is. Whoever owns Lacybourne Manor does not want a big mutt and a crazy feline traipsing around his graceful estate."

Mallory was beside himself with glee at this turn of events and drooled happily on the car's battered upholstery. Bran shifted to the floor of the passenger side while Sibyl forced the reluctant car to do what it was told, all the while muttering dire threats and foul curses at her animals.

Luckily, with only five minutes to get there, it took only ten minutes to arrive. She didn't want to disappoint the strangely intense Mrs. Byrne (who had shared her name after Sibyl had shared her own). The woman had gone out of her way to arrange this tour and, as was her style, Sibyl didn't want to disappoint her.

Unluckily, when she arrived in Clevedon proper the wind had whipped up and a fierce thunderstorm had rolled in.

By the time she made it through the gate of Lacybourne, lightning was flashing through the sky and her dratted dog and damned cat were practically jumping out of their skins.

"This is *not* a good idea," she told the animals. "I'm just going to have to tell Mrs. Byrne that I have you in the car and thank her . . ." she stopped, realizing she was talking to her pets.

She gave a brief thought to the idea that maybe she should listen to her mother, maybe she *did* need a man. She had been reduced to talking to her animals as if they could not only understand but respond.

She halted the car in the drive just before a small copse of trees. She fully intended to explain the situation to the older woman, thank the owner (if he was there) and get her pets home.

She opened her door to get out and the moment she cleared the frame, Bran flashed out of the driver's side door and Mallory, very inelegantly, trundled out right behind him.

"Bran! Mallory! Get back here!" she shouted, and as the wind whipped her hair around her face, her animals disappeared into the night. She pulled her hair back angrily with her hand, narrowing her eyes to peer through the darkness. "Damn it, you crazy beasts!" she yelled, "Get your behinds back in this car!"

Many of the lights were lit in Lacybourne upon her arrival and there were several cars in the drive. Sibyl noted with a bit of panic and rising despair that now even more lights were coming on in the house.

"When I catch you fiends, I'm going to tan your hides. Bran! Mallory!" she shouted.

She reached the very center of the copse of trees when out of nowhere Bran shot toward her, leaping gracefully into her arms. Mallory, much less gracefully, hurtled out of the darkness, skidding to a halt at her side. The big dog sat down beside her like he often wiled away his hours, relaxing calmly at her side, the wind whipping at him, the lightning tearing through the skies.

She put her hand on top of the dog's head in order to slide it down to his neck and find his collar when she heard . . .

"What in bloody hell?"

She lifted her head and at that very moment, lightning arced down behind her, the longest flash of lightning she'd ever endured in her life. Not just a scant second but entire, long, breathless moments.

And holding Bran in one arm, her other hand resting on Mallory's head and the wind whipping her hair while a faltering smile (and for Sibyl even a faltering smile came out as dazzling, much to her parents' dismay) formed on her lips, she saw, illuminated in the lightning right in front of her, the tall, handsome form of the murdered lover from her dream.

There he was, right before her, not four feet away, in real life.

The man of her dreams.

It was then that Sibyl Jezebel Godwin did something she had never done in her entire life.

She fainted.

Unfortunately, when she did so, her head smashed rather painfully against a jagged rock.

Chapter FOUR

Misunderstanding

"Call the doctor!"

Colin shouted this order to Tamara and Mrs. Byrne who were both crowding around him while he carried into the house the unconscious, unbelievable woman he'd encountered outside moments ago.

The very vision of Beatrice Godwin.

Except blonde.

Like the woman in his dream.

Not only were Tamara and Mrs. Byrne crowding him but an enormous, beige beast with a black face and black floppy ears was following closely at his heels, barking ferociously, and a fluffy, black cat was darting in and out of his legs, nearly tripping him.

"Oh my goodness! What happened?" Mrs. Byrne queried, her voice filled with concern.

"Call the damned doctor!" Colin answered, striding swiftly through the Great Hall and into the library, carrying his burden.

Tamara peeled off the scene hopefully to phone a medic. Mrs. Byrne stayed with him as he carefully deposited the woman onto the leather of a burgundy couch in the library and she leaned forward to arrange the woman's long legs in a comfortable position.

Then she looked at the woman.

"She's bleeding!" Mrs. Byrne exclaimed.

"Get a towel, the bathroom—" Colin started to explain but Mrs. Byrne was already rushing towards the bathroom (rather agilely for a woman of her age). He realized with a delayed reaction that in her role as a volunteer at Lacybourne, she probably knew the house better than he.

The dog was still barking and the cat had leapt up to walk daintily the length of the woman's body.

"Quiet!" he ordered the dog, and to his surprise the dog ceased barking immediately and sat down in a slouch where most of his body reclined against the side of his couch.

He then inclined his neck forward and licked Colin's hand.

Not quite finished, he turned his massive head and sniffed his mistress's hair before sloppily licking the entire side of her face with one long lash of his exorbitantly wet, enormous tongue.

"Down," Colin commanded and the dog settled onto the floor and, with a loud groan, rested his head on his front paws.

Colin had laid her on her back and now, gently, he leaned forward and pulled the soft, heavy hair away from her face.

Then he saw her, as he'd seen her outside, except now she wasn't exactly mimicking the pose from the portrait.

Beatrice's double, right here in Lacybourne Manor.

She was the woman in his dream.

Albeit, without a slit throat but with a bleeding head wound.

"Good Christ," he muttered, his body frozen, his eyes staring into her pale, familiar face, his mind unable to process anything but the incredible vision of her.

The cat had decided to settle smack in the middle of her chest, curling into himself and licking one of his paws.

Colin stared at her as finally Colin's mind again started working and he thought of Mrs. Byrne arriving not ten minutes ago to explain that she had, because of her extreme age and faltering memory, forgotten to call the American to tell her not to arrive for her tour.

Then they'd all heard the frustrated, shouting woman's voice rising above the storm outside.

Colin had gone out to investigate.

And in the unbelievably long flash of lightning, he'd seen her standing amongst the trees in a perfect rendition of the pose of Beatrice Godwin.

"I've called 999, they're sending someone straight away," Tamara said as she rushed into the room.

Colin didn't look at Tamara. He continued to stare at the woman on the couch.

All the years he'd waited and now here she was.

And she was blonde.

And suddenly and very strangely, he felt his body react, every muscle tightening instantaneously as he continued to drink in the sight of her. His gut clenched and his heart felt clutched in an iron fist.

"Colin?" Tamara called, her hand lightly touching his tense arm but her light touch felt like pinpricks of icicles sinking into his flesh and he experienced the strange desire to shrug her off and eject her forcibly from the house.

Before he could wonder at this reaction, he heard, "I've got a wet flannel. She'll need some ice."

Mrs. Byrne was walking quickly into the room. She pushed past Colin and sat next to the woman, leaning forward to press the flannel gently against the bloodied area of the woman's head.

Not even close to coming to terms with his shock at seeing the vision of Beatrice (but blonde), Colin stared at the older woman as she ministered to her charge in a way that Colin thought distractedly was rather familiar. Mrs. Byrne had said the woman was just an American who wanted to view the house and now the older woman was caring for her as if she was her own granddaughter.

Furthermore, Colin thought, his mind clearing quickly as he watched the scene, Mrs. Byrne had been working in Lacybourne for years. She had to have seen the uncanny, even otherworldly, resemblance of this woman to the portrait that had hung in the Great Hall for nearly five hundred years.

Colin felt a feeling he recognized very well slicing quickly through his fogged brain.

No, not this, not her, he thought.

"Who is she?" Colin asked the older woman.

Tamara's hand had not left his arm and her grip was becoming less and less light with each passing moment.

The older woman didn't appear to realize he was addressing her. Colin ignored Tamara's insistent hand and knew that instinctive, familiar feeling in his gut was something he did not very much like.

It was the feeling that he was being played.

Colin's mind fully cleared and he felt a slow burn begin.

He may be ruthless, but he was (most of the time) fair. He was normally quite controlled. Cynical, of course, but aloof. Resigned to the often annoying foibles of lower mortals (a league to which he relegated most everyone but his sacred circle). He could have, and normally would have, calmly waited for an explanation.

But now, this instant, with the unconscious woman on his couch looking exactly like Beatrice Morgan, the woman he'd waited for all his life, and Mrs. Byrne, who had, perhaps with the help of the American, staged this entire event, he felt an irrational, nearly uncontrollable fury begin to build.

"Mrs. Byrne, who is she?" Colin repeated.

Mrs. Byrne turned remarkably innocent-looking eyes to his. "I've no idea, Mr. Morgan. She came around yesterday afternoon—"

He didn't believe her for a second.

"How long have you been docent in this house for National Trust?" Colin interrupted. His voice was calm, so calm it was dangerous.

"Seven years, but I don't see—"

In that instant, he'd suddenly had enough.

"Look at her face!" Colin thundered, losing his nearly legendary patience. In fact, it seemed his increasing rage was born of something else entirely, something he couldn't control, so he didn't. "God damn it, you've seen that portrait thousands of times! Who is she?"

Mrs. Byrne jumped, the hand not compressing the flannel on the woman's head rising to her throat. She stared at him with a curious intensity as if she was a scientist marking her reaction to an experiment.

At this point, the eyes of the woman on the couch fluttered open and then darted around in a passable interpretation of panic. She reared up into a sitting position, dislodging Mrs. Byrne's hand and the cat on her chest who then went flying out of the room.

"Ow!" Her hand flew to her temple and, encountering wetness, it came away and she stared in disbelief at the blood.

"Who the hell are you?" Colin stormed, not believing her performance for one bloody, fucking second.

Her hazel eyes, a *perfectly* familiar hazel, lifted to his and blinked at him in bemusement.

With one look from those eyes, he nearly forgot himself. He nearly forgot the decades of betrayal that hardened him against these schemes.

But then he remembered and it was as if she embodied every deceitful bitch he'd ever had the misfortune to encounter.

"I said," he roared, "who *the fuck* are you?"

Tamara jumped away in shock.

Mrs. Byrne stood, her hand coming up in a placating gesture.

"Mr. Morgan, I don't think—" Mrs. Byrne began.

"Who the fuck are *you*?" the woman on the couch asked him, her own voice vibrating with anger.

And Colin could not believe his ears. He saw his vision explode in a white-hot fury he had not felt in years, maybe never felt in his lifetime.

He knew, without any doubt, that this woman and her old friend had set this up. She looked *exactly* like Beatrice Godwin and Mrs. Byrne would have noticed that in an instant. The fact that Mrs. Byrne had not mentioned it, not once during the telephone conversation or her explanation this evening, showed she was hiding something.

They would have, of course, wanted the element of surprise.

Who, in their right mind, viewed a heritage property and brought their dog *and* cat for God's sake?

Therefore, Colin was not going to stand in his own damned house and be cursed at by a blatant con artist.

"I own Lacybourne Manor and you were trespassing," he answered.

Her eyes flew to Mrs. Byrne (tellingly, he thought), then she winced and put her hand up to her temple again.

"Save the dramatics and just tell me who you are." His voice had gone from biting anger to extreme annoyance and this obvious lowering in the level of fury caused her remarkable eyes to move back to him.

"I'm Sibyl Godwin."

At that ridiculous pronouncement, first Colin Morgan blinked at her then he threw his head back and laughed.

In his angry amusement, he missed the confusion that flashed across her face but did catch her rising to her full height and his laughter faded as he noted belatedly she was definitely not petite.

She was not a lot of things.

She was not slim. She had a full, lush body that seemed absolutely built, even divinely created, for a man's hands. She did not have blemishless alabaster skin but had freckles on her goddamned nose. And she did not have sleek, shining, dark hair but had the most remarkably dramatic, leonine mane he'd ever seen in his life.

"I'd ask what's so funny about my name but I think there's been some misunderstanding here—" she started.

"There has been no misunderstanding," he assured her scathingly. "Do you have a driver's license?"

He noticed she was swaying and felt he should, out loud, give her points for her performance. She was very close to scoring a perfect ten.

Or, at the very least, he felt he should applaud.

Her dog had stood with her and was pressing his nose against her hand and Colin watched in passing fascination as she gently and distractedly stroked the dog's muzzle.

"Driver's license?" She was back to feigning confusion.

"Yes, *Miss Godwin*. I'm assuming it's 'Miss?'" His voice was like ice.

She stared at him as if he was a being from another planet.

"It's 'Ms' if you must know and yes, I have a driver's license. Why on earth—?"

"Let me see it," he demanded.

"Mr. Morgan, I don't think—" Mrs. Byrne attempted to intervene.

"That's enough out of you," he snapped at the older woman.

"Colin!" Even Tamara, who had been completely silent throughout this scene, had enough manners to object to his behavior to the older woman.

"This is . . . you are . . . I don't believe . . ." The woman who called herself Godwin was stuttering, staring at him now with eyes narrowed and flashing a brilliant green with anger.

Rather fetchingly too, he thought with some detachment.

And she was still swaying precariously.

"You need to sit down, dear," Mrs. Byrne was saying.

Ignoring Colin, she gently pushed the woman down to a sitting position on the couch.

"Where's your bloody license?" Colin roared.

The dog barked, angry and fierce, three times in a row.

Colin ignored him but the woman turned to the animal and commanded, "Mallory, be quiet!"

The dog stopped barking but the name of her pet being uttered was just too much.

The same name as the dead Royce Morgan's legendary steed.

"Priceless," he hissed, the ferocity back in his voice.

Her eyes jerked to his, the depth of green was now a hard, glittering emerald.

"If you need my license, it's in my bag, which is in my car, which is—"

Colin didn't listen to another word.

He turned on his heel and left the room, heading straight to her car.

"I NEED TO go home." Sibyl looked at Mrs. Byrne, who seemed the only sane person in the room. "There's been a terrible mistake and furthermore, that man is a raving lunatic."

There was a low, indistinct noise made by the other woman in the room and Sibyl looked into the cool blue eyes of the stunning woman who was standing five feet away from her.

The woman looked amused by this debacle.

Amused.

There was absolutely nothing funny about one damned minute of what had just occurred.

Not . . . one . . . thing.

She couldn't stay in this madhouse a second longer.

It was the man from her dream, come alive, breathing, walking, talking, *shouting*.

And he was stark raving mad.

She couldn't believe it.

It was just her luck. The moment she found who she thought was the man of her dreams, her one true love, the man she'd been waiting for her entire life, he was a screaming maniac.

Sibyl started to stand in order to escape when Mrs. Byrne pressed her back with surprising strength.

"There's medical assistance coming, you've had a nasty bang on the head, you need to rest."

"Rest?" Sibyl asked, her voice dripping with incredulity. "I'm sorry but I'm going home."

They heard the sirens when the crazy man from her dream strode angrily back into the room. He was holding her sleek, red leather handbag (a Christmas gift from her sister) and he fairly threw it at her when he arrived at their deranged quartet (quintet, if you counted Mallory).

"Your license," he gritted out through clenched teeth.

She had no idea why he needed her license. She'd never shown her license while viewing a National Trust or English Heritage site and she'd seen dozens of them.

Feeling she'd never been so humiliated in her whole life, noting that Mrs. Byrne was moving to her other side to wipe a drip of blood that Sibyl could feel sliding down her face, she tore through her bag and pulled out her wallet.

The other woman had disappeared.

She found her license and tossed it to him. He caught it without any effort and she wished (unusually waspishly) that he'd fumbled it.

He stared at it then lifted his angry clay-colored eyes to hers.

"Where's your passport?" he demanded.

"You have got to be kidding," she breathed.

She could not believe her ears.

She just wanted to see his house. It was a heritage estate for goddess's sake, not the Pentagon. It hardly required two forms of identification.

"She's right here. She's hit her head." The other woman was walking into the room leading two men in green jumpsuits and the men approached Sibyl, carrying medical boxes.

Sibyl felt like the cavalry had just arrived.

"What's happened here, then?" one man asked in a kindly tone and it took everything Sibyl had not to burst into tears.

She would *not* let the tall, good-looking madman see her cry. She didn't care if he was the man in her dream, he was not a dream man by any stretch of the imagination.

"I fell, outside, hit my head," Sibyl explained.

"What were you doing outside in this storm?" the paramedic asked, gently touching her head.

She turned imploringly towards him. "My dog . . . it doesn't matter. I need to go home."

"What year is it?" he inquired.

She lifted her eyes to the ceiling, praying for patience and counting to ten. She knew this drill, her sister was in the final years of her residency to be a neurologist and had spent hours regaling the family with information and stories filled with medical jargon, interesting case studies and detailed (and boring) explanations of testing and procedures.

Sibyl told him the year, the month, the day, the president's name, the prime minister's name, her name, her address and what she ate for breakfast (granola and fat-free, organic, vanilla yogurt).

"Did you lose consciousness?" he asked with an admiring (albeit slightly flirtatious) smile at her recitation.

Sibyl chanced a look at the man Mrs. Byrne called Mr. Morgan. He was looking now at the paramedic with narrowed eyes and a jaw clenched so hard Sibyl could see a muscle jump.

"Five minutes, at least," Mrs. Byrne replied helpfully.

She'd moved away to let the medic get to Sibyl and now she stood wringing the bloodied cloth in her hands and looking . . .

Sibyl peered closely at her . . .

Guilty.

"It's concerning, you'll have to be watched." The paramedic was cleaning the wound. "Put some ice on this immediately and keep it on for as long as you can bear it." He turned toward the maniac owner of Lacybourne. "I don't see any reason to admit her to hospital, she seems lucid and hasn't lost any memory. You'll have to observe her, make sure to wake her several times in the night—"

"*What?*" Sibyl shouted. "No! I'm going home."

"This isn't home?" The paramedic looked from her to the crazy man and went on bizarrely, "That picture in the hall—"

"This is *not* her home," Mr. Morgan's baritone voice noted drily.

"I'll take her home," Mrs. Byrne waded in courageously. "Or, my dear, I know we don't know each other very well but perhaps you should stay with me tonight. We'll come collect your car tomorrow. My cats won't mind a little company."

"She really should rest," the other medic was saying while the first one put a bandage on the side of Sibyl's forehead.

"I'm leaving," Sibyl insisted.

"You're staying," the lunatic put in smoothly.

"She's *what*?" the cool brunette snapped, finally losing her arctic composure.

"No I most certainly am not!" Sibyl shouted, making her head pound.

"I'll not have you leave this house and die in the night from a concussion and open myself up to your American family suing me for every penny I've got," Mr. Morgan noted in a calm, even voice.

"I'm not going to die," Sibyl snapped.

"You're not going to leave," he returned.

"My parents will not sue," she felt the need to add.

"You're still not going to leave," he retorted.

"Oh dear," Mrs. Byrne said.

"You're staying too," the lord of the manor stated.

"I thought that," Mrs. Byrne noted resignedly. She grabbed Sibyl's hand and patted it kindly. "I'll look after you."

Sibyl turned her eyes to the older woman and she saw the woman staring at her with a bizarre intensity.

"I want to go home, Mrs. Byrne," Sibyl told her, her tone fervent.

"Don't worry, my dear. We'll all have a good rest and we'll sort it out in the morning."

"Not likely." This, of course, was noted by the tall, impossibly handsome but utterly mad man who owned this (from what she could tell from the one room she'd actually seen) beautiful home.

Sibyl turned beseeching eyes to the kindly paramedic, thinking maybe even Mrs. Byrne had only a tentative hold on reality.

"I just want to go home," she informed who she hoped would be her savior.

He seemed to hesitate, clearly reading the mood in the room, when a radio squawked.

"Got another one," his colleague said, pulling the radio from his leg.

"Sorry," the kindly paramedic muttered. "Call me tomorrow, my name is Steve. Let me know how you're getting on." Then he winked (definitely flirtatiously, which of course was nice and all but didn't do her any good at the present moment and further was a bit inappropriate), pressed a card in her hand and followed his colleague out the door.

Sibyl looked from the small, dark woman who was staring at her with polar icecaps as eyes. Then she moved her eyes to Mrs. Byrne who was smiling at her . . . could she believe it . . . encouragingly.

Then finally to her dream man, who was looking like he couldn't decide whether to beat her to a bloody pulp or carry her up to his bedroom for something else altogether.

And that was no joke. Honestly, she could read that right in his eyes.

That last thought made her breath flood out of her in a rush and she glared at him with mutinous eyes.

If she couldn't find a way to escape, Sibyl thought hysterically, it was going to be a long night.

Chapter FIVE

Tempted

It was the longest night in Sibyl's life.

Once the paramedics left, Mr. Morgan—the raving lunatic who most definitely needed psychiatric counselling, or at the very least anger management classes—left her and Mrs. Byrne alone. He took the unnamed Ice Queen with him.

The Polar Sorceress came back shortly after with an ice pack and handed it rather ungraciously to Mrs. Byrne, completely avoiding looking at Sibyl at all.

Then she left again.

After Sibyl attempted to talk Mrs. Byrne into making a break for it (that maniac couldn't actually *imprison* them in his medieval manor house, for goodness sakes), Mrs. Byrne explained the misunderstanding and how she felt that it was a good idea to let tempers cool and talk about everything in the morning.

"I'm afraid, Mr. Morgan can be a somewhat, er . . . *difficult* man," she admitted.

Indeed, Sibyl thought but did not say nor did she bring up the fact that just the evening before Mrs. Byrne painted an entirely different picture of the man of the house.

And "difficult" she felt, was not exactly the word *she* would use.

Studying the older woman, Sibyl got the impression that Mrs. Byrne genuinely wanted the opportunity to let tempers cool so they could sort things out in the morning. In fact, it seemed for some reason this was very important to Mrs. Byrne.

The woman volunteered for the National Trust and she had, regrettably, if unwittingly, caused this bizarre fiasco. Undoubtedly, she wanted the chance to smooth things over so she wouldn't get into trouble.

As was Sibyl's wont (which always got her into trouble and she knew it but had never been able to control it), Sibyl didn't have the heart to deny the older woman this opportunity.

And anyway, Mr. Morgan may be a raving lunatic but he didn't seem to be a violent one, just a loud and angry one.

So she settled in for the long haul the night would mostly likely be and thought that her mother had never been very good at reading dreams and Sibyl herself had read the dream entirely incorrectly.

Last night's dream had not meant she needed a lover (especially not *this* lover) and it was not leading her to her dream man.

It meant she should not, under any circumstances, go to Lacybourne because its owner was certifiably insane.

As Mrs. Byrne mollycoddled her, Sibyl tried to insist she was well enough to sit up even though she was definitely feeling a bit woozy and, she had to admit, she was not at all certain she could safely take herself *and* her beloved animals home without assistance even if that opportunity had presented itself when Lady Ice, again, interrupted their *tête-à-tête* by bringing in two plates of food.

"Colin thought you might want something to eat so I prepared this for you," she announced, as if preparing food was akin to cleaning toilets at a roadside stopover in the depths of the jungles of Venezuela.

Mrs. Byrne took the food and the other woman walked out of the room again without another word.

Sibyl was left stunned that "Colin" considered their hunger at all but then, even though she'd never read the document (and didn't really wish to), she was still relatively certain that under the Geneva Convention, prisoners were entitled to sustenance.

Each small plate held a single sandwich, if they could be called sandwiches considering they were two pieces of bread that held only a wafer thin slice of ham, no condiments, no butter, nothing. They weren't even cut in half.

So much for the Ivana of the North's hostessing skills.

Sibyl set hers aside and when Mrs. Byrne noticed it (she herself tucking into the food like it was the finest delicacy) she encouraged Sibyl, "You must have something. Keep your strength up."

Sibyl shook her head, slightly alarmed that Mrs. Byrne seemed to be keen on preparing her for battle. "I don't eat ham. I'm a vegetarian."

"Oh dear," Mrs. Byrne muttered then her eyes brightened. "Well, I'll just have to go see if Mr. Morgan has anything else in the house."

"No!" Sibyl cried, yes, *cried*, desperate and everything.

And she did this because she didn't want Mr. Morgan to remember her existence at all. He seemed ludicrously averse to it. She had to get through the next twelve hours, through most of which she hoped she'd be sleeping and she did *not* want to rock the boat.

Mrs. Byrne smiled at Sibyl, a twinkle in her eye, and ignored her, setting aside her plate to go off in search of different food.

Sibyl sat back on the couch with a weary sigh and placed the ice on her temple. Bran reappeared, completely unfazed by the dramatic events, curled up on Sibyl's belly and Sibyl idly stroked his soft, fluffy fur.

She had no idea why the appallingly-attractive-but-clearly-possessed-by-Satan Mr. Morgan had reacted so horribly to her presence at Lacybourne. It was distressing and utterly bizarre. Anyone could see that Mrs. Byrne had made a simple mistake, it wasn't worth confiscating Sibyl's license (which he had done, he did not give it back and he also took her handbag with him when he left) and holding them both prisoner. It was almost as if he expected the old woman and Sibyl to be conniving to steal the family silver out from under his nose.

Sibyl could, of course, get up and walk out (albeit unsteadily). However, that would mean leaving Mrs. Byrne behind to face the towering-inferno-also-known-as-Mr. Morgan and that she would *not* do.

She did have the unusual feeling, however, that Mrs. Byrne seemed somehow pleased at these events, and not simply because Sibyl staying meant Mrs. Byrne might have the chance to get things straight with Mr. Morgan and not lose her obviously beloved role at Lacybourne. But, instead, she was pleased for other reasons entirely.

Sibyl put that strange idea down to her mild concussion.

Mrs. Byrne arrived back in the room with Mr. Morgan arrogantly striding in on her heels.

Although Sibyl did not know him very well (and what she did know of him, she didn't want to know), she could tell he was still furious. She could tell this by the muscle leaping convulsively in his rock-hard jaw.

"Is there anything else we can do for you here at Lacybourne Manor, *Miss Godwin*?" His tone was impeccably polite but he said her name like it tasted foul.

For the sake of her sanity, and her head, Sibyl ignored him.

His strange antipathy to her was only eclipsed by his extreme dislike of her name.

"A bite of cheese and some crackers," Mrs. Byrne explained, proffering a plate on which rested some rather unsavory-looking slices of cheese and crackers.

Then Mrs. Byrne sat in a comfortably worn leather chair by the invitingly worn leather couch on which Sibyl was reclining.

Mrs. Byrne appeared, to Sibyl's continued incredulity, to be having the time of her life.

"Thank you, Mrs. Byrne," Sibyl replied, taking the plate.

"You're more than welcome, my dear."

Realizing that the two women were not going to address him, Mr. Morgan turned to walk away but then Mrs. Byrne, who clearly had a death wish, called out, "Oh, Mr. Morgan!"

He looked first over his shoulder and then turned his entire body back towards them slowly, his eyes blazing, and Sibyl held her breath.

"We could use a drink, perhaps a bit of wine?" Her eyes slid to Sibyl. "Or, in your state, do you think you should have wine, dear?"

He didn't wait for Sibyl's reply, however. He simply left the room.

The Goddess of the Antarctic slid into the room not five minutes later with an opened bottle of red wine and two exquisite, full-bodied, crystal wine glasses. After plonking them down on a table, without another word, she slid out again.

"Never mind," Mrs. Byrne said to the other woman's parting back. Then, enthusiastically, she turned to Sibyl, completely dismissing the other two beings who currently inhabited the house with them and were likely plotting their bloody demise, she asked conversationally, "Tell me all about yourself. I want to know *everything*."

Sibyl, needing an excuse not to think about the freakish evening, did as Mrs. Byrne asked. As she talked, Mrs. Byrne would interrupt with strange comments such as, "Of course, your father is English," and, "Brightrose Cottage, now that's *most* interesting."

When Sibyl was finished relating her life story, drinking a glass of wine and eating her meager portion of cheese, she poured more wine (rather clumsily as she was still holding the ice pack to her head).

"Now, Mrs. Byrne," she invited, "tell me about you."

Over their second glass, Mrs. Byrne told her about her dead husband, Arthur, her two children, her five grandchildren, her three cats, her life as a librarian, her retirement ten years ago and her seven year tenure at Lacybourne Manor.

"Alas, I fear *that's* over." She shrugged eloquently, giving Sibyl another bright-eyed look, her blithe comment making Sibyl want to laugh at the same time it made her want to grab Mrs. Byrne's hand and give it a reassuring squeeze.

Sibyl had to admit, talking to the older woman was quite relaxing. She liked her immensely. Mrs. Byrne obviously adored her family and had a great sense of humor, and under any other circumstances Sibyl would have enjoyed their conversation greatly.

Then, Princess Glacier glided into the room again and told them it was time for bed.

Mrs. Byrne saw to letting Mallory and Bran out for a last minute comfort break (and Sibyl just stopped herself from encouraging the older woman to make a break for it) while the black-haired woman took Sibyl up a back stairwell to the upper floor of the house.

Sibyl would not have been surprised if she put them in the servants' quarters but instead she was shown into an enormous, beautifully appointed room filled with priceless antique furniture and a colossal four-poster bed with exquisite muted gold and sage-green drapes, coverlet and a massive quantity of fluffy pillows.

The only problem was that the room was freezing cold.

Sibyl decided she would freeze to death before she would utter one, single word.

"Mrs. Byrne will be in the room across the hall." With that, Mistress Frosty took her leave and shortly after, Mrs. Byrne let Mallory and Bran into Sibyl's room.

"You rest, dear. I'll come in and check on you every half an hour."

"You don't have to do that, Mrs. Byrne. I'm sure I'm fine."

And if she wasn't, it would be Mr. Morgan's just desserts to have to explain her dead body to Albert and Marguerite Godwin. Her dad and mom might look like a mad scientist and stereotypical archetype of Mother Nature but they both had tempers that could rival . . . well . . . Sibyl's when it was riled and that was a mighty feat.

"Please, call me Marian," Mrs. Byrne broke into Sibyl's vindictive reverie.

When the older woman left, Sibyl took a look around her at the beautiful room and decided her best bet was not to disturb anything at all.

With some pleading and a good deal of stern words, she managed to keep Mallory off the bed. The big dog sighed his displeasure and settled on the floor. Bran, however, never followed orders and curled happily at the foot of the bed.

Sibyl took off her boots and her jacket and set her jewelry on the bedside table. Laying on top of the covers in the wintry cold room, she tucked her feet under her long skirt and positioned her coat on top of her, feeling about as warm as Captain Scott must have during the race to the South Pole.

Not thirty minutes later, Mrs. Byrne came in the room.

Still awake and trying not to think of her dream of last night, the events of that evening and how they all fit together (or, spectacularly, did not) Sibyl assured the woman quietly, "I'm fine."

"You must sleep. I have a feeling you have a long road ahead of you," Mrs. Byrne whispered as she laid a comforting hand on Sibyl's shoulder.

Sibyl didn't know what to make of this latest comment that came in her current occupancy in the World of Lunacy. But she smiled, mentally promising herself to check in on the old woman after this debacle was complete to make certain Marian Byrne wasn't suffering from a mild form of dementia. Then, obligingly, she nestled her head into the soft pillows.

This happened twice more. The second time, Mrs. Byrne actually woke her and Sibyl was surprised she could get to sleep at all.

It seemed only moments after Mrs. Byrne left the room when she heard the door open again. She pretended to ignore the older lady, hoping she would cease her kind, but overly earnest, ministrations and get some sleep herself.

But this time, Mrs. Byrne entered the room and stopped and Sibyl could almost feel the lady's eyes on her. Obviously deciding Sibyl needed her rest, she left again, only to come back not five minutes later.

After she heard some rustling across the room, unceremoniously, Sibyl's jacket was pulled off of her.

She twirled around in bed to look up, not at Mrs. Byrne, but at a tall, looming male standing imposingly beside the bed.

"Get up," Colin Morgan commanded in a deep, angry voice.

"What are you—?" Sibyl started.

He reached forward and pulled her roughly out of the bed and the only way she could respond to this stunning action was to yelp.

"Did it occur to you to turn on the radiator?" His tone was caustic.

Sibyl blinked in the direction of one of several radiators in the room.

No, it actually didn't occur to her and she wondered why it hadn't, but then she'd always been a bit flighty and absentminded. However, she would never impart this information on *him*.

He didn't wait for an answer and demanded, "Put this on."

He tossed a garment to her and she had no choice but to catch it and shake it out. In the light coming in from the hall she realized it was the top of a pair of men's pajamas.

Most likely *his* pajamas.

"I can't wear this!" she snapped, ready to toss it back to him.

"Nothing Tamara has will fit you, for obvious reasons." She saw his eyes run the length of her body and she thought from the look in them that perhaps this ended up being not the cutting insult he meant to be.

Tamara must be Mother Winter's name.

"I'll sleep in my clothes," Sibyl told him.

"You'll put that on," he parried.

She glared at him and he glared right back.

He, of course, was better at it.

"Miss Godwin, you can either put it on or I'll put it on you. You choose."

His command was shocking and it was said in a voice that was dangerous and chockfull of meaning. Sibyl knew in an instant, understood it somehow to her very core, that he was ruthless enough to do it.

Strangely, and distressingly, she felt like she'd been in this exact position before, facing off against him.

And losing.

This feeling was not a little familiar, but a lot, like it didn't happen once but repeatedly.

And it was bizarre, frightening and, lastly, bizarrely, frighteningly *reassuring*.

Her energy was draining away, her head hurt like the devil and she was ready to do just about anything to make this night go a hell of a lot more smoothly until she reached its joyful conclusion.

"Fine," she bit out between clenched teeth, thinking agreement would make him go and then she could ignore his order and try to get some sleep. "I'll put it on, now you can go."

He crossed his arms on his chest as if he was settling in for a show.

Then he demanded, "Put it on now."

Sibyl's breath caught and her eyes bugged out before she breathed, "What?"

"Now," he clipped.

"You're joking."

He didn't answer but he also didn't look like he was joking.

She started trembling. She had absolutely no idea what this entire night was all about. *She* was the wounded party here, if you counted her head, literally. All she wanted to do was see his house. If he didn't want her to, he could have simply told her to go on her way. *Not* held her hostage. *Not* confiscated her purse. *Not* treated her like she was a criminal. *Not* barked at Mrs. Byrne.

She thought, somewhat hysterically, that he was supposed to be the fierce, glorious lover from her dream. The man who, when his throat was slit and she knew his life was pouring out of him, she felt such an utter sense of loss that she would have begged for the knife to slice her own throat as well rather than to live without him.

This whole scene was entirely wrong.

In fact, it felt cataclysmically wrong.

She glared at him and saw the set line of his jaw, thinking that there was a possibility, if she defied him, this would get physical.

She felt a burning shame creeping up at her total loss of power. She wanted to scream at him, rail at him, claw at his eyes.

And, unbelievably, she also wanted to throw herself in his arms.

She just stood there staring at him.

He could overpower her in a second. She was not a small woman but he was clearly fit, definitely tall and obviously far, far stronger than she. Lacybourne was just on the outskirts of town and surrounded by forest, therefore no one would hear her if she shouted. Ice Princess Tamara, she doubted, would come to her aid and Mrs. Byrne would be no help at all but would undoubtedly try, and maybe get herself harmed in the process.

And therefore Sibyl had no choice and she *hated* that.

"Okay," she gave in, feeling deep embarrassment that her voice sounded shaky. "Turn around."

He again didn't speak

He also didn't turn.

She waited a moment, realizing that his manners did not extend to allowing her a modicum of privacy, and with a strangled sound she turned herself, presenting her back to him.

She'd never been so humiliated in her entire life. She felt hot, shameful tears spring to her eyes and could do nothing to stop them, though she used every bit of her willpower not to make a sound.

As quickly as she could, she whipped off her T-shirt and pulled the pajama top over her head, not bothering to take off her bra. She undid the zip on her skirt in the back and pulled it down, hooking her fingers in her tights as she did so (careful to leave her panties in place), stepping out of both pieces of clothing at the same time and dropping them on her T-shirt.

She whirled around again.

"Happy now?" she asked, but didn't look at him, hiding behind a curtain of hair because she didn't want him to see the tears on her cheeks.

His answer was to lean forward and whip back the covers of the bed.

Bran lifted his head in ill humor, his yellow eyes indicating his unhappiness at having his slumber disturbed.

Mallory, exhausted from the evening's escapades, was lying on his side on the floor, his legs sprawled out in front of him, completely unperturbed by this new horror.

Sibyl thought with dismay that her mother had been wrong about the cat.

She clambered into the bed, doing her best to keep her back to him, and when she lay down, he whipped the covers over her. She curled into a little ball, pressed her face into the pillows, and it didn't dawn on her as she did this that he was actually pulling the covers high up her shoulder and then tucking them tight around her.

She hoped he would go now that he had his way, but he didn't. Instead, she felt his warm hand heavy at her neck and her entire body got tight.

Slowly, even gently, he pulled her hair away.

Then his mouth was at her ear.

"You should know that tears don't work with me." His voice was as smooth as velvet and completely cold.

She shivered.

She had no idea why he was informing her of this fact but it sounded like he was instructing her. Instructing her in a way that it seemed he felt she needed this information for their future relationship to go much smoother.

Like they had a future relationship!

Not on her life!

(Or his.)

She pressed her head deeper into the pillows, her humiliation complete, wondering in which of her former lives she did something so terrible that her karma included this awful night. She must have been a serial killer in a past life.

"I thought you might like to know, I have the keys to your car as well." His voice was still at her ear, still quiet, but it seemed to vibrate throughout her system.

"You're a pig," she whispered and this comment caused him to laugh softly.

He had, she thought with extreme annoyance, a very handsome laugh.

If she was a violent woman, she would have lashed out. Instead, more tears came up the back of her throat and she choked them down with effort.

Finally, he left the room and the minute the door closed she threw back the covers with such fury that even Mallory woke from his exhausted doggie slumber.

She alighted from the bed and ignored the dizzy feeling her quick movements caused.

She was going to put her clothes back on. She was going to go get Mrs. Byrne. She was going to explain that no volunteer role was worth *this*. And she was damn well going to walk home (if she had to, he didn't say he took Mrs. Byrne's keys).

But when she looked she found her clothes were gone.

Colin Morgan had taken them.

She collapsed back into the bed, wondering if she could press charges when this was all over, and holding on to her rage because it was the only thing that stopped her from crying.

And it was the only thing that stopped her from thinking, however dictatorially it came about, she was far more comfortable in his pajama top, under the covers and in the soft sheets of the bed.

And the room was infinitely warmer.

SIBYL FINALLY SLEPT but woke early. The days were still short, the sun not yet fully up in the sky.

She woke because Mallory desperately needed a comfort break and was telling her so by shoving his cold, wet nose in her face.

She had no moment of panic at her unfamiliar surroundings. The events of the night before that were burned into her memory surfaced, but she still touched her hand to her aching head in hopes that it was all a very bad dream.

It wasn't.

She had to take her dog outside. She certainly didn't want to explain a doggie accident to Colin Morgan and likely the rugs on the floor were irreplaceable.

Sibyl got out of bed and then she and Mallory, with Bran at their heels (the cat probably thinking that breakfast would soon be coming) carefully wended their way through the house.

Sibyl was making more of an effort to be quiet and find her way than attempting to look at the house she once so desperately wanted to see.

She visited National Trust properties as a pastime. It was a hobby she enjoyed with her father during their many visits to England, a hobby that she normally loved.

At that moment, the first (and she hoped last) time she would ever be a "guest" at such a magnificent estate, she was not filled with wonder and awe. She was filled with terror and tried to avoid looking at anything that would eventually make this memory more painful.

She made it to the front door and realized she couldn't exactly walk outside in a man's pajama top and bare feet.

Searching around her, she saw the almost hidden handle to a door in the carved-wood paneling in the wall of the entry. Her luck changing when she pulled it open with hopes of finding outdoor gear she could borrow, she discovered a very small room filled with a bunch of

National Trust brochures and other paraphernalia, some coats and, as with nearly every English hall closet she'd encountered, a mess of Wellingtons. She grabbed the warmest looking coat in the closet and a matching pair of Wellingtons and pushed her feet into them. Then she wrapped the enormous cashmere overcoat tightly around her body (hoping that it was not *his*, she'd had enough of wearing *his* clothes).

Outfitted, she turned and opened the front door. Mallory, who had begun whining at what he thought was Sibyl's unnecessary delay in searching for ways to stop herself from dying from hypothermia (or at the very least avoiding frostbite), shot through the door.

Sibyl and Bran followed him. The morning was bright, crisp and bone-chillingly cold. Sibyl ignored it and hoped to every goddess she knew that Mallory's morning break did not include something for which she'd have to search the house for a plastic bag.

Luck was shining on her that morning even though it was to be short-lived. Mallory finished his business (business that did not require clean up) and seemed to be enjoying the vast front garden by running around it in circles for no apparent reason. Mallory, being a big, ungainly dog, rarely ran *anywhere*. He usually took his walks making it clear he did it under duress (because Sibyl made him), got up to eat even though he made it plain he would prefer Sibyl to bring the food to him and then spent the rest of his life sleeping or with his head in Sibyl's lap getting his ears scratched.

Watching him now, Sibyl wondered with a bit of guilt if she should take him to the park more often.

"Mallory, come here, boy, come here you big, lovable, lug."

She clapped her hands and the dog ran toward her, stopped at her feet, his behind up in the air, his front legs spread and close to the ground, his tail wagging so ferociously his body vibrated with it.

She clapped again, smiling at him for she'd never seen him assume this posture, *ever*. But she loved her pup and she was game so she jumped to one side and Mallory followed her, then she jumped to the other side and Mallory did the same. Then she leaned forward and gave his head an affectionate shake.

"What am I going to do with you, you crazy pooch?" she asked and the dog stood up, accepted her kiss on his soft, fawn head and then his black, floppy ears popped up in alert.

He looked around Sibyl, ears flapping, and dashed back toward the house.

Sibyl turned and saw Colin Morgan leaning against the doorjamb. He was wearing jeans and what looked like a very warm oatmeal-colored fisherman's sweater. His arms were crossed on his chest, one bare foot crossed at his ankle. Apparently oblivious to the cold, he was settled in and watching her in a way that made it seem like he could do it all day.

"Blooming hell," she muttered under her breath and immediately felt the cold creeping up her bare legs, cold she did not feel when she was playing with her dog.

She tramped inelegantly toward the house in the floppy wellies that were too big for her and Mr. Morgan, she noted with consternation, did not appear ready to move out of her way. If he was going to deny her entry and she was going to have to suffer the indignity of walking the short distance to Clevedon in Wellingtons, a pajama top and an overcoat, so be it.

"Enjoying yourself?"

His tone was not good morning cheerful and she didn't answer as she was *never* good morning cheerful. Therefore, she cast a vicious glance in his direction.

For some bizarre reason, this caused him to throw his head back and laugh as he dropped his arms to his sides. His masculine throat was exposed and the sound was deep and rich and she liked it so much, it made her start to seethe.

She stopped two feet away from him and stared at him like he was the raving lunatic she knew him to be.

"Let me pass," she demanded once his laughter quieted.

Mallory was seated half a foot away, looking up at Mr. Morgan, his tongue lolling out of his mouth, his tail still wagging. Before Colin Morgan could reply to Sibyl's demand, the dog leaned forward and licked his hand.

Sibyl stared in disbelief.

Her dog had always, always hated men (except her father).

"Mallory!" she snapped and the dog whined then he licked Mr. Morgan's hand again. 'Mallory! Stop that!" she scolded the dog, and then to her surprise she found her arm in a vise-like grip and she was yanked through the door.

It was slammed behind her and before she could get her bearings, she was roughly pushed backward until she hit the door.

And again, before she even realized what was happening, Colin Morgan stepped into her, not even a foot away, cutting off any escape. He dipped his face to hers and he was so close she could feel the heat from his body through the coat and the warmth of his breath on her face.

"The police just called," he told her.

She blinked up at him and there was something about him being there, so close, all she could see, almost like he was everywhere and everything, her entire world. His presence simply overpowered her.

And this was an odd, frightening *familiar* sensation too. It was as if she'd looked up into his clay-colored eyes so near she could count his eyelashes and she'd not done it once or twice but countless times.

Countless.

She could also smell his cologne (a nice woodsy, musky scent, she noted with professional detachment, with hints of cedar). She could see his lashes, very thick and long. And she noticed for the first time that his lower lip was, surprisingly, sensuously full.

"I have a friend at New Scotland Yard. He did a search on you last night. It appears you are who you say you are," he was saying.

That got her attention and her gaze snapped from his lips upward. "Of course I am who I say I am. Who else would I be?"

He watched her, his eyes strange and glittering and again he had no response.

After several very long moments of silence, Sibyl realized she was holding her breath but she also knew it was either that or pant. Although she had just been out in the chill morning air, suddenly her body felt very hot and her heart had begun to pound.

"I still don't trust you for a moment," he informed her.

She had no idea what to make of that comment so she simply told him exactly what was in her mind.

"You're mad."

He proved her right by responding to her insult with, "What's that smell?"

Sibyl looked wildly around for Mallory, hoping that she didn't miss something during his morning business when Morgan's voice came again. This time softly, so softly she thought she could almost feel it on her skin.

"It smells like lilies."

Her eyes jerked to his and his were still glittering. But instead of anger, she was shocked to see (and her heart began pounding all the more insistently at the sight), there was an odd, sweet warmth there.

Something was happening to her, something she didn't understand and something she definitely couldn't control. She felt the tenseness slide from her body and her bones felt like they were softening. She felt compelled to touch him, to get closer to him, to move her body into his. Her eyelids lowered and she looked at him from underneath her lashes.

Her voice came out, just as soft as his. "It's my perfume."

He watched her for a second, his head slowly, nearly imperceptibly, descending to hers and she thought, hysterically, that he was going to kiss her.

And she braced for it. Ready for it.

Wanting it.

Then he stopped, she watched him blink and then, his tone back to cool civility, he remarked, "God, you're good."

And this was *not* a compliment. She knew this comment was meant to be insulting, knew it right to the very marrow of her bones.

It felt like she was sitting in a dunking booth, someone hit the bull's-eye and she'd crashed into its icy waters.

"I want to go home," she demanded and he hadn't moved away so she put her hands on the hard wall of his chest and shoved.

He didn't budge.

And finally after banging her head, having her license confiscated, being held hostage, forced to change in front of a male stranger who, according to her very faulty dreams, was supposed to be the love of her life and, most importantly, forgetting to count to ten, the full force of her temper exploded.

"I want to go home!" she shouted in his face. "Give me my damned clothes and my bag and my car keys and my license and let me get out of this crazy place!"

He did not react to her fury as she expected him to. He didn't move away. He didn't seem offended or angered.

If anything, he moved closer.

Sibyl completely ignored it and announced, "Mr. Morgan, if you want me to leave here and not press charges then you better step back, let me take my animals and go home."

"What if I told you I'm tempted?" he replied bizarrely, his gaze hooded and he looked (goddess help her, *she* was going insane too) unbelievably sexy.

"Tempted by what?" she squeaked.

"By you."

Her eyes rounded, she sucked in her breath so deeply her chest expanded and she shoved him with every ounce of strength she possessed. Fortunately this worked, he went back on a foot.

Then she cried, "You're deranged!" She pulled off the coat and threw it at him, not noticing that he caught it deftly because she bent down to yank off the Wellingtons. She'd lost it, in a rage that was completely out of control and so done with Colin Morgan, if she *could* control it, she wouldn't. "You're like a male Mrs. Rochester except *you* have run of the house."

She noticed over his shoulder that Ms. Winter Wonderland, Tamara, was staring at the scene with polar spears darting from her eyes.

"You!" Sibyl pointed at the woman. "Need to lock him up before he does any damage." Then she stomped (as much as she could stomp in bare feet) into the Great Hall. "Now will someone give me my fucking clothes?" she shouted at the top of her voice.

"I'd be delighted," Tamara returned, her voice calm and smooth.

In an ungracious tone, Sibyl replied, "Thank you."

"Follow me," Tamara invited.

Sibyl did and gratefully, Mallory following closely behind, his tail still wagging.

MRS. BYRNE HAD witnessed this scene and was left watching Colin from across the Great Hall as Sibyl (looking *very* appealing in his pajama top) and Tamara disappeared up the stairs.

Colin carelessly tossed the expensive coat over a chair and saw the older woman look up at the portraits then back at him, and he knew he was meant to understand her meaningful glances.

They stood that way, squaring off like opponents on a battlefield as moments turned to minutes and then Sibyl, struggling to pull her shirt over her head while, impossibly, her jacket and boots where tucked under her arm, stamped down the stairs, muttering to herself such phrases as "loony bin" and "danger to society."

Sibyl stopped, shrugged into her jacket then bent over to pull on her boots, and then she strode angrily to Colin. He stared down his nose at her.

He'd seen her earlier that morning, out the window, in her ridiculous outfit (an outfit that still managed to look enticing on her) and it was almost as if he couldn't control himself. It was almost as if an invisible force pulled him to the front door to watch her cavorting with her damned dog.

She was (he knew, as he was a connoisseur of women) unbelievably beddable. His hands itched to touch her, his mouth was dry with the effort not to kiss her. Last night, when he found her stubbornly shivering in her sleep, he had the strong urge he almost couldn't beat back and very nearly warmed her with his own body.

Earlier, every time she'd said "Mallory" it made his gut twitch because it sounded so familiar, as if he'd heard her say it before, many times before.

It didn't help matters, when the dog licked his hand, *that* seemed bizarrely familiar and welcome as well.

Now, she was standing before him, her eyes flashing that intriguing green when five minutes before, when he looked into her eyes, they were a warm sherry, and she held her hand out, palm up.

"Keys!" she barked in his face, her clearly formidable, and just as appealing, temper flashing like lightning in the room.

He calmly pushed his hand into the pocket of his jeans and deposited her car keys in her palm.

Tamara came forward and held out the red purse to Sibyl who snatched it out of the woman's hand without a word.

Colin slowly, taking his time, looked between the two women.

Tamara was his type, dark, petite, thin, sophisticated and cool.

Sibyl was not his type. She was golden, lush, curvy and tempestuous.

To his stunned surprise, there was absolutely no comparison. Tamara, he found, was sadly lacking.

Colin decided in that moment that Sibyl was rather magnificent, even if he felt certain that every movement was a studied performance. He had no idea what she and the older woman wished to gain but he was beginning to think that it might be rather diverting to turn the tables on them.

Especially if Sibyl Godwin (if that was, indeed, her real name as the police had assured him the resident of Brightrose Cottage, the address on her license, was named) was as splendidly hot in bed as she was out of it.

The other option remained that she *was* Sibyl Godwin, the reincarnation of the legendary Beatrice. The fact that option existed, even minutely, Colin knew meant it had to be explored.

He noticed throughout her act that she didn't even glance at the portraits and he didn't know what to make of that when Sibyl interrupted his thoughts by speaking.

"Mrs. Byrne, I'd love to have coffee somewhere far, *far* away from Lacybourne. Please call me if you'd like to do that sometime," she said to the older woman, her voice lower and more controlled.

"I would be delighted," Mrs. Byrne replied.

"And as for you," she turned to Colin, her eyes shimmering emeralds, she finished hotly, "I hope I never see *you* again!"

Colin studied her knowing he'd see her again.

He was planning on it.

And looking forward to it.

Thus, he did not reply.

With that, and without a comment to Tamara, she stomped out the door whistling to her dog and, when outside, calling to her cat.

They heard doors slam, the car start and the gravel fly as she peeled out of Lacybourne.

"I must say, Mr. Morgan," Mrs. Byrne was talking and Colin's eyes slid to the older woman. He read, very clearly this time that her voice held a more than mild rebuke. "*That* was *not* very well handled."

Then, with great dignity, she exited the room.

Chapter SIX

Rescue

Sibyl was *not* having a good time.

Her life, since the morning she left Lacybourne, (not unusually but still upsettingly) descended into a mess.

The only shining good fortune she seemed to have was Mrs. Byrne, who she now had a standing date to have breakfast with every Monday morning. They'd met last Monday nearly a week since their first encounter on the steps of Lacybourne and decided to make it a ritual. Sibyl had enjoyed the woman's company and was thrilled to have a new friend.

Social Services was very understanding about Annie and the sad state of her house but their hands were tied regarding the minibus driver.

Therefore, Sibyl decided to have a few choice words with him. Her choice words, and the hold on her calm, deteriorated to the point where Kyle had to pull her back as she began to shout into the driver's pitted, sneering face.

"You'll make it worse for them, luv, if you upset him," Kyle explained, gently pushing her toward the door to the Day Centre.

She didn't have to ride the minibus, Kyle reminded her, the pensioners did. And angering the driver would only make matters worse.

Kyle was right, of course, and after her minibus driver tirade, Sibyl sought out Jemma and collapsed in a chair in her office, sipping at a fortifying cup of coffee that Tina made her to calm her down (something Tina had become adept at doing in the past year).

"I'm out of control," Sibyl admitted to her friend.

Days before, when Jemma had asked at the bandage at her temple, she'd told her friend everything about Lacybourne. She had *not* told her mother or her sister, especially considering her premonitory dream and Colin Morgan's part in that. Both women would have been in fits (especially if she described him in every luscious detail) and likely would have wanted her to go back and explore her options, crazy man or not, especially if she'd relayed the information that he'd told her he was "tempted."

Tempted!

Insane!

Jemma's response to the story was odd.

"You say he covered you up at night when you were cold?" Jemma asked.

Sibyl stared at her but didn't answer.

"And watched you playing with Mallory?" Jemma went on.

"Yes," Sibyl drew out the word warningly, feeling the need to focus on the deviant parts of Colin Morgan's personality, not the contradictorily kind ones that seemed to underlie them.

"And made sure you had something to eat and even . . . wine?" Jemma continued.

"What are you driving at, Jem?"

"Well, his behavior *is* very bizarre, I'll grant you that."

"Why, thank you," Sibyl's voice was laced with disgruntled sarcasm.

"However, he did keep you in his home to watch over you after you banged your head."

"He didn't 'keep me,' he *imprisoned* me and he only did it because he didn't want my parents to sue," Sibyl contradicted because she thought it was important to keep the facts straight.

Jemma ignored her. "He also fed you, looked in on you in the night, gave you something comfortable to wear and made sure you were warm."

Sibyl let out an exasperated explosion of breath.

"I'm just saying," Jemma placated with a shrug.

Sibyl abruptly changed the subject.

Now, days later, in Jemma's office after the minibus debacle, Jemma watched her with her usual kindly reserve.

"Perhaps that bang on your head shook something loose," Jem suggested unhelpfully.

"I don't think I'm going to come to you for reassurance anymore," Sibyl grumbled.

Jemma laughed. "I'm a mother. We tend, in certain situations, to lean more toward honesty than reassurance."

"I'd say now was one of those 'reassuring times,'" Sibyl countered.

Jem just shook her head wisely.

The day after Lacybourne, Sibyl called Steve, the paramedic, to tell him she was all right.

In return, Steve had asked her out on a date.

Even though she didn't know him from Adam, because of her mother's advice and her continued conversations with her animals (and perhaps a bit of desperation after Lacybourne), she'd accepted his invitation, and tonight she was with him in a fashionable, popular club in Bristol.

Sibyl did not often date. No man ever met her expectations of what she'd always hoped for, or, more to the point, *knew* was her ideal. Although she loved to dance, she rarely went out to do it. She preferred doing things like breakfasts with Mrs. Byrne, chats over coffee with Kyle, Tina or Jem or her afternoon rendezvous with Meg than sitting in a pub getting snockered on pints. She spent a great deal of time in her summer house, concocting lotions, shampoos, and experimenting with the varying, complicated scents that made her spa treatments so popular.

But she thought Steve was a safe bet. He was a paramedic, which was a caring profession. Logically, she thought, being in a caring profession meant he had to have a good heart.

Therefore, being in a busy, loud club with a man who, as a paramedic, had been quite attentive and appealing, but as a date was anything but, was a form of torture.

The evening had not started on a high note.

Steve had shown up at Brightrose Cottage and Mallory nearly took a bite out of him.

Scuttling to his car while Sibyl struggled with the snarling dog, he called out from the safety of the space between the car's open door and body, "Whenever you're ready!"

Clearly, he's fearless, she thought sardonically, watching Steve quickly enter his flashy, chrome-plated Mazda and slam the door, and she gave up that little bit more of the fast-dwindling hope of ever finding the strong, brave, wonderful man she'd always thought she was destined to find.

"God, you look great!" Steve said enthusiastically when she finally entered the car.

She was wearing a pair of low slung, black trousers that had been way too expensive (even on sale) but she had to buy them since they fit her like they were made for her (something that didn't happen often with her incongruously tiny waist but generous hips and bottom).

Sibyl also had on a cherry-red satin blouse she'd stolen from Scarlett before moving to England. It had deep darts up each side of her midriff and each side of her spine, causing the blouse to fit snug around her middle and under her breasts and forcing her to keep a daring amount of buttons open from neck to cleavage.

She'd kept her hair down and slid her feet into a pair of high-heeled, sling-backed, bright-red pumps that killed her feet because of the seriously pointy toe.

With a good deal of conversation in the car from Steve *about* Steve (without him asking about her once), after Sibyl and Steve made it to Bristol, he drove around for half an hour looking for the hard-to-find, inexpensive (as in *free*) parking spot.

Once they located this elusive entity and Steve took four attempts at parallel parking into it, they walked, or more truthfully, hiked the long distance from car to club. This meant by the time they arrived they were late meeting his friends and, worse, Sibyl's feet were killing her.

At the club she stood next to Steve as his mates (who collectively seemed to have more product in their overly-styled hair than Sibyl had used in her life) appraised her. Steve held her close with his arm around her waist, something that was too familiar since they barely knew each other, and he did it like she was a trophy he was showing off.

These good-looking but too trendy men all had women who hung about behind them. It was as if the women were in some sort of cult that forced them to stand away from the masculine crowd but within earshot should the men ever require anything, like a pint. All of the women stared at Sibyl with varying expressions ranging from awe to abhorrence.

Definitely a close-knit crowd where strangers were *not* welcome.

And no one bothered to introduce *her* to any of them, not the men or the women.

They'd been talking for ten minutes and Steve hadn't even troubled himself to offer her a drink.

"I'm sorry," Sibyl interrupted quietly in an attempt to be polite. When she had Steve's attention she tipped the edges of her lips up in a smile and, when she did this, Steve stared at her mouth like it was the most fascinating thing in the world. "I was wondering about maybe getting a drink?"

She tilted her head, trying to pull his attention from her mouth to her eyes.

He blinked, looking sadly confused, then smiled and said, "Yeah! Great, babe. You blokes want anything?" When all four of the other men lifted their empty glasses, Steve turned back to Sibyl, "That'll be five pints of lager and, of course, whatever you want for yourself."

He turned back to his friends and Sibyl stood stock still, processing the fact that he just gave her his friend's drink order and expected her to go and get it.

She studied him as if seeing him for the first time. He, too, was good-looking. He, too, was trendy. He, too, was well-dressed.

And apparently, like his friends, he, too, thought he was the goddess's gift to women.

She felt the overwhelming urge to demonstrate to him (without any room for doubt) that he was *not* when she realized that if she got them all drinks, she could be away from his crowd for at least a few minutes as well as have time to figure out how she was going to make the night end very early.

Therefore, Sibyl stalked to the bar.

But not before hearing Steve say in a loud whisper, "Isn't she *fit*?"

She felt the urge to turn on her heel and run, except her shoes would not allow it.

As was usual (so usual, she didn't notice it) upon her arrival at the bar, the bartender ignored the other people clamoring for a drink and jogged up to her.

"What'll it be?"

"Five pints of lager, and a vodka lemonade with a splash of lime cordial, lots of ice and a cherry, if you have it," she answered and smiled at him.

The effect of her smile caused the bartender to nod eagerly at her strange drink order, deciding instantly that if they didn't have cherries, he'd go to the nearest store and steal a jar if he had to.

"You're pretty." Sibyl heard this come from the man who was somehow managing to be unsteadily seated on the barstool next to her, looking as if he'd lived there at least a year.

"Thank you," Sibyl said politely but then turned away.

She wasn't normally rude to people but she also didn't fancy striking up a conversation with an obviously highly inebriated man (she'd had enough troubles with men the last few days, thank you very much), especially considering her shoes would not allow her to affect a hasty retreat should she need to do so (and she vowed never to wear high heels again, or, at the very least, on a first date, something which she also doubted she'd do again).

The man swayed then righted himself before he slurred decisively, "I'll buy you a drink."

It was at this moment that Sibyl realized Steve hadn't given her any money to buy all of his friends a drink, friends who *she* had known no longer then fifteen minutes and the fact of the matter she didn't know them at all since she hadn't been given their names. Nor had he (or Sibyl herself for that matter), asked any of the women if *they* wanted a beverage.

"Thank you but I don't think so," Sibyl answered the drunk, stopping herself from going back and asking the women, none of whom said a word to her except "Heya," what drinks they wanted.

The drunk awkwardly stood, swayed again doing a full, unsteady loop with his upper body and carefully enunciated, "I said, I'll buy you a drink."

She turned toward him, saw his bloodshot eyes and then he breathed out. Even though he was still not very close, she smelled his drink-laced breath.

She tried not to wince but knew she was unsuccessful.

"I'm sorry but I'm fine. I don't need you to buy me a drink," she replied firmly.

Kind, polite, controlled and not unnecessarily ill-mannered, she was quite pleased with herself.

The bartender put her glass on the bar with a smile.

At its arrival, the drunk slammed the palm of his hand on the bar with such force that it made a loud smacking sound and she jumped. Several of the patrons close to her (and some not so close) turned around to look.

"I'm buyin' that drink!" the drunk slurred loudly and lurched toward her, leaning into her face, his fetid breath hitting her like a slap.

Sibyl immediately became alarmed, her body tensed and she took a hurried step back to flee and slammed into a solid, hard wall.

"She's with me." A voice came from behind her.

It was vaguely familiar, low, deep and absolutely lethal.

She glanced over her shoulder to see who her rescuer was and stared in disbelief (and not a small amount of shock) at Colin Morgan.

The drunk also turned to look and saw the tall, broad-shouldered man with the frightening look on his face standing so close behind the pretty girl that their bodies were touching.

"All right, mate, no need to get uptight." The drunk put his hands up appeasingly and stumbled back to his stool. "Pretty girls shouldn't buy their own drinks, thas all I'm sayin'," he garbled.

"I agree," Colin murmured distractedly as he watched five pints placed around Sibyl's drink.

"That'll be seventeen fifty," the bartender said.

Sibyl fumbled in her purse for money, still recovering from the shock of seeing Colin Morgan.

She could not believe that her dream madman was standing so close to her she could feel his body against her back. She could also not believe he'd witnessed her being semi-accosted by a drunk man and felt the need to come to her rescue. She never expected, never *dreamed* she'd run into him in a club in Bristol. In fact, she had hoped never to see him again for the rest of her natural life and even throughout her unnatural one (if such a thing existed).

She made the immediate decision to spend the rest of her days with old people, Jemma's family or in her Summer House Girlie Stuff Laboratory and never go out socializing again.

Ever.

Colin leaned in and Sibyl felt his hard chest pressing into her shoulder blade and watched as he passed a twenty pound note to the bartender.

At this gesture, she tried to remain cool and collected, though, she had to admit, it was difficult.

"Mr. Morgan, please don't pay for the drinks. They're—"

"For your date's friends, I know," he interrupted her then continued, "Your date, I might add, saw this gentleman . . ." Sibyl was not looking at him, *couldn't* make herself look at him. She wasn't even certain she wished to believe he was actually there. She noticed from the corners of her eyes that he jerked his head angrily in the direction of the drunk man. "Begin to approach you and did nothing about it."

She didn't respond. There was nothing to say.

Steve, unfortunately, was a jerk.

The drunk man said something though, straight into his nearly finished pint, "Criminal. Leave a pretty girl in the clutches of a degenerate like me." Then he giggled to himself.

Sibyl felt hysterical laughter bubbling up her own throat but she chased it down with a gulp and turned her mind to escape.

Before she could Colin Morgan remarked, "You made light work of that."

At this unusual comment, she finally lifted her eyes to the hard planes of his face, having to twist around and glance over her shoulder and she saw he was looking over his own at Steve. He obviously recognized the paramedic who'd come to his house.

Again, she didn't respond. He was still standing so close to her that his chest was resting lightly against her back.

"Mr. Morgan, if you wouldn't mind moving away," she whispered.

He apparently did mind because he didn't move.

"Jason." His voice rang with authority, and the bartender, who was listening to the orders of some patrons, turned his head immediately.

"Yeah, Mr. Morgan?"

"Get Shannon to take those pints to the gentlemen over there," Colin ordered, motioning to Steve and his group with his head. "And get her to get the women with them a drink for Christ's sake."

"Yes, Mr. Morgan," and Jason jogged off obediently to find the unknown Shannon.

Sibyl stared at Colin in dismay.

"Do you," Sibyl hesitated, "*own* this club?"

His eyes finally dropped to her and for some reason her breath caught when she felt the full force of them on her face.

"A third of it, yes," he answered.

Sibyl looked around the place for the first time.

It was jam packed. There were three bars she could see, two on the lower floor, one on a balcony that wrapped around the club and all of them were surrounded by people buying drinks.

It was clearly a hip hotspot for young, trendy people. Not the place she would expect Colin Morgan to spend his time, unless he had a penchant for under-clothed and nearly underage girls.

Her face must have told him what she was thinking for he said, "I was here for a meeting. It ran long. I was leaving when I saw you leave your medic, go to the bar and choose the unfortunate position of standing by Paul."

The drunk man lifted his glass in salute.

"You know him?" Sibyl was astonished.

"Here every night," Paul offered.

"Do you get drunk every night?" Sibyl asked, her voice edged in concern.

"Every night," Paul confirmed happily and nodded his head sloppily.

Not thinking, Sibyl grabbed her own drink and, in the tight space allowed by Colin and the bar, she whirled around then pushed him back, her hand on his chest.

One step, two then she got up on tiptoe, leaned toward his ear and whispered fiercely, "That man is an alcoholic!"

"I can hear you," Paul sing-songed and Sibyl closed her eyes in distress.

When she opened them, Colin Morgan was grinning at her.

Grinning at her.

And if she thought his voice sounded lethal several minutes before, it was nothing compared to the entirely different killer wattage of his grin.

She mentally shrugged off her highly pleasant reaction to his grin, put her hand back to his chest and pushed him back again, this time she pushed him around the side of the bar. She was so determined, she didn't process the fact that he let her do this.

"You have to do something!" she demanded when they'd stopped well away from Paul.

"About what?" Colin was watching her like Steve had watched her earlier, as if she was the most fascinating creature in the world.

Except, when Colin did it, she felt a warmth seep into her belly that she did *not* feel when Steve did it.

"About Paul," she explained, her voice showing her aggravation at his obtuseness just as it hid her reaction to his proximity. "If he comes here every night and gets that inebriated, he's clearly an alcoholic. You can't keep serving him."

The deadly-delicious grin was back. "He's our best customer."

Sibyl was appalled.

"Mr. Morgan, that is just . . . completely just . . ." she was at a loss for words then she found them, "morally irresponsible."

The grin turned into a full-fledged, white smile, the wattage amping up so high, Sibyl was nearly dazzled.

Although he was barely a foot from her, he leaned in closer.

"Morally irresponsible?" he repeated.

She could swear his tone was teasing.

Teasing!

Was this the man who had held her hostage, forced her to undress in front of him, accosted her in his entryway and shouted and cursed at her in his library?

Yes, she reminded herself, it was.

She straightened her shoulders.

"We must look after our neighbors," she lectured.

"Really?" he asked, his eyes dancing and not with the jumping lights in the club.

"Yes, especially you," Sibyl informed him.

For some unknown reason, he was walking around her and she had to turn in a staccato pirouette to follow him.

"Especially me?" he asked, stopped abruptly and took a quick step forward in a way that was predatory.

This caused her to take a step back, and when she did she hit a wall. His hand came up to rest beside her head and he leaned into her again. She had the wall of the club to her back, him to her front (*close* to her front) and his arm imprisoning her on the right.

She was trapped.

Her mind screamed for flight but she stood her ground. "Yes, especially you. As the owner of this club—"

"*Part* owner," he interrupted her, still smiling as if she was highly entertaining.

"*Part* owner," she amended quickly and steeled herself against that smile and the annoyance she felt at his obvious amusement. "You have responsibilities."

"Yes," he admitted. "You're absolutely correct. I'm responsible for keeping the money coming in."

She spluttered at this outrageous, yet teasing remark then saved herself by taking a deep breath. "You also have a responsibility to your patrons."

He leaned closer then stopped, but if he came further forward, even an inch, he'd be kissing her.

She held her breath.

Colin stared into her eyes.

Then he said, "Paul doesn't drive drunk. He has a standing order for a taxi to pick him up at midnight every night. He's a wealthy businessman who doesn't touch a drop during the day, I know because I have dealings with him. He has a wife who's an inveterate cheat and consummate liar who spends money almost as fast as he can make it and he buys a drink for every attractive woman who enters this club. He's a decent man, most of the time, considering, and is mostly harmless."

Sibyl was shocked he knew so much about Paul. She was further stunned that he took the time to explain this to her, calmly and rationally. She'd never had dealings with a calm, rational Colin Morgan. She didn't like it because she *did* like it and that played havoc on her very soul.

"Well good," she decided for her sanity their conversation was over. "Now that's sorted, I'm leaving."

"Excellent," he announced. "I'll take you home."

The hand by her head dropped and his long, strong fingers closed around her upper arm.

Alarmed, she blurted, "What?"

Colin looked down at her. "Would you like me to take you back to the medic?"

Sibyl glanced across the bar and through the crush of people and caught sight of Steve who was drinking from the pint he'd been delivered. He looked content and at ease and as if he'd completely forgotten he'd come with a date.

Sibyl had no desire whatsoever to return to Steve.

Her gaze dropped to the floor.

"I'll get a taxi," she murmured.

"Don't be absurd, you live five minutes from me," Colin returned.

This was true. And a taxi from Bristol to Clevedon would cost her thirty pounds. Not that she didn't have thirty pounds but she could think of a great number of things she'd prefer to spend her hard earned money on.

"I'll get a bus," she decided.

Obviously, he disagreed. Without a word, he turned and then started moving forward, taking her with him. Divesting her of her drink, he deposited it on the bar without breaking stride, the whole time he brought her along with him with a firm but gentle hand on her arm.

"Mr. Morgan—" she began, looking at him and having to quicken her pace to keep up with his casual advance.

"My name is Colin," he said distractedly and stopped.

She was about to open her mouth to say something but looked around as to why they stopped.

They were standing by Steve and his group of friends. Colin's hand had dropped but not away from her. His arm slid around her and settled tightly around her waist, not, she noted not so vaguely, as if she was a trophy to show off. Instead, his hold was proprietary, blatantly so. Colin Morgan was claiming her right in front of her date, an aggressive, callous move that stole her breath and any words she might have been able to utter.

Steve's friends noticed Colin and Sibyl first and their open-mouthed stares made Steve turn around.

"I'm taking Ms. Godwin home," Colin announced the minute he had Steve's attention.

Before Steve could put into words the angry, stunned surprise on his face, Colin guided Sibyl out the door.

Sibyl moved with him mostly in order not to make a scene.

When they were outside the club and walking down the pavement was when she asked angrily, "Well that . . . that . . . I don't even know what *that* was. Why did you do that?"

"I would guess he'd eventually go looking for you, I saved him the trouble." Colin had dropped his arm from around her waist but caught her hand in his as they walked.

She was too taken aback by his behavior to recognize the familiar intimacy of his hand holding hers while guiding her down the pavement. Before this dawned on her, he turned into a car park that was two doors down from the club and she was forced to admit to a secret relief that she wouldn't have to trek for miles to get to his car (even when she didn't quite understand how she'd managed to get herself in the awkward position of accepting a ride from him in the first place).

He strode purposefully, and she noticed distractedly, with immense masculine grace, towards a gleaming black, sporty, convertible Mercedes, all the while holding her hand.

She stared at the car in horror.

"You own a Mercedes?" she breathed.

He had stopped at the passenger side and dropped her hand. At her comment, he looked at her sharply.

In an about turn of everything she'd experienced a week ago at Lacybourne, that entire night he'd been regarding her with amusement and even, possibly (if she could credit it) admiration.

Now, however, he was staring at her with an expression of distaste, something about him with which she was far more familiar.

He also did not answer, possibly because the answer was obvious.

He unlocked the doors with an expensive-sounding "bleep," and without a word he pulled hers open, guiding her in before closing it with more force than he needed to use.

Once he'd settled into his seat, started the car and expertly reversed, she couldn't help herself, she'd lived too long in Mags's house to let it go, she had to say, "What kind of gas mileage does this car get?"

"I've no idea." His voice suddenly sounded bored.

Sibyl ignored his tone and persevered.

"Mr. Morgan, I know it's none of my business and I dislike people who lecture about this kind of thing, but as this is a sports car, you should know that it's likely it burns fuel like nobody's business. In this day and age, considering the state of the environment, everyone should have a car with fuel economy. You should consider a hybrid at the very least."

Even though he was driving, she felt his body go somehow still.

After a moment, in a voice not bored in the slightest, he asked, "I beg your pardon?"

Sibyl felt like an idiot, lecturing him on fuel economy and decided to stand down.

"It's none of my business," she muttered.

"Sibyl," he said her name for the first time and she felt the effect of it physically, almost as if the sound of her name on his lips, uttered in his rich baritone, pulsated through her body, and she caught her breath.

He continued without noticing her extreme, and bizarre, reaction.

"This is a high-performance vehicle. The fuel economy is excellent. You can save yourself from worrying that you will be tainted with guilt by association from riding in my car. I'm not unduly destroying the environment."

Sibyl was inordinately pleased his tone held no anger or even the slightest hint of it (not to mention the fact that he wasn't "unduly" damaging the ozone layer).

"That was rude. I apologize. My mother is an environmental activist and sometimes it spills over, but, um . . . that said, I agree with Mom that we should all do our bit."

He didn't respond and she tried not to look at him but instead felt the lovely, smooth nearly soundless ride of his "high-performance vehicle." She'd never ridden in a Mercedes (all her cars, and her family's, were jalopies that they rode into the ground before buying other, used, jalopies) and she had to admit (even though she would *never* tell Mags), she enjoyed it.

Colin deftly negotiated the difficult Bristol roads and entered the A38 at Cumberland Basin and Sibyl stared at the beautifully lit Clifton Suspension Bridge as they passed by.

"Why him?" Colin's voice came at her suddenly and she jumped.

Even the short drive in his smooth car had lulled her into a strange relaxation.

"Sorry?"

"The medic."

She sighed as she understood his question. It was none of his business. Furthermore, they (especially Sibyl) were both forgetting that he had an unreasonable loathing of her and the last time they'd spent any time together he made sure she knew it (well, most of the time).

"He asked me," was all she said and hoped he would let the matter drop.

"There is no way in hell a woman like you should be on the arm of a man like that," Colin remarked with deep meaning and supreme finality.

He exited the A38 and headed around Long Ashton toward Clevedon.

She should have stayed silent. For sanity's sake, she knew that. Rationally, logically and all good things that meant peace of mind, she understood that with certainty.

However, she didn't stay silent.

"And what type of man should I be on the arm of, as you put it?"

"Me," he answered boldly and she gasped, realizing, without a doubt, she'd entered the Alternate Colin Morgan Universe.

He ignored her gasp. "If you were with me, you would not buy your own drinks. You would not be sent off to buy mine. I would most likely not let you out of my sight. We would definitely not be in a club. And you certainly would *not*, under any circumstances, leave with another man."

Regardless of the edge of chauvinism that tainted his statements, something started fluttering in her stomach, something not entirely unpleasant. Indeed, something alarmingly *pleasant*, and she did her utmost to ignore it.

"If you were an ass like Steve, then you wouldn't have a choice."

He didn't reply, which in itself was an eloquent statement.

Feeling the need to be safely out of Alternate but Somehow Entirely More Disarming Colin Morgan Universe, she reminded him, "However, the last time I saw you, you forced me to undress in front of you."

He didn't hesitate. "Would you have done what you were told if I left?"

She felt her body jolt at his uncanny perception into her somewhat stubborn nature.

But unfortunately, everything she was would not allow her to lie.

"No," she admitted and chanced a glance at him.

She saw the flash of white from his teeth and she made a grumpy noise and looked out the window.

He chuckled.

She decided not to speak to him anymore.

He was not, however, finished speaking to her.

"You were freezing yourself to death, which was a fool thing to do, and you looked about as comfortable as if you were lying on a sacrificial slab."

"I could hardly make myself comfortable when I was being held hostage!" she snapped, instantly forgetting her vow to stay silent.

"You weren't being held hostage."

"Could I leave?" she demanded.

"No," he stated implacably.

She threw up her arms as if that settled her point. "You see! I was a hostage."

This time, it was no chuckle but a quiet, amused laugh.

Therefore she stated crossly, "I fail to see how anything about that entire evening was funny. I just wanted to see your house. You confiscated my license and called the police to check on me."

"I had my reasons."

"Yes? And what were those?" she asked, her voice short and angry and she was glad, no *thrilled* of these reminders.

Rescuer Colin was not nearly as easy to deal with as Lunatic Colin.

"You honestly don't know?" he asked back, surprise edging his voice.

"Well, it felt like you thought Mrs. Byrne and I were going to steal your favorite hi-fi, which was not a pleasant feeling. Though I think at the time she said it she was living in cloud cuckoo land, considering your reaction to my arrival at your home, she told me the day before you'd likely give me a personal tour of the house."

"Maybe I'll do that," he murmured as if to himself.

"Thank you, but no," Sibyl replied quickly. "I'm never going to Lacybourne Manor again. I think I may even avoid National Trust properties altogether," she declared dramatically then ruined it by going back on her word in case the goddess heard her statement and held her to it, so she made a few exceptions. "Except Tyntesfield, naturally. And Dunster Castle, which is one of my favorites. And Durham Park, of course." She wracked her brain to think of anything else she'd missed. "Oh! And Avebury, you get parking for free there if you're a National Trust member."

"You can't possibly be real." The warm, laughing tone in his voice made her head snap around to look at him and she saw the smile was there, full force.

"I *am* real, Mr. Morgan, it is *you*, or at least tonight's you, that I find hard to believe is real."

They were slowing down and she realized he was on the short but secluded drive to her cottage. How he knew where she lived, she couldn't fathom, unless he memorized the address on her license, which was undoubtedly what he did.

Colin stopped outside her front door and pulled up the handbrake. Then he turned to her, and by the dim lights of the dash she could see the deep intensity of his eyes.

"I'm *definitely* real," he told her.

"Which is the real you?" she asked in return. "Crazy, angry man at Lacybourne or rescuer guy in Bristol?"

"Both," he answered.

She saw the flash of his teeth and she fought the insane urge to smile back at him or throw herself into his arms, or both.

Instead, she retreated into flippancy which was a far safer place to be. "Great. Multiple personalities. Perhaps I should do an intervention."

On that, she unclicked her seatbelt and hastily exited the lovely car. She heard the purring, well-tuned motor stop and his car door opening and slamming shut. Even so, she didn't hesitate, walked directly to the front door, slid in the ancient key and opened it. Mallory bounded out with great, if unusual, enthusiasm and went tearing toward Colin.

"Mallory!" she shouted but Mallory would not be deterred.

"Stop," Colin ordered, his voice commanding but not harsh and Mallory skidded to a halt and stopped within inches of the man then leaned his muzzle forward and licked his hand.

Sibyl's eyes went skyward in exasperation. Though, she had to admit, if anyone deserved snarling, cranky Mallory tonight, it was definitely defunct-date Steve.

Colin walked toward her as she reached in and turned on the light switch that her father had rigged to light several of the lamps around the cottage, making traversing it easy upon entry with one single switch. This caused the whole glade around the front of the cottage to be diffused with soft, dim light.

Mallory followed Colin to Sibyl, snuffled Sibyl's hand in belated greeting and then moseyed off into the night to do his business.

And suddenly Sibyl felt awkward as Colin stood looking down at her. She stared up at him, noting it was rather strange doing so. Being quite tall herself, and also wearing high heels, she would normally be eye to eye or looking down at the majority of people, even men.

She hid her discomfort and tried valiantly to end the night on a good note.

"Thank you for the ride," she paused, "And the rescue."

"You're welcome." Simple, softly said in his deep voice, and unbelievably effective, Sibyl felt the shockwaves of his tone all the way to her toes.

A shiver slid through her and she shook it off.

"Mallory!" she called, turning toward the dark night. When she glanced back to say goodnight to Colin, he spoke.

"Tell me something," he requested quietly.

"Yes?"

"Your dog's name is unusual. How did he get it?"

She shrugged feeling somehow this question seemed too personal because something in his tone made it so.

She decided to give him the short version.

"My dad names my pets. I'm hopeless at it. My dad is kind of . . ." she hesitated, not wishing to share too much.

It was easy when it was banter and it wasn't dangerous.

Colin Morgan knowing personal things about her and her family, she, for some reason, felt the need to be guarded.

"A mythology buff," she thought it safe to share. "Thomas Malory wrote *Le Morte d'Arthur* and my father loves Arthurian Legend. So, he named him Mallory."

"I see."

This, obviously, was a highly acceptable answer because he stepped toward her and she read the meaning to his advance loud and clear. She began speaking in a rush to stop his progress.

"Bran, my cat, is named for Bran the Blessed, of Welsh Mythology."

Her ploy didn't work. Though he stopped, he did it close enough to her that she could feel him even though he wasn't touching her.

"Can I see you again?" he asked, he was using his soft, effective voice and her toes curled.

Sibyl was stunned to her core at his request. She would never have expected after that night at Lacybourne that he'd want to see her again.

Tonight, however, he was different. Completely different.

She used every bit of willpower she had to say what was logical and right for her peace of mind. "I'm not sure that's wise."

She saw the flash of his smile and noted with a thrill of fear that he was entirely unaffected by her refusal.

"Why isn't it wise?"

"Because I think you might be a little insane," she blurted more bluntly than she would have done if she wasn't trying very, *very* hard not to throw herself at him.

This *could* be her dream man. He was certainly acting like her dream man.

The problem was, the other Colin was most certainly *not*.

"I'm not insane," he assured her, his voice made even more effective by the addition of a teasing note.

Then he came even closer.

Sibyl stepped back.

"Mr. Morgan—"

"Colin."

"You scare me a little bit," she admitted softly.

At this pronouncement, he stopped moving toward her.

"This is a far better ending than the one we had before," she offered, her voice somewhat breathless and definitely rushed because if she didn't say it, she wouldn't.

Instead *she'd* do something insane, like invite him inside then offer him a drink then, maybe, totally lose it and rip his clothes off.

"I think we should stick with this," she finished.

Mallory came loping out of the darkness and instead of immediately entering the house after his business was concluded, as he usually did, he sat next to Colin and leaned his big body against Colin's legs.

Sibyl stared in shock at her dog.

"Mallory, get inside," she commanded and Mallory leaned forward, licked her hand and then decided that even though he liked Colin Morgan, he liked his sleep better. So he ambled into the house and disappeared.

Sibyl looked back at Colin. "Thank you again, you've been very nice tonight."

Colin didn't respond.

There was light but it was dim and she couldn't see his eyes all that well.

What she did see was his hand coming up and, before she could react, he traced a finger in a whisper-soft caress from her temple, along her cheek, to the corner of her lip. All the while Colin watching his finger's movements, it dipped and slowly traced the bottom edge of her lower lip ending on her chin.

The whole maneuver, in real time, probably lasted five seconds, but it felt like it took a blissful, beautiful, dreamy eternity and that was why Sibyl stood silent and unmoving as he did it.

It was not a goodnight kiss but, somehow, seemed far more intimate.

His eyes coming back to hers, he murmured, "Goodnight, Sibyl."

And with that, he left.

Chapter SEVEN

Bargain

Sibyl woke up the next day, her limbs hopelessly entangled with the covers of her bed.

She saw distractedly that Mallory stood beside her bed, looking curiously at her, not in his usual loopy manner, but as if he was standing at attention, awaiting her command.

She was sweating, she was panting and she remembered every vivid detail of the dream she'd just had.

"I'm going insane," she told the dog and he melted out of his unusual stance and moved toward her, his tail wagging, his body shaking, his cold nose snuffling at her hand.

She lay back on the bed and absently pet her dog.

Last night, after Colin left, she hadn't allowed herself to think about him, the night or his desire to see her again (and hers to see him). She had definitely not thought about his light caress. She figured it was simply bad luck that she'd run into him. She had managed to live a year in England without ever seeing him and she hoped she could continue with her life and never see him again (or, at least, this was what she told herself).

Unfortunately, that did not include seeing him in her dreams.

The real man was clearly unbalanced, or perhaps not, but she was not going to allow herself to discover the truth.

The dream man was anything but.

Last night, in her dream though, he had been blond. His hair the exact color of hers, golden and thick. He'd been wearing some sort of tunic, hose and high, soft leather boots with a gold, intricately linked chain settled low on his narrow waist.

She had been wearing a gown of soft, pale-blue wool. She also had a belt made of delicate silver filigree inlaid with roughly cut aquamarines tied low on her waist.

Sibyl blamed her father for her dream's medieval wardrobe.

They were riding a midnight-black steed, the horse's muscled power beneath her, her lover's same power emanating into her back as he held her close to his chest atop the horse. One of his arms was wrapped protectively and possessively about her waist.

This moment was a stolen one, her lover wending his expert way through a heavily wooded area until he found the place for which he was looking. They were not supposed to be out there alone together, some foreign part of her knew and felt the illicit excitement of it.

He alighted from the horse then dragged her off, sliding her tantalizingly down the length of his hard body.

Then he bent his head to kiss her and it was sweet and wild and beautiful and absolutely everything a kiss should be.

When he lifted his head, his eyes hooded and sexy as they had been in the entryway to his house a week before, she'd whispered, "Colin."

This made him grin a very devilish grin.

"Are you trying to make me jealous, wench? 'Colin' indeed. Say *my* name when I kiss you." Then, his lips on hers, he whispered, "Say it, Beatrice . . . Royce."

Confused and not knowing what to do, not knowing why he was calling her Beatrice, and wanting another of those kisses, she did as he commanded and murmured the name, "Royce."

The instant she did, he kissed her again and it was all the things before but now also hot with need. She felt desire flood through her as she slid her hands into his hair. He lay her down on the forest floor right next to the horse, his body settled on top of her and she gloried in his heavy weight.

The horse shifted and she felt the unsettling feeling they were being watched.

It was then she awoke, the limbs that had been entangled with his were simply wound through the sheets of her bed.

"I am going insane," she told the dog and Mallory whined.

She pulled the covers off the bed and grabbed some jeans and a sweater to wear to take her dog for a walk. She resolutely shoved the dream aside (it was only a dream, just a dream, Colin Morgan was forever out of her life, forever and ever, she vowed).

So it was a lovely dream.

So it was a particularly *delicious* and lovely dream.

It was just a dream.

She went through her morning regime, thinking only of the things she needed to think about. Walk the dog, feed her pets, brush her teeth, wash her face, take a shower and so on.

She sat at her dressing table, lightly applied her makeup and attempted to do something with her hair.

Sibyl loved her bedroom, it was (as was the whole of Brightrose Cottage, but especially her bedroom) her sanctuary, perfectly, splendidly *her*.

It had a lovely fireplace with a black, wrought iron grate surrounded by tile in a rich jade color. It had gleaming, wide-planked floors scattered with thick, pastel-colored throw rugs. The walls were painted a very pale green.

She and her father had found and restored an ornate iron bed and they'd painted it white. It was covered with very feminine, soft sheets and comforter, scattered with dainty, pastel flowers with big, fluffy pillows at the head.

The room had window seats in the diamond-paned windows covered with plump pillows and cushions. The bed was flanked with lovely French provincial bed stands and there was a matching dressing table with an oval mirror.

It was all girl, fresh and inviting and lovely.

If Colin Morgan stood in this room, his immensely masculine presence would be so out of place, the very thought made her laugh out loud. She took comfort in that thought and in her room that morning. She needed as much comfort as she could get after the fiasco at Lacybourne, the conflicting events of last night and her glorious dream.

Later that morning she walked into the Community Centre with a cheerful wave to Tina who was cooking lunch for fifty pensioners in the enormous kitchen.

Sibyl went straight to work on a grant to get their own minibus. Social Services could help Annie, of course, but even after another visit from Sibyl, they remained firm that they couldn't do much about the minibus driver.

So Sibyl had priced the cost of buying the bus and training Kyle to drive it. They also needed enough money for petrol, insurance, maintenance and a cushion in case of repairs for several years.

As she created the budget, she saw the rising amount with even more rising alarm.

They'd need a heck of a lot of money, but as ever Sibyl was determined to find it.

And she would, somehow.

It turned out Annie had no children even though she said she did. Sibyl thought that everyone had to look out for their neighbors and the best people who did that were the volunteers and staff at the Centre. Certainly, the minibus driver did not.

Kyle walked into her shabby, corner office with its makeshift tables she used as desks and the hand-me-down (most likely handed down two or three times) couch shoved against the wall. Detritus from talent shows, fayres, Easter parades and all sorts of Community Centre events crowded every corner and available surface.

His droopy moustache twitched and she found herself grinning at him after witnessing this endearing habit.

"You want me to make those deliveries for you today, luv?" he asked.

Kyle helped her deliver her girlie goods to the various stores that stocked them.

"Please. The shops in Clevedon and Clifton are out of product, they've ordered huge and the boxes won't fit in the MG."

"Great car but a death trap," Kyle commented darkly and he'd said this before, about half a million times.

Day after day, Kyle was assuming more and more of a position as Father Figure in Absence of Bertie, and Sibyl appreciated his gruff, but loving, concern.

Before she could reply, Jemma ran in, her dark hair bouncing around on the crown of her head, her face panicked.

"I've got to call 999. Meg just fell out of the minibus."

At these words Sibyl's heart squeezed painfully and her stomach lurched.

Her friend grabbed the phone while both Kyle and Sibyl flew out of the office, through the Day Centre and out to the street.

Sibyl wanted to burst into tears at what she saw.

Instead, she ran forward and skidded to a halt next to the heavy, prone body of Meg.

"Meg, honey, are you okay?" Sibyl asked, dropping to her knees and grabbing the woman's hand, a hand that closed around her own in a painful grip, expressing her acute discomfort.

"I think I've broken a hip," Meg answered on a tortured whisper and Sibyl knew Meg was trying to be strong but at this announcement, her voice betrayed a steady whine of hurt.

"Jem is calling the medics, we'll get you to hospital in no time at all," Sibyl tried to reassure her.

"Don't leave me, Sibyl," Meg begged, her hand clutching Sibyl's desperately, and Sibyl nodded her head fervently. Then Meg pleaded, "Can someone please call my son?"

"I'll call her son," Tina was standing over them, wringing her apron in concern. She stopped wringing her hands and ran off awkwardly on mangled feet to do her task as Jemma rushed toward them.

"They're on their way," Jem announced when she was close.

Hours later, the doctors reported to Sibyl, Jemma and Meg's son (who had left straight from work to see to his mother) that Meg *had* broken her hip.

Sibyl waited until she and Jemma were outside the doors of the hospital before she let her formidable temper explode.

"That bloody, *bloody* minibus driver. He *knows* Meg needs help with transfers. He *knows* Kyle or I have to be there when Meg gets out of the bus. How could he let her fall?"

"Her son is with her now. She's a strong lady, she'll be okay," Jemma assured her, her chocolate eyes melting as she watched Sibyl in full, heartfelt, outrage.

"She's *my* responsibility when she comes to that Centre, Jem," Sibyl replied, her voice rising. "And she's my *friend*! How am I going to face her after this?"

And as she spoke, Sibyl felt the same hated reminder that no matter what you did, no matter how hard you tried, things went very, very badly for people who mattered.

Jem got closer and put a reassuring hand on her friend's arm, saying softly, "You can't save everyone from every little hurt, Sibyl. You couldn't have prevented what happened today."

"I'm going to damn well try," Sibyl snapped and Jemma shook her head gently.

"Oh, Billie, mate," Jem whispered, using Sibyl's not-oft-used nickname in an effort to settle her, "You break my heart."

"I'm going to break something and it isn't your heart. It's that minibus driver's head!" Sibyl promised dramatically, hanging on to her anger in order not to feel her pain and definitely not to feel the nagging sense of guilt that *she'd* been the cause of today's tragedy.

Her and her big mouth.

Jemma laughed, giving Sibyl's shoulder a friendly shove and breaking the intensity of the moment. She then hugged Sibyl, an uncommon action from her reserved friend.

"She'll be okay," Jem whispered in her ear.

Sibyl let out a shuddering sigh. "I hope so."

But she didn't hope so.

Sibyl would do everything she could to *make* it so.

The end was nigh for the likes of Meg and Annie's anguish.

Sibyl would see to it.

COLIN DROVE DOWN the attractive lane that led to Sibyl's cottage, and as he did he saw dotted in the woods sprinkles of late-blooming snowdrops, crocuses and opening daffodils.

As he approached the picturesque, rambling, sparkling white cottage, he saw Sibyl's MG and a Ford Fiesta parked in the widened drive at the front. Without room to park out front, he drove around the house and found a parking spot by the side.

As he got out and walked to the front door, he noted that all the windows had window boxes and they'd already been planted with early spring flowers that tangled with dangling ivy.

Colin was there because of last week but mostly because of last night.

Last week, after sending Tamara away, Colin had ordered an investigation into the woman who called herself Sibyl Godwin.

"I'll need to go to America if I'm going to find out everything about her," his investigator, Robert Fitzwilliam, told him. "Obviously, that will significantly increase my expenses."

"Do it," was all Colin said.

He was happy to pay to find out everything about Sibyl Godwin's past and personally intended to find out who she was now.

Arriving home early, Colin had sent Tamara home Wednesday afternoon.

Things were very much finished with Tamara Adams, for a variety of reasons.

The idiot woman had attempted to seduce him while Sibyl and Mrs. Byrne were in the house. He could barely think with Beatrice Godwin's double lying in a bed (stubbornly freezing herself to death) two doors down from his own room, much less bear another woman's hands on him. Then she'd had the temerity to act affronted when he told her, in no uncertain terms, that he had no interest. Making matters worse, she'd flown into a jealous rage after Sibyl and Mrs. Byrne had both left the next day.

"I heard what you said to her!" Tamara ranted. "You were tempted by her. You said it, right in front of me!"

He'd simply stared at her beautiful face, not so beautiful as it was distorted with rage.

"How *dare* you!" she screeched when he'd made no response.

"It's my house, my life, my bed, I choose who I take to it," Colin replied calmly.

At this point, she'd flown at him in a fury.

That was a *big* mistake.

He'd pushed her off, ordered her out of his house and walked away.

That, he knew, was the end of Tamara Adams.

Colin would not put up with jealous rages and feminine pouts. With his usual ruthlessness, he made an instant decision. He didn't care if it took years to find a suitable replacement, Tamara would never have his ring on her finger.

After dealing with Tamara, he started piecing together what he knew of Sibyl.

The people at The National Trust told him that Mrs. Byrne had been volunteering at Lacybourne for seven years. She was retired, living on a meager pension and spending some of her days in a lavish manor house. She'd undoubtedly encountered Sibyl somewhere along the line and noted her amazing resemblance to Beatrice Godwin. Doing so, she'd probably talked the younger woman either into a con or conned Sibyl into a meeting with Royce Morgan's twin.

What they were up to, he couldn't care less, for they wouldn't succeed.

However, considering Sibyl's behavior last night, he was beginning to doubt she was a con artist trading on her resemblance to a long dead woman. She seemed genuinely surprised at his reaction to her and stunned by his behavior.

Though, Colin wouldn't put anything past a woman.

His parents were worth money, he had a large trust fund he'd never touched, substantial sums of his own, his business was worth a great deal and then there was Lacybourne. It was filled with priceless antiques, including an enormous Bristol Blue Glass collection and a centuries old accumulation of Wedgewood, all of which Mrs. Byrne knew very well, and if Sibyl's deft knowledge of National Trust properties was anything to go by, she did as well.

Beatrice Godwin's portrait and the story of Royce and Beatrice Morgan had been published often in books and was still often discussed local lore. Without having to think, Colin knew of five books he'd read himself about the doomed, star-crossed lovers. The National Trust volunteers recited the story dozens of times during every visiting day. If Sibyl so desired to see his house, she would likely know its most famous piece of history.

Mrs. Byrne and Miss Godwin could easily be on a con, which made him their target.

Unfortunately for them, he had no interest in being the target but, rather, aiming at one.

And he decided his target would be Sibyl Godwin.

It was either that, or the romantic myth of star-crossed lovers was true. It could, of course (and considering his cynical nature, he did not give a great deal of plausibility to this option), be merely coincidence that this glorious American woman, who just happened to own a fluffy black cat and an enormous mastiff, crossed his path.

Further complicating matters (but likely because he'd met her yet again), Colin had a dream the night before, a dream of her in a blue woolen gown, riding on a horse before him, kissing him in a forest. Her hair was dark in the dream, like Beatrice's, but Colin knew it was *her*.

Perhaps it all was just a misunderstanding. Seeing as she was out with the medic the night before, she could either be moving on as it was obvious their attempt with him would be unsuccessful or she honestly was unaware of their strange, historical connection.

If that was the case, he'd apologize to her, he'd charm her and he'd win her. Of that, he had no doubt.

Either way, he had to know.

And he had a plan.

He walked toward her home and noticed that her front door was open.

Then he heard a man shouting, "Don't you carry any of those heavy boxes!"

As she had company, instead of seeking her out, without hesitation

Colin entered her house through the open door.

He felt immediately welcomed (even though he probably was not) at the same time he was instantly transported back in time.

He was standing in a huge, open room.

An enormous, circular, dark-wood dining table with lions' paw feet and high-backed chairs upholstered in deep rusts and buttery yellows was to his left situated by a handsome inglenook fire place. In its center was an enormous cut-crystal vase filled with yellow roses.

The entire room was painted in the same warm, buttery yellow as was in the chairs and a huge, wrought iron chandelier hung imposingly over the table with matching sconces affixed to the walls.

There was a formidable chest against one wall, intricately, yet crudely, carved. On it were heavy, cut-crystal tumblers and sturdy decanters filled with varying shades of liquid. The decanters held chains around their necks engraved with the name of the liquor that rested inside.

There was a massive mirror on one wall, framed in dark wood. There was also the portrait of a woman hanging over the chest. She had a tumble of auburn hair, flashing blue eyes and very deep cleavage. She managed to look both friendly and severe.

There was a narrow staircase rising up the wall to his right with stout beams holding it up. It looked contradictorily like it could crumble at any second at the same time completely sound. The wood of the outside banister had been lovingly refinished and there was a rope handrail against the opposite wall, leading upstairs.

The stairway separated the dining area from the cozy living room, which was filled with deep, comfortable chairs and couches liberally dosed with tasseled pillows and soft throws, all of which surrounded an even larger, inglenook fireplace, which was the room's focal point.

Under the stairs, ancient, arched windows had been uncovered and lovingly restored with stained glass that was a swirl of ivory and buttery yellow. More heavy wrought iron was there, these being candlesticks in the window and higher ones standing on the floor, holding thick rust, ivory and yellow candles.

All the windows were warped with age, diamond paned and held window seats filled with inviting cushions. There was no television set that he could see but there were bookcases filling the entire side wall beyond the arched windows. The cases had been expertly built around two big windows and they were filled with books and unusual artefacts that invited perusal.

If a woman wearing a tall, conical, pointed hat with her face half-hidden behind a shimmering veil were to walk into the room at that very moment, he would not have been surprised.

Colin felt a slight uneasiness at the entire feel of the house. It was not where he expected an accomplished con artist would live.

Then he mentally shrugged. He knew little of where such people would live and there was a good possibility, the house close to confirming it, that Sibyl was exactly what she appeared to be—a beautiful American living in England who liked to visit National Trust houses and made poor choices on who to date.

He heard noise and voices coming from behind the house.

"I thought I told you not to carry those boxes." It was again the gruff man's voice.

Then he heard laughter that had to be Sibyl's, and at the husky, sweet sound of it Colin's body went completely still.

There was something achingly familiar about it even though he'd never heard it before in his life.

Her voice was a charming alto, he knew. Her laughter as well, was as rich as her voice and unbelievably musical.

"It doesn't weigh anything, Kyle."

Through the windows at the side of the house, opened to the unusual warmth of the spring day, Colin saw an older man with a shock of white hair (but strangely, the long sideburns were still completely black) walk by. The man disappeared around the back of the house and then Colin heard a masculine "oomph."

"Doesn't weigh anything, my arse," Kyle said.

Again, Colin heard her familiar, effective laughter.

Colin saw Kyle again, this time carrying a box and shouting over his shoulder, "How much more?"

Sibyl followed and Colin felt his body instinctively, and pleasantly, react to the sight of her.

"That's it, just those four. The two for Clevedon and the two for Clifton. You're an absolute love, I owe you one," she was saying as she walked behind the man.

Colin moved to the entryway and could easily see them outside. Kyle was loading up the back of the Fiesta and Sibyl was standing talking to him as he did so. Colin could not hear them and he found himself curious to know what they were saying, considering how intent Sibyl looked as she spoke.

She was wearing jeans, the pant legs so long the backs of the slightly flared hems were frayed from where she walked on them. A pair of kelly-green flats peeked out at the bottom and she wore a matching sweater that managed to be both lovingly fitted to her upper body and also looked fluffy and warm. She had a brightly-colored long scarf wrapped round and round her neck and her glorious hair was pulled up in a precarious bunch at the crown of her head, locks falling haphazardly from it. Around her neck and shoulders were tendrils that had never made it to the knot at the crown in the first place.

Watching her, Colin liked his plan all the more.

Because, he knew, one way or the other, he'd have her.

Just then the enormous beast she'd cleverly (he wondered if *that* touch was hers or Mrs. Byrne's) named, or renamed Mallory came loping toward him.

Colin figured the canine would bark. Instead, the dog just swung his heavy head toward Colin, stopped when he arrived at Colin's legs, sniffed Colin's thigh and then sat, resting his body against Colin's legs comfortably.

"Good dog," he whispered and Mallory turned his head and licked Colin's hand.

This too, seemed vaguely familiar, just as it had the first several times the dog had done it.

He pushed back the thought as he saw the Ford take off and Sibyl waved it on its way. She spent some time watching it out of sight then turned with a strangely despondent jerk and walked toward the house, staring at her feet, apparently lost in unhappy thought.

Colin moved deeper into the house, the dog following him. Once she was inside, she closed the door, never looking up, and she threw the bolt home.

It was then that Mallory gave a gentle woof.

Her head came around and she spied Colin.

Her eyes rounded, her mouth dropped open and she stared. Regardless of her open surprise, Colin couldn't help himself, he thought she looked adorable.

She snapped her mouth closed so fast, he could hear the crashing of teeth.

Then she breathed, "What are you doing here?"

He had planted his feet apart, and at her words he crossed his arms on his chest and didn't answer.

Her cheeks were pink and her eyes were flashing and he noticed her sweater had a lovely deep V-neck that showed a nice hint of her breasts below the drape of scarf.

"I thought I explained it wasn't wise for us to see each other again," she told him, her voice rising and the dog, who sat next to him again, stood up and let out a loud bark.

"Quiet," Colin told the dog and he sat down again and wagged his tail.

For some reason, his command to the dog made her angry.

"Don't tell my dog what to do," she snapped.

He again remained silent and watched her in appreciation, whether it was real or a fine performance, he didn't much care.

She dragged both of her hands through her hair and then belatedly realized it was tied up in a knot. She then tugged something impatiently out of it and Colin watched in fascination as it tumbled around her face, neck and shoulders.

Then she treated him to a true show.

She slid her fingers through her hair, gathering it up in a massive golden fall of tumbling waves and shaking it gloriously. She twisted it again and whatever she was holding was wound around it and it fell, looking just as delightfully messy as it was before she fixed it.

Colin felt his body jerk to attention at the sight.

"That was quite affecting," Colin commented, attempting to ignore his body's reaction to her.

Her eyes narrowed on him.

"What, on this good earth, did I do to deserve this?" she asked the ceiling, her voice convincingly disgruntled.

So convincing he felt a shimmer of doubt.

And, he had to admit, a long-dead resurgence of hope.

He dug into the pocket of his trousers and found what he was looking for. He held out his hand, turned it palm up and opened his fist, her red earrings and leather strapped pendant in his palm.

"My jewelry!" she gasped, her face showing a flash of appealing delight and she took two quick steps forward.

He closed his hand again and crossed his arms on his chest.

The dog settled into a lying position with a very loud groan.

She stopped when he closed his fist and her eyes flew to his. The delight was gone and confusion flooded in.

"Please give them to me," she requested quietly.

He ignored her tone and told her, "I have a proposition for you."

"Please give me my jewelry, Mr. Morgan. I forgot it in my extreme desire to exit your house and it means something to me." She also ignored his comment and he stayed silent so she continued, her voice rising again, in anger or panic, he didn't know her well enough to decipher. "Please give it to me. My mother gave me that pendant."

"If you want it, you have to hear me out."

Her response was surprising. He thought a consummate professional like herself would be willing to negotiate. But, perhaps, unsurprising if she was *not* the little actress most women of his acquaintance seemed to be.

She rushed to him and when she did so, the dog lumbered to his feet and started barking.

When she arrived a foot in front of him, she grabbed his wrist and tried to wrest his clenched fist open.

His other hand caught one of her wrists, easily twisting it behind her back and he crushed her body against his.

He tried to ignore his body's instantaneous reaction to her soft curves against his hard frame but he was not altogether successful. He calmly deposited the jewelry back into his pocket and caught her other hand, which was now pressing against his chest to push him away, and twisted that gently behind her too.

She struggled for a bit, and then suddenly realizing his superior strength, froze, her face lifting to his.

"You're unbelievable. I see your personality has changed again," she accused in a frosty voice that seemed entirely foreign on her lips.

He ignored her and remarked, "That's better."

"Let me go."

He shook his head.

"Let me go!" she demanded.

He shook her gently yet roughly and her fierce eyes turned frightened.

He found he both enjoyed that reaction and hated it with every fiber of his being.

It was a very strange sensation.

Her body still frozen, he finally had her rapt attention. It was time to get down to business.

"I want to fuck you," he told her calmly and bluntly and waited for her reaction.

"Oh my goddess," she breathed, her eyes widened and her mouth ended the statement parted in surprise.

With *that* strange remark, he could smell her breath, which was minty, and her scent, which was now gardenias and vanilla, and both took considerable toll on his fast flagging control.

He realized he wanted her, wanted her *now*, wanted to rip her clothes off, toss her delicious body on the dining-room table and bury himself inside her. He wanted it so badly it took a supreme effort of will not to give in to the impulse and the strength of this hunger made Colin deeply surprised. He'd never felt such a lack of control, such a feral need, not in his life.

"Jesus," he muttered. "You feel good, you smell good, you probably even taste good."

The panic flared in her eyes but her voice was quiet when she demanded, "Let me go."

"I'll pay you."

Gone was the quiet but the panic escalated.

"You'll *what*?" she screeched.

"Name your price. I'll pay for the use of that body of yours. You tell me how much you want and I'll tell you what it's worth to me." She was looking at him as if he'd grown a second head and she didn't reply so he continued, "Name your price and I'll tell you if it's worth one time, two times or a whole month of me having you whenever I want."

"You *are* mad," she whispered, staring up at him with intensity in her green eyes.

His fingers tightened on her wrists and he pushed his game. "Just name your price. If it's too high then we'll add things on. I'll have you on that table, for example," he expressed his thought from moments before.

Her head jerked to look at the table then jerked back to him, the tendrils of her hair catching fetchingly on her lips.

"Or, I'll have you on all fours," he suggested in a thoughtful attempt to help her make up her mind, driven by something he didn't understand to shock her.

At that, she started to struggle again, in earnest, anger and panic warring in her expression and she shouted, "Let me go!"

The dog, who had stopped barking, started again, backing up in confusion at this turn of events.

Colin's hands tightened further on her wrists and he knew it was painful because she ceased struggling immediately. But her luscious body wriggling against him, her eyes flashing green, Colin was definitely no saint, he lost his patience luckily before he lost his flagging control.

But he had to know.

He had to know if she was after his money or if she carried Beatrice Godwin's reincarnated soul.

The more she struggled, the longer she hesitated, the more he felt his hope grow and he had to know.

Was all that was Sibyl Godwin more than just coincidence?

Was she born destined to be his as he was to be hers?

Colin had been waiting his whole life.

He had to know.

Therefore, he dipped his head so his face was an inch from hers and growled, "Name your price."

SIBYL STARED AT him, more terrified than she'd ever been in her entire life.

Her mind was racing, her heart was beating like a hammer and panic was welling up in her chest so strongly, she thought she would explode.

This was not Lunatic Colin or any nuance of Rescuer Colin, this was *Scary Colin.*

"Quiet!" he thundered at Mallory and she jumped.

Her dog gave a soft, confused whine and then ran out of the room, up the stairs and, likely, into the corner of her bedroom.

She closed her eyes in stunning defeat at her dog's retreat.

And saw Meg lying on the ground by the minibus.

She opened her eyes again, knowing the exact figure because she had just that day worked on the budget.

She'd promised herself, whatever it took, she'd find a way.

And here Colin Morgan was, offering her a way.

It was an unthinkable, despicable way.

But it was a way.

She couldn't believe she was going to do it, this man was loathsome, hideous.

But she was going to do it.

If he agreed.

How many people had fifty thousand pounds to throw around, especially for something like this?

Thinking (more like hoping), he'd never agree to it and would be so disgusted he'd walk out the door, out of her life, leaving her in peace (forever and ever), Sibyl announced, "I want fifty thousand pounds."

That would buy the minibus, the driving lessons for Kyle, petrol, insurance and maintenance for several years, if they were frugal.

And it would buy peace of mind for Meg and Annie and all the other oldies who depended on the minibus to get them out of their homes so they could have a good meal and a few hours of companionship.

"And what does that buy me?"

His eyes betrayed both a disappointment so extreme it was tangible and a desire so strong she felt her body heat. Her stomach twisted inexplicably as he looked at her with that strange expression on his face.

"You tell me." Sibyl shot back, trying for bravado.

She felt like she was on the edge of a sharp, dark precipice, just about to jump over into the blinding abyss and it scared the living daylights out of her.

If she became this man's whore, she would never find her true love. She would never be the same again.

And she couldn't shake the constant feeling she had when she was with him that there was something else, something missing between them, something she didn't understand, couldn't put her finger on but it was something vitally important.

And, because of that, because he, too, had to feel it, she couldn't imagine he'd say yes.

"It gets me anything I want for two months," he declared.

Oh dear goddess, he said yes.

She blinked at him and felt the world falling away as she toppled into the abyss.

He stared down at her, his clay-colored eyes burning into her and she realized it wasn't done, she could take it back, order him out of her home and tell him she never wanted to see him again.

It was the moment of truth.

Could she do this vile thing?

But, her heart sinking, she knew she could.

No, she *had* to.

For Annie and especially for Meg.

She felt a pain slice through her stomach.

And she decided she hated Colin Morgan (at the same time she hated herself and her stupid temper that she vowed never to lose again).

Having come to her decision, Sibyl pressed her lips together and forced her body to relax.

It was done, it had to be. Two months of his despicable attention would mean years of safety for her oldies. It was, she tried (and failed) to convince herself, a small price to pay.

She'd gotten herself in many pickles, nothing *this* bad, of course, but in the past, it had been bad. And she'd lived through it and got to the other side.

She could live through this too.

She probably should have negotiated but she wanted him to let her go and she wanted all of this to be over, for now. She'd think about it again, later, after she learned how to kick herself in the backside.

"Done," she snapped.

Then she watched as Colin smiled, it was slow and it was lethal.

"Except—" she started to say, the panic overwhelming her.

His arms tightened painfully.

"No exceptions."

She ignored him and stated, "Not on that table. My father rebuilt and refinished that table, you'll not . . ." she paused, not knowing how to put it.

He was ever so helpful in a way she was beginning to realize with great annoyance was so very *him*. "Fuck you on the table?"

She thought she might just burst into tears.

Somehow she felt in her very soul that this was all wrong and she knew it was the dreams. They were just dreams but she felt, even hoped, deep down inside that they meant something more. That they meant her years of searching for her dream man, her knight, the other piece of her heart, were over.

Apparently, they did not.

"Yes," she hissed and controlled, with a mighty effort, her rampaging emotions.

"Fine," he relented, the pressure of his hands gentling but he did not release her.

"I want the money tomorrow," she told him.

If she was going to do this, she'd better do it now or she'd chicken out. Her mind was racing, two months yawned before her, filled with blackness.

"Then you're in my bed tomorrow night."

Her stomach clenched at his words but she nodded, her hair annoyingly falling all around her face, and with her hands held behind her back, she could do nothing about it.

"How shall we seal this bargain?" he asked, his voice had turned from edgy and intense to something else entirely and she could just not *believe* that her stomach actually did a mini-flip.

She didn't even chance a look at his face.

"Mr. Morgan, you don't touch me . . ." She had to stop because she was pressed up against him from toe to chest and his arms were wrapped around her, "Any more . . . until tomorrow."

"The name is Colin," he clipped.

She tossed her head and glared at him.

"Tomorrow," she snapped.

Surprisingly, he let her go.

She took a quick step back but her pride would not allow more. She was not going to let him know how terrified she was. Nor how devastated.

"My jewelry," she held out her hand, palm up.

This position was familiar and it seemed, now, Colin Morgan would always be holding something of hers she wanted back.

She had to gulp down her tears again as he deposited the jewelry into her hand.

Her fingers curled over it slightly and she dropped her head and poked at the precious pendant with her finger, cursing, for the millionth time, her absentmindedness that caused her to forget it in the first place.

This action also served to hide her face from his view.

She didn't want to look at him. She didn't know what she'd do if she looked at him. Probably run from the house and never stop running.

And how was *that* going to get a minibus?

She could taste the vile disappointment in her mouth that Rescuer Colin was not the *real* Colin.

And in that moment, Sibyl Godwin let go all of her wondrous dreams of finding her fated one, true, beautiful love. They flew away from her and she felt the acute pain as if they'd been torn from her physically.

His hand came out and he used the side of crooked finger to lift her chin so he could look into her eyes.

His were completely and utterly blank.

And that scared her most of all.

"I'll be here with the money tomorrow night at seven," he told her in a surprisingly soft voice.

She jerked her chin away from his hand.

Then Sibyl replied, "I'll be ready."

Chapter EIGHT

Consummation

"Oh dear," Marian Byrne said as she looked in her crystal ball.

It was milky but she could still see the shadows of two forms in its depths.

Years ago, when she first saw her crystal ball, Marian had been drawn to the clairvoyant orb, even though the crystal was flawed (which often made it difficult to see), but she'd bought it anyway. It never gave her a hint of trouble. It lay on its pillow of royal-blue velvet atop the spindly-legged, tri-footed round table in her magic room.

That night, it showed her something she did not like to see.

She turned and carefully touched the precious book, her hands wearing clean, white, cloth gloves. She, nor her mother, nor her mother's mother (and so on) ever touched Granny Esmeralda's Book of Shadows without using the greatest care.

The book was nearly five hundred years old and it was precious.

She read the ingredients of the potion Granny Esmeralda used on Royce and Beatrice (even though she'd read it hundreds of times before and had it memorized).

The protection charm was fierce, half of the ingredients you couldn't get anymore unless you visited the darkest shops.

Marian saw, however, that using the flesh and blood of the dark soul and the death blood of the lovers may now be causing a bit of havoc for Beatrice and Royce's descendants.

She knew (as every witch did) that bad things came from bad blood—violence, mayhem or simply (as was the case for Sibyl and Colin) misunderstanding and distrust.

Nevertheless, to make the potion as strong as it needed to be, Marian knew Granny Esmeralda needed all the magic she could get.

It should have been strong enough, the residual love of the wedded Morgans that lasted in the atmosphere for five hundred years. Everything was perfect. Colin and Sibyl were both direct descendants (of this Marian was certain intuitively rather than with any real knowledge). Colin lived in Lacybourne. Sibyl, for some deliciously fateful reason, lived in Granny Esmeralda's old cottage. Then there was the dog, named for Royce's horse. Marian didn't know why the lovers had exchanged hair, but she found it very touching.

But something, obviously, was wrong.

And it was likely that potion.

"Well, Granny Esmeralda, there's nothing for it. I'm just going to have to keep my eye on them," Marian told the book. "And maybe meddle, just a *wee* bit," she finished.

She knew it was dangerous to meddle but if she didn't it would likely be another five hundred years before their descendants could start again.

The book, not unusually, said nothing in return.

Marian stood and felt some pain in her knees.

"I'm too old for this," she complained to one of her cats.

The feline blinked at her.

Without further hesitation, Marian went to her vials and drawers.

She had work to do.

WHAT DID A woman wear when she became a whore?

Sibyl would have never thought in a million years, with ignorant bliss at her own eventual stupidity, that she would be asking herself that question.

Now, for fifty thousand pounds and peace of mind for the well-being of several dozen old people she really didn't know all that well, she *was* asking herself that question.

At least, she told herself, she hadn't sold her body to the devil, better-known-as Colin Morgan, for, say, just the price of petrol.

However, she found herself obsessing about whether she should have asked him for twice that. They needed work done on the stage too. And rewiring. And decent heating. And new furniture.

Of course, that may have meant *four* months of anything he wanted which was an idea not to be borne (not that her current predicament was easily tolerated, it was just a bargain she'd made and, regrettably, had to keep).

That might be the worst part of it all (in a situation where it was very difficult to assess what *exactly* was the worst part). Considering that he was a raving lunatic with a multiple personality disorder, "whatever he wanted" could be very much not worth getting paid fifty thousand pounds.

Staring in her wardrobe and not seeing anything that was "Become a Whore" worthy, she did what any girl would do in her situation.

She called her little sister.

"Little black dress," Scarlett replied instantly when Sibyl asked what to wear on a "date" (her sister didn't need to know any details) that she knew, at the end, would be a sure thing.

Sibyl didn't have a little black dress so, mainly out of curiosity, she asked what Scarlett would wear on a "date" that she was certain would *not* be a sure thing.

"Little black dress," Scarlett repeated.

"Scarlett, you do not wear little black dresses on every date!" Sibyl snapped, beginning to allow the niggling feeling of panic she'd been harboring for over twenty-four hours to bud out of control.

"Yes I do, my entire wardrobe consists of scrubs and little black dresses," Scarlett retorted.

For some reason, Sibyl believed this.

"Well, I don't have a little black dress and he's going to be here in . . ." She looked at the clock on her bedside table. Then she gulped before she finished, "Thirty minutes."

"That's okay, keep him waiting," Scarlett retorted airily.

Sibyl didn't like the idea of what might happen if she kept Colin Morgan waiting. She didn't like it *at all.*

Her sister, like her mother, could read her mood from thousands of miles away.

"Jeez, Billie, this guy sure has your knickers in a twist," Scarlett noted and finally finished helpfully. "Just tell me what you have in your closet."

Sibyl didn't want to think of twisted knickers either.

Therefore, she focused on Scarlett's offer of help and in great detail she recited her wardrobe to her sister.

Luckily, she had already done her hair (pulled it up in a severe twist at the back of her head) and her makeup (dramatic, it suited her mood).

She'd also bought a bottle of red wine, a bottle of white wine, three different types of beer, champagne (did one toast their entrance into the World of Whoredom? Sibyl was not up on the etiquette). She'd also bought brie, apples, water crackers and made shrimp cocktail. Further, she'd prepared platters of these as nibbles, just in case.

She might be careening quickly down the low road (the *very* low road) but she was not going to lose her hostessing skills in the process. Her mother would never forgive her.

He would not be getting a plate of tasteless cheese and a sad ham sandwich, although *he* deserved a big bowl of ashes.

"What was that? The last thing you said," Scarlett interrupted Sibyl's recitation and her culinary reverie (Sibyl was frantically, and possibly hysterically, multitasking).

"Silk camisole with some sequined beading," Sibyl repeated.

"What color?" her discerning sister inquired.

Sibyl fingered the soft material of a top she'd bought last year when a girlfriend from Boulder was out in England for a visit. She'd never worn it. She didn't go clubbing or out to dinner very often and it wasn't the type of thing to wear to the Community Centre. The top was too fancy and bared too much skin; she didn't want to give the old men coronaries. She had enough trouble with the damned minibus.

"Kind of a deep violet," Sibyl answered.

"Wear that," Scarlett declared decisively, "with a nice pair of jeans. Now, let's talk shoes. What've you got?"

And thus, ten minutes after she hung up the phone with her sister (the call had unfortunately included the third degree about "the guy"), and five minutes after Colin Morgan was meant to arrive, Sibyl stood in the dining area of the cottage wearing a dark-violet, silk, sequined camisole, her best jeans (that had gone a bit snug due to a day of stress-eating that was now turning her stomach sickeningly) and a pair of high-heeled sandals that consisted solely of a strip of rhinestones across her toes and a daring rhinestone ankle strap. They were shoes she had purchased to wear with a bridesmaid dress and she hadn't worn them since. She'd walked on them down the aisle and immediately kicked them off at the reception because they killed her feet.

Which they were doing now.

She thought, with fervor, that she just might hate her sister.

But then again, at that moment, she hated the entire world.

Most of all, she hated herself (and of course Colin Morgan).

And she couldn't shift the feeling that something, far beyond the fact that she'd sold her body to a man she didn't like, was terribly, *terribly* wrong.

She just thanked the goddess that she had a decent pedicure, complete with pale-pink nail varnish. She'd hate to enter the World of Whoredom with chipped toenails.

And she thanked the goddess that her mother insisted she start taking birth control at the age of eighteen (regardless that it was unneeded at the time).

She'd chosen a scent of peony with a hint of grapefruit and put in the dangling amethyst earrings one of her ex-boyfriends had given her.

And now she decided she was definitely hysterical because she was standing in her dining room wondering if she should light candles and put on music. She didn't exactly have to strike a mood, the seduction was a given.

Bran sauntered in, his tail twitching, then stopped and looked up at her.

Sibyl stared down at her pet and (undoubtedly hysterically) could have sworn her cat was watching her with grave judgement in his yellow feline eyes.

"What are *you* looking at?" she snapped.

Bran flicked his tail once before he sat down and blinked his eyes.

"Yes, well, it's only two months. That's it. He's young, all right looking . . ." Bran blinked again, this time in disbelief. "Okay, he's quite good-looking. He also has all of his teeth and—"

A knock sounded at the door and Sibyl emitted a frightened, muted scream.

Then she whispered, "Oh my goddess."

And the immediate feeling flooded through her that her whole life was going to change, not just the next two months. This thought bubbled up and nearly exploded into panic.

Luckily, Sibyl had just enough strength left to tamp it down.

Bran got up and wisely ran up the stairs.

Mallory, on the other hand, was already up the stairs and after a clamorous descent, he skidded on his paws at the bottom to take the sharp turn towards the door. In the process, he slid across the braided rugs covering the wide-planked floors, bunching them in huge messes. She saw him stop (because he crashed into the door) and then he barked loudly over and over again.

She took a deep breath and exhaled, in doing so managing to expel some of her panic and she walked forward.

You can do this, you can do this, you can do this, she repeated to herself over and over again, using her feet to right the rugs that Mallory had disheveled.

"Mallory, out of the way. Go sit in the living room," she commanded when she made it to the door (or nearly, as Mallory was in the way).

Mallory ignored her command and backed up enough for the door to be opened, but his big dog body stayed where it was, his tongue lolling, his tail wagging fiercely.

Sibyl took another breath, thinking what a cruel world it was that her dog, who hated men since she got him as a puppy, absolutely *adored*

Colin Morgan.

She threw back the bolt and opened the door.

Colin was standing on the threshold looking unfairly handsome wearing a dark suit and an electric-blue shirt that was unbuttoned at the neck.

You cannot do this, you cannot do this, you cannot do this, her brain (or was it her conscience?) unbidden, repeated over and over again.

"Come in," she invited, ignoring her brain, stepping wide and pleased her voice held no tremor.

Colin entered and Mallory went berserk, snuffling his hand (the way he normally only did to Sibyl's), his whole body vibrating with glee.

Sibyl stared out the door and considered the very pleasant idea of running into the night (or simply begging him to leave and never return, unless it was to ask her out on a real date again after promising him she'd accept) but instead she shook off these happy notions, now completely lost to her, and closed the door behind her.

Sealing her fate.

Colin was waiting for her patiently as she turned. He was also idly stroking Mallory's soft, black-faced head while the dog sat next to him in contented silence.

And lastly, Colin was carrying a briefcase.

She felt her knees go weak.

She lifted her arm to motion him toward the dining table and followed him when he moved. He still said not a word as he placed the briefcase on the table and turned toward her.

She walked toward the briefcase.

She had no idea what to do. What was next? Should she say something?

Good goddess, how did women do this sort of thing for a living?

She felt like wringing her hands but put every amount of energy and attention into keeping them still and tremor free.

Sibyl was so concentrated on this trying task, she didn't hear him approach.

Then he was there, he was so close that she smelled his cedar-spiked cologne. He lifted his hands toward her head and she flinched.

His fingers found the two carefully placed clips that held her hair up (clips it took her twenty minutes to secure). He pulled them out and her hair tumbled around her shoulders.

She turned stunned eyes to his to see his were drilling intently into hers while his fingers ran through the hair on one side of her head then on the other, pulling its mass away from her face.

"You'll not wear your hair up when you're with me." He voiced this demand smoothly, in a calm, even tone before he tossed the clips on her dining-room table.

Her mouth dropped open and she could do nothing but nod because, from that moment on (or at least for the next two months), his wish was her command.

He turned, flipped open the latches to the briefcase and inside there were carefully arranged twenty-pound notes. Just like in the movies.

Meg and Annie's minibus.

Overwhelmed with relief, not lifting her eyes from the money and not realizing how strange it would sound, she whispered a heartfelt, "Thank you."

When she eventually looked at him, he was staring at her quizzically.

After a brief hesitation, he replied quietly, "You're welcome."

She reached out and slapped the top of the case down. She wanted to grab it and throw it into the night, find a deep lake and toss it into the middle, gather all the money and fling it into his face, screaming, *"This is not really me!"* and do everything to make him believe.

Instead, she just fastened the latches.

"It warms the heart that you don't intend to count it," Colin drawled.

She closed her eyes which were still trained on the case.

She just *knew* she'd forget something.

Then she squared her shoulders and turned to him without a word. He was watching her so closely and so intently it made her entire body quiver.

Suddenly, he asked, "Where's your bedroom?"

"Um . . . what?" Her voice was scratchy, like she hadn't spoken in a year.

"Bedroom?"

"It's . . . my bedroom's upstairs."

He grabbed her hand and in three great strides he was at the foot of the stairs, dragging her behind him.

"Don't you want a drink?" she asked in desperation, trailing after him, her feet having no choice but to move quickly, reading his intent and terrified of it, but to her extreme unease, Colin made no response.

She tried to yank her hand away, tried to delay this until later, much later, after brie and shrimp cocktail and all was made right in the world again.

She tripped up the first step but found her footing quickly. She had to, he didn't hesitate. His strong hand gripping hers, he dragged her up the stairs.

He halted abruptly at the large landing and she slammed into him. The bathroom was obviously to his right, another two-step stairway several paces to the left took him to the upstairs hall. He turned left, and with some uncanny perception walked right past the two other bedrooms to the very end of the hall and up the three extra steps that led him to *her* bedroom.

He entered it without hesitation, pulling her with him.

The light was still on beside her bed (her mother would have given her a lecture about global warming if she saw it, but then again, her mother would probably have other things to lecture her about if she'd been there).

He drew her in the room and then let her go and the force of this action sent her beyond him several steps into the room.

He slammed the door shut behind him.

There went any chance at Mallory-induced interruptions.

Sibyl's belly dropped.

"Take off your clothes," he commanded without preamble.

All her breath left her in a rush and her heart squeezed.

She tried another delaying tactic.

"Mr. Morgan, can we just take a moment and talk this through? There have to be ground rules."

He took one stride, one *angry* stride, reached out and yanked her into his arms and she tipped her head back to look into his blazing eyes.

"Call me 'Mr. Morgan' one more time and I'll tie you naked to the bed for a week," he bit out, apparently for some reason livid. "Got that?"

Her entire body trembled.

"It's Colin," he clipped.

She nodded.

"*Say it!*" he barked and she jumped.

"Colin," Sibyl whispered.

It was then he kissed her.

It was nothing like the kiss the blond version of him gave her in the dream. It was hot, yes, but it was an entirely different type of wild that was heady and needy and so possessive it took her breath away and, darn it all, it did this deliciously.

Colin unexpectedly released her, and, unprepared for it, Sibyl stumbled back a step. She thought she might fall as her wobbly legs didn't seem able to support her. She threw out her hand and grabbed the foot of the bed to steady herself.

"Take your clothes off," he repeated and shrugged off his jacket, dropping it to the floor.

Her trembling hands went to the hem of her camisole.

"*These* are the ground rules," he forced the words out between his teeth and took a step forward.

Automatically, Sibyl took a step back.

He stopped at her movement, his head tilted to the side and his eyes turned menacing.

He took another step towards her. She took another step back.

He started speaking again. "You always wear your hair down when you're with me."

Sibyl nodded.

"Yes, I've got that one," she told him helpfully, trying to diffuse his strangely infuriated mood.

Why he would be angry, she had no idea. He was getting what he wanted, wasn't he?

He took a step forward. At his continued advance, her mind

blanked and she took a step back, rounding the bed.

Colin went on, "Not another man touches you while you're mine."

She nodded again and squared her shoulders to try and instill some confidence in herself, some control over her fluttering belly and her trembling legs.

"You aren't taking off your clothes," he reminded her in a dangerous voice.

His hands went to the buttons of his shirt.

She whipped the camisole off as fast as she could. Underneath it was the lacy, black, strapless bra she'd bought for the same bridesmaid's dress for which she bought the shoes.

She heard his swift intake of breath.

He tore his shirt off and the buttons flew around the room like mini-bullets.

She heard her own swift intake of breath, not only at his action, but at her first sight of the wall of his hard, muscled chest and the defined planes of his stomach.

Good goddess, but he had a beautiful body.

Her hands, now trembling, went to the button of her jeans.

Colin continued. "You do what I tell you, no questions asked."

He took a step forward, rounding the bed as she nodded.

She took a step back.

His hands went to the belt of his trousers and he kept going. "You're available to me when I say, where I say."

"I . . . I . . ." she had to clear her throat and cursed herself mentally for showing that weakness, "I have a job. What if I'm working?"

She unzipped her jeans and slid them off her hips, kicking them away and standing in front of him feeling desperately ill-at-ease and wearing nothing but lacy black underwear and rhinestone shoes.

It was at that moment she felt the most like a whore and something inside her curled up and died.

Her mother and father both told her that her big heart would be the finish of her one day.

This was that day.

He didn't answer her question about working. He was staring at her like she was a long, tall glass of ice water and he'd just stumbled out of the desert.

"Colin?"

Upon hearing her voice, with a start his eyes moved from her body to her face and they were lit with a fire that turned her bones to mush.

And it wasn't with fear.

She forced herself to go on. "My job's important to me. What if I'm working?"

"I thought I just gave you fifty thousand pounds?" he replied.

She forgot about that. How she did, she didn't know, but she did.

She couldn't exactly tell him he was buying her body in exchange for a minibus for oldies, he'd think *she* was a lunatic.

When she didn't answer he said, "You're on a two month holiday."

That thing that died inside her, whatever it was, turned to ash.

He was utterly ruthless.

She could do nothing but nod. She worked more hours than she was paid and hadn't taken a day of holiday in a year. She also made her own hours and there was always something happening at the Community Centre.

She'd make it work.

From the look in his eyes, she'd *have* to make it work.

"Is that all?" she asked.

"Would you like more?" he returned.

She shook her head vehemently.

"Take off your underwear but leave the shoes."

Dear goddess, she was going to melt in a puddle at the side of her bed. How she could be terrified, miserable and turned on all at the same time, she had no idea.

But she was.

And she did as she was told.

By the time she was finished he'd completed disrobing and stood in front of her in absolute brazen nakedness. His body was extraordinary. She'd never seen anything like it outside of a magazine. His muscles defined, the jutting bones of his hips and lower . . .

"Dear goddess," she whispered.

She totally forgot her own nakedness at the sight of his.

"Get on the bed," he ordered.

Then she remembered.

She turned, trying to hide her embarrassment with a fall of her hair. She sat down on the side of the bed but before she could push herself to the middle, he was there, his strong arms around her lifting her up and planting her back, deeper on the bed.

He pushed her to her back and his body came down on hers.

Strangely, Sibyl thought, when his weight hit her, he felt heavy and warm and unbelievably but indescribably *right*.

She trembled with fear *and* desire, and she hated herself all the more because only very bad girls enjoyed this type of thing.

What kind of woman was she?

She started, "Colin, I've—"

But she didn't finish, his head came down, his mouth claimed hers, his tongue sweeping inside—Colin Morgan kissed her, her entire body quivered and it started.

COLIN TRAILED THE tips of his fingers down Sibyl's spine, all the way to the very shapely curve of her generously rounded bottom.

He felt her tremble under his fingers.

She'd been worth every penny of those fifty thousand pounds. Even if he didn't have her again, he wouldn't regret the money. Hell, he would have paid it just to witness her standing before him in nothing but that black underwear, as ludicrous as that notion was.

However, it was true. She was just that exquisite.

She was lying on her belly, her face turned away from him, locks of her leonine hair falling on her back, her shoulders and tumbled all over her pillows.

So much for Royce and Beatrice's reincarnated souls shaking off the curse in an earth-shattering moment of glory the minute they consummated their passion.

He'd felt the earth move but it started and stopped with Sibyl bucking under him and moaning his name with her intense climax that he could not, for the life of him (even as cynical as he was), believe was fake.

It had taken him some time to settle her obvious nerves, either this was her first time selling her body or she wasn't used to it. But once his mouth and hands were on her, she melted, and even if she was truly a consummate actress, he didn't care.

She was, quite simply, the best he ever had.

And he'd had a lot.

She *did* taste as fantastic as she felt and smelled (tonight, she smelled of fruit and flowers and it was a thoroughly intoxicating scent).

He'd never felt the driving need, the insistent demand of his body to possess anyone like he'd felt the need to possess her. Colin could barely contain himself, nearly didn't have the patience he needed to calm her nerves and incite her passion before he drove into her. He was ready for her before they'd made it to the bed.

And it had been everything her luscious body, her brilliant eyes, her phenomenal hair and her fiery temper promised it would be . . . and more.

Two months of her might not be enough. If it got any better than this, he'd buy two more. He'd double the price if needed to keep that magnificent body writhing under him, her mouth on him, her legs open for him.

As he had these thoughts, she whipped her head around and her hair slid along her back.

"I have to let Mallory out."

She said this in a quiet voice, but he saw with some surprise that even though she'd obviously wiped her tears on the pillow, she'd been crying.

Something about this caused an unpleasant twinge of a feeling Colin never felt before to cut through his gut.

Before he could process the feeling, Sibyl twisted on the bed and got up. Walking quickly to her discarded clothes, she pulled on her jeans without putting her panties on. He rolled to his side and put his head in his hand, elbow to the pillow to watch her dress. He so enjoyed the show that, with disgust, he realized he'd watch her scrub a toilet and likely be aroused by it.

She reached into the wardrobe and pulled out a huge sweatshirt that said "University of Colorado" on it and yanked it over her head. Then she sat on the edge of the bed and leaned over to take her sexy sandals off.

"Are you going home?" she quietly asked the floor.

"No, Sibyl," Colin answered. "I'm spending the night."

She nodded, her shoulders slumped deeper and her hair shook with her head, shining in the light of the lamp. He had to force himself not to lean forward, wrap his fist in it and turn her head to his so he could kiss her again.

He remembered the taste of her mouth, it was just as intoxicating as the rest of her.

"Would you like me to come with you?" he asked, his voice gentle and he had no idea why.

He wasn't normally gentle with women, nor was he rough or brutal or cruel, usually simply cold or reserved. They used him, he used them, it was the unspoken deal and both parties understood.

But he had been all those things to Sibyl and he didn't understand his intense reaction to her or the reasons he was driven to these behaviors.

He was disappointed that she'd accepted his offer, proven herself to be everything every woman in his life had ever been.

However, Colin was used to that and should have been able to accept it. But when she'd slapped the lid on the briefcase, he felt the need to punish her for *not* being what he wanted her to be.

Given that, when she'd said "thank you" in that soft, sweet voice as if the fifty thousand pounds was the answer to fifty thousand prayers, for some reason his chest had squeezed and a sharp pain sliced through his insides.

He'd never had that reaction either, not to anything, but the demands of his body wouldn't allow his mind the delay it would need to understand his reactions and he'd dragged her upstairs and been anything but gentle with her.

At the current moment, though, everything about her screamed for gentle. She was walking around if she was made of glass and even a loud noise would make her shatter.

"He doesn't like his walks, he's too lazy." She was talking about Mallory. "I won't be long."

She yanked out some shoes from the wardrobe, shoved her feet in them and left the room quickly. He heard her calling for the dog as she descended the stairs.

In her absence, Colin looked around the room. Even though he'd been in it for an hour, he was seeing it for the first time.

It was supremely feminine and somehow so personal he felt he was trespassing on some kind of sacred ground.

Colin saw a photo on the bedside table and rolled to pick it up. He studied it in the bedside light.

There were four people in the picture, the gorgeous woman from the portrait in the dining room (but older), a rather funny-looking, thin, bald man, Sibyl and what had to be her sister, almost her equal in magnificence, with red hair instead of blonde, blue eyes instead of hazel.

His gaze moved over Sibyl's face in the photograph. He noted the color of her eyes and it came to him there was another reason he knew she'd climaxed. Her eyes shifted to the color of sherry the moment before it happened. He knew, he'd watched in triumphant satisfaction.

He mentally shook off the pleasant memories of watching Sibyl's orgasm and focused again on the photo.

The family was obviously loving, their arms thrown around each other. Sibyl and her father were caught amidst laughter (something he had still never seen, although he'd heard it) while the two redheaded women, old and young, were making faces at the camera.

Colin put the frame down and his eyes moved to glance around the room. They stopped at the window seat, which had a book sitting in it like someone had just been interrupted while reading. Then they went to the dressing table that had a feminine mess of cosmetics but also held a variety of delicate, exquisite bottles, all with no labels.

As he was studying the bottles, the cat jumped agilely on the bed and surveyed him curiously for about two seconds before he lay gracefully on his side and started cleaning his back foot.

Colin had the distinct feeling that something was not right with this picture.

Before he could decide what that was, there was a clamor somewhere in the house and he knew that Sibyl and Mallory were back.

The clamor spread, Colin heard it come up the stairs and then the dog bounded in the room and stopped clumsily at his side of the bed. He lifted Colin's hand with his nose and bumped it up so it was resting on the dog's head.

"Do you want something to eat?" He heard Sibyl ask.

Colin's attention turned from the dog to see Sibyl was standing at the door. Regardless of her makeup, she looked about sixteen years old.

He felt his gut clench with unease.

When he didn't respond, she went on, "Drink?"

"I'm fine, Sibyl," Colin answered, surveying her closely.

He fought his body's demand to drag her back into bed while she looked over her shoulder and out the door.

"Do you want a . . ." she hesitated, looked back at him and then tossed her head in an act of frustration, about what only she was privy, "tour of my house?"

There was something meaningful to that offer, something outside the realm of their bargain, something that made that unease in his gut spread.

He forced his tone to be gentle. "I'd very much like a tour of your house but later. Now I want you to come back to bed."

She hesitated before walking to the side of the bed. Her hands at the waistband of her jeans, she kicked off her shoes.

Something made him ask quietly, "You've never done this before, have you?"

Her eyes flew to his. They were back to the color of sherry, with but a hint of green close to the pupils.

Without a word, she shook her head.

Then she took off her clothes swiftly and, with a graceful gesture of her arm, tossed them across the room. Even more swiftly, she lifted the covers and slid under them.

She resumed her position on her belly, her head turned away from him. Even naked in bed at his side, her position closed her off to him, removing herself from him and Colin didn't like it.

At all.

He slid the covers down again to expose her back and ran the flat of his palm up from the gentle curve of her rounded bottom up to the expanse of smooth skin between her shoulders.

And again, as he did, Sibyl trembled.

He stared at her back, her hair and realized she was all his.

For two months.

And he gloried in that thought.

He pulled her hair away from her neck and kissed her between her shoulder blades.

He then lifted his lips to her ear. "You're doing very well."

She didn't hesitate in her response.

"Thanks." Her voice betrayed she meant none of the gratitude that word conveyed. "Just what every girl wants to hear."

That feeling of unease spread precariously close to his cold heart.

"Sibyl," he called.

She didn't turn to him and sighed before asking, "Can't we just go to sleep?"

"No," he answered honestly.

Sibyl Godwin, Colin had long since decided, would not get very much rest that night.

Nor, likely, for the next two months.

She rolled, dislodging his hand and lay on her side, up on her elbow. He settled on his elbow facing her while she pulled the covers over her breasts. He noticed her eyes were no longer sherry, they were back to emerald.

The effect of the color change was extraordinary.

"Well, of course, you have to get your money's worth," she snapped tartly after she caught his eyes.

"I've already had it," he replied truthfully.

At his remark, her eyes rounded and he watched in fascination as she pulled her lips between her teeth for a moment as if literally biting back words she wanted desperately to say.

And her eyes melted back to sherry.

That's when he knew he could kiss her.

Much later, when he lifted his head and she followed it with hers to keep in contact with his mouth, he finished what he meant to say.

Smoothly, in one fluid movement, he slid inside her magnificent, tight wetness and, while he did, she exposed her throat to him as she arched her back and neck in an open demonstration of the pleasure she felt at allowing him inside.

Her legs lifted up, her knees at his sides so high they were nearly tucked under his arms, and her thighs tightened against him. This action drew him exquisitely deeper into her.

"Sibyl," he called her name as he settled inside her, not moving and practically gritting his teeth with the effort, she was so splendid.

Her head righted, hair wildly tumbled on the pillows framing her passion-filled face.

"Colin," she whispered, his name from her lips, said in that husky tone of sex, caused his body to twitch involuntarily.

He fought back his response and warned, "I may have had my money's worth but you still owe me two months and I'm going to have them."

Her eyes rounded again but her hips shifted, inviting the movement of his.

"Sibyl—" he started but her hands were urgent on his waist, her nails digging into him.

"Yes, Colin, yes," she breathed, impatient. "Two months. Now, will you just please *move*?"

Colin grinned.

Then he did as Sibyl asked.

Chapter NINE

Danger

The phone was ringing.

Sibyl decided to ignore it, her answerphone would get it. She was too deliciously tired to bother.

When it stopped ringing abruptly, she smiled sleepily but her smile was short-lived.

"Hullo?"

She heard this said in a husky, baritone voice.

Instantly awake, she twisted violently in the bed, pulling the covers over her breasts, just in time to hear Colin say, "She's right here." His clay-colored eyes, rimmed with their lush lashes, slid to her. "It's for you."

Ignoring the rush of warmth in her belly at the sight of his eyes *and* him in her bed, she snatched the phone out of his hand and covered the mouthpiece. "Of course it's for me, who would it be for? Mallory?"

He smiled.

This smile was again lethal but not with danger, instead with the heady, pleasant aftermath of sex.

A lot of sex.

A lot of really, *really* good sex.

She ignored that too (and what it did to her belly, namely, making it flutter) and lifted the phone to her ear. "Hello?"

"Who was *that*?" her mother asked.

Sibyl sat bolt upright in bed, still holding the sheets to her chest. "Mom?"

"Yes, baby, it's your mother. Your sister phoned and told me you had a sure thing so I *had* to call."

Sibyl dropped her forehead into her hand, rested her elbow on her thigh and closed her eyes in despair.

Her bloody, *bloody* sister.

Her bloody, *bloody* mother.

Who else on earth had two relatives that were so interested in their daughter/sibling's sex life?

"It appears she was right!" her mother crowed ecstatically.

"What time is it there? It has to be . . ." Sibyl twisted around to look at the clock on the bedside table.

What she saw was Colin on his side, resting with his head in his hand and watching her, his eyes soft with interest.

And his eyes looked good soft with interest.

She twisted back so fast she was pretty certain she pulled something.

"It's midnight, baby, and I'm about to go out and commune with nature," her mother answered. "I thought I'd give you a buzz before I draw down the moon to see how your night went, but I guess I don't have to ask."

"Mom—"

"Is he cute?"

"Mom—"

"Did you have an orgasm?"

"Mom!"

"What? Oh, yes, you probably can't talk now, since he's there. And if I take up your time, you might miss a morning quickie."

Sibyl returned to her defeated position of head in hand and she expelled a frustrated sigh.

She loved her mother, she'd lay down her life for her, but sometimes she was just too much. And now was *definitely* one of those times.

Her mother continued, "Just know I'm glad your dry spell is over and I hope your father and I meet him in April. Will we meet him in April?"

Sibyl's body went rigid.

In all the emotional drama, she'd forgotten about her parent's visit in April. Their visit was smack in the middle of Colin's two months. Two months where he was to have her when he said, where he said.

The very thought of those words made her shiver, and she had to admit this shiver had not a thing to do with fear or gloom.

Sibyl powered through the shiver and began, "Mom—"

"I know, it's too soon. I hope to meet him though. He must be something special to catch your fancy. See you soon, baby."

Then she rang off without giving Sibyl a chance to say goodbye.

Sibyl pressed the phone off with her thumb and sat staring at it, thinking maybe she should throw it through the window.

Sibyl was not a morning person and this morning was no exception. Her mother only exacerbated the problem.

Before she could engage in her violent act against the phone, Colin slid it out of her hand.

She didn't watch him replace it in the receiver, she just plopped back on the pillows with a heavy sigh.

Her life was completely out of control and she only had herself to blame.

"That sounded like an interesting conversation," Colin remarked.

Considering the fact that she'd only uttered a handful of words, and most of them were "Mom," she threw him a killing look where only her eyes moved sideways but she didn't speak.

When she didn't, he did. "I imagine she wasn't too thrilled when a man answered the phone first thing in the morning."

"Oh no," Sibyl replied, slowly closing her eyes. "One could say she was beside herself with glee."

No response.

Sibyl opened her eyes again.

He was back to resting on his elbow, watching her with warm, inquisitive eyes.

She decided to ignore the warm, inquisitive eyes too. She didn't want to think of a warm, inquisitive Colin. If she did, she might shiver again.

"My mother is . . ." How could she put it? "Odd."

He decided that the conversation was finished and she knew this because his head began to descend.

"Colin, we have to talk," Sibyl blurted.

The descent stopped.

"That doesn't sound good." His voice was guarded.

"My parents are coming to visit me," she told him.

His eyebrows came up lazily. This, for some reason, made her stomach do a flip-flop.

Regardless, Sibyl persevered, "In April."

He still simply regarded her.

"For two weeks," she finished.

"And?" he prompted.

"And, well . . . you and . . . well . . . me . . ."

He grinned.

This grin was wicked.

She was beginning to realize Colin liked the upper hand, which he had a great deal with regard to her.

His head descended again and he brushed his lips against hers before saying, "I see."

"We'll need to take a little break for two weeks and—"

"Oh no." His lips brushed hers again, his tone firm, and he finished, "A deal's a deal."

"Colin!" She pulled her head away (as far away as it could go, resting on a pillow). "I can't exactly say, 'Sorry, Mom . . . Dad, gotta go meet my lover for a rousing round of bed play.' I don't *think* so."

"Bed play?" His voice was amused.

She sat up again and twisted around. Colin pulled away to avoid her crashing into him, settling on his back.

"Colin! This is serious!" she exclaimed, looking down at him.

"I'm taking it seriously. It's *my* two months."

"I'll make it up to you in May," she offered.

"If you want this, I'll take *all* of May and three weeks in June."

Sibyl gasped.

"That's another," she stopped to calculate it, "entire month!" she finished.

"Yes it is. And I'll want to see you sometime during those two weeks in April."

"That's not possible and that's not fair," she returned sharply and a little desperately.

"That's the only offer on the table," Colin retorted firmly.

She realized she'd started shaking and this wasn't a good kind of shaking or the scared or melancholy kind, it was the *angry* kind.

He was heartless.

She didn't think she could do it for another month. Not that "it" was that bad. In fact "it" was mind-bogglingly, earth-shatteringly good. One could even say it was otherworldly good.

And it was the best she'd ever had.

By far.

Although, she hadn't had that much but *this* was something else. It made her toes curl just thinking about it.

How she could not really like him (at all) and still find him so amazingly attractive was beyond her. Though, she had to admit, sex with Colin was simply unbelievable.

But he'd still paid for it, which still made her his whore, which made her hate herself, so much, she could hardly bear it.

She plopped back on the pillows and closed her eyes again.

She had no choice and she hated that even more than she hated herself at that moment (which was saying something).

"Fine," she snapped the word out so curtly it sounded like half a syllable.

"Nice to see you give in gracefully."

She opened her eyes to see him looming over her.

His eyes were no longer warm but instead they were hard and glittering.

Even obviously angry, he was so damned handsome, she felt her breath catch at the same time as she felt her temper unravel.

She had been wrong. Colin in her bedroom wasn't laughable. It was seductive. He was so out of place he looked like a conquering avenger, enjoying the spoils of victory.

Which he was, in a way. *She* was spoils.

"Perhaps I should remind you what you're giving in to." This was said in a smooth, even tone that she was realizing was his very-angry-but-controlling-it-by-the-skin-of-my-teeth voice.

His hand was under the covers, the warmth of it sliding across her ribs, down her belly making her muscles contract lusciously along its path.

In the face of his tone, she felt like throwing caution to the wind, one could say she'd had enough.

"Trust me, I remember."

"It certainly doesn't seem like it to me."

She turned toward him quickly, dislodging his hand, wanting him to understand (if he had it in him) at the same time as she completely lost her rather formidable temper.

"What do you want me to say? That it was good? Yes, it was good!"

He didn't seem to like being interrupted in his task, his strong hands found her hips and he fell to his back, taking her with him.

She wasn't finished, however, and she pressed her hands against his chest to lift herself, which he allowed.

Slightly.

When he stopped allowing it by wrapping his arms around her, one tight at her waist, one forearm pressing up her spine, Sibyl kept talking.

"Bottom line, you paid for me and that doesn't feel good but I need the money. So I have no choice, you're right, a deal's a deal. But I love my parents and I'm not going to tell them I have to drop everything to go be some man's whore. And you've given me no other options. So, if I'm a little pouty in the face of all of that, you'll just have to get over it!"

His eyes, already hard, turned to stone.

"I have another rule," was his response to this diatribe, and in a belated act of self-preservation she pressed her hands against his chest to pull further away, but his arm at her waist tightened and his hand slid up her spine until his fingers wrapped around the back of her neck and forced her to descend until she was but an inch away from his face. "If you call yourself my whore again, it becomes four months."

Caution was not in the wind. Caution was twirling around in a tornado.

"I'm your whore," she repeated stubbornly.

"Do it again and it's five months."

"I'm . . . your . . . *whore,*" Sibyl gritted out between clenched teeth and Colin whipped her around to her back, him on top, and pried her legs apart with his knee. When he did, she goaded, "That's it, Colin, prove me right."

His hips settled between her legs but instead of doing what he'd started, he snarled, "Christ, you're the most annoying woman I've ever met."

"And you are the most heartless man *I've* ever met," she returned.

They stared at each other and, even though they'd barely moved, both were breathing heavily.

Sibyl had the bizarre desire to scratch his eyes out and throw her arms around him and say she was sorry, both at the same time.

"You're mine for five months," he bit out, eyes blazing, face hard.

Gone was the desire to say she was sorry. Instead, she just glared.

"Is that understood?" he asked.

She continued to glare.

What would he do if she said no?

She really didn't want to find out. Therefore, she nodded but she did it while still glaring.

Colin wasn't finished. "And Sibyl, I don't ever want to hear you say that again. Is that clear?"

She bit her bottom lip so hard, she tasted blood.

She wanted to say it, just because he hated it. Just because she needed to remind herself that it was true. Just because it made her feel she had a modicum of power, even though it was simply to goad him, even though she lost more every time the words left her mouth.

She counted to ten and struggled for control.

Then she nodded.

She was already in enough trouble as it was, all of her own doing, and she hated that too.

"I'll be back tonight at the same time," he declared and then he was gone. Shoving her off his body angrily, he left the bed and stalked, naked, out of the room.

The moment she lost sight of him, Mallory loped in and woofed.

"Well, *that* didn't go very well," she whispered to her dog brokenly.

And then, for what had to be the hundredth time in a week and a half, she cried.

It was then she realized that she'd agreed to five months of Colin and not only that, he *wanted* five months of *her*.

And she didn't know what to make of that at all.

COLIN WAS STILL furious with Sibyl when he parked in front of her house that evening.

He was angry because he didn't like hearing her call herself a whore, in fact, he loathed it. Even though, for all intents and purposes, that was what she was, he vastly preferred not thinking about it and he certainly wasn't going to allow her to throw it in his face.

It annoyed the hell out of him that *she* took his fifty thousand pounds and managed to make *him* feel guilty about it.

And he didn't like that, in listening to her affectionate but obviously frustrated phone conversation with her mother, he became even more intrigued at the puzzle that was Sibyl.

Not to mention, he had the bizarre desire to meet her mother.

He didn't like that she'd announced she "needed the money," which made him wonder what the money was for in the first place. She didn't appear to lead a life of luxury and didn't look or act the sort of woman who aspired to it.

So, why did she need it?

He further didn't like that after only one (albeit satisfyingly active) night, he apparently couldn't get enough of her. He hadn't stopped thinking about her and her incredible body all day. Even so, she wanted nothing to do with him and he had to take further advantage in order to force her to spend more time with him.

This, particularly, was a concept with which Colin was unfamiliar and he detested it.

What he did like was that he'd succeeded in securing three more months of last night out of her very poorly controlled temper.

He wasn't entirely up on the code of practice of con artists and mercenaries, but he couldn't imagine it included throwing enough attitude at your mark to make them want to toss you screaming from a window.

But Colin wasn't about to argue with something that worked in his favor.

He knocked on the door and, within five seconds, heard Mallory careening towards it. Colin also knew when the dog arrived because he heard the loud thud and saw the door shake when the dog smashed into it.

This was so ridiculous and humorous, it nearly made Colin smile.

However, he was so annoyed, he did not.

"Mallory! You'll give yourself a head injury!" He heard Sibyl shout, and again he nearly smiled.

The dog was a menace (to himself) and Sibyl's affectionate acceptance of it was one of the many pieces of what Colin considered Sibyl's mystery. A mystery he spent a great deal of his day attempting, and failing, to solve.

The door swung open and she stood there, not made up like last night but wearing a pair of tan cowboy boots, brown tweed trousers, a cream, long-sleeved, scoop-necked T-shirt, some kind of elaborate silver necklace, complicated, dangling silver earrings and her shining hair was tumbling about her face.

And she was just as stunning as she was in the magnificently sexy silk camisole and dramatic makeup of the night before.

He looked at her carefully and couldn't read her mood, her eyes were simply hazel.

"I'll need a key," he said by way of greeting.

What he wanted to do was scoop her in his arms and carry her up to her bed, but he felt the need to control himself, felt the inexplicable need to control the situation in its entirety, which included controlling

Sibyl. He felt unprecedentedly out of control when it came to Sibyl and he wasn't used to that.

At all.

And he didn't like that either.

She stood, her hand on the door, regarding him warily, and she nodded.

Then something perverse, something that didn't even feel a part of him drove him to make that demand, "And I expect you to greet me with a kiss when you see me."

Her mouth parted slightly in surprise, and she hesitated a moment as mutiny played about her face and the hazel started to shift to the warning shade of green. Finally she leaned forward and brushed her lips against his.

Before she could pull away, the devil that was controlling him made him say, "I know you can do better than that."

Her head came up with a snap and he watched in grim fascination as her eyes, in the soft illumination from the lamps lit in the house, lost all hint of hazel and became blazing green.

Something about that pleased and irritated him at the same time.

She moved into him, her body touching his slightly then more as one hand came up to rest on his chest and the other hand slid into the hair at his nape. She tipped her head back and pressed her lips against his, he felt them open and he opened his in response. The tip of her tongue came out softly and touched his own.

He felt heat sweep through him at the touch of her tongue but before his arms could close around her, she ended the kiss and moved her head away.

Her hands still on him, her voice managing to be both warm and cold, she asked, "Is that better?"

In answer, he ordered, "Get your coat."

She blinked at his sudden change, her hands falling away. "What?"

"Your coat," he repeated.

He hadn't even crossed the threshold. Nevertheless, she stepped away and grabbed a scarlet-colored trench coat from a peg by the door and pulled it on. As she did, Colin turned on his heel and walked to his car.

He heard the dull thud of the heels of her cowboy boots as she rushed to catch up to him.

"Where are we going?" she asked.

He didn't stop as he strode purposefully to the car and jerked open the passenger side door to help her inside.

"Dinner," he answered curtly.

They didn't say another word until after they were seated at the seafront restaurant in Clevedon and he'd ordered a gin and tonic. She ordered the extraordinary drink of vodka lemonade with a dash of lime cordial, a maraschino cherry and ended this litany with the instruction, "And lots of ice."

After ordering, she smiled at the waiter and Colin felt his chest seize.

She'd never, not once, smiled at him, except that very first moment where their eyes met in the storm while she was acting out Beatrice's portrait.

Her smile, he noted in a vaguely dazed way, was arresting, sensational and the waiter nearly tripped over himself in a rush to do her bidding.

When her gaze slid to Colin's he scowled at her and didn't know why. He knew he was still furious but why her smile would cause such a spectacular reaction made no sense to him.

He realized in that moment that he didn't know a lot of things when it came to Sibyl, *and* his reaction to her, and he found that *supremely* annoying.

They studied their menus in silence and they ordered their meals after the drinks were brought to the table.

She spent a great deal of time pretending he wasn't there and looking out the windows at the sea.

He spent that time watching her.

The waiter brought Colin's steak and the bottle of wine Colin ordered. He also set some dish down in front of Sibyl that looked entirely concocted out of mushrooms.

Colin made no comment and Sibyl did the same.

They ate in silence.

When he was finished, he sat back in his chair, stretched his legs out in front of him, crossing them at the ankles, and continued to watch her while drinking his wine.

She valiantly attempted to finish her meal but then set her fork down and sat back herself, sipping her wine nervously, her eyes darting anywhere but to him.

"Do you want dessert?" he asked politely and she jumped in surprise at the sound of his voice.

She looked at him. The restaurant was illuminated with a romantic, candlelit ambiance so the lighting in the room was dim, and therefore Colin couldn't see the color of her eyes.

She shook her head.

He took his money clip from the breast pocket of his suit jacket, peeled off enough notes to pay for dinner and tossed them on the table.

He stood and Sibyl stood too.

He moved behind her, took her coat from her chair and helped her put it on. He felt her body was stiff under his hands.

This annoyed him even further.

The waiter scurried to their table looking alarmed.

"Is there anything wrong?" he asked (Colin noticed, with still growing irritation, the waiter asked Sibyl, staring at her like a lovesick puppy).

"We're leaving," Colin answered in clipped tones.

"Everything was lovely, thank you," Sibyl assured the waiter and smiled at him again.

Colin's irritation grew even more at her smile, another smile *not* directed at him. Without another word, he grabbed her arm and pulled her out of the restaurant.

Once outside, she yanked her arm away and quickened her step in an attempt to avoid him, something that some force inside him was driving him not to allow. As they hit the pavement, Colin's fingers curled around her upper arm just as he saw a flash from the headlamps of a car parked not two car lengths away.

Without warning, the engine revved and the car shot forward.

Sibyl was a step ahead of him, ready to cross the road to get to the Mercedes, when the car came directly at her like it was aiming.

Instinctively and swiftly, Colin dropped his hold of her but hooked his arm around her waist and snatched her from the street, pulling her into his body with such strength that her head crashed against his chin. He ignored the jolt of pain and at the same time took two deep steps backward. This meant the car narrowly missed them both as it flew past, two of its tires up on the pavement, and kept going without braking.

He set Sibyl down in front of him but held her, the warmth of her back pressed tightly against his body, and he could feel her heavy breathing. His arm, which had been about her waist, had slid up and was closed around her ribcage, her fingers were clutching it as if she'd never let him go, and he could feel her heart beating wildly. Both of their heads were turned, staring after the car for a long moment even after it disappeared before Sibyl lifted her hand to touch the back of her head distractedly where it had smashed against his chin.

"My goodness, he narrowly missed you. Are you all right?"

This came from an elderly lady who was rushing toward them and to Colin's irritated surprise, it was Marian Byrne.

"Mrs. Byrne!" Sibyl gasped.

"Sibyl!" Marian Byrne replied, and Sibyl broke free of his arm and gave the woman a tight embrace.

"Did you see that?" Sibyl exclaimed when she ended the embrace. She swung toward Colin, her evening's silent treatment a memory. "That lunatic driver nearly hit us. It was like . . . it was like he was *aiming* at us."

Colin stared at her then swung his head to where the car had gone, his thoughts racing.

She was correct. It seemed exactly as if the car was aiming at them.

Marian Byrne obviously agreed. "*I* saw it and it *did* look like he was aiming at you. My goodness gracious, goodness, goodness gracious," Marian Byrne chanted, her voice filled with alarm.

Colin turned his head again and stared at Mrs. Byrne.

Regardless of what seemed to Colin like a telling coincidence—these two women tended to "run into" each other with alarming frequency—Marian Byrne looked genuinely distraught.

"Mrs. Byrne, you need to sit down." Sibyl had moved toward the older woman and slid her arm around her.

Carefully looking both ways, she guided Mrs. Byrne across the street to a bench under a streetlamp that faced the sea. Colin followed silently and watched as Sibyl crouched down next to the older woman once she was seated.

Sibyl looked up to him.

"Should we take her back to the restaurant, get her a drink?" she asked and in the light of the streetlamp he could see her face was awash with concern.

"I'm fine, I just need to take a few deep breaths," Marian answered.

"Mrs. Byrne, why are you out tonight?" Sibyl voiced the question to which Colin wanted an answer. "It's late. You should be home. What if *you'd* been in the path of that crazy man? You wouldn't have been able to get out of his way." She glanced hesitantly at Colin and whispered, "*I* nearly didn't get out of the way," and he realized that was the closest he would likely get to any expression of gratitude.

Marian gave a deep shudder and replied, "I'm restless. I think it's this unseasonable weather. England is never this sunny and warm in March. At least not in my many years of experience." She smiled wanly and her hand lifted to pat the hand that Sibyl was resting on her arm.

Finally Colin spoke. "I'll take you home."

"Oh no, Mr. Morgan, I live not a five minute walk from here, ten at the most."

"I insist," Colin said in a voice that seconded the words he'd uttered.

When Mrs. Byrne looked like she was going to protest, Sibyl moved closer to her, shifting awkwardly on her crouched legs. "Let Colin take you home, Mrs. Byrne. Please? For me?"

Sibyl smiled at the other woman and Colin noted this smile was not dazzling but faltering. She was still reacting to the near-miss with the car and it became clear, even though he had thought differently moments before, that both of these women had nothing to do with the events of that night.

Marian turned to Colin and gave in to Sibyl's plea. "Thank you, Mr. Morgan. That would be very kind."

Colin looked at Sibyl. His car was a two seater and she'd have to wait until he returned from this errand.

"Go to the restaurant," he ordered curtly, "I'll be back for you in ten minutes."

Without a word in protest, she nodded and then gracefully stood. She helped Mrs. Byrne to the car and Colin waited to get in himself while he watched Sibyl, again with great care, her head swinging from side to side as she scanned the road, crossed the street. He didn't get into the car until he saw the restaurant door close safely behind her.

As he drove off, Marian Byrne gave him quick directions and then asked, "Are you quite all right, Mr. Morgan?"

He lied gruffly, "I'm fine."

"That was a nasty scare," she noted on a trembling sigh. "Drivers these days. So impatient. You must promise me you'll be most careful."

He nodded.

"I take it things with you and Sibyl are on a much better footing now?" she asked, her voice tentative and polite.

She knew it was none of her business.

"That depends on how you look at it," he replied honestly at the same time not giving her very much information.

"Well, Mr. Morgan, considering my tenure at your house and what I know of its history, I look at any time you spend with that delightful girl to be a very, *very* good thing, if you understand my meaning."

His eyes slid to her briefly then back to the road.

"So you admit to arranging our meeting?" he inquired bluntly.

"Of course!" she confessed, her voice losing its tremble and becoming more cheerful. "I thought you'd figured that out on the night."

"I did," he told her then demanded, even though he thought he knew, "What was Sibyl's part in it?"

"Oh, she has no idea." Her tone was very cheerful now but her words rocked Colin. "What I find most amusing is that she spent an entire night at Lacybourne, even had her little, shall we call it an 'episode?'" She laughed softly to herself, finding this all very amusing, something that grated on Colin's nerves. "Doing that right underneath the portraits and never once spared them a glance. Have you told her yet?"

He hesitated.

"About Royce and Beatrice," she prompted.

"No."

"Oh my," Mrs. Byrne sighed. "*Are* you going to tell her?"

"I don't know." And, at this news, he not only didn't know if he was going to tell Sibyl about Royce and Beatrice, he didn't understand *why* he didn't know if he was going to tell her or why, if she was not in partnership with Mrs. Byrne, Sibyl had taken the money and lastly, and most annoyingly, he realized he didn't know much of anything.

And he didn't like that either.

"Well, I won't say a word," she surprised him by assuring him and he surprised himself by believing her. "I'll leave it in your hands." Then she murmured, "It's right here," and motioned to an elegant, well-kept house on Victoria Road. "Thank you, Mr. Morgan, you've been very kind. No," she said when he started to alight, "I'm quite fine, get back to Sibyl, she seems a bit shaken."

For some reason, he did as he was told (though he waited for the elderly lady to make her way up her walk, enter her house and the light in the front room to come on), and five minutes later he pulled up at the restaurant, leaving the car to collect Sibyl who had seen him arrive and was walking from the restaurant to the car.

He opened her door and made sure she was safely inside before he went to his side and they took off.

They didn't speak a word the entire way to her home but he noticed she was clasping her hands together so intensely he could see the whiteness of her skin by the dash lights.

He hadn't given her the time to lock the door to the cottage so when they arrived she turned the latch, shoved it open and pushed inside. Instead of taking her coat off, she grabbed the dog's lead. Mallory came lurching excitedly into the room before she'd cleared the lead from the peg.

"I have to take Mallory for a walk," she explained to Colin, her voice soft and still a bit shaky.

"I'll go with you," Colin replied, his voice hard, his mind preoccupied with their near-death experience and what it might mean or if it meant anything at all and was just an accident.

Her head jerked up to look at him and then it tilted while she studied him. He noticed her eyes were more sherry than green.

Colin didn't know what to make of that.

She nodded, clipped the lead on Mallory's collar and they walked out into the night.

And as they walked, Colin noted that Mallory didn't seem like a dog who didn't like his walks. He seemed thrilled to be outside, smelling every blade of grass, and, as they made it down the secluded drive and turned onto the pavement, every car tire, post and inch of pavement he traversed. He was so excited Colin noticed that Sibyl was having trouble controlling the lead.

"Give it to me," Colin ordered and didn't wait for her to act. He took it from her hands.

"I don't understand. This is how he behaves during his morning walks sometimes. He *never* likes the evening walks. He just does his business as quickly as he can and we go home," she explained.

As if realizing they were talking about him, Mallory stopped. The dog looked down the length of his enormous body at them both, and Colin could see that Mallory's mouth was hanging open in what looked like a version of a canine smile. A long sliver of drool slid off his lip and plopped on the pavement.

"We're going home," Colin told the dog and Mallory, just as happy with this idea as he was with the walk, immediately turned around and headed back to the house.

"Utterly bizarre," Sibyl muttered under her breath.

Colin did not reply.

Mallory decided on the pillar of a streetlamp and took care of his business on the way home, and the three of them walked down her dark lane in silence (except for Mallory's excited panting). Sibyl pushed open her door when they arrived, and once inside, Colin unhooked the dog's lead and hung it on the peg while Sibyl took off her trench coat.

Without a word, his mind occupied with both the events of the evening (including the near-miss with the car *and* his strange conversation with Mrs. Byrne) and his continued anger at Sibyl, Colin walked up the stairs and straight to her bedroom. He was shrugging off his suit jacket when she arrived in the room.

"Colin?" Her voice was hesitant.

He turned on the bedside lamp, settled his eyes on her but didn't answer and started to unbutton his shirt.

She stood across the room from him nervously then started to speak.

"You should know something about me," she announced.

He stopped unbuttoning his shirt to study her, wondering what she had to say. Wondering if he'd believe what she had to say. Wondering if he'd be further annoyed by what she had to say. And thinking that he likely would not (to the former) and definitely would (to the latter).

Then, to his surprise, she crossed the room and halted not a foot away from him.

She lifted her beautiful face to his and her eyes were sherry. When she spoke her voice was low and intent and almost urgent.

"My mother and father are both redheads, I didn't get their hair but I got their temper. I always say things I regret when I lose my temper and I'm always in a foul mood when I wake up. I'm so sorry I was such a terrible shrew this morning. Please don't be mad at me anymore."

When he didn't reply to this stunning announcement, an announcement that, backed by the shade of her eyes (something she likely couldn't control), he believed for they were a warm sherry, she closed the distance between them and hesitantly rested both her hands on his chest.

"I like it when you're yelling at me or ordering me around a *lot* better than this. Not that I like you ordering me around but I couldn't bear five months of this," she declared and at the earnest look on her face he finally felt his chest, which had been tight since the moment he saw her smile at the waiter, relax.

He also felt the anger ebb out of him and decided on the best course of action to work the rest of his tension at the evening out of his system.

Therefore, he ordered, "Take your clothes off, Sibyl."

She nodded, her shoulders drooped, she dropped her head and began to step away from him.

"No," he changed his mind, "I think tonight I'd rather do it."

Her head snapped up and his hands went to her hips, sliding around, pressing in to pull her to him and she rested her hands lightly on his shoulders.

"Can I take it that since you're ordering me around again that you aren't mad at me anymore?" she asked, her alto voice sweet and, if he heard it correctly, hopeful.

Colin studied her.

Sibyl Godwin was definitely an enigma and this was a new, enchanting element to her puzzle.

He bent his neck and brushed his lips against hers.

Then he said against her mouth, "No, Sibyl, I'm not mad at you anymore."

And that's when it happened.

She relaxed, leaned into him, locked her sherry eyes with his and smiled.

And Colin knew, in that instant, he'd never forget that smile for the rest of his life.

MUCH LATER, COLIN woke from a deep sleep, mainly because Sibyl had kicked him violently in the shin.

He pulled himself onto his elbow to see she was still asleep. They hadn't closed the shutters and he could see her in the moonlight, she had moved away from him in the night and was lying on her stomach. He could tell she was agitated, something wasn't right.

"Sibyl?" He reached out to touch her, to wake her from what was obviously a nightmare.

Before he made contact with her body, she reared up violently then she flew from the bed and raced across the room.

Colin noted distractedly that Mallory, who had been lying on the floor by Colin's side of the bed, was now up as well, standing still and fierce and not barking or vibrating with his usual big dog energy.

But Colin's attention was focused on Sibyl, she'd halted by the window and stood panting as if she'd just run a race. Her body was tense, her arms held out, bent at the elbows, palms up in a defense posture. She was looking around, her head tossing this way and that, like she expected someone to attack her.

On guard at her strange behavior, Colin exited the bed and approached her slowly.

"Sibyl," he murmured quietly and her head jerked to him.

"Colin," she whispered achingly and he felt his gut clench at the terrible tone of her voice.

She sounded sad and defeated and, somehow, lost.

He reached her and slid his hands carefully around her waist, slowly drawing her body to his and wrapping her in his arms.

"It's all right, you had a nightmare," he told her and she shook her head, tossing her mane of hair. "Sibyl, it's all right," he assured her firmly.

She pulled back slightly and gazed at him. He could not see her eyes in the moonlight but he could feel their intensity.

Then she did the strangest thing, something that moved him at the same time it sent a sense of fear searing straight into his soul.

Lifting a trembling hand, she touched his throat in a feather-light caress and his body completely stilled. The light touch was somehow fervent, even reverent. Then she leaned forward, pressed her lips against his throat and kissed him there.

At her kiss, his still body froze.

Except for when she'd laid her hands on his chest in apology and, after, on his shoulders when he held her, she'd not touched him, and definitely not kissed him, unless he'd commanded it or they were having sex.

But he knew, instinctively, this was not a game, this was not an act.

This was something else entirely.

"Sibyl, what's happened?" he asked.

"It's just a nightmare," she whispered in a way that sounded like she was trying to convince herself of the truth of her words. She tucked her head under his chin and wrapped her arms around him so tightly that it almost felt as if she wanted him to absorb her into his body.

It went without saying that she'd also never hugged him and this embrace was not simply an embrace. It was profound and it was desperate.

Automatically, his arms tightened around her.

"It's all right," he repeated, not knowing what else to say, completely at a loss of what to make of this latest, spectacular event.

She nodded her head against him, causing her hair to slide against his chest, and even though he would not have thought it possible, her arms tightened further around him. He reciprocated, pulling her even deeper into his body and resting his chin on her head.

Colin opened his mouth to speak, to ask her questions about her nightmare but he felt a tremor go through her and decided against it.

It was not for tonight, when it was dark and whatever dream she had was fresh. He would ask her in the morning. Now, he needed to take the fear away.

And therefore Colin Morgan and Sibyl Godwin stood by the open window, their naked bodies bathed in moonlight, holding each other.

THE DARK SOUL stood hidden in the trees and watched the cottage. The soul saw the flash of movement as the body came flying to the window, a woman's body, a woman with unforgettable hair.

Then a man come to her to hold her, gently, carefully, as if the naked woman was an exquisite, fragile piece of priceless crystal.

At this sight, the dark soul seethed.

Chapter TEN

Perfect Fit

Marian was not cheerful when she entered her house after Colin brought her home.

Marian was frightened.

What she witnessed outside the restaurant was no accident. It was not an impatient driver.

It was something else.

She'd followed Colin and Sibyl there and she'd been watching the restaurant (in between bouts of doing her grocery list and writing a letter to a friend) for over an hour. She saw the car drive up. She noticed that it didn't park or turn off its motor but she didn't know it was waiting to run down her precious charges.

She did know it was a black BMW although she had not seen the driver (who never exited the car), if it was a man or a woman, and she did not note the number plate.

She'd let down the side.

Marian should have been watching carefully. She should have had her eyes peeled for anything, however, she had no idea that dark soul would make a move so soon.

It had been only at the last second, when she *felt* the malevolence, that she used some of her cheapest magic and blinked her eyes to light the headlamps of the car in warning to the couple.

If she hadn't, likely the two, who both seemed deep in thought, would have been mowed down.

Marian herself had no idea of the state of play between Colin and Sibyl.

Sibyl had been pretty adamant about her feelings regarding Mr. Morgan a few days before at breakfast (these feelings were that he was a raving madman). Marian was relatively certain that they were still in combat mode from what she saw in her crystal ball. She was pleased as punch that they seemed to be out on a date. Though Colin's stony face was a bit unwelcoming, that wasn't exactly unheard of with Mr. Morgan, and Sibyl looked bemused, poor girl.

But that car had been waiting for them and aiming at them with the desire to run at least Sibyl, but likely both of them, down.

Marian was going to have to work faster. She was going to have to get some charms together to protect both Lacybourne and Brightrose. She'd likely have to do something to protect both their cars. And she needed to get to work on some potions that took time to mature, just in case she needed them.

On top of all this, she was going to have to be very vigilant.

She really hoped that Mr. Morgan was the charmer that many of the National Trust volunteers gossiped to her that he was. He was going to have to make swift work of it with Sibyl.

Why Colin didn't tell Sibyl about the ill-fated lovers, Marian could not understand. Sibyl's kind heart would have melted straight away.

He didn't though and Marian was willing to give him his lead, for a while.

But if this dragged on, and they didn't realize they were destined for each other, destined to fall in love and then consummate it after that realization, they were in big trouble.

SIBYL WOKE UP, aroused.

Not just aroused, *highly* aroused.

And the reason for this was a light touch at the skin of the small of her back, an area always sensitive, an area that no lover had ever truly discovered or, when they did, made appropriate use of.

Until now.

She was on her side, facing the fireplace, away from Colin, and her eyes fluttered open.

She could feel the heat of his body even though only his fingers were touching her, drawing delicate figure eights and zigzags on the small of her back, dipping tantalizingly every once in a while to her bottom.

This light touch caused waves of glorious sensation to shoot down the insides of her thighs, up her back and zoom straight between her legs.

"Are you awake?" Colin's husky voice sounded in her ear.

She nodded her head against the pillow and could only say, "Mm hmm."

She did this because she didn't trust her voice. She was about to whirl and attack him. She clamped her legs together and tried to think unsexy thoughts but the pulsating heat between her legs made this task impossible.

He kissed her shoulder lightly.

"How are you feeling?" he asked.

Oh goddess, he knew, he knew exactly what he was doing to her.

"Fine," she muttered but the word was shaky.

His body moved closer, his hand at the small of her back flattened, smoothing over her bottom and she felt a sense of relief that he was going to stop. Then it started its distracted figure eights and zigzagging again.

Her body tensed.

"Tell me about it," Colin encouraged.

"About what?" Sibyl answered quickly, confused and wondering what he meant.

Did he want her to explain how it felt, what he was doing to her?

"About your dream," Colin murmured in her ear, using his stubble-roughened chin to move the heavy hair away from her cheek.

"What dream?" she whispered, her mind not processing anything but the fact that her bones had melted to water and her blood had heated at least one hundred and fifty degrees. Even her breasts had swelled and were aching for his touch, though he hadn't even so much as looked at them.

She was beginning to panic.

Did he know about her dream man? Did he know about her idea of one true love?

"Your nightmare last night," he answered and went on, "It's all right, Sibyl, it's over, it's daylight now and you can talk to me about it," he assured her gently.

Even the reminder of the horrible nightmare didn't distract her from what his hand was doing. The nightmare was the same one she'd had over a week ago, before meeting him.

Her body continued to react to what she realized now was what he intended to be a soothing touch, though it very much was *not*.

"Colin?" she asked, and she heard the tremor going through his name.

She had wanted to ask him to stop, but his lips were close to her ear and he mumbled a vibrating, "Mm?" and, already aroused, the sound of it thundered through her and she was done.

Before she could stop herself (or even *think* of stopping herself), she whipped around, pushed him on his back and attacked him.

She maneuvered her body, swinging her leg over his hips to straddle him and before he had a chance to react, she leaned into him, tilted her head and kissed him, *hard*.

She didn't even try to be gentle. She was primed and ready for him.

Now.

Her mouth opened, as did his, her tongue darted inside and she moaned just tasting him.

Goddess, even first thing in the morning, just like always, Colin tasted *divine*.

He, to her extreme pleasure, immediately deepened the kiss.

Tearing her mouth away, she realized his hands had settled on her waist. She rained kisses on his eyes, his cheeks, sliding her tongue down the column of his throat to dip it into the space between his jutting collarbone. She felt his hands slide up her sides then into her back where they separated, one going up between her shoulder blades, one down to cup her bottom, all the while scorching a lazy trail of fire.

She dragged her lips down his chest and ran her teeth across his nipple while one of her hands went between their bodies to wrap around him and she was thrilled beyond rationality that he was already hard.

She heard his sharp intake of breath.

"Sibyl," this was a groan but she was beyond responding.

She lurched up, releasing him and running her fingers down his arm, pulling it away from her until she found his hand, and as she did she kissed him, again ravenous. She wanted to devour him, her body was on fire for him, and she kissed him greedy and hungry as she pressed his hand between her legs, whimpering as his fingers slid against her wet, sensitive flesh.

"I want you, Colin," she whispered against his mouth, "now."

The minute he touched her wetness, he understood. Then she watched his lips form a deeply satisfied, even smug, smile. While they did this, he slid a finger inside her.

"Thanks be to the goddess," she breathed and closed her eyes in rapture as his finger filled her.

At her words, the finger disappeared and he flipped her on her back in one smooth move. Parting her legs expertly, Colin didn't hesitate, he drove into her.

Sibyl cried out at the ecstasy of it.

Even though it had been only minutes since they started, it felt like she'd waited an eternity for him. She lifted her hips to receive his thrusts as she wrapped her arms about his waist, holding on to his tight, muscled behind, her nails digging in. She buried her face in his neck, tasting him there while one of his arms curled around the top of her head, giving him leverage to pound into her, harder and deeper.

It was glorious.

"Yes," she purred in his ear. "Harder." She nipped him there and her hips lifted to meet every thrust, each one deeper, sending spirals of desire shooting through her.

He stopped thrusting and started grinding and she caught her breath, ready, right there.

She knew it was going to happen, she knew it was going to be intense, beautiful, like always with Colin, and right before she exploded she whispered reverently, "Goddess, Colin, you fit me . . . perfectly."

Then she gasped, arched her neck and cried out as everything in the world but the space where their bodies joined was obliterated, and she felt the shudders of pleasure course through her with pure, sweet violence.

So consumed was she in her own climax, she missed his but vaguely noted he'd wrapped her legs around his waist in his final moments.

After they both came down, still deep inside her, Colin gave her his weight and both of them lay panting and speechless.

Finally, he came up on his forearms and looked down at her.

"That's quite a way to combat a morning mood." His voice was low, sexy and rough with residual desire and his handsome face was soft with approval.

As the last waves of pleasure subsided, she felt them immediately replaced with acute embarrassment.

What *on earth* was she thinking?

More to the point, what was she *doing*?

She'd just attacked him!

She closed her eyes and turned her face away at the same time she tried to push him off by pressing against his chest.

It was one thing for him to buy her body and an entirely other thing for her to attack *his*.

Goddess, she was a raving wanton! What must he think?

She needed to escape.

She pressed against his chest harder.

He didn't move.

"Sibyl," he called.

"Colin," she said to the wall, her eyes still closed, "Please get off me."

He still didn't move.

"Sibyl, look at me," he demanded.

She shook her head but his hand came to her face and forced her to do as he said.

"Open your eyes," he ordered.

She did and hers were filled with rebellion mixed with a good dose of humiliation.

"What just happened?" he seemed to see only the rebellion and she knew this because his voice was still low, sexy and rough, but his face was no longer soft with approval and his eyes were intense with scrutiny.

"You were *touching* me," she explained, her tone accusing, deciding her best course of action was to place blame quite squarely on his very broad shoulders.

"Touching you, yes, seducing you, no. What just happened?"

She shook her head.

"Sibyl," he was using his smooth, even voice that meant he was close to losing his cool.

"I told you, you were touching me," she repeated.

He waited but the expression on the hard planes of his face told her it wasn't patiently.

Sibyl, again, obviously had no choice but to give him what he wanted.

"In a very sensitive spot," she admitted reluctantly.

At her words, he looked startled. She should have been pleased at that but instead she felt all the more embarrassed.

"A *very* sensitive spot," she stressed.

He simply stared at her but the intensity in his eyes was quickly fading to something much less hard and far warmer.

"I get somewhat," she hesitated, fighting for the right words, "out of control if someone touches me there for any length of time."

"Does this happen often?" Completely gone was the intensity and in its place was something entirely satisfied and more than a touch amused.

"Never quite like this," she confessed, his hand on her face had relaxed and she looked away again. "But no one else had done it so," she hated to say it but there it was, "*well.*"

He kissed the exposed line of her throat (but not before, out of the corner of her eyes, she caught sight of his mouth twitching) and he murmured against her skin, "I'll have to remember that."

"I shouldn't have told you."

He lifted his head and, there it was, right there in front of her, his lips *were* twitching. "You don't think I would have discovered it eventually?"

"No one else has," she informed him, straightening her head to look at him again.

And that was when she saw his eyes start dancing with hilarity, absolutely *dancing*. At that look she lost all embarrassment and became instantly grumpy.

"Then they weren't very good at it, I'd already suspected. You jump and moan every time I touch you there," Colin told her.

Sibyl grunted with ill humor.

"Or lift your ass to meet my hand," he continued informatively. "I was already intrigued."

"Thanks, Colin," she gritted between her teeth. "You can stop talking now. I think I have the picture."

He grinned at her before his head dropped to nuzzle her neck.

Then he suggested, "Let's talk about your dream now, shall we?"

Her body went rigid.

She could *not*, under any circumstances, tell him about her dream.

She could provide an entire list, even in writing (if he were to require) of every sensitive spot on her body (behind her ears, the skin underneath her breasts, and so on).

But she could not tell him about her dream. She could not tell him she'd seen him in her subconscious before she'd ever even met him. He'd think she'd lost her mind.

This meant she was going to have to lie to him.

And Sibyl hated lying. It wasn't a very nice thing to do and she wasn't at all good at it. One could get caught up in lies but Sibyl *always* got caught up in them. She was too absentminded to remember what she'd said, she always had been.

"It was nothing," she muttered, trying to blow it off.

"It was enough for you to kick me, rather forcefully, in the shin and drive you from the bed and across the room."

Her eyes rounded at this news. "I kicked you?"

Colin nodded.

"Did I hurt you?"

"Surprised me, I was dead asleep when it happened."

Without her volition, her hand went to rest on his waist.

"I'm sorry," she said quietly and she meant it.

His body became quite still as he watched her face. He seemed captivated by something there, so much so he was lost in whatever it was.

"Colin?" His body jerked at her calling his name and his eyes cleared.

"Tell me about it," he commanded, his voice now strangely husky.

"What?" she asked.

"The dream," he persisted, rather annoyingly, Sibyl thought.

"I said it was nothing."

"Tell me," he urged.

"I'd rather not. I don't want to think about it," she demurred, beginning to get panicky.

And anyway, why, exactly, did he want to know so badly?

"Sibyl, tell me." The huskiness had vanished and he was lapsing into his smooth, angry voice again and she decided he was not going to let it go.

So she gave in, in a way.

"I've had it before. It's just . . . not nice."

"Yes?" he prompted.

"In it, I'm sleeping." Her mind was racing, she was going to have to make something up and decided, in case it came up in the future, or she dreamed it again and kicked him or hurt him in some other way (which she hoped she never did, indeed, she hoped never to have the awful dream again), she would remember what she said. "Peacefully, alone . . . I mean, by myself, sleeping by myself . . . all alone . . ."

"Go on," he prompted when she'd trailed off, his eyes assessing. "You were alone, by yourself, sleeping."

Sibyl nodded. "Then someone, or it feels like more than one person, I never see them, they don't have faces, drags me out of bed and they slit my throat. That's it."

"Christ," he swore immediately after she finished speaking, dropping to his side and taking her with him. Once there, he pulled her deep into his body and repeated, "Christ."

She tipped her head back to look at him, feeling guilty at her white lie and somewhat surprised (in a funny, happy way) at his reaction. He seemed so concerned, it was almost touching (well, it was actually *very* touching but she didn't want to consider that).

He dipped his chin to look at her.

"Last night, you touched and kissed *my* throat. Why?"

Oh goddess, she'd forgotten she'd done that.

"I don't know," she fibbed for she bloody well *did* know. "Maybe just a spontaneous reaction. I was kind of out of it at the time."

He was watching her closely, *very* closely, and she was fairly certain he knew she was lying. It wouldn't be hard to figure out, she was *the worst* liar.

"That's all?" he asked, his voice showing his doubt.

She thought it best not to utter another word so she nodded.

He seemed to decide to let it go and tucked her head under his chin as his hands roamed her back. This she found soothing, even though she still felt guilty for lying to him.

"Do you want breakfast?" she asked against his throat, wishing to be on another subject.

"What?" he queried distractedly.

"Breakfast," she forced her head back and he again dipped his chin to look at her. She noticed he looked lost in thought and she explained teasingly, "You know, the first meal of the day. The most important meal of the day. Breaking your fast. The French call it *petit dejeuner*. The Spanish call it *desayuno*."

He awarded her one of his fabulous grins and, at the sight of it, Sibyl felt her entire body relax and warm.

"I know what breakfast is," he told her, his voice low and effective.

"Would you like some?"

"I've got to take a shower and get to the office."

For some reason, Colin's announcement made Sibyl feel a vague sense of disappointment.

Well, if she was honest, not all that vague. It was more like a *keen* sense of disappointment.

She hid it by pushing her face into his throat again and then she worked with every ounce of strength in her to push the disappointment aside.

This, she had to remember, was a *temporary* arrangement. He'd paid for this, paid for *her*.

This was not boyfriend and girlfriend having a morning quickie and an affectionate chat.

This was not that *at all*.

And with those thoughts firmly (kind of) planted in her brain, she whispered against his skin, "I need to take Mallory for his morning walk."

Then she shoved away from him and started to leave the bed but he caught her forearm.

Half in, half out of bed, Sibyl looked back at him.

"I'll be back tonight," he told her, his grin gone. He was watching her and she felt as if he could see past everything, straight to her heart.

"Same time?" she asked and the words made her feel wrong. They made her feel like what she was to him, a word she was not allowed to say but she should never allow herself to forget.

"Yes," he replied.

She nodded and with a rough movement jerked her arm away. She had to get away from him, now. She could get lost in him, she knew, especially when he turned into sweet, teasing Colin. When he was like that, Sibyl could start pretending that this was more than it was and she mustn't ever do that.

Ever.

She snatched her robe off the hook on the back of the door, shrugged it on, grabbed some clothes and ran out of the room.

She dressed in the bathroom.

Then, with effort, throughout her errand of the morning, she kept her mind carefully blank.

After she arrived back from Mallory's walk, Colin was gone.

Chapter ELEVEN

Reprieve

"I'm dreaming about him."

It was the next Monday morning and Marian was having her breakfast with Sibyl.

Marian was also realizing that Sibyl clearly needed a confidant.

"Yes, my dear?" Marian prompted. "Who?"

Sibyl looked distracted, the streak of fine weather had broken and the day was gray, rainy and cold, and Sibyl was gazing moodily out of the diamond-paned windows. They were eating in a small breakfast nook in Sibyl's warm and cozy yet elaborate kitchen. Marian had visited Granny Esmeralda's abandoned cottage many times when the last owners left it unoccupied for years, but she had not been there since the unknown (now known) Americans had bought it and refurbished it as a holiday home.

She'd been delighted when Sibyl suggested they not meet at a café but instead asked Marian to come to her house and Sibyl would cook for her. She'd been captivated by the loving renovation that Sibyl explained she and her father had done to Granny Esmeralda's sweet cottage. It felt welcoming and warm and Marian was immediately relaxed and at peace there.

And her young friend was an excellent cook, making Marian homemade American pancakes with maple syrup and big bowls of bite-sized pieces of ripe, delicious fruit.

Now, food consumed, Sibyl was on her second cup of coffee and Marian was finishing a pot of tea.

"He's away in London for three days," she changed the subject, or at least Marian thought she did.

"Who?" Marian asked again, thinking she knew who but uncertain.

Sibyl started and seemed to come back to the room. She blinked at Marian and gave her a feeble smile.

"I'm sorry. It's Colin. You should know Colin and I are together now," Sibyl hesitated, then finished. "Well, sort of."

Marian smiled encouragingly. "I guessed that when I saw you two the other night but, how do you mean, 'sort of?'"

Sibyl shook her head and gently changed the subject. "And I'm dreaming about him, all the time, nearly every night. Except he's blond and he's . . ." She paused then stated, "This is going to sound stupid."

But at her words, Marian's heart skipped a joyous beat.

What did she mean, he was blond?

Was she dreaming of Royce?

Dear goddess, was Sibyl Godwin clairvoyant?

"Go on, nothing's stupid. You can tell me anything," Marian urged, her voice betraying her excitement (she couldn't help it, it *was* exciting).

Sibyl shuddered and then forged ahead. "It's like he's from another time. I'm there too, always. We're wearing old clothes . . . not old as in age, a different style, clothes from a different time period, a long, long time ago. But the dreams are so vivid, so clear they almost seem real." Sibyl turned to Marian. "Marian, I know you're going to think this sounds a million kinds of crazy, but they don't seem like dreams at all," she leaned forward, her eyes intense but confused, "they seem like *memories*."

Marian's mouth parted in surprise.

She *was* a clairvoyant.

Hallelujah!

Sibyl, clearly oblivious to Marian's elation, kept speaking.

"He makes me call him Royce in the dreams and he refers to me as Beatrice. And I get this very bad feeling that although they're beautiful together, their story is not a happy one. I know that sounds even more stupid, considering they're only in my mind, but I just get this sense, you know? Just like Colin and I will not end well."

Marian closed her eyes to hide her joy, her heart skittered again, and when she opened them she smiled reassuringly at the younger woman.

"You're falling in love with Colin, aren't you?" she said sagely.

"No!" Sibyl exclaimed instantly and strangely somewhat desperately.

Her forceful cry made Marian rear back.

Sibyl, being the sweet girl she was, noticed Marian's reaction and immediately apologized.

"I'm sorry Marian, but no, I'm not falling in love with Colin. I can't," she announced firmly.

This was not good news, nor was it what Marian expected to hear.

"Why on earth can't you?" Marian's voice had just the slightest edge and it, too, was desperate.

"He's not the one. I'm supposed to . . ." She stopped talking, closed her eyes tight, and when she opened them she continued, "All my life I knew there was one perfect man out there for me. A man like Royce is to Beatrice. My match. I have a space in my heart that only this person fits into." She bit her lip, her expression pained before she finished, "And it's not Colin."

Marian's heart felt light at this news. It was all too right.

"How do you know it's not Colin?" Marian asked, trying to appear calm.

"Trust me," Sibyl answered, her voice sounding awful, "I know."

Marian's mind whirled with what to say.

This was all perfect, dreaming of the doomed lovers (without even knowing they existed!), living her life yearning for the special man that fits in her heart. It was perfect, beautiful, sublime.

Marian wished she could tell Sibyl about the legend, she *itched* to tell her. But she'd promised Colin. She had a tentative hold on his trust already; she certainly shouldn't fall at the first hurdle. Marian could see in her crystal ball that things were still not quite right with the pair.

Although, she could never hear the words they said, there was just something wrong.

Marian believed, though, that true love would find a way.

It did with Royce and Beatrice, even though, at their beginning, they'd had a time of it.

Just, it seemed, like Sibyl and Colin were.

"Do you want to tell me about it?" Marian invited in a soothing tone.

Sibyl shook her head. "I don't want to talk about it. He's gone for three days and I'm glad." Marian noted she didn't sound glad, she sounded positively gloomy. "I can't seem to get my head around things when he's around. He's overpowering. He fills a room . . . no, the entire *house*, with his presence. He didn't let me out of his sight all weekend."

Marian thought this was a strange turn of phrase for a young woman of this modern age to use the word "let" in regards to her boyfriend. Sibyl was spirited and she had free will, Colin Morgan didn't own her.

"You feel suffocated," Marian surmised.

"I feel safe, protected and taken care of, sometimes even precious." Marian was surprised to hear her reply. "My mother would have a heart attack," Sibyl muttered under her breath then she continued, "He's a perfect gentleman, impeccable manners, very respectful, even, goddess, am I going to say this?" she asked herself then said, "*Gallant.*"

With that she dropped her face into her hands and rested her elbows on the table with despair.

At Sibyl's words and her contradictory actions, Marian was genuinely confused.

"I'm sorry, I don't understand the problem."

Sibyl spoke to the table, "It's temporary. I don't *want* to like it. I know he's going to go away."

"He doesn't have to go away."

"Oh yes he does."

This was said with a finality that was absolute and completely conflicting.

Although Sibyl was making no sense, Marian felt her spirits plummet.

"Are there times when he's cruel to you?" Marian asked gently.

Colin Morgan was, Marian knew, a somewhat difficult man.

This, for some reason, made Sibyl laugh, bitterly. A sound like that coming from a woman like Sibyl grated on the nerves, it was borderline obscene.

She lifted her head and her expression looked defeated. "Every second he's with me, even though it's unintentional. He doesn't mean it, doesn't even know it, I just feel it. And I did it to myself."

This *really* didn't make any sense.

"Sibyl, just tell me what's troubling you. Maybe I can help," Marian urged.

Sibyl stared at her for a moment and Marian felt hope that she would further confide in her. She had promised Colin not to tell Sibyl about Royce and Beatrice but she *could* help here.

Then Sibyl gave her a sad smile and said, "I don't think you'd understand, and if I told you, you would likely not want to have breakfast with me again."

Marian covered the woman's hand with her own. "I'm not sure *you* understand either, dear. And nothing you could tell me would make me feel the slightest bit different about you. I think you're terrific."

Finally, Marian made Sibyl smile. It was not her usual dazzling smile, it was tremulous, but it was something.

"I think you're terrific too," Sibyl whispered but shared no more.

Sometime later, after Marian left Sibyl's cottage (it was now firmly entrenched in Marian's mind as *Sibyl's* cottage and she felt sure that Granny Esmeralda would approve of that), she went to her magic room to check her fermenting potions. Several of them she was likely going to have to use after all.

The only good thing that came of her visit with Sibyl was that obviously the girl had magic of her own. This could be most helpful. The fact that she was feeling memories from her past soul was a good sign.

And Marian still held hope that the feeling behind most of Sibyl's words (even though the words themselves were rather dire) meant that whatever it was that was standing between the two young lovers was an obstacle that could still be climbed.

"WE GO TOGETHER . . ."

Sibyl was sitting in the Community Hall with Jem watching her girlie quartet sing a song from *Grease* while Jemma sewed a poodle onto a child's full, felt skirt.

"The choreography is fantastic, Jem," Sibyl whispered as we watched.

The girls, it seemed, were having a blast and they looked great.

"What?" Annie shouted, sitting beside her. "What's happening now?"

"They're dancing and singing, Annie," Sibyl raised her voice so Annie could hear her.

Kyle and Tina, Sibyl, Jemma and a couple of the other volunteers had a rota to go once a week to tidy Annie's house, fill her fridge and spend some time with her. That afternoon was Jemma's afternoon but it was also talent show practice. Annie decided to wait it out. Far better sitting in the Hall with kids rushing around and music blaring than sit at home in virtual silence and complete blindness.

"Wearing poodle skirts!" Annie shouted and Sibyl smiled.

"Black ones, with white poodles that have pink bows," Jemma yelled.

"I used to have one of those," Annie informed them of something that might, or might not (as Annie told tales) be true, and neither Sibyl nor Jem responded.

The girls sang as Annie, Jemma and Sibyl lapsed into silence while Sibyl also lapsed into reflection.

Colin's three day trip turned into a five day trip. He'd called and told her he wouldn't be home until, at least, Friday.

Today.

She found she missed him, even though she knew that was wrong so she tried not to think about it . . . and failed.

The good thing was that he couldn't claim back this time and she desperately needed it to get her head straight.

Her time with him had been good, sometimes (she hated to admit it, but it was true) wonderful, and always she'd forget who she was to him.

Then he'd do something unintentional to remind her.

Mostly, he would order her about which, she thought, considering the frequency he did it could be a part of his nature but she wasn't in the place to test it.

For instance, once, after a long day in her Summer House Girlie Laboratory, she had put her hair up to get its heavy weight off her scalp. She'd forgotten it was up when she walked into the front room from the kitchen after he'd used his key to enter the front door. Mallory was all over him, but the minute he turned his attention to her, his eyes shifted to her hair. He didn't say a word but she lifted her hands up to tear the clip out immediately.

It was times like those, although infrequent, but always painful, she knew exactly what she was.

"How is your new young man?" Annie shouted, taking Sibyl out of her thoughts and she saw Jemma's eyes shift to her.

No one knew about the arrangement but she had told Jemma, Kyle and Tina about Colin. She had to, in case he called her away or she couldn't get to work for some reason. Jemma knew something was wrong, but in pure Jem Style she didn't push it. If Sibyl wanted to tell her then Sibyl would choose the time.

But of course, news this meaty ran like wildfire through the Community Centre and all of its patrons were agog. Not once in over a year had Sibyl had a boyfriend.

"He's been away," Sibyl shouted back.

"When're we going to meet the lad?" Annie yelled.

The idea of Colin being addressed as a "lad" made Sibyl burst out laughing. The idea of him confronting all the oldies at the Pensioners' Club nearly made her double up with laughter. He'd scare the pants off them. They'd have to have a row of ambulances available to whisk the oldies directly to hospital, all of them suffering from a rash of strokes and heart attacks.

After she stopped laughing, she yelled back, "He's a very busy man, Annie. I don't know."

"Miss Sibyl, your phone's ringing," Ben, one of the boys who was practicing a somewhat alarming rendition of a rap song (although neither she, nor Jemma, really understood the words so they couldn't judge) in her office, stood by her and held out her mobile.

She saw who it was on the display and quickly got up. As she engaged the phone, she ran into the Day Centre without looking back and, once there, slid the doors closed behind her.

"Hello?" she greeted.

"Sibyl," Colin returned tersely.

It was Colin, and with that one word she knew he was angry.

"Colin."

"Where the fuck are you?"

Sibyl was struck dumb at his tone *and* his question.

He had no idea she worked at the Community Centre.

Indeed, in all their time together, he knew nothing personal about her except from what he could tell through observation and from the photographs scattered about her house.

And Sibyl did everything she could to keep it this way.

If she let him in, she knew somewhere deep inside her, she wouldn't want to let him go. Even with what she was to him, there was no denying the otherworldly strength of her attraction to him or that bizarre connection she felt between them.

She knew this and she hated it just as much as felt strangely safe in knowing it.

"I'm—" her mind raced to find a lie.

"You sound like you're at a club." His voice was short, curt and obviously furious.

"I'm not—"

"A bad one," he interrupted.

She felt a hysterical giggle bubble in her throat and she gulped it down.

"I've been calling for an hour," he went on.

Her eyes rounded and she took the phone away from her ear to stare at its display.

Blooming hell, she'd left it in her office.

When she put it back to her ear, he was still talking, " . . . home right away."

"I'm sorry?"

"I want you home right away."

Her heart stopped and her stomach plummeted.

Her girls were on the stage.

"Where are you?" she asked.

"At the cottage, where I've been for an hour." His voice was ice cold.

You're available to me when I say, where I say, he'd said.

Bloody, *bloody* hell.

"Colin—"

"Now," he said simply.

"I'm at work," she explained, her voice a plea.

"I don't care," he bit out.

"Colin, I can't—"

"Now, Sibyl," and without another word he rang off.

She stared at the screen.

Three missed calls.

Bloody hell.

She ran to the Hall just as the girls were jumping off the stage.

"Miss Sibyl," Flower was calling to her, her voice plaintive, "we can't get that last part right."

"We'll *never* get it right," Katie moaned as the four of them stopped in front of Sibyl.

Sibyl was in a panic. Flower, Katie and their two friends, Emma and Cheryl, were staring at her with need and expectation.

And it was Colin or four little girls. She had to decide in a split second who needed her most.

It took her less than a second.

Colin would have to wait and Sibyl would have to suffer the consequences.

She turned off her phone, buried it in the back pocket of her cords and took a deep breath.

"What part is giving you trouble?" she asked Flower with an overbright, shaky smile.

SHE ARRIVED HOME nearly an hour later even though the drive from work was twenty minutes.

She could, of course, lie and say that it took her that long to get home. Colin had no idea where she worked.

But Sibyl couldn't lie, she'd already lied to Colin once and if they kept stacking up she knew she'd get them messed up and get caught in one of them one day.

She pushed open the door to her house, feelings of dread seeping through her body.

Colin was standing in the living room staring out the back window, emanating rage even though he didn't move a muscle.

He had a drink in his hand. Gin and tonic. Once she knew that was his preference, she made certain she stocked it in her house, just like she made certain she had Diet Coke and rum when her sister came around, good Scotch when her father was there and margarita mix and tequila for her mother.

The minute she entered the cottage, he turned around.

"Where the hell have you been?" he demanded.

"I told you, Colin, I was at work," she replied softly.

He processed this and she could tell by the muscle leaping in his jaw that he did not like it one bit. Then he put his glass on a table and started toward her.

"Your phone is off," he informed her.

"Yes, I . . . well, I had to turn it off."

She really wished she was a good liar. It would certainly help in this situation.

"Why is that?" His voice sounded curious, curious and cold and very, *very* menacing.

He'd reached her and when he did, his hand came up to curl around the side of her neck. This could have been a loverly gesture, but at that moment it was most definitely not.

"I was in the middle of something urgent and—" she started, his eyes turned to stone and immediately she stopped speaking.

"Did you forget the rules?" he asked in a quiet, scary tone.

No, she didn't. Though she had been harboring some, small,

lingering hope that he had, until that moment.

She shook her head. "Colin, I—"

"Be quiet," he ordered softly, dangerously and thus she felt a tremor slide through her and instantly ceased speaking.

She was already in enough trouble. She was not stupid enough to throw fuel on what appeared to be a rather blazing fire.

He looked away from her, lost in thought, lost in *angry* thought. All of a sudden his eyes focused on something and he smiled a wicked smile.

Sibyl, in a panic, looked behind her but all she saw was the dining area.

She longed to say something, even tell him why, share a piece of herself, maybe he'd understand. But she didn't want to speak, didn't want to make him any angrier than he already was.

Colin angry, she'd already learned, was a very bad thing.

He put pressure on her neck with his hand, bringing her toward him, and as he did this, he tilted her face up with his thumb on her jaw.

His head descended but he didn't kiss her.

Instead, with his lips against hers, he said, "I've been trying to think of a suitable punishment for you breaking the rules. I paid fifty thousand pounds for this privilege, Sibyl. If you were an employee of mine, I'd sack you."

"Okay," she agreed shakily and perhaps a little foolishly. "Maybe you should sack me."

"Then you'd have to pay back the fifty thousand pounds."

Her eyes rounded in alarm. She'd already "anonymously" donated it to the Community Centre for the minibus.

He watched her expression closely.

"I didn't think so." His voice was smooth as silk but *not* in a good way.

"What are you going to do?" she asked, her voice so far from silky it was ludicrous.

His arm closed around her as his other hand caressed her cheek using the backs of his fingers. She felt a shudder go through her as he drew her against his hard body.

Once his arm was tight around her waist, her body pressed firmly against his, his lips still against hers and his eyes heavy-lidded, he said, "I'm going to fuck you on the dining-room table."

She jerked her head back, shock, fear, anger and hurt all at once coursing through her.

"No!" she cried.

"Oh yes," he returned smoothly.

"No!" she repeated and started to struggle against him.

She couldn't believe this, he wouldn't be that cruel.

"Stop struggling," he commanded.

"Colin, you can't do this! You promised."

"I can, I will and you're going to let me. In fact, you're going to beg me to do it in the end. I'll see to that."

This was a promise, a promise she was pretty certain he could keep and she felt panic and despair sear through her body.

"Colin, don't do this!" she pleaded, feeling every bit of the years of Mags's gently-bred empowerment of her girls flying out the window. "Please, don't do this."

"Maybe you should try tears, Sibyl. They won't work but it might be amusing," he taunted in an ugly voice.

Sibyl glared at him and she hated him in that moment.

In so doing she felt fury rage through her system. She completely forgot her vow never to lose her temper again and she didn't even consider counting to ten.

Therefore, she shouted, "Let go of me!" and very nearly wrenched herself free but his hand at her cheek dropped and his arm sliced around her, slamming her back against his body.

"I said, stop struggling," he ground out.

"They're little girls, Colin!" she yelled and he immediately stilled at her words but she was so angry, she didn't notice. "They're little girls and they needed me. I couldn't run out on them. I would have, I promise you, at any other time, but they *needed* me."

She pulled free of his now loosened arms and sucked air through her mouth, expelled it through her nose like a bull and she stared at him with all the hatred she felt for him at that moment.

"They needed me," she repeated. "I picked them over you. I did it on purpose because they needed me more. So, okay, you want to fuck me on the dining-room table, you want to make me beg for it? Do it! I understood the consequences. But you should know *why*!"

He was watching her and she was breathing heavily and this went on for longer than Sibyl could endure.

"Do it!" she shouted.

"What little girls, Sibyl?" he asked quietly and her body jolted at the words.

"I . . . what?"

Good goddess, she'd said too much.

Her stupid, *stupid* temper!

"Who are these girls who needed you?" he pressed.

She threw back her shoulders at the same time she tossed her hair off them and her guard immediately came up.

She wouldn't let him in, *couldn't* let him in.

"They're a part of my life, a part you've no place in, so it's none of your goddamned business," she informed him truthfully. "You didn't pay your fifty thousand pounds for *that* privilege."

Something flickered in his eyes at that pronouncement but she was too caught up in her fury to register it and nowhere near a place where she would allow herself to understand it.

"What are you waiting for?" she demanded.

To her stunned surprise he turned and walked back across the room. Once there, he picked up his glass and resumed his stance at the window.

She stood there for what seemed like an eternity, watching him, but he didn't move, although the muscle in his jaw did.

Her fury started to drain out of her (though not entirely) and she stalked to the kitchen.

She was pulling food out of the fridge and cupboards to make dinner, just to have something to do while Colin considered her next torment. She might as well be fortified enough to suffer it.

Bran came through the cat door and looked at his bowl of food that was full of biscuits. His expression showing his distaste for this repast and he looked at her. His meaning was clear.

"You aren't getting any more wet food, you had some this morning," she snapped at her cat.

Bran regarded her haughtily for a moment then, although cats couldn't shrug, still it seemed Bran did so and he trotted out of the kitchen.

"Greedy little minx," Sibyl muttered under her breath as she slammed a pot on the stove. "He'd weigh two stone if I didn't dole out food like a prison warden."

She knew she sounded like a lunatic, muttering to herself, but she also didn't care.

A movement at the doorway caught her eye and her head jerked up to see Colin leaning against the doorjamb watching her.

"What now?" Her words where sharp.

"Sibyl, a warning," Colin replied softly. "You've had a reprieve, you should be careful with it."

"Meaning?" she retorted.

"Meaning, if I were you, I wouldn't push me," he replied.

"No, I mean the reprieve," she prompted.

"I promised not to take you on the table, I won't take you on the table. That's what I mean," he explained.

Instantly, her eyes locked with his, Sibyl felt something in her shift.

It was slight and if she wasn't in a heightened emotional state, she might have missed it.

But she knew he wasn't giving her this reprieve because of a promise. He was doing it because he was a decent person. He had a temper that could rival hers (even best hers most of the time) but having the thought of doing something cruel, and voicing the thought, was nothing at all to *doing* the thought.

If he had done what he said he was going to do, she would never have forgiven him.

And he knew that so he didn't do what he said he was going to do so that would never stand between them.

Relief flooded through her but she carefully tucked it, and her thoughts, away.

Instead, she asked, "Do you want some dinner?"

She was not going to thank him for not "taking" her on the table but offering him dinner was the closest she would get.

"Will it be vegetarian?" he asked mildly.

"Of course."

"Then we'll go out," he decided.

COLIN DID PUNISH her, although not by having sex with her on her father's table.

He excruciatingly slowly made her climax with his hands and mouth while he watched, and through it all he refused to allow her to touch him, kiss him or turn to him, nor did he slide inside her, no matter how much she begged.

It was magnificent.

And after, when she'd whispered not-at-all-convincingly, "I think I hate you," *then* he'd taken her, her fully sensitized body so raw and open she'd actually cried out the second time she came and he feared she drew blood when she bit him on the shoulder.

That had been beyond magnificent.

Earlier, he'd been so furious with not being able to contact her, he couldn't think of anything else. In fact, for a week without her when he was in London, he couldn't think of anything but her. The minute the train came into Yatton, he drove directly to the cottage, not even stopping at Lacybourne.

He didn't intend to wait another moment to have her in his arms.

He was even dreaming of her, except he knew he was Royce and she was Beatrice, dark hair and medieval clothing. She called him Royce in the dreams and she stared at him with all the love in the world in her eyes.

He had them every night and they were the most vivid dreams he'd ever had.

But she had not been at the cottage when he arrived and was not answering her phone.

Colin was not used to not having what he wanted the moment he wanted it. And he didn't like that at all.

He also didn't like that he seemed to have an insatiable desire not only for her body but for her company, however, she much preferred to be somewhere else, even after days apart. He'd always been pursued, chased, seducing only when that game needed to be played. He was a target, a trophy, all the woman of his experience grasping and sucking everything they could from him. Not once had Colin met a woman who had her own life, her own interests or anything outside her pursuit of him. He had *never* been in this position and found he contradictorily loathed it and admired it.

When she'd shouted at him about her "girls," something shifted in him through her speech.

Her eyes were furious, blazing with an intensity he'd never seen the like on her or anyone. Even though she refused to allow him into that part of her life, had been for days keeping him at arm's length, carefully guarding anything personal, he knew those girls, whoever they were, were so important to her she'd likely lay down her life for them.

Or throw fifty thousand pounds at them.

He knew from her expression this afternoon that the money was gone, and he also knew, most likely, she hadn't spent it on herself.

It was time to find out just who the hell Sibyl Godwin was.

Robert Fitzwilliam was due to make a report in a week.

Colin was going to give him until Tuesday.

Chapter TWELVE

Potion

Marian Byrne slid behind the wheel of her car and told her windshield, "Sometimes, it's good to be old."

The windshield, as with many of the inanimate objects Marian found herself talking to since her husband Arthur died, didn't answer back.

She started the car, put it into gear and thought about the last hour of her life.

No one questioned an old lady wandering around the office. No one said word one when she walked through, giving a breezy wave to the security guard, and headed (slowly) up the three flights of stairs to Colin Morgan's office.

When his harried secretary ran into the kitchen to make Colin a cup of coffee, Marian was waiting, sitting at the table and knitting. Although she didn't knit and didn't know what she was doing, no one really noticed anything but masses of yarn and the clicking of the needles. Knitting was what stereotypical old ladies did, and since Marian was in disguise she felt it was a good prop.

She was right. The secretary barely reacted when Marian spoke.

"Would you like me to make that for you, dear?" she'd offered in her kindliest, old lady voice.

She knew it was Colin's secretary, Mandy. She'd been paying close attention to a lot of things about Colin Morgan's Bristol offices since she began her stakeout some time ago. Colin worked later than everyone, his secretary left the building a quarter of an hour before him every night.

Mandy's startled eyes came to Marian.

"Who are you?" she asked.

"Oh, I'm Neil's mother. Come for a visit," Marian lied.

She knew a Neil worked there, on that very floor. She had sat next to him at lunch one day in the busy café down the street. There were no other tables and she was "forced" to ask him to share his table with a tired, old, talkative lady who just needed a cuppa and a rest of her weary feet. Being a polite young man, he'd agreed. He'd also (somewhat magically, Marian had to admit) talked a great deal about the comings and goings at the office and how a girl he liked, the boss's secretary, was too tired to go out to drinks after work because her boss always worked her later than anyone else.

"I'm making coffee for Mr. Morgan, he's kind of picky about his coffee," Mandy explained, breaking into Marian's thoughts.

Marian had no doubt Colin Morgan was picky about his coffee.

Marian thought the young secretary looked like she had a great many other things she would prefer to be doing rather than making coffee.

"I think I can handle coffee, dear. How does he take it?"

The girl hesitated only briefly before her expression changed and she looked thrilled to have one less task. With vows of gratitude, she gave Marian instructions and left.

Marian carefully made the coffee, not wanting Mandy to get into trouble and definitely needing Colin to drink it. When she was finished, she surreptitiously took the vial from her old lady handbag (she didn't normally carry such an unfashionable handbag but she was undercover). She tipped the concoction in the drink and stirred. Colin liked his coffee strong—a splash of milk, no sugar, the potion wouldn't change the taste one bit (she hoped).

Mandy rushed back in and Marian handed her the steaming mug and was flashed a grateful smile.

Job done, Marian made good her escape, again without anyone even looking at her.

Now, wending her way through the hated Bristol traffic, Marian went through the ingredients of the potion in her mind.

It would take a while to work. Hopefully he would be back to Sibyl by the time it happened.

Of course, it *could* start working earlier, or later, or do something entirely different than it was supposed to.

She liked to call it her "volatile cocktail." Marian thought that was amusing and she vastly preferred to be amused than to be consumed with worry about all the appalling things that could go wrong with her cocktail. This was very advanced magic and could backfire easily.

It was a huge risk but Marian felt it was a risk she had to take.

Hopefully, the coffee made it to Colin. She'd hate to think what would happen if some other person drank it. Someone with, perhaps, a rather unsavory past life who might go on a killing spree and would genuinely not remember it.

Never mind, Marian thought.

These were the risks one took when in pursuit of facilitating true love.

Marian resolutely set these thoughts aside and hummed to herself the rest of the way home.

SIBYL WAS WORKING in her laboratory in the summer house in her back garden.

Janis Joplin was blaring from the radio and Sibyl was singing with Janis about Bobby McGee. It was six o'clock and the days were much longer since daylight saving time began. They were also back to being unseasonably warm. The cold, gray spell had started the day Colin went away but it cleared the evening he returned. The sun was shining day after day, the tulips were out, the trees were budding, the hyacinths had opened and life was good on this green earth.

Well, mostly.

Colin would soon be at her house, arriving sometime between seven thirty and eight, the way he was nearly every night except the weekends. The weekends, he stayed with her almost all the time (the weekend before, most of this spent in bed). This past weekend, he went into the office for several hours on Sunday.

But on Saturday, he took her to Durham Park. When they arrived at the ticket counter, Sibyl was shocked to find he was not a National Trust member and therefore forced him to buy a membership on the spot (she did this by attempting to buy one for him, which he refused to accept). This he did with ill grace and then muted anger when she announced to The National Trust volunteer that he was the owner of Lacybourne.

"Imagine!" she'd fumed. "He owns a National Trust property and he isn't a member! It's a crime!"

The volunteer had agreed wholeheartedly and gratefully accepted Colin's money.

Colin had punished her for this episode by kissing her, quite thoroughly (to shut her up, he said), in front of a busload of pensioners who looked on with avid curiosity. When Colin was done, a couple of them even clapped.

He later took her out for the most delicious dinner she'd ever had at a French restaurant in Bath. The owner was French and, upon hearing Sibyl's pronunciation of her order, came forward from behind the bar and, in French, asked if she spoke his language. Sibyl forgot herself for a moment, told him she did and they had a hilarious five minute conversation (somewhat stilted, as she was out of practice, but he was very patient) about the episode at Durham Park.

When the owner clapped Colin on the back, shook his hand and left, Colin turned speculative eyes to her. She immediately regretted losing herself in the conversation.

"Sorry, it's been so long since I've practiced, I was all over the place. I . . . um, speak French by the way," she informed him, feeling somehow exposed at letting her guard slip and wishing she'd kept her mouth shut.

"I gathered," he replied drily but said nothing else on the subject.

They spent a great deal of time together but in all that time he never once took her to Lacybourne.

And for this she was glad for it meant he, too, was guarding himself from her.

She needed that.

Something had changed between them, something had shifted, something dangerous to the health of her heart.

That morning after her breakfast with Marian, even though it was her day off, Sibyl had taken a trip in to the council estate to visit Meg and because Kyle was bringing back the minibus. The volunteers and oldies had all been elated and everyone signed up to ride the new bus. Kyle was finishing the driver's course and Jem's art group were going to use it for some outings. It was the talk of the estate. The bus would be in action in a week and Sibyl was thrilled.

In order to have a visit and share this news, Sibyl took some food to Meg who was not doing very well, finding recovery difficult.

"Oh don't look that way," Meg admonished softly when Sibyl's face filled with worry. "I'm old, Billie, and I'm not in pain. I'm resigned to the former and happy for the latter."

Sibyl knew that Meg was lying. She could see the deeper lines of pain that had formed around her friend's mouth but she didn't say anything.

Now, in her laboratory, Sibyl was pouring some perfumed salts into wide, fat glass jars, affixing their black lids and labeling them with a white label with "Wicked Apothecary" (her brand name, chosen by her dad) in bold, emerald-colored, calligraphy script. The label had the picture of a black cat with its back arched and its bushy tail straight up (chosen by her mom). She wrote the scent of the salts on the jar in her handwriting (a personal touch) this batch was ylang-ylang and lavender.

Throughout doing this, Sibyl was singing with Janis, now about a Mercedes Benz, when with no warning and for no reason the CD stopped right before the door to the summer house crashed open.

She whirled around to stare.

Colin was there.

Except, with one look at him, she knew it wasn't Colin, even though it was.

She studied him and felt a shimmer of fear run up her spine, alongside it an evocative thrill.

She knew in an instant, looking at his face, into his eyes, that it was Colin but it was also someone else entirely.

And because of this peculiarity, and the familiar look in his eyes she couldn't quite place, she braced.

"What are you wearing?" he barked and Sibyl jumped at his fierce tone.

He didn't even sound like Colin.

Yet he did.

She was wearing a white, lacy, gypsy camisole with wide straps edged in lace and a pair of her oldest jeans that had a rip in the knee and a tear just below the right cheek of her bottom. Her feet were bare and her hair was screwed up in a clip.

Her hands went immediately to the clip and tore it out of her hair. His eyes followed the action as her hair came down in a tumble around her face and shoulders.

And it was then, he roared (yes, *roared*), "*What have you done to your hair?*" and he did this as his eyes narrowed dangerously so Sibyl jumped again.

"Colin?" she asked in a timid voice.

He was across the short space to her in one angry stride, pulling her to him with his hands closing around her upper arms so painfully she cried out. He ignored her and crushed her to his body.

"Why do you use this name when you're with me?" His voice was full of warning and his eyes were hard. "I no longer find it amusing."

His hands were biting into her flesh and she stared at him, filled with terror.

She'd looked into those eyes before.

She knew those eyes.

"Royce?" she ventured.

At the sound of her uncertainty, he pushed her slightly away and shook her roughly. So roughly that her teeth clattered together and her head snapped back.

She grabbed his upper arms to steady herself but as quickly as he shook her, he stopped.

He seemed to notice where he was and she watched as he stared around the room. He took in her jars and bottles, the essential oils neatly labeled and stacked on shelves. The vats of ingredients carefully lined up on the floor. The huge mixing bowls and paddles she used. The rolls of stickers with which she labeled her products.

"What is this? You're at the witch's cottage. Are you a witch? Have you bewitched me?" he rapped out these questions in quick succession, his voice low and even. The same voice Colin used when he was very angry but controlling it with an effort of will.

"Royce, you're—"

She stopped speaking when she saw that something was changing in him. It changed his eyes, his face, even the line of his frame. It was something even more otherworldly than before.

Then, suddenly, his hands gentled, his eyes warmed and they roved over her face. They did this as if he hadn't seen her in years.

Indeed, as if he hadn't seen her in centuries.

As if she was the most precious creature in the entire universe.

Her stomach did a somersault.

He lifted one hand to her hair. Capturing a tendril at the side of her face, he twirled it in his fingers tenderly.

"Oh, Beatrice," he murmured, his voice thick and throaty but she knew he was not speaking to her, he was talking to someone else. Someone who wasn't there. And his voice so filled with pain that Sibyl felt a lump form in the base of her throat. "I gave you my hair."

She had no idea what he was talking about, but at the tender ache in his voice, the pain stark in his eyes, she felt compelled to lay her hand on his cheek. "Royce?"

His gaze slowly shifted to hers.

"You're so like her." His voice was now soft, his eyes unbelievably warm. "So like her." He cupped her face worshipfully in his hands, making her knees go week. "But not her."

"I know you," Sibyl whispered to him. "I've seen you in my dreams."

"And I saw you in her." He smiled a beautiful, heart-wrenching, sad smile. "You called me Colin when you were her. I thought she was attempting to vex me."

Her heart lurched at the sound of adoration in his tone when he spoke of "her."

"How can you be here? Is it me that's doing this to you?" Sibyl asked.

He shook his head, she knew it was not in the negative but telling her he didn't know.

"Where are you from?" she asked urgently.

"I know not," he answered.

"Another time? A different place?" she pressed.

"Not here," he told her the only thing he knew.

"Royce, who's Beatrice?"

His look turned intense and he whispered, "She's you."

And then, before she knew what he was about, he wrapped his fist in her hair and pulled her head back with a gentle tug, his arm gliding around her waist, and he kissed her.

And his kiss was sweet and wild and beautiful and everything a kiss was meant to be, because it was filled with yearning and love.

Experiencing the sad joy and intense beauty of the kiss, she relaxed into him and felt tears burn the backs of her eyes then roll down her temples. When she opened them after he'd lifted his head, she knew in an instant Royce was gone and Colin had returned.

"What the hell is going on?" he clipped.

Releasing her, he stepped back and looked about him.

"Colin?" she queried, staring at him in disbelief, her heart in her throat.

A tremor went through her as he looked around with angry bemusement.

Sibyl's mind was awhirl.

This was not right, not *real* and very, very wrong.

Did she do this to him? Her mother tried to be a witch, believed in magic. But even though Sibyl had grown up around the pagan religion, she'd never truly believed in magic.

Except, of course, to think it would one day bring her a soulmate.

With her strange, lifelike dreams, meeting Colin and all that had happened since Lacybourne (and now this), she was beginning to feel that there was some other power at play here and it could be, maybe *had* to be, magic.

"What's going on?" Colin thundered, masculine confusion morphing into anger very quickly.

"You need to sit down," she told him gently.

"I don't need to sit down, I need to know what . . . *the fuck* . . . is going on," he returned slowly and through gritted teeth.

"Do you remember anything?" Sibyl asked and stepped toward him.

His eyes took her in, sweeping the length of her and they stopped on the way up.

"What's happened to your arms?"

She looked down at her upper arms and saw the dark, angry, red welts that had risen up where Colin/Royce had grabbed her.

"You've been crying." It was not a question or a statement but an accusation.

Sibyl took a deep breath.

How to explain?

"You . . . Colin, you grabbed me and you shook me," she told him quietly and then took another step toward him when his face blanched.

"*I* did that to you?"

She laid her hand on his chest and made honest excuses for him, "You weren't yourself."

"Christ!"

Sibyl winced because that one word was an explosion. His hand went to his hair and tore through it before he continued speaking.

"I don't remember anything. I was in the kitchen, wondering where you were and I heard the music. I was going to come out and the next thing I knew I was kissing you."

She used the hand on his chest to push him back carefully. He didn't resist and fell into the flowered cushions of a wicker chair she kept in her lab.

She hated to see him this way and wished things were different between them. She wished they were such that she could comfort him in the way she wanted, *needed* to comfort him.

Instead, she said, "I'm going to get you a glass of water. I'll be right back."

Then without delay, Sibyl ran from the summer house, feelings of guilt tearing through her.

She couldn't help but think she was responsible for this. Maybe her mother *was* a witch. Maybe that made Sibyl a witch. Maybe these dreams she was having were coming to life. Or, she'd always felt there was something strange and magical about Brightrose Cottage, maybe it was the house.

She flew into the kitchen and grabbed a glass. A phone was ringing and she saw a mobile on the kitchen counter. Without thinking, she grabbed it, engaged and put it to her ear.

"Hello?" Sibyl uttered the greeting distractedly and turned on the tap, her eyes moving to look through the window in the back door to ascertain if she could see Colin, but she couldn't.

There was no response on the phone and when Sibyl was about ready to disengage, a refined woman's voice said, "I'm sorry, I thought I was ringing Colin Morgan's phone."

Sibyl froze.

Was it Mistress Freeze, the long-since-absent Tamara?

Colin had told Sibyl that she could not allow another man to touch her while she was with him, but he made no such promise to her. She'd entirely forgotten the other woman in the extremes of her drama and he'd just spent a week in London.

Dear goddess, he could have been with *her*.

Sibyl felt waves of sickening jealousy she was not entitled to feel crash through her and said hesitantly, "This is Colin's phone. He's . . ." she peered through the window again and still could not see him, "out back. Um . . ."

She was at a loss of what to say.

"This is his sister, Claire. Who's this?" Her voice was friendly and engaging but, even so, as her concern fled that she was talking to Tamara, Sibyl's body jerked at the thought of speaking to Colin's sister.

She didn't even know he had a sister.

In fact, Sibyl thought that Colin was akin to a quicksilver god born of the elements, not having parents or siblings or anything mere mortals would possess.

Before Sibyl could reply, Claire asked chattily, as if they were going to spend the next hour in pleasant conversation, "You're American aren't you?"

Sibyl put the glass under the tap not believing this was happening, especially not now, considering the fact she had unawakened witchy powers and Colin was angrily recovering from an episode of real multiple personalities.

"Yes, I'm American," she answered.

"Oh, where are you from in America? I *love* America." Then before Sibyl could respond Claire went on, her voice sounding amused and *very* sisterly, almost exactly like her own sister, (except less annoying). "*You* must be the reason no one has heard from Colin *in weeks*."

Sibyl pulled the glass from under the faucet and turned it off.

As an answer, she hedged, "Perhaps I should get Colin."

"Sure," Claire agreed happily. "Here I am, monopolizing the conversation, as usual. I didn't get your name."

Sibyl opened the back door and walked stiffly through the garden. She loved her garden, with its flagstone paths and beautifully laid flower beds that were carefully created to look wild.

At that moment, however, she didn't even see it.

"Sibyl Godwin," she replied without thinking and heard the woman's shocked gasp.

Her *extremely* shocked gasp.

"What did you say?" Claire whispered, her voice sounding strange in Sibyl's ear.

Why everyone that had anything to do with Colin (although, if she was honest, it was really just Marian, Colin and now his sister, then again, those were the only people Sibyl knew who had anything to do with Colin) reacted so strongly to her name was beyond her.

She didn't have time to consider it. Sibyl had made it to the door of the summer house.

Colin was still sitting in the wicker chair, his forehead resting in his hand, his elbow resting on his knee.

He glanced up at her when she arrived and instead of repeating her name to his sister, Sibyl told her, "He's right here."

Claire didn't reply and her silence was deafening.

Sibyl extended the phone to Colin and announced, "It's your sister."

He took the phone but stared at Sibyl intently. She had no idea what her face looked like, but she could tell by his look that he could read her dazed reaction to the phone call clearly.

"Claire," he said by way of greeting, his eyes never leaving Sibyl's face. Then, on whatever his sister was saying, they closed, slowly, and when they opened again, they rolled to the ceiling of the summer house in exasperation.

Sibyl stood motionless inside the doorway. But at his rolling of eyes, she moved jerkily forward, set the glass of water on a counter and went to finish with the salts.

She heard him talking behind her and felt his eyes on her back.

"Claire, can you be quiet for one minute?" Silence and then, "Do *not* call Mum." More silence. "Claire, if you tell—"

He must have been interrupted because, seconds later, she heard the electronic beep of him disconnecting.

Before he could light into her, she quickly and defensively explained to her salts, "I was thinking about you. I heard the phone ringing and I just grabbed it. It was a reflex action."

She felt him come up behind her but she didn't turn.

Instead of his voice being angry as she expected it to be, it was soft when he asked, "What are you doing?"

She was surprised at his question and the curious tone behind it.

"Making bath salts. I have a small business," she answered.

He made no reply.

Then she felt his finger run gently along the marks on her right arm and the skin tingled where he touched it. She felt him move closer to her back.

She continued talking to her salts; she'd completely filled the jars and was now screwing on their lids. "Have you ever had an episode like that before?"

His reply was immediate. "Never."

She felt the word on her neck and then, to her complete surprise, she felt his chin settle on her shoulder as his arms slid around her belly.

She sucked in breath. It was a moment so tender, so unlike anything she and Colin had ever shared, Sibyl froze.

And in that moment, she knew she should tell him everything but she decided there was the good possibility that if she informed him that she thought she was a latent witch, expunging magical powers through her dreams or possibly her home (or both) and he was bewitched, he would think (perhaps rightly) she was a screaming loon.

Furthermore, she didn't want to do anything that would make him pull away from her when he was holding her like that.

Therefore, instead she remarked, "You should see a doctor."

This was true, he probably should, but she knew in her core Western medicine would probably not be able cure this ailment.

"I'm sorry I hurt you." His voice was warm and she felt a shiver pass through her not only due to his tone but also due to the guilt she felt. "I don't remember it, not a moment, but that's no excuse."

It *was* an excuse, since he had been possessed by some other being, but Sibyl couldn't tell him that.

Therefore, she could do nothing but nod her head and whisper, "It's okay."

His arms gave her a gentle squeeze then he queried, "Did I say anything to you?"

At that, she shook her head and lied, "I just knew, the minute you arrived, you weren't you."

With that, she shrugged her shoulders as if to indicate it was a matter of little importance.

"What did I say?"

"Nothing that made sense." That was almost true. "Nothing important." That was most definitely *not* true.

"Why was I kissing you?"

She smiled to herself at the memory of the kiss, a secret smile she hoped he couldn't see.

She had broken a rule, she knew, not blatantly but she still broke it. She had allowed another man to touch her and kiss her, even though it was Colin, it was also not.

She lied again on a whisper, "You always kiss me."

Colin was silent a moment before he said softly, "If this was as unimportant as you wish me to believe, why aren't you looking at me?"

At his comment and the soft accusation in his tone, she turned quickly and he loosened his arms and lifted his head so she could do so. The minute she was facing him, his arms tightened around her again, drawing her into his warm, hard body. She lifted her eyes to his, he stared into hers and must have seen something there because she felt his body instantly relax.

There was something intensely sweet about his reaction for she knew he was concerned.

She worked desperately to quell the even sweeter feelings this realization sent surging through her and managed it (just).

"I'm sorry about answering your phone," she told him. "I wasn't thinking."

His mouth came down and brushed hers lightly but swiftly before his head lifted and he replied, "Don't worry. I can deal with my sister."

As if on cue, his mobile began to ring again. Instead of ignoring it, he pulled it out of his pocket and glanced at the display. When he did, he sighed and took the call. Without letting go of her, he put it to his ear.

"Mum," he said as greeting.

Sibyl's body stiffened, and in response his hand traveled up and began to stroke her back. This was done without thinking, she could tell, a spontaneous reaction to her tenseness and the thoughtfulness made her pull in her breath to mask her reaction.

"Yes," he answered some question while she watched his face change expressions from wary to exasperated before he shuttered it from her. "Yes," he said again then, "There is absolutely no need—" Then, the short conversation apparently over, he ended the call with a heavy sigh.

"I've caused a problem, haven't I?" she asked, feeling even more guilt.

She had no idea what was happening with his family and she knew it was none of her business. She also knew his sister had jumped to a conclusion about what Sibyl was to Colin and now Colin had to find some tactful way to explain.

"I'm going to have to go. My mother and sister will be descending on Lacybourne. They're leaving within the hour."

Sibyl felt a rush of gloom at his leaving.

"My parents are coming next week," she blurted and had no idea why she felt compelled to tell him a piece of information he already knew, except to prolong his departure.

"I know." His answer was distracted, he'd already pulled away from her and she already missed his arms.

He tipped up her chin and kissed her but that was distracted too.

She wanted to do all the things a girl would normally do when her lover was going to spend his first night away from her while both of them were in the same town.

She wanted to give him a kiss.

She wanted to ask him if she could come with him.

But she did neither of these because that was not what she was to him.

Instead, she walked to her roll of labels to finish the jars.

He was watching her.

"How are you getting to Heathrow?" he asked as if he'd just thought of it. "You can't be taking the MG."

Even though it would have been physically impossible for herself, her father, her mother and their luggage to ride the two and a half hours back from Heathrow in the MG (not to mention, the MG would never make the trek), his statement was not exactly what the words said.

He said "can't," he meant "won't."

"Hire car," she answered. "I pick it up the night before."

"Cancel it. I'll arrange for a car to come 'round to get you."

She felt her mouth part at this announcement before she informed him, "I've already booked the car."

"Cancel it," he repeated, still distracted but clearly issuing a command.

She felt both irritation and tenderness at his domineering. It was beginning to dawn on her that many of his commands had something to do with her protection, safety, convenience or comfort (but, of course, not all of them).

"Colin, is that an order?"

He was watching her affix the labels, for some reason regarding this act as if it was fascinating, but, at her voice saying his name, his eyes came to hers.

"Yes," he replied shortly.

She glared at him and, having no choice, nodded.

For some reason, this made him grin.

And the grin was unlike any grin he'd ever given her before.

It was a Royce-like grin, teasing, playful, knowing and intimate. As if he found her amusing and adorable. She felt her body instantly react and had to fight against the overwhelming desire to throw herself across the room into his arms and kiss him senseless.

But maybe he *was* Royce again. Maybe, she thought with alarm, that Royce was back.

Her head tilted to the side and tentatively she called, "Colin?"

"Yes?" he answered.

A gush of relief spread through her, then her body tensed again because it was Colin giving her that grin, not Royce.

She didn't know what to make of that.

"Nothing," she muttered and continued writing on the labels.

He came forward and kissed her shoulder in a gesture so fond Sibyl had to steel herself against it.

This was not Colin, nothing like him.

Maybe, she thought, there were residual Royce-waves floating through him.

This was not arm's length.

This was real, heady, wonderful, couple-like stuff.

Maybe he felt guilty about hurting her.

That had to be it.

"I've got to go," he said.

She nodded, wanting to be alone to think about all of this.

At the same time wanting to throw herself at him, beg him to spend the night and make love to her. *Not* have sex with her but make love to her.

"Sibyl."

Her body jolted at his voice and she turned her head to him. The look on his face was now definitely the Colin she knew.

"I'll take a goodbye kiss now."

Definitely the Colin she knew.

She moved forward and gave him what he demanded.

Regardless of the fact that when she first met him he behaved like a deranged madman then he had charmed her and she thought he was her dream man *then* he'd bought her body, and she thought she hated him—despite all that, despite how she knew it was very, very dangerous—she was beginning to have feelings for him. Strong, wonderful, scary feelings that were no good for her at all.

And because of that, when she kissed him, she pressed her body to his and pulled him to her by wrapping her arms around his sides and pressing hands between his shoulder blades. She went up on her toes and kissed him with all the strong, wonderful, scariness she felt. She opened her lips under his and slid her tongue in to taste his beautiful mouth and when she did, his arms swept around her, pulling her deeper into him, and at the touch of her tongue against his he took over her goodbye kiss.

It wasn't Royce's beautiful kiss, but it was a goodbye-for-now kiss that she would never, ever forget.

As she stood, shaken and trembling from the kiss, watching him walk with his masculine grace back through her garden, she heard his mobile ring again.

MARIAN SAW COLIN walking toward his car and would have been alarmed at his much-earlier-than-usual exit had she not seen the look on his face.

Colin Morgan looked quite content with the world.

He got in his Mercedes and deftly maneuvered down the lane.

Marian was about to follow when she saw something out of the corner of her eye.

Marian was hiding in the wood outside Sibyl's house.

And so was someone else.

She stared, looking closely at the place where she saw the movement and she stood stock still.

It would not do for *them* to see *her*.

Minutes passed but she saw nothing else.

An evil shiver slid through Marian's body because she knew she was in the presence of the dark soul that, in this time, crossed the lovers' stars.

She had been planning to follow Colin but she decided it was best to spend a little bit more time watching over Sibyl.

Just to be certain everything was all right.

Chapter THIRTEEN

Realization

Colin Morgan had made up his mind about Sibyl Godwin.

And when Colin made up his mind, that was that.

For the last two weeks, she'd resolutely kept herself guarded and distant from him.

She was not wheedling her way into his life. She was not using her rather considerable feminine wiles to force some avowal of feeling from him. She made no demands, never dissolved in tears, didn't ask to go back to Lacybourne and never mentioned Beatrice or Royce.

She had her own life, her own interests, her own business and a job somewhere for which she obviously felt a great deal of passion.

She was not, he decided, a scheming bitch like all the other women of his acquaintance.

She was just . . . Sibyl.

Colin had no idea why she needed fifty thousand pounds but he knew she had not spent it on herself.

She had not bought a new car (which she definitely needed, how she could lecture him on fuel economy and drive her petrol-guzzling wreck, he could not fathom, though she referred to her MG as "recycling").

She was not surrounded by bags of new clothes. She didn't wear expensive jewels. She always dressed well (albeit often endearingly bohemian) but she clearly did not have expensive tastes.

She didn't drink too much and he'd spent enough time with her to know she didn't take drugs. She was a resolute vegetarian and the first morning she'd presented him with a breakfast bowl filled with a hideous concoction of organic Weetabix mixed with yogurt, honey and strawberries, he'd known she was likely not the type to start drinking or taking drugs.

Her home was well-presented, well-kept and sound and she needed nothing to fill it and did nothing to it. He'd seen an open credit card statement and utility bill and shamelessly looked at them. Both were paid up fully and current.

It seemed her only extravagance was that she always kept expensive fresh flowers on her dining-room table, this, he thought (correctly), was an unconscious show of love to her father, but as lovely as they were, she was not spending fifty thousand pounds on them.

She was definitely fit and energetic, except in the mornings when she was quite hilariously moody, and he couldn't see that she had any ailment that needed treatment.

He had no idea what she did with her days but he knew she worked somewhere, somewhere that meant a great deal to her. He'd discovered last night that she had her own small business, and the fact that she was still working meant she hadn't taken the money so she could quit and spend her days shopping or doing whatever it was that women who didn't work did with their time.

It could be she'd taken the money to invest in the business, though it seemed a relatively small operation from what he could see, considering it was run out of a chalet in her back garden.

With a temper like hers, he could imagine she'd gotten herself into some kind of trouble with someone but he couldn't imagine how or with whom.

Whatever she needed the money for, it was likely not for her.

This all made Colin believe there was a reason Sibyl Godwin had come into his life.

And, even if she was an excellent actress hiding a deceitful, larcenous heart, (although this option, day to day, was seeming less and less viable) she was still the vision of Beatrice Godwin, she was still extraordinary in bed, she was always surprising him (speaking French, looking, while eating chocolate mousse, (nearly) like she did when she reached orgasm) and he was still going to have her for as long as he wished no matter what it took.

Five months would not be enough. Two weeks hadn't done a thing in assuaging his lust for her. If anything, after two weeks, he wanted her *more.*

He didn't question it and didn't care to, all he knew was that if he wanted more, he'd get it.

And he wanted more.

He'd never met a woman like her, regardless of who she was and what she was. In reality, he knew there were few women who didn't have deceitful, larcenous hearts so he might as well spend his time with one who was open about it.

Or at least open enough to ask for fifty thousand pounds.

Once.

Since then, she'd tried twice (after the second time he'd ordered her to stop doing it and, with her usual mutinous expression, she'd agreed) to pay the bill at a restaurant when he took her to dinner. She never hinted she wanted presents, nights out, to jet off on holiday or more money.

She also never asked about his work, his family, his life and did not share any information about herself.

She kept him at arm's length with everything.

Except in bed.

There she was fiery and responsive and utterly magnificent.

He had lied to Sibyl only once, when he told her he didn't remember anything about the episode in the chalet in her garden the night before. He *did* remember kissing her. Not the start but definitely the middle and obviously the end.

It was like a kiss he'd never given a woman in his life, it was almost unbearably sexy, even going so far as being moving.

Whatever had made him kiss her like that, he could not imagine, but her reaction to it was strange.

Receiving a kiss like that would have been the perfect excuse for any woman to wheedle nearer to him, but Sibyl seemed to want to hide it, hide her reaction to the kiss and hide the fact that it had happened at all. She set it aside as if it was unimportant, even though her behavior said it was anything but.

She was more intent on taking care of him and apologizing for answering his damn mobile than talking about the kiss, the episode or the rather upsetting fact that he'd apparently physically abused her (another advantage she did not seem willing to turn).

Colin was concerned he'd had a snatch of his life he didn't remember, but with his strange dreams and all that had happened between him and Sibyl, Colin was more interested in her reaction to the entire episode and especially that remarkable kiss.

And she had lied to him once, he knew, about her nightmare. She was a spectacularly bad liar, another part of her puzzle that made the option of her being a scheming mercenary less feasible.

However, what she had told him was enough for him to realize that something was connecting them and it was much more than magnificent sex. He wasn't ready to believe it was something else, a legend or myth brought to life in the form of a tall, curvaceous, annoyingly adorable American woman with leonine hair, but it was something.

Something was definitely not right about Sibyl Godwin. She was not what he expected her to be, and he was going to find out what, exactly, she was.

When he walked into his office the morning after the incident in the chalet he expected to see Robert Fitzwilliam, the investigator who he had sent on Sibyl's trail. He'd set the meeting as his first order of business.

Colin did *not* expect to see Marian Byrne in his outer office, nor to see his secretary glaring at the older woman with barely concealed distrust.

"Mr. Morgan," his secretary, Mandy, popped up the minute he entered the room and said, unnecessarily and unusually forcefully, "Mr.

Fitzwilliam is here to see you."

"Thank you, Mandy, I can see that," Colin replied but his eyes were on Mrs. Byrne who seemed quite content and smiled happily at him.

Before he could greet the older woman, Mandy continued.

"And *this woman*, who, by the way, was here yesterday and said she was Neil's mother but now says she's not, is Marian Byrne and she says she needs to speak with you urgently. I explained you have a very busy morning but she said she would wait," Mandy announced, her words coming out in an angry rush.

Colin raised his brows at the Neil comment, wondering why on earth Marian Byrne would pretend to be one of his employee's mother.

She was still smiling and shrugged her shoulders nonchalantly, giving nothing away.

He'd decided he'd find out soon enough.

"I know Mrs. Byrne. I'll see her after I speak with Mr. Fitzwilliam." He turned his attention to the investigator and motioned to the door to his office, inviting, "Robert." Then Colin walked past Marian Byrne and nodded politely at her in greeting, saying, "Mrs. Byrne."

She calmly returned the gesture.

Colin had just settled into his desk chair when the door opened and Mandy brought in a tray of coffee, her usual morning task. She set it on his desk, handed Colin his cup and gave one to Robert and left without a word.

Colin ignored her.

"Shall we start?" Colin invited, ready to hear some answers.

Robert took a sip and put his cup on Colin's desk.

"Pretty basic stuff, you'll be pleased to know," he began.

His words slightly surprised Colin, and Colin watched him pull a thick file out of a briefcase.

"Sibyl Jezebel Godwin," Robert started and something shifted inside Colin as Robert read out her full name, her real name—truly she was a Godwin.

Some part of him never believed that, for some reason. To have it read to him so calmly felt like a blow.

Christ, did Beatrice Godwin's descendant walk into Lacybourne three weeks ago?

Dear *Christ*, had she done so only to have him shout at her?

"Born to Albert Godwin, an Englishman." Robert lifted his eyes to Colin and the other man's were benign. They showed no signs that anything he was about to say would be life changing even though, with the two pieces of information he'd given Colin, they already were.

Sibyl's father was English.

She *could* be descended from Beatrice's family.

Robert continued, "Her father was born in Wells. He teaches Medieval History and took his first post in Arizona where he met his wife, Marguerite. She was born Marguerite Wilhemina Den in Sedona, Arizona. Bit of a wild one, is Marguerite. An aging hippie, studies witchcraft, been arrested seven times, mostly during demonstrations for civil rights, women's rights, anti-war, stuff like that. Nothing serious."

Colin sat in stunned silence as the pieces of Sibyl's puzzle flew together.

Everything about her fit, the damned granola she always seemed to be eating, her lecture about fuel economy, her pets' names.

Not to mentions Sibyl's bizarre muttered comments of "Oh my goddess" were because her mother had brought her up Wiccan.

Robert went on, "Albert and Marguerite had two children, both girls, yours, of course, Sibyl, and a younger daughter, Scarlett. They both were straight A students, honor role, Who's Who, barely missed school, traveled a lot with their parents as the father went from university to university. Never showed any signs of trouble with all the moving around, as kids sometimes do. Though Scarlett is a bit of a wild one, like her mother. Sibyl seems less, er . . . prone to that, or at least in that way. Sibyl has two degrees, a Bachelor of Arts in languages and another in social work. Scarlett is finishing up the final months of a neurology residency."

Robert kept talking and Colin felt his gut clench painfully as the information flowed at him, something about Customs and Immigration, something else about a domestic abuse charity and something alarming about an animal shelter.

Sibyl owned Brightrose Cottage outright, deeded over to her by her parents on her move to England over a year ago.

She had only had three boyfriends that Robert could find, a fact Colin could hardly believe.

She had close relationships with family and friends, a fact Colin definitely believed.

She currently worked part-time at a Community Centre on a deprived council estate in Weston-super-Mare (which must be the source of "the girls" who needed her).

Robert only imparted one small piece of information to Colin that he already knew. Sibyl ran a small, but rather lucrative business on the side making bath salts and shampoo. It would have been very lucrative if she didn't divide forty percent of her profits between Amnesty International and a small, local animal shelter that took in abused cats that couldn't be re-homed.

"From what I heard, they love her at the Centre and she spends more time there than she gets paid for. Pretty tight with the family that runs the place as volunteers, a Kyle and Tina and especially their daughter, Jemma. There was a little bit of trouble a few weeks ago but you saw to that, obviously," Robert finished and nodded at Colin, with what, Colin thought, was a strange gesture of respect.

Colin stared at him.

He had no idea what the man was talking about. He hadn't even known Sibyl worked at a Community Centre.

Therefore, he asked, "Sorry?"

"The minibus. Your girl was making some waves about the local minibus company the council had contracted with to transport the pensioners. Some issue with a blind lady who was living in squalor, your girl found out about it, cleaned up the woman's house and set up a rota to look after her. She raised hell with Social Services that the driver didn't report it. They couldn't do a thing and your girl was furious. She lost her nut with the minibus driver when she saw him. A few days later, during a delivery to the Day Centre, one of the pensioners fell out of the bus, broke a hip. Apparently this lady was a particular favorite of Sibyl's and she took it hard. Then, out of the blue, there was a convenient 'anonymous' donation, clearly from you, fifty thousand pounds.

Bang, new minibus, enough to train one of the volunteers as a driver, insure the bus, well . . . I don't have to tell you."

Colin felt his heart squeeze painfully and he found he was having difficulty breathing, but Fitzwilliam wasn't done.

"Lucky she met you. Found herself a nice patron, you two make a striking couple if you don't mind my saying. Of course, investigating her I had to watch you for a while, you understand, since you spend so much time with her. Can't say I blame you . . ."

Colin wasn't listening to him, he was thinking of Sibyl, who she was and what she'd done.

Sibyl had sold her body for a minibus for old-age pensioners.

Not only that, she'd quit her job (before she could be fired) at the domestic violence charity because she'd been found sitting on the porch of a client training her father's shotgun on an abuser who had dared to approach his estranged wife's house in the middle of the night.

And what had Robert said about what she did to the people who brought in the dog who'd been burned by cigarette butts?

He didn't want to think, couldn't think, all he could remember was her staring at the money in the briefcase and saying, "Thank you," like it was the answer to her prayers.

Clearly it was the answer to *a* prayer. A prayer for a bunch of old people to whom she was not related, who simply came to her Centre. People who were in the hands of a thoughtless driver who wasn't responsible for them but should have had enough feeling to at least take note and some care, and didn't.

So, Sibyl did.

"Christ," he said under his breath.

"What's that?" Robert asked him.

A memory came to Colin and his tight chest seized.

"What was the date of the accident with the woman who broke her hip?"

Robert looked at him curiously and told him the date, a date Colin remembered very well. He remembered Sibyl talking earnestly to her friend Kyle, her body stiff and jerky as she walked back to her house, her mind consumed with something unpleasant.

The date he'd made her his whore.

"Christ," he clipped viciously, shook his head and found when he looked down at his hands on his desk they were shaking.

He clenched them into fists.

This woman, *his* woman, walked into his home innocently for a tour and he'd treated her like a common criminal.

Then she'd sold her body to him to make a group of old people safe.

And he'd made her feel like a whore so she could do it.

Money was scarce in the voluntary sector, he knew that, his company received dozens of requests a week for donations, and he personally was asked to become a benefactor on a regular basis.

It would likely take a small community centre on a deprived council estate years to raise the funds to buy a bus.

Sibyl had seen her chance and grabbed it.

"You should know you have two tails." Robert was continuing. "The woman out there . . ." He jerked his head to the door of Colin's office. "And I think someone else, though can't get a lock on them. Both have been watching you and Miss Godwin pretty closely. Do you want me to find out why?"

Colin was reeling with the information he'd learned, the fact that Beatrice Godwin, reincarnated had finally walked into his life and he could barely process any more.

"Look into the other one," he ordered distractedly. "I'll talk to Mrs. Byrne and I'll phone you if I need anything further."

Robert put the file on his desk and stood. "Can I say, Mr. Morgan . . . ?"

Colin was staring at the file, knowing Sibyl's remarkable life was inside.

He opened it randomly somewhere in the middle.

He saw a copy of a newspaper clipping announcing, "Local Girl Wins Volunteer of the Year Award." A younger Sibyl was shown in the photograph, holding up a plaque and smiling at the camera with her dazzling smile.

"Mr. Morgan?"

Colin's head came up sharply. "What is it?"

His voice was impatient. He had things to do.

He calculated the time.

Colin's mother and sister were at Lacybourne now, meddling and needling him about the American woman named Godwin. A woman he had not expected, three weeks ago, that they would ever meet.

Now, he knew, they most definitely would considering they'd be grandmother and aunt to that woman's children.

Robert continued, "I know it isn't my place to say but your Sibyl, she's a bit . . . well, she's got her heart in the right place but sometimes . . ." He stopped and then repeated himself, obviously uncomfortable, "Again, it isn't my place but you should keep an eye on her. She gets herself into trouble sometimes. Well . . . a good bit of the time."

Colin nodded distractedly.

That, as well as many other things about Sibyl, was now stunningly clear.

"Please send Mrs. Byrne in on your way out," Colin ordered.

Dismissed, Robert left and Colin sifted through the file on his desk, watching Sibyl's life pass by. On the last page there was a picture of her with four young girls aged around ten or eleven. They were staring at her with rapt attention as if she was the center of the universe and she was smiling at them, her arms in full gesture, almost like she was dancing.

They needed me, she'd said.

"Jesus," he growled.

"Mr. Morgan?"

He looked at Mrs. Byrne who was walking into his office.

"Please have a seat, Mrs. Byrne," Colin invited, firmly controlling his thoughts, all of which damned him to hell, and he closed the file carefully.

She was watching him but she sat in a chair opposite his desk.

"Before you tell me what's so urgent you're here first thing in the morning, could I ask you one question?" he inquired politely.

"Certainly, Mr. Morgan," she replied agreeably.

"Your story about Sibyl, you met her the night before she came to my home, is that true?"

She watched him for a moment and then she nodded.

"I told you, I know you may not believe me—" she began.

"Oh, I believe you," Colin said smoothly.

This announcement startled her but she recovered quickly.

"But the reason I'm here is to tell you what my part is in all of this," Mrs. Byrne explained.

"All of what?"

"You, Sibyl, and Royce and Beatrice Morgan," she announced.

He did not show any reaction to this.

Colin had a great deal to do and did not have the patience to sit through this interview. Considering she was just a meddling National Trust volunteer who had very clumsily, not to mention with the addition of unneeded mystery, instigated a meeting with him and an American woman who looked like the portrait of Beatrice Godwin, Colin lost interest in her.

"Do you know of Esmeralda Crane?" Mrs. Byrne asked.

That got his attention and his eyes focused on her.

Of course he knew Esmeralda Crane. Anyone with any knowledge of the legend of Royce and Beatrice knew it was Esmeralda Crane, the local midwife rumored to be a witch who discovered the bodies of the newlyweds. She was also rumored to be the one who cast the spell on them, linking their souls for eternity.

He sat back in his chair and raised his eyebrows but did not respond.

She inclined her head. "I'm her great, great . . . let's just say, many 'greats' granddaughter."

Colin decided the old woman sitting across from him was clearly unbalanced.

"You are?" he asked out of politeness because he was not at all interested in her tale and was trying to figure out a way to get rid of her.

Quickly.

"Yes, Mr. Morgan. And I, like my mother and her mother and so on, back to Granny Esmeralda, am a witch."

Yes, Colin decided, clearly unbalanced.

He lost his patience but held on to his good manners.

Barely.

"Mrs. Byrne—"

She interrupted him.

"Did anything unusual happen to you yesterday, Mr. Morgan?"

Colin froze.

She was watching him knowingly. What she saw while regarding him answered her question.

"I was in your offices yesterday, as your secretary told you. I should apologize for what I did but I don't think there were any unpleasant consequences. It has been vowed down the line of Granny Esmeralda to do whatever needs to be done to—"

"What were you doing in my offices yesterday, Mrs. Byrne?" Colin cut into her rambling.

She fiddled with the straps on her handbag and hedged, "It was for a good cause." But when he leaned forward menacingly she rushed on, "I put a potion in your coffee."

She couldn't have surprised him more if she got up and danced a jig on his desk.

Then he realized what she was saying and the implications and he began to lose his temper.

His tone was low and even when he asked, "What kind of potion?"

"A magical potion to bring forward a past life, in your case the life of Royce Morgan," she explained.

He stared at her in disbelief.

There was, he knew, no such thing as magic.

She carried on, "For a time, a brief time, Royce, through you, would be in this world again. Using your body to exist in this time, he would be you but he would be you as Royce."

Colin felt his fury building as he stared at the woman and understanding dawned.

The kiss.

If this bizarre explanation was true then he had, as Royce, been in Sibyl's small chalet in her back garden most likely kissing who he thought was Beatrice.

And Sibyl had kissed him back.

You weren't yourself, Sibyl told him.

He *wasn't* himself. He was Royce fucking Morgan, kissing Sibyl. Kissing Sibyl in a way that made tears come to her eyes.

Colin felt a searing jealousy tear through him even though he knew it was ridiculous, because it had been him but also, it had not.

Fury he could no longer contain made Colin slowly stand.

Mrs. Byrne watched him, her calm never leaving her, and she stood as well.

"I had to do what I did," she defended herself. "You and Sibyl did not have a very good start and things were *not* progressing very smoothly."

His hands were clenched into fists but he held himself in check, though his voice was dangerous.

"Do not *ever* do that again, particularly, do not give such a . . ." he could barely make himself say it because he could barely believe it, "*potion* to Sibyl."

"Of course not! I wouldn't dream of it!" she cried, clearly affronted at the very thought.

"But you not only dreamt of it, you *did* it, to *me*," he shot back.

"You're a bit more difficult than Sibyl. She's a sweet woman," Mrs. Byrne replied calmly.

"I know that!" Colin thundered, and surprisingly, in the face of his fury, Marian Byrne smiled.

"Well, finally. I thought you thought we were a couple of con artists. Hardly complimentary of myself but certainly not Sibyl . . ."

He stopped listening to her, sat back down in his chair and buried his head in his hands, resting his elbows on his desk.

This, although he didn't know it, was a posture Mrs. Byrne was familiar with as she'd seen Sibyl do precisely the same thing.

His carefully controlled life had just turned over.

He was sleeping with a real-life avenging (if somewhat misguided) angel, willing to raise shotguns at abusive husbands and sell her body for old people.

This same angel was, apparently, the living reincarnation of the woman he, and his entire family, thought would magically enter his life at some point, not only to be his wife, but also to fulfil some longstanding legend of true love.

He was right then sitting across from a "witch" who thought she was, and could even be, the descendent of the famous Esmeralda Crane. And she'd given him a magical potion that evidently worked, very well.

He'd just decided to marry Sibyl, though he could not imagine, considering her spectacular temper, how she would react to all of this.

And in the midst of that, how he'd convince her to bind herself to him in holy matrimony at the end of it, considering what he'd done to her.

Mrs. Byrne cut into his thoughts by asking, "Mr. Morgan, are you quite all right?"

His head came up with a jerk.

"Mrs. Byrne," he started, making a quick decision, "what are you doing for dinner next Tuesday evening?"

Colin had finally broken her steady calm and she blinked in surprise.

"I . . . I . . . don't have any plans," she stammered.

"Good, then you'll be able to join my family, and Sibyl's, at dinner at Lacybourne."

She stared.

She smiled.

She accepted.

"I'd be delighted."

Chapter FOURTEEN

Real Dream Man

It was sing-along day at the Day Centre Pensioners' Club.

Not that the oldies ever sang along. Every once in a while the organist would play something they liked and they'd all sing but that only happened about once a month. They usually just talked and smoked but they always clapped for the hardworking organist after she'd finished a song.

Sibyl never got any work done on sing-along day. The organ was too distracting.

Today, she was simultaneously creating a flier that advertised the talent show while she was writing a letter to the Council to beg them to rewire the building.

Neither of these were going very well.

She was also considering the astonishing possibility that she was, and always had been, a witch with magical powers.

She was also thinking about what happened in her Summer House Girlie Laboratory with Colin, this she seemed to be able to concentrate on (with great focus).

Lastly, she was just plain old thinking about Colin and this she seemed to be able to concentrate on very well (with even *greater* focus).

And Royce, of course.

But mostly Colin.

Last night, she'd picked up the phone to call her mother (and then put it down) at least a half a dozen times. She desperately wanted to explore the idea of magic, dreams and premonitions but her mother would eat it up. She'd be too excited actually to help Sibyl make any sense of it and Sibyl desperately needed it to make sense.

Since she couldn't ask Mags and she couldn't look in the phonebook under "witch" or "magic" or "clairvoyants" to get a professional opinion, she was on her own.

This all so prayed on her mind, Sibyl was considering coming clean with Colin, telling him about her nightmare and all the dreams since.

But if she did, he'd leave her. He'd think she'd gone around the bend. Even though she had the feeling he liked being with her (and definitely knew he liked being in bed with her), she wasn't certain (indeed she was quite uncertain) that was strong enough to withstand her admitting to him she thought she had magical powers.

She shouldn't worry about him leaving her, but she did. Especially after how he'd treated her yesterday in that strange, sweet way.

And that was all there was to it. She couldn't deny it and she couldn't lie to herself about it, although she really wanted to.

She had months with him, and she decided she was going to hold on to them and then . . .

Well she'd worry about life after Colin when it happened.

"Hey, Billie," Jemma was at the door of her office, "come out here for a second."

Her friend's eyes were dancing and Sibyl smiled despite her unhappy thoughts.

"What is it?" she asked, following Jem into the Day Centre.

"Just come into the Day Centre, I'll be back." Jemma walked behind the huge tables that were all shoved together in the middle of the room.

The oldies sat around the tables to have their lunch and then lounged the hours after in conversation. Jem waved at the people who called out a greeting to her, gave Sibyl a gesture that told her to wait and sidled through the sliding doors.

Luckily, the organist had stopped and was basking in her weak, distracted applause.

"Sibyl, is that you?" Mrs. Griffith, sitting in her customary seat by the Day Centre doors, shouted over the clapping from across the room.

Sibyl walked down the tables, touching a few of the oldie's shoulders lightly while she passed, and when she arrived at the old lady's side she crouched down beside Mrs. Griffith.

Mrs. Griffith was another of her favorites (Sibyl had to admit, she had many favorites). She was a crotchety old bird who complained about everything, could go on for hours about her ill health and disliked everyone.

Except Sibyl.

And she liked Sibyl for one reason. Because Sibyl had brought her animals with her from America. Mrs. Griffith liked pets and once she heard Sibyl had not left hers behind, that was it. Sibyl was on the (very) short list written in Mrs. Griffith's Good Book.

Mrs. Griffith had the habit of grasping on to Sibyl's hand in a death grip whenever Sibyl talked to her.

This she did now.

"I heard your new lad is too busy to come visit us. This, Sibyl, is *not* a good sign," Mrs. Griffith announced in a dire tone.

Sibyl smiled despite the fact that Colin seemed everywhere, even here, where he should not be and replied, "Annie talks too much, Mrs. Griffith."

"Tell him he *must* come," Mrs. Griffith demanded. "I want to have a look at him. If I don't like him, I'm writing a letter to your mother."

Mrs. Griffith often threatened to write to Sibyl's mother, but, as yet, (to Sibyl's knowledge) had not done so even though she'd demanded to have and received Mags's address.

"I'll see what I can do," she promised her friend on an utter lie.

The last two words were drowned out by Jemma who was now standing at the sliding doors that led into the hall.

And as Sibyl straightened and looked her way, it appeared Jem was making an announcement.

Sibyl vaguely noticed that the door behind her opened and closed, but she, as well as all the oldies, was captivated by the usually very quiet Jemma Rashid making any announcement.

"Ladies and gentleman, I'm proud to present a sneak preview to Cadbury Community Centre's Talent Show. I give you, Flower, Katie, Emma and Cheryl, the Greasy Girls!"

And that was when the girls made their entrance wearing saddle shoes, bobby socks, poodle skirts and fluffy pink sweaters with black scarves wrapped around their necks. Their hair was pulled back in ponytails and they looked adorable. They stood giggling and posing and Sibyl felt pride sweep through her at the sight.

Sibyl, who could not sew, bought all the clothes, shoes and socks, and Jemma had made the skirts from the fabric and other bits and bobs that Sibyl also purchased.

And Sibyl stood, with Mrs. Griffith still clutching her hand in a death grip, and smiled, every bit of her pride showing.

All the oldies were shouting their compliments as Sibyl gently disengaged her hand from Mrs. Griffith and walked around the woman, clearing the tables and standing several feet in front of the door.

And as she did she clapped and shouted, "I love it! You girls look *great!*"

The girls noticed her and all came rushing forward jumping around her with excitement.

"Do you love it, Miss Sibyl? Do you think we look okay?" Katie asked.

"Oh, Katie, you look fabulous." Sibyl bent over and kissed the top of girl's head then straightened and caught Katie's chin in her hand. "I'm going to get you some redder than red lipstick and some blue eye shadow and the pinkest blusher I can find. It'll be perfect!" she announced, thinking Katie would go agog at the idea of makeup.

But Katie was no longer listening to her or, for that matter, looking at her. Instead, the girl was looking behind her.

Sibyl noticed belatedly that the excitement had died to a very strange (for the Day Centre), eerie quiet.

"Who's *he*?" Emma breathed, also peering behind Sibyl.

It was then Sibyl smelled it, a woodsy scent liberally spiked with cedar.

She whirled and there stood Colin, wearing a handsomely tailored dark suit and an expensive looking deep-lavender shirt opened at the collar. He looked like a movie star who had come on a Make-a-Wish errand, standing powerful and strong and exuding all of his sex appeal in the drab and worn (but cheerful) Day Centre.

"Colin!" she cried, her heart skipping three beats before it began racing like a wild thing.

What on earth was he doing here?

"Sibyl," he replied calmly, staring at her like . . . like, she didn't know. She couldn't put her finger on it but whatever "it" was made her stomach go funny, her knees go weak and her heart stop momentarily before bouncing around in her chest, out of control.

There was no other way to put it.

It was a Royce Look, pure and simple.

"What are you doing here?" she forced herself to voice her thought.

Before he could answer, Marianne, the Centre's bingo caller, shouted throatily from the back, "Billie, is that your young man?"

After voicing her question, Marianne collapsed into a fit of smoker's cough, and once she finished she sucked another drag off her ever-present cigarette.

Everyone was looking at Colin, at Sibyl, at both of them.

And Sibyl wanted to run. She wanted to scream. She wanted to know what the hell he was doing there.

This was not a part of their bargain. *This* was not to be touched by him. She needed *this* when he was gone, *not* memories of him here.

"Introduce him, Sibyl," Mrs. Griffith was demanding (loudly), twisting around in her chair to get a better look. "Don't keep us all waiting."

"It's about time he came to call!" Annie shouted, apparently just being informed that Colin was there.

Sibyl stood awkwardly, not knowing what to do. She noticed Jemma watching her carefully, ready to come to her aid should Sibyl make the slightest indication that she needed it.

Which, of course, she could not do.

No one could ever know.

Kyle and Tina had come in from the kitchen and were watching the unfolding drama with speculative eyes.

Sibyl cleared her throat.

"Everyone," she announced loudly, "this is Colin. Colin," she continued, feeling idiotic and throwing out her arm to encompass the room, "this is everyone."

A cacophony of greetings emerged from the room.

"Are these your girls?" Colin asked after he'd arrogantly inclined his head to the elderly assemblage.

His voice was quiet and his eyes were on the four girls who were staring at him as if he'd just stepped out of a movie screen.

"Um . . ." she started (bloody, *bloody* hell), "yes."

"I'm Colin," he introduced himself to the quartet.

"I'm Katie." Cheeky Katie didn't miss a trick and shot forward to shake his hand, a shake which Colin returned solemnly.

"Cheryl," Cheryl offered but she was not nearly as bold, though she wasn't going to be left out, thus no hand shake.

"Emma," definitely not bold, Emma said her name in a timid squeak and kept her distance.

Flower, however, was staring at Sibyl.

"Did you really call us 'your girls,' Miss Sibyl?" she asked breathlessly.

Sibyl looked at Flower who was staring at Sibyl with her heart in her eyes and Sibyl's own heart melted.

She forgot Colin (or, at least, ignored him) and crouched next to Flower. "You *are* my girls so of course I did."

Flower, who had no decent woman-figure in her life, save Jemma and Sibyl, threw herself in Sibyl's arms for a quick, embarrassed hug and then ran from the room.

The three other girls followed, trailing giggles.

Sibyl watched them go and wanted to take that opportunity to shove Colin out the door and scream at him at the top of her lungs but her torture was not complete.

"Come here, young man. I have a few things to ask you," Mrs. Griffith demanded imperiously.

"Don't do it," Sibyl hissed under her breath, straightening, but Colin simply cocked his head, regarding her with eyes filled with amusement and something warm and tender, something she had never seen before.

Something that made her bones feel like jelly.

And then he totally ignored her demand and strode toward Mrs. Griffith.

Sibyl counted to ten. After she did, she went up to twenty for good measure.

"Yes?" he said to older woman, looking down at her.

Mrs. Griffith looked up at him.

"You're tall," Mrs. Griffith announced, wanting him to crouch at her side but too proud to ask.

He didn't crouch and he also didn't reply. There was no need, she was stating the obvious.

Even though she didn't get her way, Mrs. Griffith persevered and she did this by snapping, "Do you have a good job?"

"I believe so, yes," Colin answered without hesitation.

"Do you have a healthy diet?" Mrs. Griffith fired off and Sibyl's eyes searched the ceiling, praying for deliverance.

"Not really, no," Colin replied.

Mrs. Griffith gave a short harrumph of displeasure at Colin's answer.

"When you go out, who pays for dinner, you or Sibyl?" she demanded to know.

"Me."

"Always?" she went on.

"Of course."

"Do you work hard?" Mrs. Griffith carried on with her mini-interrogation, undaunted by his short, uninformative answers.

"My mother thinks I do," Colin returned.

This was apparently a good response and, lightning quick, Mrs. Griffith made up her mind and turned to Sibyl saying, "He'll do."

"Thank you, Mrs. Griffith," Sibyl muttered, wanting a hole to open up in the floor and swallow her.

Colin was smiling one of his killer, white-flash smiles at Sibyl made all the worse by a hint of smugness.

When Mrs. Griffith turned back to him and caught his smile, she announced, "He'll *definitely* do."

And that was when Sibyl had had enough. She grabbed Colin's hand and started marching toward her office.

Surprisingly, he followed.

The Mistress of Luck was not smiling on her that day because as they passed Annie's chair, Annie's hand shot out as if guided by a mystical tractor beam because surely she couldn't see them and she caught Colin's forearm.

"Sibyl's my daughter," she announced in a very loud voice when Colin stopped and looked back at her.

He turned fully to the old lady, his brows rising. He was now holding Sibyl's hand (rather than the other way around, in other words, she couldn't get away) and he pulled her back to Annie.

"Is she?" Colin asked politely.

Annie didn't respond and Colin stood patiently watching her.

"She's mostly deaf," Sibyl whispered with a tug on his hand, which he ignored.

"Is she?" Colin asked, in a louder timbre but not exactly a loud voice.

"I'm Annie," she told him.

"I'm Colin," he returned.

"Children take care of you." Annie was on a roll but not making any sense whatsoever.

"Annie—" Sibyl began by shouting her name.

"That's why you're my daughter," Annie said to some point over Sibyl's shoulder. Then she guesstimated (badly) where Colin might be and declared dramatically, "I'm starting legal proceedings to adopt her. Tomorrow, I think, I haven't decided. She's going to be my adopted daughter because she takes care of me."

Sibyl's already racing heart started its rocket thrusters.

Colin didn't need to know this. Colin knew too much already.

Way too much.

"Oh, Annie . . ." she murmured, half with her heart in her throat, half horrified.

This time Colin crouched next to Annie.

"What does she do?" Colin asked, his voice still vibrating strongly enough for Annie to hear, and Sibyl wished she could pull him up and away, but she couldn't.

"She talks to me," Annie explained. "And she cleans my house and she gets me my favorite kind of custard. Then, when she puts things in the refrigerator, she always takes me there and puts my hand on everything so I'll know where to find it when I need something and I don't knock it on the floor, like I used to."

Colin was still holding Sibyl's hand and his seemed to contract spasmodically then it gentled.

Annie wasn't finished.

"I never had children but children are supposed to take care of you. That's why I'm going to adopt Sibyl. I can't adopt Jemma because she already has parents." She leaned forward conspiratorially. "Though I'd like to, she's a very nice girl too."

Tina came to the rescue by announcing the minibus was going to be there in five minutes and those who rode it would have to be ready.

Therefore Annie immediately lost interest in Colin in her haste to get prepared. The minibus driver didn't dally and he had no patience (the screaming jerk).

Sibyl seized her opportunity to drag Colin to her office, and once there she closed the door.

When she did, she whirled on him only to find him staring around with an expression that could only be described as extreme distaste.

"You work *here*?" he muttered, his voice mimicking his expression.

She ignored his question. She wasn't in a good mood and she had bigger fish to fry.

"What are you doing here?" she snapped angrily and his eyes cut to her.

"Sibyl—" he began, his voice patient.

"Don't you 'Sibyl' me. What are you doing here?" she demanded.

He came toward her but she backed away and he halted.

"This isn't *your* place, this is *my* place," she informed him hotly. "You aren't supposed to be here. How did you find out about this?"

Before he could answer a knock came at the door and Kyle poked his head in.

He looked at Sibyl then at Colin and asked, "All right, mate?"

Colin inclined his head.

Sibyl, feeling the bizarre need to act politely (for Kyle's sake), said, "Colin, this is Kyle. He's our caretaker. Kyle, this is Colin."

She didn't give Colin a role. Colin *had* no role that she'd share with anyone at the Centre.

"Colin, good to meet you, mate," Kyle greeted and his eyes shifted to Sibyl. "Bus's comin'," he announced.

The door closed again and Sibyl closed her eyes and muttered, "Bloody, *bloody* hell."

"Listen to me," Colin demanded but she opened her eyes, sent him a savage glare and interrupted him.

"I have to go help get the oldies on the bus. We'll talk later." She was walking to the door as she spoke but stopped, and then her glare turned murderous. "Unless there's something you require?"

He watched her closely for a moment, his expression unreadable then he shook his head.

Instead of leaving, like she should have done, she ranted, because that was what she did when her temper flared out of control.

"This isn't fair, this isn't right, this *isn't* a part of our bargain and you know it," she told him on an infuriated whisper.

"Come here," he ordered gently.

She stood where she was and continued glaring.

"Sibyl, come here." This was said in a tone that could not be defied.

She walked toward him but did it in a way that showed she didn't like it.

When she arrived close enough to Colin, his arm stole around her waist, and with his other hand he tipped her face up to look at him with a crooked finger under her chin.

"I was curious how you spent your days." His voice was low and soft and he was looking at her like he'd looked at her in the Centre.

To her dismay, and against her will, she felt her body react to it by relaxing.

She fought against her body but, it must be said, didn't entirely succeed with her struggle.

"I'm very angry with you," she announced in an effort to control her emotions.

"I can tell," he grinned, completely unaffected by her words.

She sought refuge in fury.

"Don't you grin at me, Colin Morgan. You haven't heard the last of this."

With that, for her sanity (and for the oldies), she tore free of his arm and stalked out of the office.

Several of the oldies were still packing up but she could see the minibus was already there and some of them were getting panicked.

Colin had followed her and she was helping Marianne pack up her cigarettes, lighter and a variety of napkin-wrapped food she hadn't eaten at lunch and would consume for dinner (Tina always gave Marianne a little extra because Marianne didn't have much and would skip dinner if she didn't).

Sibyl took Marianne's heavy carrier bag filled with whatever Marianne (or any of the oldies, most of them seemed to lug around bulky carrier bags) carried with her all the time, turned around and saw Colin staring out the windows at the bus.

"Make yourself useful," she ordered grumpily and began to hand him the carrier bag, but uncharacteristically impolitely he didn't take it and she lifted her eyes to his face.

Now he was staring out the window and whatever he saw made the warm, tender expression he was wearing moments ago fade to one of complete fury.

Then he turned without a word and, with long, quick, ground-eating strides, headed for the door.

She whirled to see what had made him react in such a way and saw Annie trying to alight into the bus.

Annie, blind and reaching, was not having a good time of it and all the while the minibus driver stood not two feet away, smoking a roll up and not assisting her, even though it was clear Annie was having trouble.

Sibyl, still carrying Marianne's bag, ran after Colin. She exited the door in time to see Annie catch her foot on the step of the bus and stumble. Her heart tripping in alarm, Sibyl sucked in her breath just as Annie righted herself at the last minute.

Kyle was at the back loading a folded wheelchair so he couldn't see what was happening.

The minibus driver flicked his butt into the grass.

"What in bloody hell is going on here?" Colin demanded while Sibyl raced up behind him.

At his deep, angry voice, most jumped and everyone turned to stare

"Everyone, get off the bus," Colin ordered.

Sibyl's mouth dropped open in shock but before she could say anything, Colin turned to the driver.

"What's your name?" he demanded in his smooth, even tone that said, in about two seconds, the driver was about to have Colin's fist in his face.

"Who're you?" The driver, clearly not that bright, didn't read Colin's tone.

"I said, *what's your goddamned name*?" Colin roared.

Sibyl (and pretty much every one else) jumped again. She quickly put down Marianne's bag and ran to help Annie away from the minibus.

"Why'd you wanna know?" the driver asked on a mini-sneer.

"I want to know," Colin enunciated every word with perfect clarity, "because I'll need to be certain I get the right man sacked."

The minibus driver stared at Colin goggle-eyed and everyone gasped (including Sibyl).

"You can't get me sacked!" the driver snapped.

"Would you like to bet?" Colin's voice was still smooth, dangerous and had a very sharp edge. "Did you not see that woman struggling to get into the bus?" he demanded.

The minibus driver shrugged, thinking it was a good idea to throw fuel on the fire. "Not my job."

"You're not only incompetent, you're negligent. You drive a bus for elderly people," Colin informed him. "That *makes* it your job."

"Have you read my job description?" This time the driver outright sneered. "I don't think so."

"Your job description will be changed by five o'clock tomorrow night. Unfortunately, you won't be *in* the job to see it." That said, Colin turned his back on the driver and said to Sibyl, "Get everyone out of the bus."

Regardless of the fact that his eyes were blazing, carefully, Sibyl said, "Colin, this is their only way home. It would take Kyle and I—"

While she was talking, he pulled his mobile out of his jacket, engaged it and jabbed twice at the screen.

Once he'd done this, he spoke into it.

"Mandy, get me . . ." He surveyed the crowd that was now exiting the minibus, gathering around and staring at Colin with avid fascination. "Fifteen taxis to the Community Centre at Cadbury Council Estate in Weston. Right now. Have them do a docket and bill it to us." He paused. "Yes. Right *now*."

At his deadly tone, Sibyl felt a chill go down her spine just as she felt a soft flutter in her heart.

He disengaged the phone.

"Don't bother me, mate. Makes my afternoon easier," the minibus driver remarked.

Colin looked over his shoulder at him. "Get used to it. You're going to have a great deal of free time on your hands."

Something about the way he said it made pretty much everyone believe it, except those who couldn't hear what was going on, but when they were told, *they* believed it too.

"Think you're the big man, get me sacked. *She* couldn't get me sacked," the minibus driver taunted, making it known he most definitely did not have a very high IQ *or* enough instinct to last an hour in the wild.

Colin slowly turned back to the man, so slowly it was crystal clear he was doing so to keep himself in rigid control.

Sibyl held her breath.

When he spoke again, Colin's voice was as rigidly controlled as his body.

"If you ever get the chance again, which you will not, you will refer to her as Miss Godwin. And *Miss Godwin* doesn't know seventeen councillors on North Somerset Council, all of whom I'll be having my staff calling in five minutes and telling about *you*. If they don't hand me your job by nine o'clock tomorrow morning, I'll have every paper, TV and radio station in Weston and Bristol all over this estate. The councillors will undoubtedly listen at that point as they won't want to be the ones who allowed an incompetent, uncaring, thoughtless bastard to look after their community's grandparents."

After this stunning declaration, Mrs. Griffith shouted, "I know two councillors and I'm calling them in five minutes too!"

"I know three!" a gentleman (another one of Sibyl's favorites) named Gilbert called.

"I don't know any but I'm calling them anyway," Marianne yelled.

Before the oldies jumped the minibus driver and brained him with their carrier bags, Kyle, ever the peacekeeper, snapped open the now unloaded wheelchair and shouted, "All right, everyone back into the Centre!"

Colin engaged his mobile, dialed his two numbers again and said, "Mandy, I want you and every administrator on staff to call every North Somerset Councillor in my Rolodex and tell them . . ."

Sibyl didn't wait to hear what he said. She helped Annie to the Centre, scooping up Marianne's carrier bag along the way, all the while her mind whirling in an attempt to process what had just occurred.

Did Colin just make a scene in front of the Day Centre, battling her hated minibus driver nemesis and conquering him for a bunch of elderly people he didn't even know?

She couldn't quite believe it. She wanted to but she couldn't.

And this was because *this* was the kind of stuff a dream man was made of.

And, because of what she'd done and who she was to him, Sibyl had lost all hopes of ever being his dream woman.

Dazed, she helped everyone settle back into the Centre, vaguely noticing they were all watching her closely.

She didn't pay attention.

Instead, she was thinking there would be, soon, a life without Colin and not always, but increasingly often, he acted like her dream man.

Most especially that day.

But there was nothing she could do about the day when her life would be without Colin.

In the meantime, however, it was a life *with* Colin, and in those moments she saw him tearing into her evil nemesis she knew that she was going to make the most of every damned second of the time she had.

FOURTEEN (COLIN HAD made a *slight* error in counting) oldies, Kyle, Tina, Jemma and four ten-year-old girls all crowded around the big windows that looked out on the patch of worn grass in front of the Day Centre.

They saw their adored, beautiful, American girl wander across the grass slowly toward the tall, dark, broad-shouldered, handsome man who was talking angrily on his mobile.

They watched as she approached him, stood in front of him toe to toe, then she leaned in and rested the top of her head against his chest, placing her hands lightly on either side of his waist.

They watched, too, as he slid one hand up her spine to curl it around the back of her neck.

He pulled the phone from his ear and bent his dark head to kiss her honey one.

Then he put the phone back to his ear and kept talking.

Everyone in the room decided they made a striking couple and felt, considering what they knew about Sibyl and what they'd seen of her man, that they were the perfect match.

"I think we know who our anonymous donor is," Tina whispered to her husband and Kyle nodded.

"I'm writing to her mother," Mrs. Griffith declared.

"I'm going to adopt *him* too," Annie shouted.

And then fifteen taxis started arriving at the Centre.

Chapter FIFTEEN

Tranquillizer Dart

Colin was in his office on his phone.

He'd gone back to Bristol after visiting Sibyl at the Community Centre to return phone calls and make certain the incredible ass who drove the minibus was indeed, sacked (which, as Colin threatened, a number of councillors assured him, he would be, first thing in the morning).

Once he'd heard the news from the bus driver's line manager directly, Colin felt a strange, intensely pleasant sense of satisfaction.

He didn't question it, he didn't have time. He had other things to do.

That task completed, Colin also phoned a surveyor to have a look at the Community Centre as a whole. From what he could see, the place was a fire trap, a health hazard and needed significant renovations.

Not to mention better furniture.

And, likely, fumigation.

And finally, he called a contractor, told him to go to the Centre and give Colin a quote on how much it would cost to build an extension so Sibyl could have a decent office, one that didn't look like a salvage yard.

All of this Colin was going to finance and he didn't care how much it cost.

It was ridiculous that those people were forced to spend their time in that dilapidated wreck, and he certainly wasn't going to allow Sibyl to do so.

He'd had a few words with the councillors about that as well.

He wished, two weeks ago, when she'd slapped the briefcase shut on the fifty thousand pounds, that she'd told him then what the money was for.

However, he had to admit, he probably wouldn't have believed her.

She was, on the whole, quite unbelievable.

He'd thought that before Robert Fitzwilliam had told him about her. This feeling solidified after witnessing her in her element at the Centre. He could still see the look of shining adoration in "her girls" eyes as they stared at her and he could hear the esteem in the pensioners' voices when they spoke to her.

He finished his call, quickly scanned some correspondence that Mandy had left for him to sign and tried not to think of how he felt when Sibyl had rested her head against his chest.

Except for the night she'd had her nightmare and the morning when she'd attacked him because he was caressing her "sensitive spot," she rarely touched him of her own volition.

And Colin liked it when she did. Very much.

Further, there was something nearly precious about the feeling that he'd done something she approved of.

With a good deal of effort, he'd finally convinced his mother and sister to leave Lacybourne and come back next week when he was ready to introduce them to Sibyl and her family.

They were both beside themselves with the idea of a walking, talking American Godwin wandering around Clevedon. Not to mention the fact that she was in Colin's life. They didn't even know yet what she looked like, and he hadn't told them or they would never have left Lacybourne. They would have hunted her down and forced a Morgan Family heirloom ring on her finger, he had no doubts about that.

Colin had a great deal of work ahead of him winning Sibyl's trust. His meddling mother and equally troublesome sister would likely disrupt his many, varied, rather complicated and extraordinarily fragile plans.

Colin felt (quite rightly) that he'd made great strides that day and that hadn't even been part of his plan. He found after talking with Robert and Mrs. Byrne that he couldn't wait a moment longer to see her, which was the only reason he'd gone to the Centre.

Colin's reaction regarding the minibus driver was instinctive. When he looked out the window at the elderly blind woman who wanted to adopt Sibyl trying to alight while the bastard stood, disinterested and smoking a cigarette, he'd temporarily lost his mind. He hadn't intentionally gone charging in to score points, although he was happy to accept them if they were a means to his desired end. He'd help every blind lady he encountered if it meant he got what he wanted.

It only made Colin all the more satisfied that the person who had inadvertently pushed Sibyl into selling her body was now to be punished, regardless if the driver knew his flagrant negligence had cost Colin weeks in winning Sibyl and cost Sibyl something even more dear.

But he needed Sibyl right where he wanted her before she learned of Royce and Beatrice, magic and myth, his lifelong knowledge of it, her place in it and especially him keeping it from her. She was likely to lose her temper (justifiably) and Sibyl's temper, he'd learned, once lost, was rather difficult to get under control.

His mobile rang and he glanced at it distractedly not wishing to talk to another North Somerset councilor. He saw Sibyl's name on the screen.

He stared at his phone.

She'd never phoned him. Not once.

He grabbed it immediately and took the call.

"Sibyl," he greeted.

There was no response but he could hear her breathing. At this oddity (oddities being nothing new with Sibyl), he patiently repeated himself, calling her name.

"Colin," she whispered.

His back instantly straightened at the tone of her voice. It was tremulous and she sounded frightened.

"What's happened?" he asked.

"Colin," he heard a catch in her voice, "someone's been in my house."

Before she was done speaking, he was already walking toward the door and a queer sensation seized him, something akin to panic.

"Where are you?" he demanded.

"Sitting outside, with Mallory."

"Have you called the police?"

There was a pause. "No, I didn't think of that." Now she sounded both exasperated and frightened.

Colin found Sibyl's frequent absentmindedness both amusing and annoying. Especially now, with the exception that now he didn't find it amusing.

"Call them," he ordered as he exited his office and walked right past Mandy without looking at her.

"Colin, I think," she hesitated and then her voice dropped to a whisper, "oh my goddess, I think they've done something to Mallory."

He was surprised at his strong reaction to the thought that something had happened to her dog. It felt like someone had kicked him in the stomach.

"Why?" he asked cautiously, jogging down the stairs.

"He's lying here, not moving, not awake. He's breathing and I feel a heartbeat but he won't wake up no matter what I do."

"Sibyl, call the police," Colin ordered. "I'll be there in fifteen minutes."

When he heard her shaky, "Okay," he rang off and lengthened his strides.

It took twenty-five minutes, on a good day when the traffic gods were smiling, to get to Sibyl's house.

That day, the traffic gods were unhappy and Colin still made it there in fifteen.

There were three police cars outside her house as he pulled up.

After he'd exited his car, he saw Sibyl talking to five officers, all men, all hovering around her like she was a female rock god and they were her male groupies.

This was not surprising considering she looked like a rock star with her hair a shower of golden tangles. She was wearing a long, full, chocolate-brown skirt with a heavy, silver-looped belt hanging low on her hips. She accompanied this with her red cowboy boots and a bright red, long-sleeved T-shirt with a collar so wide it dipped off one shoulder.

At the sight of Sibyl and her law-enforcing entourage, Colin kept hold of his temper by a thread, but he managed this only because Sibyl noticed him and immediately ran to him.

When she reached him, she threw herself at him so forcefully it rocked him back on a foot.

This was the third time she'd touched him affectionately of her own volition (at that precise moment, he began counting).

She wrapped her arms around him, tucked her head under his chin and cried into his lapel. "Colin! Someone shot Mallory with a tranquilizer dart!"

She imparted this extraordinary fact on Colin with a voice that was part furious, part incredulous and part scared.

Colin's arms went around her and he automatically stroked her back and he did this while all the police were staring at them like they were a piece of performance art.

Colin lost patience and barked, "Don't you have something to do?"

The police all jerked into motion but Sibyl seemed not to notice his angry outburst. She leaned back against his arm and peered up at him, a heartbreaking look in her very confused hazel eyes.

"Who would *do* something like that?"

He looked down at her pale, beautiful face and shook his head in answer because, of course, he had no idea who would do something like that and he understood now that Sibyl *definitely* wouldn't know.

At that moment, he finally noticed Mallory lying on his side close to the entry of the house, his big dog body completely still.

Colin had never seen the dog when he at least didn't thump his tail and he felt something slice through his gut at the sight.

He carefully pulled out of her embrace, and linking his fingers in hers he guided her over to Mallory. Once there, he crouched down and felt the dog's chest, noting a strong heartbeat and steady breathing.

Other than that, the dog was motionless and, from far away, could even appear dead. Colin couldn't imagine the shock that Sibyl'd had when she arrived home.

"Christ," he muttered as he absently stroked the dog's head, fury beginning to burn slowly in him.

"They called a vet to have a look at him. He hasn't moved a muscle in ages. I'm kinda used to Mallory being relatively motionless but this is terrifying," she told him, her voice still shaky.

Colin made no comment as he watched a police officer come toward them as the other four stayed where they were, pretending to be busy but still staring at Sibyl.

"And who might you be, sir?" the officer asked when he arrived.

"I'm her boyfriend."

He felt ridiculous saying it but not after he heard Sibyl's swift intake of breath, noted her quick, round-eyed glance and, most especially, when he caught the look of deep disappointment that passed across the policeman's face.

"Oh, right." He made an effort at recovery while Colin straightened, put his arm possessively around Sibyl and pulled her against his side, a gesture which made his role in her life *perfectly* understood. "There appears to have been a break-in," the policeman continued.

"I already know that," Colin informed him.

"And the dog has been shot by a tranquillizer dart."

"I already know that too," Colin said, his tone making it crystal clear his patience was quickly ebbing and that was not a good thing. "Can you tell me something I don't know?"

The policeman shifted uncomfortably under Colin's irate glare, belatedly, but correctly, assessing that Colin was not someone to be trifled with.

"We just made it to the scene a few minutes ago. We've ascertained there's no threat. We have an officer checking the house now to see if there was anything obviously stolen, forced entry, that kind of thing."

"Wouldn't that go faster if all *five* of the officers standing out here checked the house?" Colin suggested sarcastically, inclining his head to their audience.

"Um . . . right," the officer agreed, and after a glance at Sibyl and a brief hesitation he trotted off to his colleagues who disbursed, some going to their cars, others going into the house.

Colin watched the sudden action and muttered with distracted irritation to Sibyl, "You're too damned beautiful for your own good."

When he finally swung his gaze to her, she was staring at him with eyes no longer hazel, but a warm, liquid sherry and her mouth was parted slightly in surprise. Then, as if wishing to hide her response to his comment, she turned in his arm and pressed herself against him, burying her face in his chest.

That was when he felt she was shaking.

"I can't believe someone shot my dog," she whispered.

His fury built and spread as his free hand went to her hair and stroked the heavy mass.

There was nothing to say, he couldn't believe it either.

They stood that way for some time. The longer they did so, Colin found the fury flowed out of him and he became rather contented. Sibyl, however, continued to tremble until his hand at her hair stroked the tremors away. Minutes ticked by then another officer exited the house and approached them.

"Seems like it's just vandals," he informed them upon his arrival. "We'll have to ask Miss Godwin to walk through the house but the stereo's still there, there's some jewelry sitting on the chest of drawers, untouched. There have been some pillows destroyed, feathers everywhere. Some crockery broken. No real damage."

"Has this happened before?" Colin asked.

"What, sir?" This officer, more intelligent, was the one who had been checking the house when Colin arrived as Colin hadn't seen him before.

"This kind of thing at another house in the area, tranquillizer darts, vandalism?" Colin prompted.

"No, nothing." The officer shook his head. "I'll need to take Miss Godwin through to see if she can determine if anything's missing."

It was then that Mallory made a move, a slight lift of his head then it fell again. Instantly Sibyl dropped to her knees, pulled the dog's head in her lap and started murmuring comfortingly as she stroked his soft, black and beige head.

Colin crouched beside her and muttered gently, "Sibyl, go with the officer. I'll look after Mallory."

She lifted her sherry eyes to him and asked, "You promise not to leave his side?"

He stared directly in her eyes and said quietly, "I promise."

She nodded and, with obvious reluctance, she left with the policeman. As promised, Colin stayed crouched by the dog who was waking, just not very quickly.

While Sibyl was inside, another police car came up to the house, possibly unloading lab men, or, more likely, a new set of groupies called in to have a look at Sibyl. Then another car came up the drive but this was not a police car. Colin watched as it stopped with a dramatic shower of gravel and then Marian Byrne came flying out.

She ran toward Colin, her face a mask of worry.

"Where's Sibyl?" she demanded to know by way of greeting.

"Mrs. Byrne, what are you doing here?" Colin asked, straightening from his crouch.

Mrs. Byrne didn't answer.

Instead, when she took in the dog, she cried, "What's happened to Mallory?"

"He was shot with a tranquillizer dart," Colin replied.

Mrs. Byrne gasped, her hand flying to her throat in surprise. "What on earth?" She breathed then asked more forcefully, "For heaven's sake why?"

"We don't know."

"Is he going to be all right? Is *Sibyl* all right?"

"A vet is coming to look at Mallory," Colin responded. "Sibyl's in the house, checking to see if anything was stolen."

"So she's fine?" Mrs. Byrne queried, her face still troubled.

"Yes, shaken but fine. What are you doing here?"

"I was . . ." she looked back at her car then turned to Colin again, "baking for a bake sale. I have a Victoria sponge. Sibyl loves Victoria sponge so I made her one especially." Her tone was odd in the way that any discussion about Victoria sponge in the presence of a bizarrely tranquillized dog and four police vehicles would be odd.

At that point, Colin noticed Sibyl's cat daintily picking its way through the grass towards them as if grass was a ground cover far beneath his lofty pedigree and he would prefer to be treading on velvet. He made it to one of the flagstones surrounded by cushions of turf that created a winding path from the drive to the front door and stopped, sat and swung his tail in a wide sweep. He stared at Mallory with an expression that Colin could swear communicated his disdain that the dog had put himself in the way of a dart.

"It's the dark soul," Mrs. Byrne whispered.

"I'm sorry?" Colin asked, his attention going back to her.

She moved forward and put her hand on his arm. "Colin, dear, someone's following Sibyl. I saw them."

Colin's eyes narrowed on her face, vaguely wondering when his status to her had elevated to being her "dear." He was also thinking about what Robert Fitzwilliam said that morning.

"Who?" he inquired. "Did you see him?"

"No, I just caught a movement when I was, er—"

"Following us yourself?" Colin finished for her.

"Well," her eyes widened at his comment and then she said guiltily, "yes. It *is* my job as Granny Esmeralda's descendent to look after you, you know," she defended herself and then hurried on before Colin could speak. "But it's the dark soul, I know it, I felt it. Destiny is against you—"

"Mrs. Byrne!" Sibyl was at the door and she came toward them, stopping only to scoop up Bran, who gave a mew of righteous protest at the indignity. "What are you doing here?"

"I baked you a Victoria sponge," Mrs. Byrne told her after Sibyl gave her an awkward embrace considering the cat.

"Oh, Mrs. Byrne. That is *so* sweet."

The intelligent officer had followed her and was taking in this bizarre exchange with a disbelieving expression on his face that mirrored exactly what Colin felt.

"Miss Godwin can't find anything missing," he told Colin. "We'll be a while and the vet is nearly here. She can't spend the night here, the door needs a new lock, the last one looked approximately four hundred years old so wasn't much of a deterrent. It was easily broken."

Instantly, Mrs. Byrne offered, "You can stay with me, dear."

"She's staying at Lacybourne," Colin put in and ignored Sibyl's stunned eyes flying to his face.

To hide her reaction, she dropped the cat who ran off without hesitation, clearly this scene was beneath him, and bent over Mallory who was now struggling to sit up.

Colin went on, "Mrs. Byrne, can you take Sibyl for something to eat? I'll wait here for the vet and then bring Mallory to Lacybourne with me. I'll leave when the police are finished. I'll phone and ask Mrs. Manning to leave the back door open so you can get in that way."

"Colin, I couldn't eat anything—" Sibyl started to say but Mrs. Byrne interrupted her.

"I suppose that the Great Hall is still being, er . . . done up, so we shouldn't go in there, is that the case?" Mrs. Byrne asked mysteriously.

Colin stared at her nonplussed and she continued.

"You know, *the portraits* being cleaned. That type of thing."

She was a sly old fox, Colin thought as he caught on and nodded.

"Yes, avoid the Great Hall if you would," he muttered.

Sibyl watched this exchange mutely with a befuddled expression then she gave Mallory's dazed head a scratch and stood.

Before she moved away, Colin pulled her to him for a quick kiss and then commanded gently, "Go, pack a bag and then have something to eat. I'll meet you at Lacybourne."

She nodded and, without a word, walked back into her cottage, Mrs. Byrne trailing behind.

Shortly after they left the vet came and declared Mallory fine. The dog was unsteady on his feet but it was only a shade worse than normal as he wasn't the most graceful of canines at the best of times.

While he waited for the police to finish, Colin considered the attractive idea of what it meant that Sibyl had phoned him first. That she had phoned *him* before any of her friends at the Centre or any of the nameless, faceless people he did not know that must inhabit her life in

England. She'd even phoned him before she'd phoned the police.

He decided to take this as a good sign.

Colin exchanged his, rather than Sibyl's, contact information with the police, deliberately misleading them as to the nature of their relationship. It wasn't exactly a lie, as they *would* be getting married soon. It was just that Sibyl didn't know that yet.

The police were preparing to leave when his mobile rang again.

Sibyl's name was on the display.

"Sibyl," he said in greeting.

"Colin, I'm ordering you a curry. What do you like?"

"I'll find something at home."

There was a pause then Sibyl said quietly, "Colin, would you please just tell me what kind of curry you like?"

Something about her soft tone told him she was not exasperated but curious. She was finally asking him something personal about himself and it was about what kind of Indian food he preferred.

"Lamb vindaloo," he answered shortly.

She gave a faint laugh and whispered, "Of course, vindaloo," before she rang off.

After the police left, he checked that the house was secured, or as secure as it could be. Then, once he had the big, groggy dog in his car, he went home.

They were there before him and he found them in his huge kitchen drinking tea as if they did it every night of their lives. Or, at least, Mrs. Byrne was drinking tea. Colin saw the yellow box with flowers and Oriental writing on it and smelled the pungent, weird aroma and knew that Sibyl was drinking the Asian organic hot drink she sipped on a frequent basis.

Whatever it smelled like, if he kissed her after she drank it, she tasted of flowers.

Sibyl started when she saw him and then ran to him then she ran right past him and Colin was, for the first time in his life, upstaged by a dog.

"Mallory!" she cried, crouching low, and gave her dog a hug and a kiss on his head.

In turn, Mallory gave her cheek a sloppy lash before the dog's backside collapsed as if he could hold it up no more. He sat there, looking mystified and a slim, glistening line of drool slid off his lip only to hang there in suspended animation.

"Let's get you cleaned up," Sibyl told the dog and Colin was relieved to hear amused affection rather than worry in her voice.

As Mrs. Byrne prepared Colin's food, Sibyl wiped the dog's mouth with a paper towel with an efficiency borne of years of practice. For some bizarre reason, Colin found this act fascinating.

Once Colin was eating, standing in front of his kitchen sink with his hips resting against the counter, Mrs. Byrne announced, "I must be going. It's terribly late. Sibyl, tell me if you learn anything about what happened." She gave them a look that encompassed them both and she looked pleased with her handiwork as, weeks ago, she'd attempted to orchestrate exactly this scene. She glanced at the counter where Colin belatedly noticed a cake stood. "Enjoy the sponge."

And with that she was gone.

He watched Sibyl clean out the teacups as he finished his food.

"There's a note and an envelope on the counter for you," she told him.

He threw the food carton in the rubbish bin and noticed that Mandy had couriered the correspondence he'd left behind when he went to see to Sibyl. Mandy had written an unhappy note about how the letters were supposed to be in first class post *today* but if he didn't *mind* seeing to them *tonight*, she'd have them *couriered* first thing *tomorrow*. This emphasis was achieved through dramatic use of underlining. He might have been annoyed if Mandy wasn't so efficient, and more importantly Sibyl wasn't in his kitchen rinsing out teacups.

"I've some work to see to. Do you have something to do?" he asked Sibyl, tearing open the envelope.

"I've brought a book," she replied, watching him.

She seemed guarded and it dawned on him that she didn't have the best memories of Lacybourne. Considering this dilemma, Colin decided to act business as usual in an effort to curtail any unpleasant emotions she might have considering her already difficult night and her unhappy memories of his home.

"Good, you can read in the study while I finish this."

She nodded then went to her bag which was sitting by the entry to the back stairwell, undoubtedly Mrs. Byrne's gentle reminder not to use the staircase in the Great Hall, and pulled out a book.

Colin led the way to the study and Sibyl and Mallory followed him. He counted it as a good sign that Mallory only ran into the wall once on their short journey.

He settled behind his desk while Sibyl sat on the couch in front of the enormous fireplace, looking around with obvious interest.

"I'll give you a tour of the house another time," he offered, watching her. "These were meant to be in today's post."

She hid her interest in the room and said quickly, "That's okay. I don't need a tour." Her eyes dropped to his work and she finished on a whisper, "I'm sorry that I took you from work."

He let her first comment go. She'd eventually have to have a tour, considering it would one day be her home, but it was highly precipitous to mention that at this juncture.

To her second comment, he replied softly, not taking his eyes from hers, "I'm not sorry."

At his words, she pulled her lips between her teeth, but as she did this she stared at him inquisitively as if she didn't know quite what to make of him before tearing her eyes away.

Mallory put his head in her lap as she sat then the dog lost his battle with his lethargy and his forepaws slid forward until he was lying down. Sibyl opened her book and Colin turned his attention to his papers.

A half an hour later when he was done, he glanced at her again to see she was staring with unfocused eyes at the wall, her book in her hand which was resting on the couch. He could see her thumb was curled inside, holding her place.

"Sibyl?"

He'd startled her and she jumped, swinging her eyes to him.

And when her eyes hit his, she asked, apropos of nothing, "Someone shot my dog and attacked my toss pillows. How bizarre is that?"

He set his finished work aside, got up, walked around the desk and stood before her.

"Get up, Sibyl," he ordered quietly.

She flipped her book face down on the couch and rose immediately, emitting a deep, weary and slightly mutinous sigh. Mallory, whose head was resting on his paws, shifted it so it was resting on Colin's shoes.

Colin ignored the dog as Sibyl came within touching distance and he pulled her forward so she was leaning into him. Then he lifted his hands to her hair, gathered the thick, tawny mass and lifted it away from her neck. Once he'd accomplished that feat, considering Sibyl had a great deal of hair, he bent forward and kissed her neck where it met her shoulder.

"Your hair is remarkably heavy," he murmured against her skin in an effort to take her mind away from tranquillizer darts and assaulted toss pillows.

He felt her relax into him and gladly took on more of her weight. His body pleasantly reacted to her full breasts pressed against his chest but what she said next chased away all evidence of the heat she was producing.

"I know. It gives me headaches sometimes, pulls at my scalp."

Christ, he was an ass.

He felt his body become fixed, his hands freezing in position as they held the weight of her hair. Then he dropped it and buried his face in her neck as he pulled her closer with his arms tightly wrapped around her. She smelled of something he could not name, a complex flowery scent that was both delicate and alluring.

At that moment he could barely stand himself and couldn't imagine how she could.

"I'm rescinding one of the rules," he murmured against her neck, his voice to his own ears strangely hoarse.

It was her turn to go still. "What?"

He lifted his head and looked down at her.

"You can wear your hair however you want," he told her quietly and watched in sheer fascination as her hazel eyes melted liquid to sherry within an instant.

Before she could respond, he announced, "We're going to bed."

IT WAS MUCH later, indeed it was the dead of night, when Colin heard the phone ringing.

When he woke he was surprised to feel that Sibyl was snuggled against his side, her legs tangled with his. Until that night she always pulled away and slept with her back to him. Now, her arm was resting on his chest, crooked so that her elbow was at his stomach and her hand was dead center. Her head was on his shoulder and he could feel soft tendrils of her hair everywhere.

He shifted slowly as he felt her stir, reached out to grab the phone and put it to his ear.

Before Colin could speak, he heard a man's voice say, "Next time I shoot, it won't be the dog and it won't be a tranquillizer. Tonight's your last night with her. Tomorrow, you say goodbye and you won't see Sibyl Godwin again."

The phone went dead in his hand.

He lay stock still as the unfamiliar and immensely uncomfortable sensation of dread chased through his body, this feeling fleeting, being replaced by anger.

He felt Sibyl's head lift from his shoulder. "Colin?"

Her voice was husky with sleep and his arm, which was wrapped around her with his hand resting on her hip, tightened reflexively.

"Who was it?" she asked.

"Wrong number," Colin lied as he replaced the phone, forcing his body to relax.

Then he remembered.

It's the dark soul, Mrs. Byrne had said and Colin's body went back to tight.

Sibyl's hand moved from his chest to encircle his waist and she pressed her soft, warmth closer to his side.

"Are you cold?" Her voice was still husky and without waiting for an answer, her hand moved to pull the covers up over her shoulder and his chest. It returned to its place around his waist as her weight settled into him and he knew she was again sleeping.

She was already responding to him, he knew.

This was very good, he knew.

But if indeed he was Royce Morgan's reincarnation, he was never meant to have her.

Though, he *did* have her in a way that Royce had never had Beatrice, there was something missing. Something that made Colin uncomfortable, something that he and Sibyl needed to find before the curse of star-crossed lovers was lifted, if it even existed.

No one ever knew who killed Royce and Beatrice Morgan or why.

The theory was it was an enemy of Royce's. He'd made many of them with his exploits and successes on a variety of bloody battlefields.

Myth said that the dark soul would follow them, would stop them through eternity from finding each other or finding whatever it was that would forever protect them and break the curse.

And Mrs. Byrne believed the dark soul was watching them.

Colin didn't believe in lore, myth, magic and curses and he certainly didn't believe in dark souls coasting through eternity on vengeance.

But he took middle-of-the-night threatening phone calls after an attack on a dog and a break-in deadly seriously.

What Colin knew was that he hadn't lived a sainted life, as, apparently, the misguided angel who was lying pressed to his side had. Colin had made people angry, he'd made enemies—enemies who might use Sibyl to get to him.

All Colin knew was that Robert Fitzwilliam said the same thing Mrs. Byrne had said—that someone was watching them. It now became apparent that someone had tried to run them down with a car. And now someone had shot Sibyl's dog and ransacked her cottage. All of this, for what seemed like no apparent reason at the time, but now Colin thought it was to warn him.

Colin came to a decision.

Tomorrow, Colin would call Robert Fitzwilliam and task the man with watching Sibyl, protecting her and finding out who was behind these plots while Colin kept steady at his task of winning her.

Chapter SIXTEEN

Hope

"It's rather nice of your young man to send a limousine," Bertie Godwin told his eldest daughter.

Sibyl stared at her father and used every ounce of willpower not to scream at the top of her lungs.

Sibyl Jezebel Godwin was in a carefully controlled rage. This was unprecedented, considering that Sibyl's rages were usually considerably uncontrolled.

However, yesterday while she was standing outside customs in Terminal 4 at Heathrow Airport waiting for her parents to come through the doors, her mobile had rung.

It was Colin.

After she'd answered, without even so much as saying hello, he commanded, "I want you and your parents to come to Lacybourne for dinner tomorrow night."

Sibyl felt her heart constrict painfully and she stared unseeing at the people marching tiredly through the doors of arrival dragging their luggage behind them as she listened to Colin's inconceivable order.

"Please tell me you aren't serious," she'd breathed.

For the last week things had been different between them. Entirely different. So much so that part of her feared her magical powers were forcing Colin away and bringing Royce out of the dream world and into the real.

But this order was from the Old Colin.

Their relationship was temporary. She knew that. He knew that.

Why on the goddess's green earth would he want to meet her parents?

It was cruel.

He interrupted her careening thoughts. "I'm very serious."

"Is this an order?" she asked, her voice sharp.

He didn't hesitate. "Yes."

Her breath, and her sharpness, went out of her.

"Why?" she whispered, that one word, she hoped over the miles, expressed the many nuances of her question.

"Just be at Lacybourne at seven thirty," he'd replied, and if she could credit it (which she decided later she could not), he sounded gentle.

And therefore she didn't even say goodbye, she simply hung up.

The very idea, the very *thought* of her parents meeting Colin tore her heart to pieces.

They wouldn't understand, they'd probably even like him (they always liked the men in her life).

Her father, she knew, even though he never said, wanted her to find herself a mate, a partner, a husband partly so she wouldn't be alone and partly because her father wanted to know she was protected and safe.

Her mother wanted her to be intellectually and sexually gratified (and often). Not to mention, her mother already was hinting broadly, and sometimes asking straight out, at wanting to meet Colin every time she'd called in the last three weeks.

And this meant Sibyl was going to have to sit through dinner knowing what she was to Colin with her parents sitting right beside her.

She hadn't been reminded of *that*, of what she really was to Colin, since he'd yelled at the minibus driver.

The situation became worse when her parents walked through the arrival doors.

Mags saw her daughter and shouted, "Surprise!"

And behind her mother struggling with a fair amount of duty free shopping bags was Scarlett.

At the sight of her sister, Sibyl's heart plummeted just as it sang with happiness.

Sibyl loved her sister, loved her to death. But her parents were one thing. Scarlett, being Scarlett, was going to be a problem. She read men like books, dissected them with her mind like a psychological biologist. She was good at it because she'd had a *lot* of practice. Sibyl would not be able to hide what she was to Colin from Scarlett.

There was plenty of room for them in the huge Mercedes sedan that Colin sent for her to use, a sedan that came complete with driver. Sibyl had, that morning at nine o'clock when she'd first clapped eyes on it, considered this an act of extreme thoughtfulness. Her parents could ride to Clevedon in complete luxury after a trying plane trip.

Now she wished she could send the driver home and troop her family into a bus just to be contrary.

Obviously, she could not.

Although her family seemed surprised at their chauffeur driven transport, they took one look at her set face and knowingly let the matter slide.

Luckily the sedan had a huge trunk for all of her family's luggage and Scarlett's shopping. Scarlett sat in front with the driver and Mags, Bertie and Sibyl sat in the back. As usual, conversation was tangled and loving as they caught up. When they were nearly to Clevedon, Sibyl was forced to break the news.

And pretend to be happy about it.

And, considering her poor talents at prevarication, she was surprised she got away with it.

"We have plans for dinner tomorrow night," she'd announced, trying desperately to sound cheerful and she must have succeeded because her mother and sister pounced on this right away.

Mags turned to Sibyl, her eyes bright.

"Really?" She drew this word out dramatically, her dancing green eyes alight with excitement (yet Sibyl had the strange sensation Mags was hiding something).

She had no time to assess this sensation for Scarlett twisted in her seat to stare at Sibyl, her blue eyes not bright with excitement but as usual teasing. "Well then, does this mean we'll finally learn this mystery man's name?"

Sibyl asked the goddess silently for patience but said with forced levity, "His name is Colin Morgan and he'd like us all to come to his house for dinner."

"How delightful," Bertie murmured, trying not to look too pleased all the while watching his daughter carefully.

"Where does he live? Does he live in Clevedon?" Scarlett asked.

"Yes." Sibyl hated this whole thing but she knew she hated what she was going to say next the most. "Dad," she called and her father turned kind eyes to her, "he's the new owner of Lacybourne Manor."

Her father, usually rather staid and mellow, gasped and his cheeks went pink with pleasure.

"Lacybourne Manor? What's Lacybourne Manor?" Mags asked.

"Sounds like a house in a Daphne du Maurier book," Scarlett commented.

"It's a great manor house, built in medieval times . . ." Bertie started to explain, breathless with excitement but as usual the rest of the women tuned him out the minute the word "medieval" passed his lips.

The Godwin Girls always tuned Bertie out when he started instructing them on medieval history.

For her part, Sibyl, who was usually the only one who listened to him (sometimes), found she'd rather spend her time seething, which she did.

Shortly after, when her family were ensconced in their rooms at the cottage, all of them having naps to fend off jetlag, Sibyl searched through her bag and took out the business card Colin had given her weeks ago.

She grabbed her phone and went into the garden with Mallory and Bran close on her heels. She sat on one of her sun loungers and Bran jumped into her lap, pressing against her and purring. Mallory collapsed beside the lounger, exhausted from his amble which consisted of the great and taxing distance from living room to garden.

For the life of her (and she wasn't actually going to *ask*) she could not fathom why Colin had done this. He had said he wanted to see *her* while her parents were in England but he'd never said he wanted to meet *her parents*.

She would never have agreed to that.

Never.

Sibyl turned her face to the sun and let her thoughts wander in an attempt at procrastination.

She'd called him without thinking after she couldn't wake Mallory the night of the break-in, and he'd done exactly what she needed him to do. He took control and handled things while she coped with the bizarre and frightening situation.

But he'd gone beyond that, being possessively, even fiercely protective. When he'd crouched by Mallory and gently stroked him muttering a curse in a tone that exactly matched Sibyl's mood, she'd nearly come undone. She wanted to hurl herself in his arms, promise to pay him back every penny if they could go back to the beginning and start new.

But she couldn't do that. They couldn't do that. That time had long since passed.

She simply had to take what she had for as long as was left and be happy with it.

The morning after the break-in, she'd stood in his bathroom brushing her teeth and thinking how different it was this time at Lacybourne. It was normal, *he* was normal (not even a hint of a personality disorder). It felt safe. It felt *right*. It felt pleasantly, weirdly and wonderfully like she was home.

Helping it to be more pleasant and wonderful, Colin had come up behind her, kissed her shoulder and turned her into his arms.

"I like you in my bathroom," he'd whispered in a voice so hot, his eyes blazing with intensity, she instantly relaxed in his loose embrace.

As if this wasn't enough, he went on.

"And in my kitchen," already reduced to goo in his arms, those arms tightened and his face came close before he finished, "And in my bed."

He then gave her a hard, closed-mouthed kiss (even though her mouth was filled with toothpaste foam) and he'd walked away, carelessly wiping the back of his hand across his lips to swipe away her foam.

It took her at least five minutes of holding the sink basin to recover from this heated yet tender barrage and every bit of self-control she possessed not to rush into the bedroom and pounce on him like a demented wanton.

Her teeth had gone a whole shade whiter.

The day after the cottage break-in, Colin sent a locksmith to put new locks on the front door *and* the back door. Not happy with this, he also sent out an alarm specialist to see to putting in an alarm. However, as the cottage was a listed building, everything would need to be approved by the heritage council before it was installed. Since Colin knew seventeen North Somerset councillors (he reminded her rather arrogantly, as was, she'd learned, his way) this would not be a difficult proposition.

"But Colin, I can't pay for an alarm system," she'd informed him at the time.

"I'm hardly going to allow you to live at Brightrose when there's a lunatic running around with a tranquillizer gun," he'd replied, like it was as simple as that.

"But Colin, I can't *afford* an alarm system," she somewhat repeated, thinking the different word might permeate his dictatorial brain.

"You aren't paying for it, I am."

"But Colin—"

"It's either that or live at Lacybourne with me."

At that alarming juncture in the conversation, she'd given in, though not gracefully.

He'd also, to her surprise (and hidden delight) had a survey done of the Community Centre and had some builder "pop round" to look at building an office extension for her.

The oldies were beside themselves with delight and Kyle couldn't believe his luck at the possibility of no more patched wire jobs and blocked toilets.

When she approached Colin about this he'd said, "The place is a health hazard. If something isn't done, it'll crumble down on your head and I happen to like your head as it is."

Well.

How could she respond to *that*?

She didn't know so she didn't respond at all and couldn't really, since he'd brushed his lips to hers, turned from her and walked into the kitchen.

Furthermore, a rubbish truck arrived last Friday and carted away the old, ratty chairs and couches that littered the Day Centre (and nearly every stick of furniture in Sibyl's office).

It was replaced within a half an hour with new, plush easy chairs and a three piece suite. There were brand new, sturdy yet attractive tables on which the oldies could lunch with far more comfort, not to mention safe chairs all around the tables.

Sibyl herself had a new desk, a swivel chair that could only be described as luxurious and a lovely, comfortable couch in her office.

"I'm *definitely* writing your mother about this," Mrs. Griffith proclaimed, settling contentedly in a new, plump, mauve chair covered in soft velour.

Sibyl had been so beside herself with glee, she didn't know what to say or do. When she saw Colin again after the new furniture was delivered, he passed it off like it was nothing even though she knew it had to be worth thousands of pounds.

She thought he'd demand his pound of flesh, another month, maybe two, but he didn't say a word.

Not a single word.

Instead, the whole time he treated her like she was, well . . . his *girlfriend*.

The very idea of him having a girlfriend was ridiculous. Men like Colin didn't have girlfriends. They had arm candy, glorious, sunken-cheeked, catwalk-model-type lovers. When he'd described himself as her boyfriend the night Mallory was shot, she'd been stunned but she thought it was simply his way of describing the indescribable. He couldn't say what she *really* was to him.

However, for the rest of the week, although he was constantly authoritarian (as per usual), his usual politeness and gallantry had melted to something that was far more tender.

Sibyl didn't know what to make of this, how to handle herself with this new Colin or who she was to him anymore. She was confused and felt vulnerable, and he pressed this advantage aggressively, asking her questions about her life, her work, her friends. She couldn't bear up against it, telling him things she never meant him to know, inviting him into her life where she never meant him to be.

She'd even told him about the incident with the animal shelter, something she promised her father she'd never speak of again, in her whole life, under threat of death or certain torture or, at the very least, being disowned.

She was on dangerous ground for this Colin, who she thought of as Royce/Colin, was something new and different and entirely wonderful.

And she feared that she was making him thus simply because she wanted it. Simply because she had decided that she was going to make the most of the time she had with him and *she*, as an untapped, untrained witch, was turning him into something he was not, using a power she could not control.

Of course, she could never tell him this. She could not tell him of her dreams of Royce (dreams she still had, every night) or the beautiful kiss they shared. Colin would call in the men with the straight jacket and have her carted off immediately.

Or, worse, turn away and walk out of her life forever.

But that was then and this was now and Colin was no longer Royce/Colin of the possessive, protective, tender, loving variety. He was back to Colin of the annoying, imperious, crazy variety.

Sibyl phoned his office, not his mobile, meaning only to leave him a message because she did not want to speak to him at all. She'd never phoned his office before and didn't relish the thought. As she dialed, she even entertained the notion (quite contentedly) of spending the next four months sleeping with him but never speaking to him again.

A woman answered, "Colin Morgan's office."

Something about this greeting made her seethe more.

"Hello, this is Sibyl Godwin. I'd like to leave Mr. Morgan a message."

"Oh, hiya, Miss Godwin. I'm Mandy, Mr. Morgan's assistant. He told me to put you through immediately if you called. One moment."

Before she could get a word in edgewise, Sibyl was put on hold. This gave her the golden opportunity to seethe even more and she took it. She did not spend one second (well, maybe *one* second) thinking what it meant that he'd instructed his secretary to put her through the minute she phoned.

Faster than she expected, she heard his rich, attractive voice saying, "Sibyl."

She tried not to react to the sound of his voice and without preamble she began, "Colin, you should know, for dinner tomorrow night—"

"Sibyl, I don't—"

She interrupted him as he interrupted her. "I'm just calling to tell you that my sister is here too."

He was silent.

"It was a surprise," she explained, wishing she could be more excited about her sister's surprise visit and blaming Colin for that too.

"I'll inform Mrs. Manning of the addition," he replied, though he sounded strangely pleased.

Sibyl seethed even more.

"Mrs. Manning?" Sibyl queried, her voice curt.

"My housekeeper," he answered calmly.

"Oh." Of course, *Mrs. Manning*, the housekeeper.

"I'll send a car to collect you," he added.

"Fine," she bit out, knowing it was an order and not feeling she had a tight enough rein on her temper to fight him on it.

"Sibyl—"

"I've got to go," and with a great deal of courage, she hung up on him.

Luckily and unfortunately, he did not call her back. Luckily, because she didn't wish to speak to him. Unfortunately, because not calling her back meant she had to worry if he was angry with her for hanging up on him.

Her family's first evening in England was spent, to Bertie's despair (although he quickly found himself listening to a comedy program on BBC's Radio 4), in Sibyl's bedroom with Scarlett and Mags inventorying Sibyl's wardrobe. Apparently, after Sibyl's phone call several weeks before, Scarlett became alarmed at the state of her older sister's apparel and decided it was high time for a fashion overhaul.

With clothes and shoes everywhere, Scarlett turned from the wardrobe to Sibyl, who was lying on the bed, and proclaimed, "Girl, you *really* need a little black dress."

"And some of those peasant shirts. They're very 'in' right now," Mags added helpfully, sitting on the floor and sifting through piles of clothes.

"The dress is priority," Scarlett decreed, her face contorting in hilarious distaste at the thought of a peasant shirt.

"And maybe some of those flowing gypsy skirts," Mags ignored her younger daughter.

With the state of Sibyl's wardrobe declared at a level Scarlett told her was called "dire," the next day, while Bertie took the MG and went to Clevedon Library to research Lacybourne and do the other things professors did when they lost themselves for hours in libraries, the women took a taxi to the train station and went to Bath in search of a little black dress.

They found three, as well as four new pairs of shoes (for Sibyl, Scarlett bought herself two). Scarlett relentlessly added two skirts, three pairs of trousers, a pair of jeans, several expensive, designer T-shirts, four blouses and a good deal of lingerie and sleepwear to Sibyl's massive shopping take of the day.

Which meant Sibyl (and Scarlett) were both wearing little black dresses to Lacybourne.

Sibyl would have liked to have been wearing a potato sack to make her feelings about the evening perfectly clear, but instead her dress was halter-necked, the narrow, deep V showing more than a hint of cleavage (indeed, it went nearly to her midriff) and the hem of the skirt hit her two inches above the knee ending in a short, perky ruffle.

The ruffle, Sibyl found, was the most annoying part of her outfit as she felt anything but perky. Her legs were bare and shone with some kind of lotion-slash-oil that Scarlett forced her to try (and, Sibyl thought, with professional detachment, she should add it to her spa inventory). Her feet were encased in a pair of beautiful, yet painful and extremely expensive, spike-heeled, elaborately strapped sandals.

Scarlett and Sibyl had nearly come to blows when Scarlett demanded Sibyl wear her hair up and Sibyl dug her heels in and wore it down.

This was done in order to irritate the now-despised (Sibyl was telling herself) Colin. Once he found out the weight of her hair gave her headaches, he had begun the habit of bunching her hair in his fist and lifting its weight while kissing her, holding her and, once, just plain old standing close to her.

She *had* thought this lovely. Now, since she fully intended to wear a pained expression the entire evening, she'd aggravate his conscience at the same time.

And now they were in the car driving through the slowly darkening night to Sibyl's doom.

Lacybourne.

Bertie was going on about some star-crossed lovers who used to live at Lacybourne, but Sibyl wasn't paying attention even though Mags and Scarlett were listening to this dramatic story with unusually rapt attention. Sibyl was too busy with her new favorite pastime of controlling her temper and trying very hard not to cry.

The driver of the sleek, black limousine turned into the gates of Lacybourne and Sibyl held her breath.

She felt, inexplicably, that her life was about to change (yet again) and she convinced herself that it was *not* for the better (yet again).

The weather was holding out even though a storm was, for the first time in weeks, threatening, and luckily this time there was no rain, thunder, lightning or misbehaved pets. As the car halted, Sibyl touched the place at her temple, just under her hairline, where a small, only slightly still pink scar was the physical souvenir of her first visit to Lacybourne.

The driver let out Mags and Scarlett on one side. Sibyl exited the other side with her father's assistance. Once they'd alighted, Mags and Scarlett stood staring in wonder at the dramatically grand and beautiful manor house that lay before them.

Sibyl didn't notice it and started toward the front door but her father stopped her by not releasing her hand and not moving.

When she turned to her father, he got close.

"Sibyl, my love, is there something not right between you and this Colin?"

Bertie was studying her intently and she realized he was very tuned in to her mood, as per normal. She and her father had a close bond; they always had for as long as she could remember.

She shot him a false smile and hoped she fooled him (she didn't).

"I'm fine, Dad. It's fine. We have a kind of . . ." she searched for a word that would not worry her father, "an unusual relationship."

He looked at her with searching, faded blue eyes and then nodded. She felt that he did not, at all, like what he saw and she hated herself for kind of lying to him.

Bertie escorted his daughter to the imposing door, his hand firmly at her elbow, his demeanor nowhere near his normal, relaxed, mellow self.

He knocked loudly, uncharacteristically taking control as her father and the man of the family. Mags and Scarlett trailed behind.

Sibyl steeled herself against the sight of Colin on the other side.

Instead a beautiful, older woman, with graying dark hair swept back in a chic chignon, kind, cornflower-blue eyes and flawless skin opened the door. She was wearing her own version of the mature woman's little black dress and she wore it well.

The woman looked first at Bertie and smiled an obvious warm welcome. Then her eyes skittered to Sibyl, and upon seeing her the older woman's mouth dropped open, the color drained from her face and her hand went to her throat in a gesture that seemed meaningful in its profound surprise.

Sibyl didn't know what to make of this bizarre reaction nor did she know who this woman was.

Thinking she was Mrs. Manning, the best dressed housekeeper in the world, she said with a small smile, "Hello, we're here to have dinner with Colin."

At Sibyl's smile, the woman's eyes actually filled with tears.

Yes, *they filled with tears*.

At the sight, Sibyl stepped forward instinctively, detaching herself from her father as Bertie stared in confusion at the other woman's outlandish reaction to his daughter.

Sibyl put her hand on the woman's arm in concern and asked, "Are you okay?"

The woman blinked once then twice. She finally nodded her head and smiled a smile that was faltering but it was warm.

"Yes, my dear girl, I'm definitely okay," she replied in a breathy voice filled with what sounded like wonder. "You must be Sibyl."

"Yes," Sibyl responded and squeezed the woman's arm reassuringly, awarding her with the force of a full smile.

Then she said something that nearly made Sibyl faint for the second time in her life.

"I'm Phoebe Morgan, Colin's mother."

It was Sibyl's turn to react in a bizarre manner as she stared at Colin's mother in obvious distress.

Vaguely she heard noises behind her. Her father made some kind of indistinct murmur, her mother chuckled and Scarlett muttered, "Now *this* is interesting."

"Good God, woman, don't stand in the doorway. Let the people in."

This was a booming, deep voice and it came from a tall man who could only be Colin's father.

Sibyl dazedly watched as he moved into the entryway. He was a few inches shorter than his son, he had thick, attractive, salt and pepper hair and nearly Colin's exact bone structure. His eyes, however, instead of the rich clay of Colin's, were a deep, warm brown.

"You must be Sibyl," he commented knowingly and he was smiling with what appeared to be extreme, almost unnatural, delight.

Sibyl felt a hysterical bubble of laughter rising up as both of Colin's parents said the same thing in greeting and were both now staring at her as if she was an unusual and intriguing creature but one from another planet.

"Come in, come in." He gestured magnanimously and pulled Sibyl gently into the entryway that not long before had been the scene of Colin's first audacious indication that he was attracted to her. "Colin just phoned. He's been detained at the office but will be here shortly. We'll have a few drinks, have a chat, get to know one another, the usual." He let go of Sibyl and walked to her father. "I'm Mike."

"Albert," Bertie responded, also looking a bit dazed.

Sibyl noted with distracted eyes that Mike was wearing a superbly-tailored suit.

Her father looked, as usual, like the absentminded professor. He was in a brown suit that had seen lots of wear but never really better days. Her mother was dressed flamboyantly in an outfit she had bought that day, pairing a bright-pink peasant blouse (which she tried to get Sibyl to buy herself, an effort that failed mostly because Scarlett would not allow it) and a deep-purple gypsy skirt complete with little metal dangles that tinkled when she walked.

Phoebe and Mike Morgan were the stylish and tailored opposite to Albert and Marguerite Godwin's eccentric and showy. Yin and yang, night and day. Sibyl's heart sank and she hoped her parents felt comfortable in the face of this new horror.

Sibyl knew, at that moment, that this night was doomed to be a disaster.

"It's all going to be fine, absolutely fine," Scarlett whispered in her ear as if sensing her dismay then Scarlett moved forward to interrupt Phoebe and Mike introducing themselves to Mags.

"I'm Scarlett, the prodigal sister," she announced and Sibyl felt the desperate desire to run screaming as far away as she could get in her strappy heels, which she had to admit would not have been very far, and she wondered, somewhat distractedly, what happened to her vow never again to wear high heels and she re-vowed to learn her damned lesson.

Instead, she and her family were swept into the Great Hall, swept in *and* through, with somewhat alarming speed, into the library. Bertie was desperately craning his neck to have a look around but Mike was crowding him strangely and practically pushing him forward.

"Drinks!" Mike boomed once he'd slammed the doors firmly shut to the Great Hall behind them, his tone sounding strangely slightly desperate. "We need drinks."

"I'll get them, Dad."

Sibyl halted with a jerk several feet into the library when she heard these words.

Phoebe Morgan's younger, stunning, equal stood in front of them smiling a warm, vivacious smile and also wearing a lovely, little black dress (it seemed Mags would be the only little-black-dress-less female of the evening).

"Hi! I'm Claire," she introduced herself coming, without even a moment's delay, right to Sibyl. "We talked on the phone?"

At this reminder (not that she needed one) Sibyl nodded, feeling she'd left the land of the real, normal and sane and had been rocketed, kicking and screaming, into some other, frightening, bizarre world where she did not, at all, wish to be.

What was Colin thinking?

His parents, her parents, his sister, her sister. Why on earth was he engineering a meeting of their two families? What would motivate him to introduce his family to the woman with whom he paid to have sex and who he would, in a little more than four months from now, likely leave without looking back?

Claire leaned into Sibyl and kissed both her cheeks.

After doing that, she grabbed Sibyl's hands, squeezed them tightly and announced, what sounded genuinely, "I'm *so* glad to meet you!" Her eyes wandered Sibyl's face, and if Sibyl hadn't totally lost her mind she could swear she saw tears shimmering in Claire's eyes.

Claire suddenly broke away.

"Is this your family? Hi!" she repeated. "I'm Colin's sister."

Scarlett, for some reason, burst out laughing.

Sibyl glared at her sister.

"Drinks!" Mike boomed again, cottoning on quickly to the weird overall mood. "Don't worry, Clairy-Berry, I'll get them."

Sibyl was coping with Colin's father's familiar endearment to his daughter, just like they were a normal, adoring family, which was something she never expected in a million years that Colin would have (what she expected he would have, she had no idea, she'd never considered it, she'd never thought she'd have the opportunity to meet them much less have drinks and dinner with them, with *her* family also in attendance no less), when she heard, "Hello, Sibyl dear."

She jumped, whirled and stared as Mrs. Byrne melted out of the woodwork and came toward her.

"What are you doing here?" Sibyl rushed to the other woman and, once there, pressed her lips to the still smooth skin on her cheek, thrilled beyond belief that she had an ally in the room even though she couldn't imagine why Mrs. Byrne was there, not to mention even Mrs. Byrne didn't know what Sibyl was to Colin.

"Why, Colin asked me to come. Wasn't that kind?"

Kind?

Mrs. Byrne thought Colin was *kind*?

And Colin had asked her to come?

The last time he'd had Mrs. Byrne and Sibyl in this room, he'd roared at them both like a raving lunatic.

It was then Sibyl knew that she was currently residing in an alternate universe.

Heart racing, Sibyl turned woodenly from Mrs. Byrne to take in the scene. She watched as Mike poured drinks, Phoebe fingered the material of Mags's skirt admiringly, Scarlett and Claire were giggling, actually giggling, like high school chums reunited when they'd known each other all of five minutes and Bertie was staring with rapt admiration at some crossed swords and a chest plate from a set of armor that was affixed to the wall.

"Mrs. Byrne, do you know what's going on here?" under her breath, Sibyl asked the other woman.

"Just have faith, have strength and trust Colin," came what Sibyl considered her mentally unhinged reply. "Our Colin knows what he's doing."

Our Colin?

Sibyl's eyes rounded and then Mike was standing close, pressing a drink in her hand. He hadn't even asked what she wanted but one look at the tall, thin glass with a maraschino cherry sitting on the top told her what it was. She sniffed it anyway and smelled the lime cordial.

It was chock full of ice.

She felt a shimmer she didn't comprehend go down her spine.

Something was happening, something she didn't understand, something she feared but also something that her crazy mind and crazier heart told her just might be hopeful.

"Mrs. Byrne," she whispered to the other woman as Mike moved away, but before Mrs. Byrne could answer Phoebe was speaking.

"Albert, Marguerite, how would you feel about a tour of the house before dinner?"

Scarlett and Sibyl were, pointedly, not invited, which, Sibyl thought, was pointedly peculiar.

At that moment, Sibyl decided to give up attempting to understand what on earth was going on and walked to the comfortable, inviting couch that had been the center point of the scene that was her *last* nightmare at Lacybourne. She decided it, as well as any, was a good place for her to spend her time experiencing this latest one.

She told herself it was only a few hours, just a few, short hours. Whatever was happening, she could cope. She'd been through worse, she told herself, she'd get through this.

"Please call us Mags and Bertie, everyone else does," Mags invited as she hooked her arm through Phoebe's and they turned to the door.

Bertie didn't reply. He was speechless with excitement at getting a tour. The older people went off, leaving the four women together, but again Mike firmly closed the doors to the Great Hall behind him after they'd gone through.

"Sibyl, are you okay? You look a bit pale." Her sister, the soon-to-be-fully-practicing neurologist, pointed out the not-so-medically obvious.

Before Sibyl could answer, Claire noted, "Scarlett, I don't think you've met Mrs. Byrne."

The four women wiled away the minutes, all but Sibyl joining in easy conversation while Sibyl tried to decide why, on earth, Colin had arranged this hideous tableau.

And what she decided eradicated that hope she'd felt earlier.

For, she decided, she had been right about their first encounter.

He had to hate her. Whatever reason there was for him to hate her, she knew there could be no other reason for him to do this to her. This whole thing was simply . . . well, she'd never been the paid sexual plaything for a man but she couldn't imagine it was *de rigueur* to invite her family to meet his parents (and sister). In fact she was pretty certain it was the exact opposite. He'd spent weeks lulling her into a false sense of security and now he was going in for the kill.

"Sibyl, you aren't saying a word," Claire noted, her blue eyes looking concerned. "Are you quite all right?"

"No," Sibyl stood, her heart was fluttering in a funny way that felt almost like pain and she replied honestly, "No, I don't think I'm all right."

All three women stood with her, glancing at each other with concerned eyes and Sibyl felt a great wave of nausea building inside her.

She was no longer seething, no longer angry.

She was humiliated and defeated.

"Sibyl," Mrs. Byrne said, her voice full of weight, urgency and a meaning Sibyl did not understand. Sibyl heard their parents coming back into the room as Mrs. Byrne went on, "Did you hear what I said to you earlier? Did you understand me?"

Sibyl wasn't listening. She was staring at her parents.

It looked like her mother had been crying but they were joyous tears and there was a smile, a smile the like she'd never seen on Mags's face and Sibyl had seen many smiles on Mags's face.

It was a smile that made Mags's face illuminate with happiness.

For his part, Bertie looked stunned and pleased as punch, as if Mike had told him there was an ancient archaeological ruin in the backyard that no one had ever touched and it was all his.

"What's going on?" Scarlett asked, clearly also noting the buoyant looks on their parents' faces.

"A word in the hall, Scarlett." Bertie had recovered first and promptly commanded his younger daughter in a tone he rarely used but both girls had obeyed for a lifetime.

Scarlett followed her father out of the room.

Sibyl stood stock still.

"What's going on?" Sibyl repeated her sister's question.

Mags walked to her daughter, her eyes shining with a beautiful light that, for some reason, made Sibyl feel even more frightened and sick.

Mags grabbed Sibyl's hand and squeezed.

"Will someone tell me what's going on?" she whispered to her mother and Mags simply leaned in, looked into her daughter's eyes with her own still bright with tears then she turned her head and kissed Sibyl on the cheek.

At this, Sibyl started to shake. She felt that the world had tilted and she was the only one remaining upright.

She was about to scream blue bloody murder when she heard Phoebe Morgan exclaim, "Colin! Finally, you've arrived," and relief was palpable in her words.

Sibyl's head snapped around and she saw Colin, wearing one of his dark suits with a deep green shirt, as usual, unbuttoned at his throat.

He looked around the room, seeming tense, until he saw her. Then he relaxed, took one look at her face and strode forward, straight to her.

She felt like fleeing, she felt like screaming at him, she felt like bursting into tears, but instead, she held her ground.

He ignored everyone else in the room even though everyone else was watching.

Avidly.

"Colin," she whispered when he was close enough to hear her. She was physically unable to make her voice any louder.

He stopped close to her, too close, closer than was seemly in front of his parents, her parents (well, maybe not Mags), everyone.

Then he did something strange.

He took both her hands in his.

Then he did something even stranger.

He dropped his forehead to rest it against hers and murmured in a low, intense voice filled with urgency and a meaning akin to Mrs. Byrne's, meaning she didn't understand, "Trust me, Sibyl."

She shook her head in a panic and his hands squeezed hers.

It was then she noticed his eyes, the look in them, a look that immediately melted away her fear and nausea.

He'd called her Sibyl but this wasn't Colin.

Not at all.

It was Royce.

"Trust me," he repeated.

She gulped.

As she stared, close up, into his beautiful eyes, her heart fluttered again, dangerously, but the feeling had a soft edge, which was a weak sense of hope.

Sibyl latched on to the hope.

Then she leaped off her second precipice in a month, leaped into the great unknown.

And she nodded, and, even in front of her parents, his parents, their sisters and Mrs. Byrne, Colin came even closer and brushed his lips tenderly against hers.

Chapter SEVENTEEN

The Story Comes Out

Throughout the introductions to Sibyl's family, Colin kept her close by holding her hand. Then his father gave him a gin and tonic and Colin stood drinking it, keeping her close with an arm about her waist. He also kept her close, his arm consistently wrapped around her, as he chatted amiably with everyone. Even though she was struck practically mute while everyone else seemed bright and cheery (irrationally so), Colin seemed to make little of all this and behaved as if this was your normal, average, everyday dinner party.

Which it most definitely was not.

He was Royce.

Though he answered to the name Colin, he was someone else.

Relaxed, amused at Mags and Scarlett's hilarious behavior (which seemed somewhat desperately hilarious), respectful to her father (regardless of Bertie's expression, which lapsed consistently into one that could only be described as astonished), familiar with his family and possessively demonstrative to Sibyl—this was not mercurial Colin, this was loverly Royce who couldn't get enough of her and didn't care who knew it.

Somehow, Royce had taken over Colin.

Completely.

They eventually headed in to dinner, Colin/Royce allowing the others to precede them. While they wandered ahead, Colin pulled her back down the hall a few steps and then did the first Colin Act of the entire evening.

He pushed her against the wall and kissed her breathless.

The kiss was definitely different, far more loverly-sexy-Royce than sexy-lover-Colin and Sibyl's heart started racing.

She'd done it. She hadn't *meant* to do it, but with her mystical powers, she'd nearly obliterated Colin and replaced him with a dream lover.

When he lifted his head, he murmured, "I've been wanting to do that since the minute I saw you in that *very* charming dress."

Sibyl, recovering from the kiss and the inconceivable knowledge that she could change a man's personality with her magical powers, blinked at him.

"Are you all right?" she asked.

He smiled, a white flash against tanned skin. All his smiles tended to be disarming in one way or another, but she was not certain he'd ever smiled at her the way he was doing now. He was smiling like the cat who'd managed to snag a couple of field mice, a juicy bird *and* came home and got his cream.

Her racing heart skipped a beat.

"Perfect," he responded, his deep voice like velvet.

"You're not . . . ?" she began to ask him if he was having another episode, but he wouldn't know. The last time he didn't remember a thing. Though the last time it had lasted minutes, this seemed to be going on forever.

What if he came back to Colin in the middle of dinner, spitting mad and wondering who all these people were and why they were eating his food?

She was uncertain what to do or say, thinking he might be unstable. Thinking she should call a doctor. Wondering how she could find a *witch* doctor. She laid her hand against the side of his face (a thoughtful gesture that masked her checking his temperature, just to be sure he wasn't in the throes of some kind of walking, talking fever that rendered him partially delirious).

"You're sure you're okay?" she asked.

"I'll explain later." He moved into her, pressing her against the wall. "Stay with me tonight," he whispered, his voice smoothing along her skin like a silken caress but the words sounded like a request, *not* an order.

"I . . . is that an order?" she queried, confused at how to proceed.

He smiled his devastating smile again and shook his head. "No, I'm asking you to stay the night."

Her heart skipped to a stuttering halt and then started beating again, double time. She was going to have a heart attack, at thirty-two years old, in the hallway of a National Trust property.

Definitely Royce.

"My family—" she started.

"I'll have the car take them home and return in the morning for you, early if you like."

If she liked?

She opened her mouth and then closed it.

What could she say? She *wanted* to be with *this* Colin. She knew it wasn't fair and it wasn't right, she was practicing an insidious voodoo against her will and his (well, maybe not against hers).

Perhaps she was going to have to bring Mags in to deal with it after all. Her mother couldn't actually do anything but she might know someone in her loopy collective that had some knowledge of how to exorcise a dream man from a real, flesh and blood man.

"Sibyl?" he prompted.

"Colin?" she returned.

She was testing him, saying his name to see his response. His head tilted and he watched her with an expression on his face that even blind Annie could have seen showed he thought she was adorable.

Her heart still racing, she now caught her breath.

"Now that we've ascertained we remember each other's names, perhaps you'll promise me that you'll spend the night with me, here at Lacybourne, in my bed, no matter what happens tonight."

She'd stopped listening on the word "bed."

She let her breath out in a gush. "Where's your family staying?"

"Here."

"I can't stay with you while your family—"

"Trust me, they don't mind."

This was a bizarre statement in a bizarre evening. They were both consenting adults but it wasn't seemly, especially not the first night she'd met his family. They'd think she was a screaming slut.

She was, of course, his paid-for sexual partner but *his parents* didn't know that.

"Colin."

"Sibyl, promise me."

His voice was silk. His eyes were warm. His lips were less than an inch away.

She was no match for that combination.

"Okay."

He grinned, his grin filled with triumph and then he kissed her breathless.

Again.

When he released her mouth, he turned and guided her to the dining room. Distractedly, she heard the hushed conversation, but the minute they entered hand in hand all talk ceased and everyone stared at them. Covering, they rushed on with what seemed like great determination to appear natural and at any other time in her life Sibyl would have found it curious and, probably, hilarious.

Now, she did not.

Colin's seat at the head of the table was vacant. Phoebe sat at the foot, to her right sat Mrs. Byrne, to her left, the only other empty chair next to Mike. On Mike's other side sat Mags, who sat to Colin's right. Scarlett (to Sibyl's despair) was to Colin's left then Bertie then Claire coming full circle to Mrs. Byrne.

It was the Seating Arrangement of Doom.

Sibyl took her chair and a young man in dark pants and a white shirt immediately entered carrying a tureen of soup to the side table. Sibyl watched, captivated at the idea of having a waiter at a dinner party in your home.

"Sibyl, I hear you make lotions and bath salts," Phoebe forged in while the waiter served soup. "You smell divine, is your perfume one of your creations?"

"Yes," she shared, leaning back to allow the young man access to her place setting. "If you like, I can make you a goodie basket of my products," Sibyl offered and then wondered why she did and *then* gave herself a mental forehead slap.

"She makes *the best* goodie baskets," Scarlett put in helpfully, and if she'd been close enough Sibyl would have kicked her sister. There was a small chance that Phoebe would have demurred.

"Oh, I'd like one too," Claire said exuberantly.

Gone was the small chance.

"Of course," Sibyl murmured.

"Tell us about your work at the Community Centre," Mike boomed so loudly, Sibyl started.

Everyone stared at her curiously, even her family who knew all about her work at the Community Centre. Therefore, she had no choice, so she did. While everyone ate their soup, Sibyl talked about the oldies, their bingo and sing-a-longs, and the kids, their art projects and their talent show. She talked and pretended to eat while she felt Colin's eyes on her. Then she gave up all pretense of eating to focus her attention to pretending she didn't feel his eyes on her.

Once she'd petered away on a story about Mrs. Griffith using her cane on an unsuspecting neighbor with an overly loud dog (Mrs. Griffith was feeble, it didn't hurt her neighbor . . . too much) the waiter came in and whisked away the bowls, quietly asking if Sibyl was done with her nearly full one.

She nodded mutely and he swept it away.

"So, what do you do Colin?" Bertie inquired.

Sibyl turned startled eyes to her father then to Colin, realizing, with a hysterical feeling rising inside her, that *she* didn't even know what Colin did for a living.

"I buy and sell companies," Colin replied.

This was met with complete silence and Sibyl tensed.

If Mike and Phoebe were posh, tailored yin to Mags and Bertie's oddball, unconventional yang, Colin's profession was the Antarctic in relation to Sibyl's Arctic Community Centre.

"He's very successful," Mike offered hopefully into the silence.

"What does that mean, you buy and sell companies?" Mags asked dubiously.

"It means he's a corporate raider, Mom," Scarlett offered and Sibyl held her breath at *that* explosive comment, definitely wishing she was close enough to kick her sister.

"Not exactly," Colin muttered, his eyes on Sibyl.

"The corporate raid stopped over a decade ago," Mike boomed in defense of his son as the waiter walked in carrying salads this time.

"What *does* it mean?" Bertie asked, every liberal bone in his body rankling and Sibyl wished the floor would open up and swallow her.

And Colin, of course. She couldn't leave him behind at the Table of Doom.

"I buy mismanaged companies, clean them up and sell them for a profit," Colin answered patiently.

"Sometimes not still in one piece, I assume?" Scarlett asked sweetly, perversely loving every minute of this.

Sibyl hoped that the Morgans would realize that Scarlett was annoying in the extreme, even to her own family, and especially to her sister.

Colin opened his mouth to answer but instead, Claire, desperately burst out, "Colin saved a girl from drowning when he was sixteen."

All eyes swung to Claire.

"Remember that, Colin, at the club?" Claire continued courageously. "She nearly died. Colin had to give her CPR and everything. It was quite something," she told the table at large.

Mike laughed, remembering. "Yes, of course, you dated her for six months after that. Remember son? She was quite a looker."

Sibyl was in the middle of them and therefore caught a bit of the polar freeze that came from the frosty glare Phoebe directed at Mike. Sibyl realized Phoebe would also very much like to be in kicking distance of her husband and quickly tucked her legs beneath her chair.

Everyone turned their attention to their salads. Sibyl saw Mrs.

Byrne smile at her reassuringly after Sibyl had rearranged several walnuts and pear slices in a more decorous display on top of the spinach leaves.

"I know!" Phoebe exclaimed, making everyone jump. "You brought that puppy home. Do you remember, Colin, the one someone abandoned?"

Every pair of eyes moved to Colin hopefully.

"That was Tony, Mum," Colin reminded her and Sibyl watched as a muscle leaped dangerously in his jaw when he clamped his mouth shut after speaking.

Phoebe muttered a dejected, "Oh."

Sibyl felt her stomach sink.

"Who's Tony?" Mags whispered to Mike.

"Youngest son," Mike answered softly and Sibyl was surprised to hear that Colin had a brother.

It was at this point that she decided to enter the fray.

Someone had to.

"Colin saved me from the advances of a drunk man at a club," she said quietly to her salad and felt, rather than saw, all eyes turn to her. "He also got a terrible man, whose inattention was borderline abuse, a man who drove a minibus of oldies, fired by getting his secretary to call seventeen councillors to do it." She continued fiddling with her food and didn't once raise her eyes. "And he just bought all new furniture for the Day Centre so the oldies would have somewhere nice to eat and relax away from home."

This was met with an even more profound silence and Sibyl continued in her pursuit of making certain every leaf of spinach was finely coated with dressing.

The waiter reappeared to collect the salad dishes but Colin's authoritative voice stopped him. "Miss Godwin hasn't finished her salad, Peter."

"Yes, sir," Peter replied and slid back out of the room as Sibyl turned her eyes from her food to Colin.

He was leaning back in his chair, the comfortable lord of the manor, smiling at her like they were the only two people in the room. She felt the warmth of his smile tingle all through her body, from the top of her head straight to the tips of her curled toes.

She smiled back and was so immersed in the moment that she missed all the air being sucked out of the room as their audience pulled in their breaths at the fascinating (and hopeful) sight before their eyes.

"Now that my character has been assassinated and redeemed in the expanse of ten minutes, perhaps we can give Sibyl a chance to finish one of the courses by moving away from the third degree, shall we?" Colin suggested in only the way Colin could suggest, which meant it wasn't a suggestion at all.

"That sounds like a fine idea," Mike agreed readily.

But Sibyl was now watching her father, and to her surprise, after the corporate raider declaration, she saw Bertie looking at Colin with what appeared to be approval.

The rest of the dinner progressed relatively well (considering its start meant it couldn't get much worse). Course after course followed, a nice goat's cheese wrapped in puff pastry with red onion marmalade and then a huge, succulent portobello mushroom cap topped with puy lentils and minced garlic drenched in olive oil with a side of sugar snap peas.

Sibyl was finishing an utterly delicious passionfruit gateau when she realized, belatedly, that the entire meal was vegetarian.

And that Colin had eaten it.

After all the dishes had been whisked away by Peter and everyone was drinking the last drops of their full-bodied, dry red wine, Phoebe announced, "Let's finish the evening in the library, where it's more comfortable. Peter will be serving cheese, liqueurs and coffee."

Everyone seemed to think this was a smashing idea. So much so that, with nary a word, all chairs scraped backwards almost before Phoebe finished the word "coffee."

Colin hung back at the door and grabbed Sibyl's hand so she would do the same.

When everyone had left, Colin ducked his head and whispered into Sibyl's ear, "Thank you for defending me."

She gulped, a tremor of awareness went through her even as she was feeling somewhat ill-at-ease with this exciting new Royce / Colin hybrid. "You're welcome."

He turned so he was fully facing her then glanced over her shoulder at the table.

"Are you . . . is everything okay?" she asked, still feeling somehow timid.

She couldn't say she knew Colin all that well but she definitely didn't know Royce and *most* definitely not Colin / Royce. It was almost like this was a first date. And anyway, who knew when Colin would wake out of his magical slumber and how he would react when he did.

His gaze came back to her and what she read in his eyes made all thoughts fly out of her head and her knees went instantly weak.

"I was wondering, for future reference of course, if *this* dining-room table was fair game?" he asked.

Her lips parted, her eyes widened and her head jerked around to look at the table. She felt her stomach flip and little tingles spiral delicately throughout her body.

Her head came back around and she saw his lips were twitching.

He was teasing.

"You're a brute," she whispered but her tone was teasing and her mind, somehow, was put at ease.

"You haven't answered my question," he drawled.

"Did your father build it or refinish it?" she queried mock seriously.

"No."

"Your mother?" she continued, tilting her head.

"Of course not."

"A beloved godfather?"

The twitching lips spread into a grin and he shook his head.

She countered by nodding hers.

"I take it that's a yes?" he pressed.

She smiled her yes then caught her bottom lip between her teeth while his eyes dropped to watch.

His face turned serious.

"Sibyl, before we join the others, I want to show you something. When you see it, I want you to promise me that you'll let me finish what I need to say before you fly off the handle."

Her eyes widened at this sudden change from flirtatious-mode to deadly-serious-liberally-mixed-with-ominous-hints-mode.

Even so, she focused on something else and declared in self-defense, "I don't fly off the handle."

His eyebrows lifted mockingly.

At his eyebrow lift, she sighed and said, "Okay, maybe I do, but *why* would I fly off the handle?"

"Just promise me."

She felt a shimmer of dread slide up her spine at his still serious tone and she started, "Colin—"

He cut her off, demanding, "Promise."

He was using his silky voice and his warm eyes but they weren't working on her this time because his look was so intense, it was scaring her half to death. She needed no more shocks tonight. She didn't know if she could endure them.

But this was Royce, wasn't it?

And even if it was Colin, she told herself she could trust him. He'd taken care of her tranquillized dog, for goddess's sake. He was buying her an alarm system. He bought a bunch of furniture for her oldies and she couldn't forget the luxurious swivel chair. And, even though tonight's dinner seemed doomed to failure for a variety of reasons, that didn't happen and it wasn't all *that* bad.

Yes, she could definitely trust him.

Couldn't she?

What could he want to show her that might make her angry?

Whatever it was couldn't be all that awful. Especially if he could explain it.

Taking yet another chance that night, Sibyl decided to trust him.

Therefore, looking into his eyes, she nodded and for this, she was rewarded with one of his killer-watt smiles, a smile that told her it was going to be all right.

She drew in a deep, steadying breath as Colin led her down the hall, and instead of turning to the library where everyone else had gathered he took her to the Great Hall.

They walked through the big room and Colin stopped her right in the middle.

She'd been there before, of course, she'd just never really looked at it because she was mid-diatribe the last time she'd spent any time there.

It was huge and stunning.

Right in the middle was an enormous, heavy table made of wood so dark, it was nearly black. Twenty large, ladder-backed chairs surrounded it.

In the stone walls, the room had dozens of deep windows with warped panes of glass. Two of the windows were semi-circular, one filled with a sculpted bust on a half column, the other with an immense, antique globe. In the center of each window were breathtaking stained glass *fleur-de-lis*.

There were old-fashioned wooden chairs sitting at precise intervals along the walls, almost like sentries standing at attention. There was also a massive mellow-colored stone staircase built up one wall, a thick, red carpet runner in the center held to each step by a brass rod.

The room was decorated with suits of armor, flags floating from the ceiling beams, pennants dripping from brass rods and crossed swords affixed to walls.

She felt a shiver of apprehension as she stood there, not only because Colin wasn't speaking a word as she looked around but also because she felt something familiar about this place. Almost like she'd been there before and not when she had her blazing tirade weeks previously.

She noted somewhere in the back of her mind it was now raining, the water streaming down the glass of the windows, the sky dark and threatening.

She did a slow pirouette, mainly because she couldn't help herself.

"Colin," she breathed, "it's love—"

She didn't finish.

And she didn't finish because she saw Royce.

Royce!

Royce depicted in a portrait, hanging on the wall in the Great Hall at Lacybourne.

She took two steps toward it, her hand flying to her mouth.

"Royce," she whispered as she gazed in shock at the portrait.

She vaguely heard Colin ask, "What did you say?" in a tone that was far more Colin than Royce.

But she wasn't listening.

It was Royce, stunningly handsome even though he looked fierce, even angry. He was standing in front of a shining black horse with a wild mane, a horse Sibyl knew very well because she'd ridden on his back.

She felt her heart squeeze in a mixture of horror and delight.

"My goddess," she stared, "My goddess, Colin, it's . . ." but she stopped again because as she was about to turn to Colin, her eyes fell on the *other* portrait, the one beside Royce's.

She gasped and took two steps *back*.

It was then that thunder rumbled and, seconds later, lightning split the sky.

"Sibyl," Colin was saying but she interrupted him and took another step away from what she saw.

"That's . . ." she raised her arm and pointed a trembling finger at the portrait.

A picture that showed exactly what Sibyl saw in her mirror every morning, except with dark hair. It even had Mallory and Bran in it.

"That's me!" she cried and swung confused eyes to Colin who, she saw, was watching her closely. "Why do you have a portrait of me in your house? How? Why?"

"Do you know Royce Morgan?" Colin asked and she heard a thread of accusation in his tone.

"Why do you have a painting of me in your house?" she returned, her voice rising with hysteria. Then she processed what he said, her stomach clenched and she breathed, "Royce *Morgan*?"

"Yes." He glanced swiftly at the portraits and then back to Sibyl. "Royce Morgan and his wife, Beatrice, born Beatrice Godwin."

She felt as if she'd been struck, all her breath went out of her in a whoosh.

Beatrice *Godwin*.

She stumbled back another step, throwing her arm out for something to steady her and catching one of the ancient chairs around the ancient dining-room table that was known to her because she had sat there and eaten a meal.

A meal that happened in her dreams, which took place in ancient times when the table was *new*.

"Beatrice Godwin?"

When Sibyl spoke her voice was loud and it was shrill.

Sibyl felt rather than saw someone come into the room but she didn't turn to see who it was.

"Beatrice and Royce Morgan," Colin explained tersely. "He was the owner of Lacybourne and they were married for a few hours. On their way home to Lacybourne after their wedding, they were murdered."

"Oh my goddess. Oh my goddess," Sibyl was blathering, her hand clutched the chair like a lifeline. "Oh my *goddess*! He . . . he looks like *you*! And . . . and, she . . . she looks like . . . *me*!" Sibyl shouted her last.

It was then Sibyl remembered her father talking about the lovers who never got the chance to live at Lacybourne because they'd been killed. She hadn't listened to much of what he said, but she remembered the story was famous, a tragic, romantic tale of true love lost.

What had her father said?

"Oh my goddess," she whispered.

They'd had their throats slit.

Just like in her dream.

Without thinking, hysteria filling her, she turned to run, to escape, to get far away from Lacybourne and Royce and Beatrice, Colin and her dreams and what this meant to her.

She'd asked Royce, when he was Colin, who Beatrice was and he'd said it then.

She's you.

She'd manage to run two steps when she was grabbed at the waist by Colin. He swung her effortlessly around to face him.

"Do you know Royce Morgan?" Colin asked, hanging on to his temper, but, she could tell distractedly, just barely. He was staring at her with narrowed, angry eyes.

"Colin, don't!" Mrs. Byrne cried from somewhere in the room.

"Of course I do! I see him every night in my dreams," Sibyl yelled in his face, struggling against his arm. "Every night. But they aren't dreams, they . . . they're *memories*!" she cried frantically. "I'm Beatrice in my dreams."

It was then Sibyl felt her face pale.

Oh dear goddess, she might even *be* Beatrice in reality.

Royce had said, *You called me Colin when you were her. I thought she was attempting to vex me.*

"Oh my goddess. Oh my goddess." Sibyl was back to chanting.

"Sibyl, calm down," Colin commanded and her eyes flew to his.

His were no longer irate, they were concerned. His hands were no longer grasping her bitingly but had gentled.

That's when *she* became irate.

"Calm down? *Calm down*? Are you mad? You have a portrait of a dead medieval woman in your house. A woman who had her throat slit. A woman that looks exactly like me, I even think she *is* me in a way and . . ."

She stopped and her body went utterly still.

He had a portrait in his house that looked like her. A portrait that likely had hung there for hundreds of years.

She stared at him and then her eyes cut to Mrs. Byrne.

Lightning split the sky.

Mrs. Byrne had been working at Lacybourne for years.

Her eyes cut back to Colin.

"You knew!" she cried and heard others entering the room.

But she couldn't think about anything else because thoughts, memories, visions, snippets of dreams, her first meeting with Mrs. Byrne (who was *very* keen to have Sibyl come to the house), her first meeting with Colin and his maniacal behavior all came crashing into her brain and she understood.

She finally understood.

"You knew I looked like her and you knew you looked like him." Her eyes went back to Mrs. Byrne. "You both knew and you never said a word."

"Dear—" Mrs. Byrne began placatingly.

Sibyl cut her off.

"You knew! I even told you about my dreams and you knew!" Sibyl shouted at Marian. "Why didn't you say anything to me?" Her head swung back to Colin who was close, very close, holding her against the warmth of his body and staring at her, a muscle working in his jaw but this time, not with anger. "Why didn't *you* say anything to me?"

"I thought you were—" Colin started to say, but with a forceful jerk she pulled out of his arms and quickly took several steps away from him, putting needed space between them.

The dawning light finally rose in her dim brain and it all made startlingly clear, hideous sense.

"I know what you thought," she hissed. "I know *exactly* what you thought. You thought I knew who *she* was." Sibyl's hand flew to point at the portrait of Beatrice. "And that I was after the family silver. *That's what you thought!*" She screamed these last words, her fury completely out of control, her voice ringing in the hall.

She held tightly to her rage, if she didn't, she would likely curl up and die.

This was not a dream. This was magic but it wasn't the light airy-fairy kind.

This was dark and ugly and she wanted no part of murdered, star-crossed lovers, the male half of which reincarnated into a misanthropic beast.

Colin started toward her as Mrs. Byrne called out, "Sibyl, you must listen."

Sibyl didn't respond, she was watching Colin.

"Don't come near me! Don't you even *touch* me!" she warned but Colin didn't stop. Indeed not only didn't he stop but he was coming at her with grave purpose. "You wanted to punish me?" she asked acidly. "Well you did! You got my family here to make a fool of me, to humiliate me and you made me your . . . *oomph*!"

She didn't finish because she had his shoulder in her belly and she was being lifted. Her breath was knocked out of her as he threw her over his shoulder and carried her toward the stairs.

She recovered quickly and struggled, shouting, "Let me down!"

He didn't stop and he didn't let her down.

She lifted her head, her hair falling away from her face and as he carried her up the stairs, she saw her family *and* his family watching their ascent in fascinated, horrified silence.

But no one came to her aid.

Chapter EIGHTEEN

Real Life Magic

Colin put her down in his bedroom and the minute her feet touched the floor, Sibyl started to run toward the door.

He grabbed her by hooking an arm about her waist and yanking her back against his body. She crashed against the length of him and he wasted no time. He reached out, leaning into her, his upper body pushing her torso forward, and he slammed the door.

"Sibyl, five minutes. Listen to me," he demanded, his mouth at her ear.

"No!" she shouted and struggled, tearing at his hand at her waist.

Her mind was whirling, her head was spinning. No one down there helped her, not even her family. They *all* knew before she did, that was what they were so damned *cheerful* about. That was why they were all acting so strange.

She felt, at any moment, she was either going to cry, scream the house down or be sick.

Or all three at the same time.

He caught one wrist and twirled her out then used her arm to jerk her forward. She slammed against his hard body while he twisted her arm carefully behind her back. Her other hand came up to push against his chest but he grabbed that too and it joined the one behind her back.

She was pressed full-frontal against his body and completely powerless.

This, of course, made her angrier.

She tipped her head back, her hair flying everywhere.

"Let go of me!" she yelled in his face.

He shook her, a gentle but rough gesture that caused her no pain but further angered her all the same.

"Listen to me!" he commanded, his voice an urgent rumble.

"No!" she repeated. "You have nothing to say that I want to hear."

"I dreamed of you, the night before I met you."

She became instantly still.

Perhaps that was something she was willing to hear.

"What?"

"I dreamed of who I thought was Beatrice, but she had your hair. It was you. I was making love to you and then you were torn from my arms and I was held back as someone slit your throat."

Her mouth dropped open and she gaped at him, completely at a loss for words.

What on the goddess's green earth was going on?

She'd dreamed of him too. The same exact dream. Except it was *his* throat that was slit.

"Does that dream sound familiar?" he asked, watching her closely.

She blinked and shut her mouth so fast, her teeth clacked together.

Damn, she always got caught in her lies.

"Sibyl, I know you were lying about your nightmare that night. You're the worst liar I've ever met."

She stayed silent, not ready to let go of her rage and instantly deciding she did not want to hear any more of this latest revelation. Really, how much could a girl take?

"You've had the same dream, haven't you?" Her eyes went to the door with visions of escape dancing in her head but he shook her again. "Haven't you?"

"It doesn't mean anything," she told the floor to her side.

His hands released hers but he didn't let her go. His arms tightened around her, holding her to him even as her hands went to his chest and tried to force him away. She didn't lift her eyes above his throat as she pushed with all her strength.

All this work was to no avail. He didn't shift an inch.

"Stop struggling and talk to me," he demanded.

Her eyes lifted to his and she obliged, "You made me your whore."

He flinched as if she'd struck him, and he seemed for a moment genuinely to be in pain. And she felt, to her surprise and annoyance (for a moment), upset for him.

"You were never my whore," he murmured gruffly, his eyes drilling into hers.

"I felt like it," she informed him with complete honesty, still trying to pull away.

His arms tightened. "I'm sorry for that but I never thought of you that way."

"You did that first night," she corrected him.

"All right, I never thought of you that way after that first night," he conceded through gritted teeth.

She knew that. Rationally, logically, looking back at all that transpired between them. She wasn't exactly hip to how paid sexual partners were treated but she doubted their men took them out to dinner and on jaunts to National Trust properties on the weekend.

She knew all of this but she wasn't rational or logical at that moment.

Far from it.

"Then how did you feel about me the night you threatened to fuck me on my dining-room table?" she pushed, her voice nasty.

Now she was out of line, he'd threatened it but he didn't do it.

He didn't apologize for threatening it but he still didn't do it.

She wasn't going to feel badly about being out of line. *He'd* been lying to her for *weeks*.

She told herself that but what he said next made *her* feel like an absolute heel.

"I'd been away from you for days. I wanted to see you and you weren't home. So, I suppose what I felt was that I missed you." he clipped, his patience with her beginning to wear and it was showing.

At his words, she stopped pressing against his chest to get away.

"You *missed* me?" she breathed, her eyes rounded in surprise.

He just stared at her and she (wisely) let it go.

"Why didn't you tell me about the portraits?" she rushed on. "And, why did you offer me fifty thousand pounds to sleep with me? I mean, who *does* that? And—"

"Why did you take it?" he cut in, and at his turning of the tables she clapped her mouth shut.

It was her turn to stare at him.

Unlike her, however, he actually intended to get an answer.

"Would you care to answer me?" This was voiced as a request however it was anything but.

Sibyl mentally kicked herself for again, after the many times in the past, not learning her lesson. How she managed to get herself in these tricky situations, she did not know. She had two degrees, got straight As, graduated with honors, she kept her home tidy, managed to take care of her pets, hold down a job, keep a business, pay her bills, but her life was (always) an absolute mess.

She decided to remain silent. She figured it was her best option at that point.

"Christ, for someone as beautiful and warm-hearted as you, you're truly the most annoying woman I know," Colin ground out, looking over her head rather than at her.

She was now staring at him in wonder.

She'd kind of heard the word "annoying" but she was stuck on "beautiful" and "warm-hearted" so she didn't fully process the "annoying" bit.

It was then that there was a knock on the door.

"Come in," Sibyl called automatically.

"*Go away*," Colin barked at the same time.

Of course, since it was the sisters, they listened to Sibyl and opened the door.

Looking over her shoulder, Sibyl watched Claire and Scarlett walk in, Claire watching them with her heart in her eyes, Scarlett's eyes were scrutinizing.

"We came to see if you were all right. That was quite a scene down there and we were a bit worried," Claire announced, walking fully into the room, her gaze swinging worriedly from Colin to Sibyl.

"*I* came in a medical capacity. After carrying Sibyl up the stairs, I thought you might need me to check if you'd sustained a hernia," Scarlett drily informed Colin.

At that, Sibyl's head snapped back around to look to Colin.

"Would you like to amend your comment about the most annoying woman you know?" she quipped angrily.

His arms loosened around her as one corner of his lips twitched tellingly. Sibyl stepped away from him, breaking the hold of his arms and gave him a look that told him *she* did not think her sister, or any of this, was amusing.

"I'm fine. He's fine. We're fine. Everything's fine," Sibyl curtly assured Claire who was still looking as if one, the other, or the both of them was about to spontaneously combust and she didn't want to be in the way of flying body parts.

"We were hoping to have a private conversation," Colin said pointedly then glanced at the door.

Scarlett ignored the glance, walked toward the fireplace and turned one of the comfortable armchairs there around to face the room.

As she did, she noted, "*You* clearly wanted to have a private conversation, but as you carried my sister to your bedroom like a Neanderthal, it is somewhat debatable if *she* wanted a private conversation with you." Then she sat, crossed her legs and groaned. "These damn shoes are killing me."

"Scarlett—" Sibyl started, her voice edged with warning.

"You must know, it isn't easy for him," Claire burst out.

Everyone's eyes turned to Claire who was standing, her arms straight down at her sides, her hands clenched in fists. She was upset about something and Sibyl thought for a moment she was angry at Scarlett (deservedly so), but her eyes were directed at Sibyl.

"Who?" Sibyl asked, thinking maybe she was confused.

It wouldn't be surprising if she was confused, considering her whole world had been turned on its head.

However, Sibyl could not imagine Claire was referring to Colin. *Everything* seemed easy for Colin.

"Colin," Claire answered and Sibyl's eyes widened.

Sibyl looked at her sister and Scarlett shrugged and turned her attention to Claire.

"It's just that every woman he meets—" Claire began but Colin interrupted.

"Claire, I don't think—"

"Wants her pound of flesh," Claire finished stubbornly, looking at Colin with a rebellious gleam in her eye.

"Pound of flesh?" Sibyl echoed.

"Yes. Her pound of flesh," Claire repeated.

"Claire," Colin said again, this time *his* voice held a warning.

"Really, Colin, I'm not entirely certain what all this intrigue was about tonight but we went along with it. Though, it's obvious something isn't right with the pair of you," Claire retorted.

"Yes, that's one thing that *is* obvious," Scarlett muttered under her breath but loud enough for everyone to hear.

Claire ignored her, which Sibyl thought showed great diplomacy and Sibyl's already high estimation of Colin's sister climbed another notch.

"So someone has to tell your side of things," Claire went on.

"His side of things?" Sibyl parroted, beginning to feel like she sounded like a fool.

"Yes, Sibyl. Colin doesn't trust very easily, especially women, which isn't surprising, since every woman he's ever met was out for something," Claire explained.

Colin made an exasperated noise or an annoyed noise or a furious noise. Sibyl wasn't certain, she'd never heard him make it before. Whatever it was, it showed he was losing what was left of his control.

"Perhaps you should carry *Claire* out of the room," Scarlett helpfully suggested to Colin.

"Scarlett, will you shut . . . *up*!" Sibyl snapped then she swung around to face Colin and asked, "Out for what?"

Scarlett laughed and Sibyl found herself whirling around again. "Sibyl, girl, I really need to introduce you to Manolo Blahnik. I'm pretty certain most of the women Colin's dated are intimately acquainted with him and wanted to remain so, indefinitely."

At Scarlett's words, Claire actually clapped.

"That's *exactly* what I mean!" On that she nodded emphatically, smiling beatifically at Scarlett as if she'd met her soulmate.

Sibyl was pretty certain they were speaking in code and stared at them, trying to decipher it. Then she gave up, it was all too much, this, the whole night. She no longer had the energy.

"How could Colin help them with shoes?" Sibyl queried.

At this, for some unhinged reason, Colin threw his head back and roared with laughter and all three feminine pairs of eyes swiveled to him. As he got himself under control, his body still shaking with mirth, his arm shot out, curled around Sibyl's waist and he tugged her toward him. She could feel, against her own body, the laughter still rumbling through him even as he kissed her soundly on the lips.

When he lifted his head, his eyes were smiling (hers were dazed, and not just from the kiss). She had the impression that something profound just happened, she just didn't know what.

"I *will* amend my statement, your sister is definitely annoying, you're just adorable," he told her.

"Oh dear goddess, don't let Mags hear you call her adorable. There'll be hell to pay," Scarlett warned.

Sibyl was beginning to feel a prick of irritation.

The last two days, she was on pins and needles wondering what was happening with Colin. Finally, after a rather frightening dinner, she discovered she was likely the reincarnation of a woman who was murdered centuries before and Sibyl's lover was the doppelganger of that woman's dead husband. Two people she cared about lied to her about this bizarre fact for weeks. And now, in what seemed like the blink of an eye, she and Colin were something else. Something other than what they had been. Something that made that thing that curled up and died inside her weeks ago start to feel some life again.

And they were talking about shoes.

"I think I'm missing something here," Sibyl told the room at large.

"Look around you, Billie. Look really closely, what do you see?" Scarlett prompted, her tone was no longer wry but gentle.

Sibyl looked around.

Colin had a very nice bedroom. It was rather large and richly painted with matte, slate-gray walls and accents of ivory and midnight blue. There were fantastic white cornices and intricate ceiling roses. There were deep-seated, diamond-paned windows with heavy drapes. The bed was an enormous four-poster covered with a fluffy comforter in midnight blue and she already knew the ivory sheets were soft, lush and divine. There was a marble-edged fireplace with an elaborate mantelpiece that had two comfortable chairs at angles in front of it (at least, when Scarlett wasn't sitting in one of them). Several gleaming chest of drawers and gigantic wardrobes were against the walls.

Off to one side was a door to a pristine bathroom that used to be a dressing room, which contained a fabulous round tub big enough for two.

Off the back corner of the bedroom was a small room, sunken by several steps, that used to be a consecrated sanctuary, complete with stained glass windows, but was stripped of its blessing centuries ago and was now a rather glorious reading room, complete with a chaise lounge covered in gray velvet.

Sibyl felt somewhat uncomfortable as she looked around the room, standing in it with a man who actually owned and lived in a National Trust property.

Notions were coming to her fast and sharp.

He drove an expensive Mercedes.

He wore tailored suits to work, suits that, after years of living with Scarlett, Sibyl knew probably cost a month of her salary (if not more).

He hired someone to wait on the table at a dinner party at his house.

He could afford, in a day, seemingly without effort, to acquire a suitcase full of fifty thousand pounds worth of twenty pound notes.

And refurnish a room in a Community Centre days after he'd

bought a new alarm system for her house.

The light finally dawned and she looked at Scarlett mainly because she was avoiding looking at Colin.

Then she breathed out the word, "Oh."

She could imagine every woman he met took one look at him, his clothes, his house, his car and saw nothing but his bank account. The fact that he was magnificently handsome, protective, intelligent and could be gentle and even tender was just a bonus. A very nice bonus, but a bonus all the same.

She couldn't leave it at that, she had to know so she lifted her gaze to Colin.

"You were testing me, weren't you?"

She was referring to the fifty thousand pounds.

He knew what she was referring to and nodded.

Her heart sank.

"I failed, didn't I?" she whispered but she knew.

She'd not only failed, she'd done it spectacularly.

"Sibyl." His voice was quiet and there was something else there, something that might have been easier to decipher if they didn't have an avidly watching audience, but before he could say more another knock came at the open door and Mrs. Byrne was standing in it.

"Am I interrupting?" Marian asked.

"No," Scarlett offered as an answer.

"For God's sake," Colin muttered under his breath.

"Sibyl, dear, I just wanted to be certain you weren't angry with me," Mrs. Byrne said, looking anxious and coming into the room.

"Oh, Mrs. Byrne, I was just in shock," Sibyl answered, pulled from Colin's arms, walked to the woman and gave her a fierce hug. "I'm not angry with you," she reassured her.

"Perhaps we should have the cheese and coffee served in the bedroom?" Colin drawled.

"Great idea," Scarlett agreed. "Do you have a bell pull up here so we can call the young, strapping Peter?"

Colin cut an acid look to Scarlett and Sibyl moved to stand between them in case he was driven to physical violence.

"I need you to know my part in all of this," Mrs. Byrne told Sibyl, thankfully drawing her attention away from her sister.

"I want to hear this!" Claire cried and then threw herself on the bed, stretching out on her side, her head in her hand and she settled in excitedly.

Colin watched as Mrs. Byrne sat primly on the edge of the bed and then his eyes shifted to the ceiling as if praying for deliverance. Realizing there was none, he walked toward the chair next to Scarlett, swiftly pivoted it around, leaned forward and hooked Sibyl (again) about the waist and settled into the chair. He pulled a surprised Sibyl onto his lap and when she squirmed he muttered impatiently, "Sit still."

Sibyl watched as Scarlett took this all in, raised her eyebrows and grinned.

She ignored her sister and did as she was told. Colin was giving the impression of a caged lion who would undoubtedly attack given his first opportunity and she was the first in line of assault.

It was then Mrs. Byrne started talking.

Of witches.

And magic.

And horses named Mallory.

Of ancient spells linking lovers for eternity and present day potions that brought old souls back to life in new bodies.

She went on and on about Granny Esmeralda Crane (whose old cottage Sibyl now inhabited), the results of the grisly murder she happened upon, Esmeralda's Book of Shadows, Royce and Beatrice and how she, Marian Byrne, was here—after a long line of witches who'd waited in vain to bring together the new lovers and end a nearly five hundred year old curse of doomed—true love.

What she did *not* talk of was dark souls, this, unknown to Sibyl, Colin had demanded she keep to herself.

"So, you see, Sibyl, it was my destiny to bring you to Colin. As you've learned, he's a bit, er . . . difficult, so I was trying to be clever. I was not so clever as I thought and it made things hard on you and for that, I apologize," Marian finished with her hands held up in front of her in supplication.

Sibyl stared at her in astonishment.

There was nothing else to do but stare . . . in . . . complete . . . *astonishment.*

Finally, she whispered, grasping onnto the thing that least affected her sanity and she felt Colin's arm tighten around her waist when she did so. "Royce's horse was named Mallory?"

"Indeed, it was, my dear." For some reason Marian was smiling at her and her next statement would explain why. "You see, in so many ways, you and Colin were meant for each other, one could even say *born* for each other. Do you take my meaning?"

Sibyl felt her sister's eyes turn to her just as she experienced something raw and unexplainable rip at her heart.

And she immediately felt panic.

Sheer, unadulterated panic.

Because she might be getting what she'd always wanted, what she always knew was waiting for her and instead of being joyful, it scared the living daylights out of her.

Or she might not get it at all and that frightened her more.

"I need to go home," she whispered urgently.

She had to think. She had to get away and think without an audience, without Colin's hard thighs under her and his warm arms circling her. She tried to stand but Colin's hands prevented her.

"Let me go, Colin," she said softly, turning beseeching eyes to him. "I need to go home," she repeated and she hoped he understood, prayed for it.

He didn't. Instead, his eyes slid sideways toward her sister, communicating to her sibling silently.

Sibyl heard as Scarlett said, "Story time over, folks, time for us to leave," and she was shocked at her sister's ready defection but too overwrought to do a thing about it.

Sibyl tried to stand again as she heard the others quietly exit with nary a word to the couple. Colin kept her where she was, his hands hard at her waist.

"Please let me go," she whispered as she heard the door close softly behind the other women.

"You promised me," he told her, his eyes moving back to her after watching the door close behind their family and friend.

"Promised?"

She was near tears, holding on to her careening thoughts with waning energy. She was frightened to the core of her being by what she'd seen and heard that night.

And mostly what it meant.

"To spend the night with me, you promised," he reminded her, his eyes were searching her face but his own was set and unyielding.

"That was before. You must understand." Her voice was pleading.

"No matter what happened, you promised me that."

"I wasn't in my right mind!" she cried. "I thought, just like when we were in the summer house, that tonight *I'd* turned you into Royce with my magical powers."

She stopped speaking for he looked at her like a third eyeball had suddenly popped out of her forehead.

Then he asked incredulously, "Your what?"

She immediately felt a fool (or more of a fool than she already was). She should never have told him that. She closed her eyes slowly and wished she could grab the words and stuff them back in her mouth.

She was tired—no, exhausted, bone weary and not to mention frightened out of her mind. She wasn't thinking clearly, didn't have her guard up.

This was too much, *he* was too much.

Apparently, he *was* her dream man, the one she'd been destined to find, the one who she was fated to be with for five hundred years. He'd tested her fortitude, resolve and moral perspicacity and she'd fallen at the first hurdle by taking his money (a great deal of his money) the third time she'd ever seen him.

And for what?

A minibus for oldies.

If he knew, he'd think she lost her mind, if she ever had one in the first place. He'd likely be disgusted, it was almost better to let him think she'd used it on herself. Considering his history with women, *that*, at least, was something he'd understand.

"Please let me up," she pushed against his hands, not able to take a moment more.

"Will you stop fighting me and *talk to me*, for Christ's sake?" he exploded.

Obviously, he'd reached the end of his tether and her head snapped around to look at him.

"Well I didn't know!" she cried.

"Know what?"

"That you'd been given a magical potion! I thought, well, I'd grown up with Mags always telling me that there was magic in the air, in the trees, in the rivers, yadda, yadda, yadda, and I was dreaming of Royce and Beatrice and *I didn't know*. I didn't know who they were. I thought it was *me*! I thought *I'd* brought Royce out in you."

Colin changed the subject and his voice was lethal when he stated, "You knew it was him and you let him kiss you."

It was her turn to look to the ceiling and make quick, desperate promises to the goddess for rescue. When no otherworldly aid arrived, she tugged once more at his hands, using her legs as leverage, and she surged up, but unfortunately he followed her.

"Why did you let him kiss you?" Colin pressed.

She was *not* going to tell him about her dream lover, that she thought she was creating Royce because she needed to believe. She had no idea what this all meant, to her, to them, and she didn't trust him enough with that knowledge. It was too close to her heart, she barely knew him. Until tonight she didn't know what he did for a living or that he had a brother. He could have twelve more siblings for all she knew. She knew his body intimately, but Colin, she barely knew at all.

Selling her sexual favors for minibuses and living her life thinking she was destined for another was pure lunacy. He wouldn't want anything to do with her.

He was night and she was day. His parents were posh and hers were weird. His sister was sweet and caring and hers was . . . well . . . *not* (exactly).

They didn't suit.

She had to guard her heart, or, at the very least, she had to know what this all meant to *him*.

"What am I to you?" she asked in response to his question.

"Don't change the subject, Sibyl," he warned, his voice dangerously smooth.

"You want an answer then you answer my question. I deserve that and you know it. What am I to you now?"

"Why did you take the fifty thousand pounds?"

"Goddess!" she exploded, throwing out her arms. "Can't you answer a single question?"

He glared at her.

She glared back.

Then she gave up.

"I'm going home," she declared and turned to leave, tired, sick at heart and wanting nothing but a nice mug of hot cocoa and her mother's shoulder to cry on. She didn't even care how pathetic that seemed for a thirty-two-year-old woman. Luckily, fortune smiled on her (belatedly) and made it so that her mother wasn't over a thousand miles away but was right downstairs.

She had forgotten, briefly and absentmindedly, how ruthless Colin could be when he wanted something.

And three steps away from the door, she was swung up in his arms. She emitted a stunned cry as he swiftly strode back across the room and then she was thrown on the bed. Before she could get her arms and legs under control and scramble off the other side, his weight settled on her, pinning her to the bed.

"Do I have your attention?"

His voice was calm, his eyes were not. His chest was against hers, his heavy, muscled thigh was thrown across both of hers and he was up on one elbow, his other arm stretched across her and he was scowling down at her with blazing eyes.

She gritted her teeth and stared at him. It was futile to struggle. He had twice her strength, maybe more.

When he lifted his brows arrogantly, silently demanding a response, she snapped, "Yes!"

"Good, now you're going to answer some questions."

She pulled both her lips between her teeth to stop herself from saying something foolish.

"Why did you take the fifty thousand pounds?"

"I can't tell you."

"Why can't you tell me? Is it illegal?"

"No!"

"Are you in trouble?"

"No."

"In debt?"

"No."

She was losing her patience but unfortunately so was he, and his lost patience was a tad bit scarier than hers.

"Sibyl."

"I just can't tell you, you'll think I'm . . ." she hesitated.

"What?"

"Crazy!" she cried.

"Crazier than you thinking you turned me into Royce Morgan with your magical powers?"

She groaned, horrified and humiliated.

Then she replied what she thought was relatively logically, considering they were discussing a real life, magical potion, "Well, it's hardly crazier than how you actually *did* turn into Royce Morgan or any of the other things that I've learned tonight."

He decided to ignore that and persevered with his interrogation. "Why did you kiss him?"

She bit her lips again.

"Am I going to have to make you talk?" he threatened silkily.

Her eyes rounded.

She had no idea how he would do that but she doubted, seriously, that it would include physical violence.

However, she did not doubt that it would include *something* physical.

Then, for some reason, the words flew out of her mouth, almost against her volition, and she said something truly stupid.

"It was between him and me."

His eyes darkened dangerously and a muscle leaped in his jaw, and she knew in that moment that she was really in trouble.

Before he could say anything, or worse, *do* anything, there came another knock on the door.

Colin closed his eyes in angry frustration.

When he opened them, they were blazing and Sibyl held her breath at the sight of them.

"Do . . . not . . . bloody well . . . *move*," he bit out, shoved away from her and stalked to the door.

She thought it best to do as he said.

The caged lion had definitely been freed.

He pulled the door open and, luckily, it swung in such a way as to hide Sibyl from whoever was on the other side. Sibyl closed her eyes as she heard the conversation.

"If anyone else comes up here—" Colin's voice was barely controlled.

"Your mother, Claire and I are going to Walton Park Hotel. I'm going to take the Godwin's home first." Sibyl heard his father's voice speaking, his tone indicating solemn understanding at Colin's plight.

"Fine," Colin gritted out.

Sibyl sat up and looked across the room at the back of the door, her face flaming.

"Is Sibyl all right?" Mike asked quietly, his voice now filled with concern.

"She is right now," Colin answered his father, his words filled with foreboding.

There was a hesitation and then muttered goodbyes.

Colin closed the door with a finality that rocked Sibyl and caused her to scramble to her knees as Colin angrily moved toward the bed.

And, in an extreme act of self-defense, she blurted out a semi-fib that was part truth and part lie, "I'm not telling you about what happened between Royce and me because . . ."

He stopped at the side of the bed and stared down at her, his face a mask of fury. "Yes?" he prompted.

"Because of Royce, he wasn't even kissing *me*. He was kissing *her*."

She wasn't entirely certain that was exactly true, but she thought it sounded good. "It was his moment to say goodbye and it seemed . . ." She stopped, not able to find the word as Colin's angry face didn't change one iota. She finally found it, "Private."

"Sibyl." He voiced her name quietly.

"Yes?" she asked hopefully, wishing very much to get in the car with Mike and her family and go home to her bed, her thoughts and figure out what was to become of her future.

"You're a very bad liar." His voice was lethal.

Gone was her dream of escape.

Especially when his arm shot out and dragged her forward.

"Colin."

He didn't answer. To her disbelief, he'd located the zipper at her back and, expertly, slid it down.

"Colin!" She pushed against the arm that was still around her waist as his other hand pulled her dress up.

She could just not believe he was undressing her.

They were arguing, for goddess's sake!

His eyes locked on hers. "If you fight me Sibyl, I swear to God—" he started.

"What am I to you?" She had to know.

"Until you decide to start talking, our deal stays as it is, you're mine . . . for five months."

Her mouth dropped open.

Nothing had changed.

Not one thing.

Except, she knew she was the one who could stop it if she just told him who she was, what she was, why she took the fifty thousand pounds and all about her dream of a true love.

And none of this she could tell him. Not now, and, until she could trust him, maybe not ever. She'd rather him leave her later, than now. She'd rather have a few months of him, even angry, than just a few weeks. She couldn't bear to think of how he'd react if he knew the truth.

"It's four months," she retorted as the skirt of her dress slid over her hips.

"Now, it's six."

She gasped.

"It's four!"

"Seven," he bit out.

She clamped her mouth shut and he pulled the dress over her head, forcing her arms up with it. He tossed it aside, his hands settled on her waist and then slid, sending tingles in their wake, up her sides. He watched his hands move on her as she struggled valiantly against the tingles (and still lost).

"Are you stopping at seven?" he inquired with mock politeness as if he was an auctioneer and she was deciding what to bid.

She nodded, her head jerking angrily.

"I bet Royce didn't do this to Beatrice."

She had no idea what drove her to say it, it was ugly (not to mention stupid) and it didn't sound right on her lips.

But Colin reacted strangely, he chuckled, but instead of sounding amused it sounded grim.

"He should have, if he had, we wouldn't be in this fucking mess."

Then he pushed her to her back and landed on top of her.

And then he did a variety of delightful things to her where she didn't have to think anything at all.

Chapter NINETEEN

The Storm is Over

Colin awoke before dawn knowing something wasn't right.

He rolled from his back to his side and opened his eyes to see Sibyl sleeping all the way across the expanse of the large bed, her back to him.

Regardless of the fact that he was still half asleep, this annoyed him immensely.

In the beginning she had always slept with her back to him. However, since Mallory had been tranquillized, she'd taken to curling her warm, soft body against his every time they'd been together.

This was *not* a step in the right direction.

Last night had definitely not gone to plan mainly due to Sibyl's extraordinary temper (even though he knew this about her, he still underestimated it) and her refusal to trust him with the truth about herself.

Colin was not about to take any responsibility for what happened, he had kept Royce and Beatrice from her for a reason which she had cottoned on to quickly and his sister had helpfully, if rather irritatingly, confirmed and then explained.

He, however, had taken great pains to break it to her gently, with her loved ones around and Marian Byrne there to impart the whole story (or the parts Colin felt Sibyl should know). Not to mention, Colin showing her that she had his family's full support as well.

None of which, he marked with irritation, she actually noticed.

He couldn't understand her reaction because he knew she didn't have a thing to hide. This was something, however, he'd never tell her. If she found out he'd investigated her, there would be hell to pay.

He felt no compunction at keeping this from her. He felt no compunction about doing anything that would make this rough ride smoother, for both of them. The fact that she had nothing to hide made it further difficult to understand why she continued to keep it from him.

This, he could only assume, meant she didn't trust him.

Which meant he had more work to do.

Luckily, he now had *seven* months in which to do it. She seemed willing, with only the mildest form of protestation (something that he found very telling) to allow him to demand further time from her.

He pinned his hope on this.

Her refusal to discuss Royce was a different story. How Colin could feel such searing jealousy for a dead man, he could not fathom, but he did. She'd shared something with Royce in her chalet and Colin damned well wanted to know what it was.

And what Colin wanted, he found a way to get.

He reached out and dragged her across the bed. She made an endearing, sleepy mew in her throat but didn't wake. The moment she hit his warmth, she turned and curled against his side, wrapping her arm around his waist.

This was *much* better.

Then, listening to the soft rain against the windows for a few moments while Sibyl nestled deeper into him, Colin fell back to sleep.

COLIN WOKE AGAIN, hours later, to an empty bed.

Instantly alert, he nearly threw the covers back, thinking she'd crept away while he was sleeping and determined to find her (wherever she was), drag her back and keep her there until they had things sorted.

The way things were, obviously, could not go on. He wouldn't allow it. They needed to straighten everything out between them. He didn't need to battle her while protecting her against whoever was out there trying to kill her. He still took the threat seriously even though there had been no further contact and no report of suspicious activity from the team that was following her.

Then he saw her coming from the bathroom wearing the green shirt he'd worn last night. His body momentarily stilled at the sight and then he settled back into the bed and allowed some of the tension to ease out of him. He watched her without saying a word, deciding that he liked, very much, the look of her in his shirt.

She was holding it together with one hand at the front and looking about the room with what appeared to be confusion. He watched with interest, wondering what she was up to as she walked to one of his dressers, pulled open first one drawer then closed it then another, and found what she was looking for. Closing the drawer quietly with her thigh, she shed his shirt with her back to him and pulled one of the T-shirts he used to work out in over her head. As she was quite tall, it engulfed her in width but barely covered her rounded bottom.

There was something profoundly intimate about her wearing his clothes, not only wearing them but rooting around in his dresser to find them.

If any other woman had dared to do this, he would have found it an unacceptable invasion. With any other woman, it would have been a line not to be crossed.

With Sibyl, he not only accepted it, he welcomed it and decided he liked this item of his clothing on her even better than the other.

She walked back to the bed, clearly preoccupied. She didn't even look at him to notice he was watching her openly, lying on his side and up on his elbow. She slid between the covers, close to the edge of her side and settled with her back to him.

The instant she was settled, Colin's arm shot out, hooked around her waist and dragged her (again) across the bed.

This time, awake, she made an *angry* mew of protest and whirled mid-drag so she faced him head on.

"You're awake!" she cried, accusation in her voice, as if he was trying to keep this fact from her, which he was not.

"I thought you'd left," he returned.

Expressions chased across her face from surprise to exasperation.

"I didn't think of that," she muttered and he could tell she was cross with herself.

He nearly smiled at the thought of her absentmindedness finally working in his favor.

Instead, he kept his mind steadily on his latest task.

"Are you ready to talk this morning?" he inquired smoothly.

Her eyes shifted to his face and they narrowed just as her lips puckered. The room was dim with early morning light but he could still see they were growing emerald. Quickly.

He had long since found her transforming eye color a boon. She wasn't likely ever to be able to hide anything from him when it was written, so clearly, in her eyes. Not to mention the fact that she was an incredibly and often hilariously poor liar.

"No," she answered abruptly, everything about her showing she was definitely deep in her early morning grouch.

It was then the idea came upon him. A very pleasing idea. An idea that would make this morning's anticipated skirmish go in Colin's favor and likely be immensely enjoyable in the process.

And Colin wasted no time putting it in action.

One of his arms was under her body. He wrapped it around her waist and bunched the material of the T-shirt up in his fist so it slid slowly up her bottom. He felt her tense as he ducked his hand under the shirt while his other arm went around her back, pulling her even closer to his chest. Before she could try to escape, he threw his leg over both of hers.

"What are you doing?" she asked suspiciously, moving her legs under his thigh, and he knew she was trapped when she made an aggravated noise in the back of her throat.

He didn't answer as his hand started to move on the soft skin at the small of her back, leisurely forming figure eights on her body's (nearly) most sensitive area, and her head snapped back to look at him just as her frame froze.

"Colin, what are you doing?" she repeated.

Her voice was now slightly desperate, definitely tinged with panic and she lifted her hands to press them against his chest.

"Making you talk," he answered lazily.

"No!" she cried, realizing his intent.

"Yes," he retorted.

She moaned, it was partially a frustrated sound but partially something else. He felt his own body begin to respond to the moan, not to mention her fidgeting.

Christ, but no woman had ever had this effect on him. The sight of her, the feel of her, the smell of her never ceased to make him nearly desperate with wanting her.

Resolutely keeping his mind on his aim, he dipped his hand to smooth it over her lushly curved ass and suggested, "Let's start where we left off last night, hmm?"

She closed her eyes, bit her lip and pressed against him. She didn't say a word, just shook her head on the pillow.

"Sibyl, look at me," he commanded.

Her eyes flew open and they were no longer emerald but changing swiftly to sherry.

He grinned in anticipated triumph and went back to his figure eights.

"The fifty thousand pounds, what did you need it for?" he asked, his voice low.

Not giving her time to answer, he brushed his lips against hers, and tasting a hint of toothpaste, but mostly Sibyl, he felt himself start to harden with need.

She remained silent.

"The fifty thousand?" he prompted relentlessly.

She shifted and dipped her chin low, nearly knocking his chin with her head as she did so. He could feel she was no longer trying to escape but instead trying to control her body's reaction to him. He moved his other hand up under the T-shirt and brushed his knuckles on another sensitive area he discovered, the satiny skin beneath her breast, and he heard her suppressed moan.

"This isn't fair," she whispered to her chest, her voice breathless.

"I'll stop when you talk to me."

She shook her head and he didn't know if she was shaking it to tell him not to stop or that she wasn't going to talk. Either way suited his purpose. He was vastly enjoying this sensual torture and he moved his hand to cup her full breast, softly brushing his thumb over a nipple and feeling it harden in response. All the while, his hand moved languidly and tantalizingly at the small of her back.

Her head fell back and she licked her lips then pulled them between her teeth.

Still, she remained silent.

"Not talking?" he queried.

She shook her head stubbornly, her hair fell into her face, sliding gorgeously down his chest and his already stiffening body turned rock hard.

He recognized then that he wasn't going to be able to play this game very long. Heightening her arousal was doing the same to him.

He needed answers from her. He needed her to trust him with those answers, and, as she writhed against him, he felt the blood pound through his veins, quickening his own breath and licking fire through his body. He decided he didn't much care how he got those answers just that he got them soon.

Colin dropped his head, pulled the T-shirt up to her chest and lifted her breast to receive his mouth. The minute his lips closed around her nipple, drawing it in gently, she made an appealing sound deep in her throat and he smiled as desire strummed through him.

"Do you like that?" he asked against her nipple and then blew on it, watching in fascination as it rose and puckered, tremendously satisfied that he could illicit the same easy reaction from her that he felt for her.

He heard her head move on the pillow again and lifted his to watch her.

"No?" His tone was teasing.

"I'm never going to forgive you," she whispered, her eyes sherry and her face flushed.

"I think you will," he countered and then dropped his head again and pulled her nipple into his mouth, rolling his tongue around it.

Gratified when he felt her body buck and jerk against him, he drew her nipple in further, sucking gently, then more adamantly, demanding a further response and she didn't disappoint him. She arched her back, forcing herself deeper into his mouth. This caused havoc in his own body, her squirming against him and her mute, seductive displays of desire. He had a pressing urge to plunge his hand between her legs to see how ready she was for him.

When her hands slid into his hair, holding him to his task, he realized he was finally getting somewhere.

He lifted his head and she made a noise of disappointment that thrilled him in an almost primitive way and he interrupted his game by crushing his mouth to hers. He needed to taste her, allowed himself this moment of sheer pleasure before carrying on with his goal. She opened her lips immediately, inviting his tongue inside, and happily he obliged. The kiss was hot and wild and he pressed his hips against hers, showing her his blatant arousal. She groaned into his mouth the moment she felt his need and her hand slid down his back, over his ass then fluttered around his hip to find him.

He caught it easily and shifted it behind her back.

"Not yet," he warned. "Not until you talk." This he said against her mouth, his breath was coming fast but hers was faster. His hand at the small of her back never ceased moving and she was, of her own accord, pressing her body against him, pushing her hips insistently against his.

He let go of her hand, and before she knew what he was about, he lifted his leg off hers, pulled one of hers up to hook around his waist and slid his hand between her legs, finally touching her right where she needed it.

The minute he did, she gasped deliciously and his own body jerked at the sound and the evidence of her need.

Christ, she was amazing.

Colin lost several notches on his control.

"Talk," he growled impatiently, needing this to end soon so he could take care of the both of them.

He pressed his fingers against her, wanting his cock to be where his fingers were, just as she pushed her hips against his hand.

"What . . . what do you want to know?" she breathed, delightfully losing her battle.

"The fifty thousand pounds," he reminded her through clenched teeth, too far gone to glory in his triumph then, needing the feel of her, Colin slid one finger inside.

He watched her immediate reaction. Her lips parting, she pulled in her breath delicately and he nearly lost himself in the seductive beauty of it.

Christ, he was going to come without her even touching him.

She emitted a deep, lusty groan and finally capitulated. "I gave it to the Community Centre. For . . . a . . . a minibus."

Not finished, he wanted it all, so he continued his torture.

He slid his finger out of her silken wetness, sensing victory and then back in again.

"Why wouldn't you tell me?"

"I thought . . ." She pressed against his hand and he took his finger away from her when she hesitated and her half-closed eyes flew open. "Colin, I want it back."

Her voice was throaty and her hands were moving all over him. They felt hot, fevered, and wherever they went, they sent shafts of lust straight through him.

"You'll get it back," he promised and she'd get more than that, he knew. "Finish telling me."

She shook her head but started talking anyway. "I thought you'd think I was crazy. I thought, if you knew I'd sell my body for a minibus, you'd leave me."

That was not what he expected to hear and it so surprised him, he momentarily forgot his desire.

"Why would I leave you?"

Her dazed eyes found his.

"Who in their right mind sells their body for a minibus for oldies?" she burst out breathily, frustrated, tracing his arm to his hand to force him back to where she wanted him but he was now more interested in what she said than what they both wanted. She swiftly reminded him, "I told you, Colin, and you promised. Now I want it back," she demanded, and he pushed her on her back and loomed over her, spreading her legs with his thigh and pressing against her.

"You didn't want me to leave?" he asked.

This was definitely something he wasn't expecting and he found himself enjoying an entirely different sense of triumph.

Her gaze was soft on his face, her expression filled with longing but he could see fear there as well.

"No," she whispered.

"Why?" he pressed.

"Colin, please. Don't ask me these things."

"Why didn't you want me to leave?" he demanded, ignoring her request, now wanting more than ever to hear what she had to say.

Indeed, he found he *needed* to hear it.

"Because I thought you might be . . ."

She stopped, her hand drifted down his abdomen with seductive intent and he grabbed it and pulled it to his chest.

"Sibyl—"

"Someone special!" she suddenly shouted, losing her battle against him, her stubbornness and her body's desire. "I thought you were someone special and I didn't want you to think I was some crazy woman and leave. I mean, it isn't every day someone sells their body and with it their soul and all they feel is good and right about themselves for a minibus! Don't you find that odd? Strange? Utterly ludicrous? Do *you* want to be with a woman like that? I think not," she snapped, not letting him react.

Her words tore at him, lacerating his heart.

All they feel is good and right about themselves . . .

All of his desire to torment her fled as he stared at her, his insides clenching with guilt.

He had nothing to say except to point out the very important fact that she was *exactly* the kind of woman he wanted to be with but she didn't give him the chance to say it.

She reared away from him, yanking her wrist out of his grasp, but he caught her and rolled to his back, pulling her on top of him, his thigh still pressed between hers and he lifted his knee.

"I've got to get out of here!" she cried desperately.

She was near tears, he could see them shimmering in her eyes.

"Sibyl."

He knew then that, regrettably, he'd lost control of the situation and she'd lost control of her emotions. This wasn't about desire anymore but about something else, something he was powerless to control, something that was totally Sibyl. The only thing he could do was ride it out.

"What?" she snapped. "You're ruthless, you know. Just plain old mean."

Not allowing him to respond to those true, awful (but also rather adorable) statements, she tried to pull away again and grunted with the effort then stopped at once, for seemingly no reason, caught in her own turmoil, her weight collapsed on him and this time, he grunted.

"My parents warned me, after the animal shelter debacle, they warned me I'd end up doing something stupid and here I am. I should have said yes to you when you asked me out after the night at the club. But how was I to know you were, well . . . *you*!" she cried. "That you were the type of man who could, and would, with a couple of phone calls, have gotten that vile minibus driver sacked. Or that you could be gentle and tender, sweet and generous. I didn't know who you were, what you could do or that you'd even do it! I would have done anything in these last few weeks to take all of this back so you wouldn't think I was a worthless, money-grubbing slut. But, back then, I thought *you* were insane. Now I know everything and—"

She stopped abruptly, deciding again to fight. She pushed against him then just as suddenly gave up and crumpled on him, promptly lost control and burst into tears.

Finally given the opportunity to get a word in edgewise, he was speechless at learning what he did in her shouted, abject confession. He could do nothing but hold her as she cried against his chest, moving only once to press her face between his shoulder and neck. Her body was wracked with her tears, tears wrought by something far beyond her confession, something deeper, more painful. He was not certain he understood it and definitely didn't know what to do about it.

Colin was not used to not knowing what to do. In fact, he was pretty certain there was never a time when he *didn't* know what to do.

When she started speaking again, her words were stunted and jerky with tears.

"It was just Meg," she said and this made him all the more confused because he didn't know who the hell Meg was, until she spoke again and it became dreadfully clear as to what had been tormenting Sibyl for weeks.

And what Sibyl Godwin said next began to melt Colin Morgan's brittle, cold heart.

"When she broke her hip falling out of the bus. I yelled at the minibus driver a few days before, letting my stupid, *stupid* temper get the best of me. Kyle told me I would make it worse for them if I upset the minibus driver and I did. I made it worse! So much worse! And Meg got hurt because of it. *Because of me!* It was all my fault so I had to fix it, no matter what it meant. I had to fix it. And then *you* came in and gave me a way to fix it and it was the *worst* way possible but I had to take it because it was the only choice I had and it was *all my fault*!"

His arms tightened around her and he rolled her to her back. Stretching his long length down her side he lifted himself on his elbow to look at her. Then he gently moved the hair away from her face but she threw her arm over her eyes, dislodging his hand and turned her head away from him to hide her emotion.

And Colin felt his heart squeeze at her anguish. It was clear she'd been holding on to this for weeks. Blaming herself for something she could never possibly have prevented, something she could not have caused, something that was beyond her control.

"What happened to Meg wasn't your fault." He tried to reason with her, thinking it the best way.

She shook her head determinedly. "It was."

"It wasn't your fault, Sibyl. These things happen."

She took in a shuddering breath and slid her arm away from her eyes, allowing it to drop in defeat at her side and her tear-brightened gaze moved to lock on his. At the sight of her desolation, his gut clenched.

How could one person take on such a world of pain? It wasn't even *her* pain.

What was it like to live in that head of hers?

"Christ, Sibyl," he muttered because he could think of absolutely nothing else to say.

"Old people die after breaking their hips, Colin," she told him.

"Did she die?" he queried cautiously.

"No," she answered and took another fractured breath. "But she's been very hurt and she isn't getting better very fast."

"Did she blame you?"

"No, of course not!"

He ran the back of his fingers gently along her jaw, trying physically to soothe away her hurt. "Then, sweetheart, you have to stop blaming yourself."

"Don't you see?" She threw up her hands in exasperation at what she considered his extreme obtuseness. "I did that with the minibus driver, which hurt Meg, and then you came to my house and offered me money and you don't trust women easily—"

"Sibyl—" He tried to interrupt her rampaging train of thought and its hysterical bent toward self-recrimination and failed.

"No!" she cried. "And I played right into your hands so I'm *double* trouble, breaking old people's hips and making you think even worse of my sex. Once you found out . . ." She stopped and then blurted out, "Of course you'd leave me! Hell, *I'd* leave me!"

At this outrageous assertion, he couldn't have helped it to save his life.

He chuckled.

She was whipping herself up into a drama, so caught in everyone else's troubles she couldn't see what was happening around her.

She couldn't see that he, long since, had stopped using her and started courting her.

She couldn't see that even though she pretended she wanted less of him, she never left, not last night, not this morning, not the first night they met, not any time before and not now.

She couldn't see that she hid something splendid (if a little warped and certainly a habit he needed to break her of), an act of such selflessness it was breathtaking, when telling him would have ended their battles days ago.

At his chuckle, her eyes flared.

"What's so damned funny?" she snapped, in a flash moving from despair to anger.

"Would you have taken the money from Paul and slept with him for it?" Colin asked, watching her closely, knowing her answer and trying to hide his mirth.

"Paul?" She blinked, momentarily confused.

"The drunk from the club."

"No! How could you even think—?"

"Your medic?" Colin persisted.

"My . . . Steve?" Her eyes narrowed. "Of course not. And he's not *my* medic." This was said with extreme distaste as if the thought was beyond foul.

Her reaction satisfied Colin tremendously.

He shook it off and charged on, "Can you think of anyone, besides me, who you would have taken the money from, sold your body to for a minibus?"

This stopped her. She froze and glowered at him. Then her eyes narrowed again and he could swear (to his immense relief) he saw the dawning of understanding.

To his surprise and extreme displeasure, she said, "Yes."

"Who?" he clipped.

"Clark Gable!" she announced and tried to slip out from under him but he hauled her back, this time he was no longer chuckling but laughing, his entire body shaking with it.

When he had his humor under control, Colin informed her helpfully, "I think, darling, you'll find he's dead,"

"Well," she muttered huffily, "I would have taken it from him when he was alive, of course, during his *Gone with the Wind* years."

"I'm in good company then," Colin muttered as he dropped to his side and pulled her against his body.

"It's time for *you* to answer some questions now," she demanded, recovering quickly from her drama and spearing him with her eyes.

He dipped his chin to look at her, giving her his full attention.

"What do you want to know?" he asked without hesitation.

"This Royce and Beatrice business, you and me, what am I to you now? What does that mean to us?"

"We have seven months to figure it out."

Her body stilled and her eyes, emerald before, started shifting back to hazel. This, he was beginning to interpret, when not just her norm, was when she was confused, mildly upset or melancholy.

"So nothing has changed?" she asked.

He shook his head and she bit her lip, her eyes sliding to the side, away from his, trying to mask her disappointed reaction. It took every ounce of his willpower not to grin.

"I will warn you," his tone was mock severe, "it might take eight months for us to figure it out."

He tugged gently on her hair to pull her head back and he ducked his own and kissed her throat, his other hand moving to the small of her back to form its lazy figure eights.

Her body jerked.

"Eight?" she breathed.

He noted, again, she said it in (weak) protest but she didn't bloody well mean it.

He had her. He knew in that moment, she was definitely *his*.

"Yes, maybe nine or even ten," he replied.

"Do I still have to do what you tell me to do?"

"Yes."

He felt her slump and he grinned against the skin at her throat then he slid his lips up her neck to taste the area just under her ear.

Sibyl trembled.

"Obviously you can't see anyone else but me," he warned, moving his mouth to hers and he brushed his lips there, feather-soft.

"What if I don't agree? The original bargain was two months. You keep changing the goal posts. Now you know what I did with the money, and you obviously don't mind, you can get a tax break, that ought to buy back some time."

He ignored her thoughtful suggestion (although he mentally filed it away). "You never know, it could take a year."

She gasped.

"I'm not doing this for a year!" she cried.

"No?" he asked, his hand slid back under her T-shirt and his finger swirled around her nipple.

She gasped again, this one much different than the last.

At her reaction, he gave her a smug smile as he felt his body tighten and he kissed her freckled nose.

And she gasped again, this one soft and, finally, full of understanding.

"Colin," she whispered, "You called me 'sweetheart.'"

Colin didn't reply.

Her eyes liquefied instantly to sherry.

"Colin?"

He stared her straight in the eye. "Yes?"

"Do I have to be where you want me, when you want me?"

"Not if you don't want to."

He felt her relief as she moved into him, wrapping her arms about his waist and pressing her soft, sweet body against his as a reward.

"So, can we start over?" she asked, her voice gentle and honeyed, and, if he heard it correctly, happy.

The glorious sound of it nearly made him groan.

Nevertheless, he answered her honestly, "No."

She looked startled.

"Why?"

"Because I like what's happened before."

"Well, I—"

"Stop thinking about it Sibyl. *That* part of it was over almost before it started."

She hesitated and he watched as she struggled briefly with it and finally, with a valiant effort of will, let it go.

And then he listened as she pressed her advantage. "So I *don't* have to do what you tell me to do."

"Of course you do." He rolled her onto her back, sliding his thigh between hers.

"What if I don't want to?"

"You suffer the consequences."

At this, she smiled, one of her heart-stopping, devastating, bedazzling smiles.

This time he rewarded her for the smile and he kissed her.

Without hesitation, she melted beneath him.

Several long, heady minutes later, when she was again wet and ready for him, he dragged his mouth from hers and warned, "We'll talk about Royce later."

Her desire-drugged eyes rounded with anger *and* alarm.

And he finally, with immense satisfaction, slid slowly inside her, her anger and alarm fled, and she was blissfully, completely, all his.

It was then, outside, even though neither Colin nor Sibyl noticed it, the sun started shining.

Chapter TWENTY

The Calm before the Second Storm

Colin pulled the BMW out of the garage, on his way to pick up Sibyl and her family to take them to the Community Centre's talent show.

Last weekend, when Colin arrived in the BMW to transport the five of them on a day trip to the Cotswolds, Sibyl walked out of the cottage and had been shocked at first sight of the car.

"Colin, I didn't even think. You had to rent a car!"

He just stared at her and she quickly, and accurately, interpreted the stare.

"How many cars do you own?" she asked with narrowed eyes.

"More than one," he'd answered carefully.

She'd sighed dramatically as if she was in fear for his mortal soul.

Then she suggested, "Let's just not tell Mags, agreed?"

Spending time with Sibyl's mother, Colin had swiftly learned that he could have told Mags he had twelve cars, with half of them being Land Rovers, as well as a number of sweat shops in the deepest regions of Vietnam, and Mags wouldn't have cared as long as Colin continued to service Sibyl sexually.

Nevertheless, for Sibyl's peace of mind and to reward her for being the only woman of his acquaintance who thought owning more than one vehicle a *fault* in his personality, he'd agreed.

Sibyl's surrender had been complete.

Colin instantly recognized just how much she had been holding back when she opened her heart to him fully. He found the offer of it into his care a gesture so precious, he wasn't certain how to handle it but he was certain that he would not, under any circumstances, let it go.

Regardless, the last two weeks of Sibyl had been a form of torture.

True, most of it was a splendid kind of torture, but it was torture nonetheless. He couldn't imagine a lifetime of it, just as he was looking forward to it. He was pleasantly contemplating their children (lots of them) and then old age. Sibyl could use some wrinkles, a few extra pounds (perhaps a stone or two) and a dozen children to slow her down.

If she didn't slow down, she'd likely kill him.

And if she didn't (or *he* didn't) control her rampant benevolence, she'd kill them both.

The sweet torture had started immediately after their morning at Lacybourne.

Before he had learned about her, he had planned to catch up on work while her parents were in England. He wanted to give her some private time with them therefore, he'd set up meetings in Manchester and Leeds the first week, and the second he was to be in London for an entire week of nearly back-to-back meetings he'd postponed since Sibyl.

The first week they were in town, he attended only one dinner with her and her family.

Claire had gone home the night after dinner at Lacybourne (or, as Sibyl described it, "The Dinner of Doom") to return to her family. Phoebe and Mike had stayed on to spend some time with the people who they knew (as Colin had told them) would soon be part of their extended family.

Colin had arrived late at the Indian restaurant and they'd all been ensconced in a huge booth and tucking into their starter.

The minute Colin arrived at the table, Mags or Phoebe wouldn't hear of Colin sitting anywhere but right beside Sibyl. As Sibyl was to the back at the very inside of the booth next to a window, Scarlett, Mike and Sibyl had to shift out so Colin could slide in.

Once he was in, he was crushed against the wall with Sibyl practically in his lap. She'd ordered a starter for him and another upheaval was caused when everyone handed their plates around to each other.

Forced to rest his arm along the back of the booth in order to accommodate himself and Sibyl in their spare space, he ate with one hand, his left.

He had no problem with this, it left his right hand free to stroke the skin at the nape of Sibyl's neck and feel her delicate shivers beneath his fingers.

During dinner, the conversation was tangled, Scarlett, Mike and Mags in a fierce verbal battle of one-upmanship as to who could tell the most outrageous story (Mags won by a landslide).

Not in the line of fire, Colin kept to himself, enjoying the feeling of Sibyl pressed contentedly against his side while, any time she'd want to share her humor with him, she looked over her raised shoulder, resting her chin against it as she prized him with one of her gorgeous smiles.

Bertie, seated opposite him, noticed Colin's absence from the conversation and took it upon himself to draw him into a private one of their own. At first a *one-sided* private conversation where Bertie explained to him (in detail) how he felt about what he described as the "Henry the Second and Thomas Becket fiasco."

Colin eventually found himself drawn into Bertie's passion for his subject and into a discussion about it, thinking Bertie was undoubtedly a popular professor considering both of these things.

When they left the restaurant and arrived at their assorted cars, Mags said to Sibyl, "I'm guessing you want to spend the night at Lacybourne."

This was not so much a guess as a command when she produced (to Sibyl's stunned glare) a small overnight bag that Sibyl obviously didn't pack and knew nothing about. Mags handed it to her daughter with a meaningful look.

Bertie sighed.

Phoebe and Mike looked dumbstruck.

Scarlett chuckled.

Colin could have kissed her.

Sibyl took the bag with a killing look at her mother and slid into the Mercedes.

"I told you my mother was odd," she announced when he reversed out of the parking spot.

"I'm not complaining," he pointed out, maneuvering the car out of the lot.

"You wouldn't," she grumbled, clearly embarrassed.

"Would you like me to take you back to Brightrose?" he queried politely even though he had no bloody intention of doing any such thing.

"No," she mumbled.

"Are you sure?" he couldn't keep the smile out of his voice.

She made an irate noise.

"You have better *sheets* at Lacybourne," she told him and he burst out laughing.

He spent the rest of the week letting himself into Brightrose in the dead of night, calming an always excited Mallory and then sliding into bed beside her long after she went to sleep. Once there, she would snuggle against him or, more to the point, he pulled her into him. He usually left long before she or her family woke or just in time to give her grumpy morning face a kiss before leaving to get to work.

Saturday and Sunday were days of revelation.

Mike and Phoebe had gone home on Friday morning after exchanging addresses, phone numbers and e-mails with the Godwins.

Saturday morning, Colin took Sibyl and her family to Bourton-on-the-Water and the morning passed in peaceful tranquility (if you didn't count Sibyl shouting like a drill sergeant at her lagging family and marching them into the newly discovered BMW).

Then, late morning, Colin's tranquility fragmented.

While in a fudge shop, Sibyl saw a young boy at the counter trying to buy a box of fudge and coming up short by twenty pence. Sibyl sidled up beside the boy and slid the twenty pence to the clerk. This not being a kind enough gesture, one Colin would never think of doing, she then handed the boy a two pound coin.

"Don't want to be caught short, again, do you?" she'd asked with a wink.

Then she so bedazzled the boy with one of her winning smiles, he'd walked straight into a display of candy. The entire display (which was a foot taller than him) came crashing in a great clamor to the floor.

Scooting him kindly on his way to his parents, Sibyl (with Mags and Scarlett) spent a quarter of an hour helping the clerk right the candy stand while chatting amiably and becoming the best of friends with the clerk in the process.

As they walked the streets of Bourton, every person she passed who had a dog on a lead, no matter how grand or ugly the dog was (indeed, she lavished more affection on the ugly ones), she would stop the owner with a joyful cry and beg, "Can I pet your dog?"

Unwilling, or more likely, unable to decline her friendly request and her sunny smile, the owners would acquiesce. She'd then crouch, ruffle the dog's fur and accept sloppy kisses all over her face and hands. All the while she cooed at the dogs and she and the Godwins would engage the owners in friendly conversation about any subject that came to mind—the unseasonably warm weather, the beauty of Bourton, dogs and what they thought of the ever-increasing danger of the greenhouse effect.

Then they'd stopped at a tea shop for cream teas on the way home. As they were all relaxing over their scones, clotted cream and jam, Sibyl was staring out the window with rapt attention.

Moments later, without a word, she abruptly ran from the table and out into the sunny back garden. As she approached she startled a family who were lazing in the warm day at a picnic table. She was talking intently and gesturing carefully and then she herded them solicitously into the tea shop. To Colin's stunned surprise, the family joined him and the Godwins for tea, crowding around a too small table, while they thanked Sibyl profusely for warning them of the beehive that nestled in the tree above their picnic table.

Not done, Sibyl sought out the owners of the tea shop to inform them of the hive. After doing this, she stood outside in the garden with the owners and Bertie and Mags, discussing (at length) what was to be done about the beehive while Colin sat with Scarlett, his legs stretched in front of him and crossed at the ankles, as he took in the scene.

He was prepared, if necessary, to haul Sibyl, kicking and screaming (he had no doubt), to the car if she tried to climb a ladder and see to the hive herself.

"Nothing to say?" Colin offered Scarlett her opening, not taking his eyes from Sibyl.

"Not right now," Scarlett answered, not taking her eyes from Colin.

Sunday he went to work in the morning and at noon he left to meet Sibyl and the Godwins on the seafront. When he arrived he found Bertie seated on a blanket in the grass with the remains of what appeared to be a vegetarian picnic. Mags was five feet away, talking animatedly to two women who both had babies in prams. Colin took in Mags, her red hair not faded but streaked with comely shafts of white, wearing a bright, gauzy concoction that looked delicate enough to disintegrate at a hint of wind.

After greeting Bertie, Colin asked, "Where are Sibyl and Scarlett?"

Bertie tilted his head across the green and Colin saw both sisters (Sibyl wearing a tight-fitting, faded, oft-worn Grateful Dead T-shirt and her daringly torn jeans, Scarlett wearing a pair of black capri pants and an emerald-green fitted, scoop-necked T-shirt) playing Frisbee with five men.

Colin watched for precisely thirty-eight seconds (Bertie timed him). Then he saw one of the men semi-tackle Sibyl, wrapping his arms about her middle and whirling her away from the Frisbee she was trying to catch. Her deep laugh filled the air at what she thought was friendly frolicking and Colin knew was anything but.

Without hesitation, Colin prowled toward them and Sibyl caught sight of him.

"Colin!" she cried as she smiled and ran to him, skidding to a bare-footed halt inches away, her golden hair flying in an attractive mess about her shoulders. She touched him with a hand at his waist, hooking her thumb in a belt loop at the side of his jeans and leaned in to ask playfully, "Do you want to play Frisbee?" And she asked this as she pulled her heavy, gorgeous hair away from her face with her other hand.

"No," he stated shortly.

Her face fell and he ignored it, dragged her against his body and kissed her hard on the lips.

When he lifted his head, she stared up at him, stupefied, before she breathed, "What was that for?"

Colin looked about the green at five crestfallen male faces and Scarlett's knowing one and said, "Just making things clear."

He dropped his arm, not waiting for her reply, turned and walked back to Bertie, settling down beside him on the grass, one leg stretched out, one knee bent, his wrist dangling on his knee.

Bertie was silent for a moment, before saying thoughtfully, "Welcome to my nightmare."

Colin's eyes reluctantly left Sibyl, slid to her father and he asked, "I'm sorry?"

Bertie again indicated his two daughters playing what was now a far more lackadaisical game of Frisbee and Colin glanced that way. Regardless if the men took Colin's possessive gesture in the spirit it was intended and backed off entirely, that didn't mean the magnificent sight of Sibyl and Scarlett racing around after a Frisbee wasn't the height of entertainment for most of the men on the seafront.

"I must say, Colin, I'm happy to have you around," Bertie told him.

"Why's that?" Colin inquired, giving Sibyl's father his full attention.

"A problem shared is a problem halved, in my case, literally."

At his comment, Colin threw his head back and laughed, as did Bertie.

When he'd controlled his hilarity, Colin told the older man with a hint of admiration, "I can't imagine how you did it for all these years."

"I've lost three inches and all my hair, so count yourself warned," Bertie stated then asked, "Do you have a plan?"

"I'm taking it day by day," Colin answered on a smile.

Bertie nodded with approval. "That's a good plan."

"What are you talking about?" Mags queried as she joined them.

"Nothing," Bertie replied after he accepted a swift, but rather ardent, kiss from his wife.

"You were laughing," Scarlett also sat with them and Colin looked up to see Sibyl drop to her knees beside him.

She awarded him a flush-faced grin, and to his deep satisfaction, she didn't hesitate a moment before she settled on her back with her head on his outstretched thigh, her hair falling haphazardly all over his lap.

"You must allow us our private little joke," Bertie murmured.

"About us girls? I don't think so," Scarlett parried.

"Enough, Scarlett," Bertie warned.

Sibyl shifted to her side but didn't lift her head.

"You were joking about us?" she asked her father.

"You joke about men all the time," Bertie defended.

Colin noted his tone was far less strict with his firstborn.

"That's true. Men, as a whole, are our private little joke," Scarlett confirmed cynically.

"Scarlett! Be good." It was Mags's turn to chastise her daughter but it was clear she didn't mean it and this was made clear by her blue eyes dancing wickedly.

Sibyl moved again to her back and caught Colin's eye.

"*You* aren't *my* joke," she assured him, her eyes dancing but not like her mother's, her gaze wasn't wicked but warm and sweet.

"Colin isn't *anybody's* joke," Scarlett declared, for the first time giving Colin an indication of her blessing and she collapsed on her side and popped a grape in her mouth.

"With practice, you'll learn to ignore her," Sibyl confided to him and froze her sister with a glance.

Colin leaned back on an elbow. He had Sibyl's head on his leg, her hair spread across his lap, the sun was shining on them and she'd just indicated he'd be around long enough to learn to ignore her sister. He'd long since been ignoring Scarlett as well as the envious looks he was getting from most of the men in the vicinity, and had, for longer than he could remember, perfected the art of ignoring the looks from the women.

He couldn't call up even a hint of irritation because at that precise moment, all was right in Colin Morgan's world.

They went to Brightrose shortly after, Colin driving the lot of them and their picnic paraphernalia in the BMW as they'd walked to the seafront. While Mags cooked dinner, Bertie, Scarlett, Sibyl and Colin spent the rest of the afternoon playing Trivial Pursuit.

Colin lost, soundly. Bertie knew everything about everything. Scarlett, a neurologist, also had an amazing knowledge of entertainment and sport. Sibyl's subjects were history, art and literature and geography. The whole game, Bran spent tucked in Sibyl's lap while Mallory lay by Colin, his head, when he was given the option, resting on Colin's feet.

Mags stepped out of the kitchen and announced that dinner would be ready in five minutes.

At her announcement, Sibyl gave a panicked cry, dropped her cat and sped into the kitchen. After a great clamor, Mags came out of the kitchen again and announced with a grin that dinner would be in *twenty-five* minutes.

Colin made Bertie and himself a gin and tonic and they settled on the couches while Scarlett went to help in the kitchen.

"Sibyl says you have the dreams, just like she does," Bertie noted.

Colin had confided in Sibyl that he, too, was dreaming of Royce and Beatrice. This was confided in an effort to soften their eventual discussion about her time with Royce in the chalet. A discussion Colin still fully intended to have but only after she was more comfortable with him and in their relationship.

"Yes," he answered.

Bertie leaned forward excitedly. "What's it like, being back there, being in that time?"

Colin regarded his soon-to-be-father-in-law, a medieval history professor who undoubtedly thought this of extraordinary interest, and answered honestly, "It isn't like anything. I don't pay attention to it. I only pay attention to Beatrice. My dreams aren't like Sibyl's, she's participating, Royce knows there's a difference in Beatrice when she's with him. I've always known who I was when in the dream, why I'm there, because I knew where I was, who *she* was. I just experience it."

"Does it feel like a memory?" Bertie asked.

Colin thought about it and had been thinking about it a great deal lately, mainly because of how Sibyl described her own dreams. She'd hinted that Royce had recognized her, knew who she was that afternoon in the chalet. This lent an added, unknown dimension to their meeting in the present time and, possibly, their kiss, a thought Colin did not particularly relish.

"It's too vivid to be just a dream, so yes, it must be a memory."

"Superb," Bertie muttered.

"Dinner in five minutes!" Scarlett called from the kitchen door.

Mags set a bowl of what looked to be tofu, black beans and barley liberally mixed with onions and parsley, an enormous salad and a bowl of spiced couscous on the table. Sibyl slid a pair of succulent chicken breasts, rice pilaf and steamed broccoli in front of Colin and he realized what caused the delay in dinner. Sibyl had prepared a non-vegetarian option specifically for him.

No one uttered a word about this considerate gesture likely because they were used to such gestures from Sibyl.

Colin, however, was not.

"I could have eaten the tofu," he whispered to her as she settled in beside him at the round table.

"Do you *like* tofu?" she asked with an engaging grin.

"Not particularly," he admitted, responding to her smile.

She didn't reply, just nodded her head as if that was that and accepted the bowl of couscous from her sister.

Later that evening, after Mags's much more enticing raspberry pavlova, Colin made to leave as he had to wake even earlier than usual to catch his train to London and he didn't want to disturb any of Sibyl's family.

When he made his move, Mags disappeared swiftly up the stairs.

Sibyl was walking him to the door when Mags descended, carrying an overnight bag as well as canvas carrier bag.

"I took the liberty to buy some bits and pieces you could keep at Lacybourne, baby," she told her daughter with a challenging glance at Colin, to which he acceded without a hint of rancor, indeed, biting back a smile. "You don't want to keep lugging things back and forth."

Sibyl opened her mouth to say something but Mags interrupted her with an admonishing tone. "We aren't going to see Colin until Wednesday, you're surely not going to allow him to leave town without an uninterrupted evening of privacy, are you?"

Sibyl clamped her mouth shut.

"Give her a good tumble, Colin," Mags urged audaciously, pushing a stiff-with-humiliated-fury Sibyl out the door ahead of Colin. "She'll need it to keep her in good spirits for the next couple of days."

At that, Sibyl pulled out of her freeze, yanked the bags out of her mother's hands and stomped to the car.

"She's too much!" she declared while Colin slid into the driver's seat.

"Are you unhappy about spending the night with me at Lacybourne?" Colin asked, turning toward her.

"No," she snapped grumpily, staring straight ahead.

"Then what's the problem?"

"My *mother* told *you* to give *me* a good *tumble*!" she cried then ended on a mumble, "My goddess, it's embarrassing."

"Why?"

She twisted to look at him. "You don't think it's embarrassing?"

"No," he replied frankly.

"Really?" she asked, her voice filled with disbelief.

"Really."

She watched him in the fading light of the evening and then, slowly pulling in both of her lips (an endearing habit of hers he was getting used to), she considered something important to which Colin wasn't privy.

He didn't push but allowed her to sort it through.

Finally, she smiled, leaned forward and gave him a soft kiss.

Then she whispered, "Thank you."

"For what?" he asked, lifting his hand to graze her cheek with the tips of his fingers before sliding it through her soft, lustrous hair and around her nape to keep her close.

"For accepting my crazy family. I'll warn you though, they're holding back. They're actually a lot weirder than this."

He found that hard to believe but didn't voice this comment and ended the conversation with a swift, hard kiss that held a promise of what was to come.

Upon arrival at Lacybourne, Sibyl wasted no time in presenting her reward for his acceptance of her bizarre family. Silently, she wandered away from him deep into the house as he dropped her bags at the foot of the stairs in the Great Hall.

He followed her and found her in the dining room.

He stood in the doorway watching her as she moved a chair away from the table and then pressed her palms on the top, putting her weight into it.

With her back to him, she inquired with mock-innocence, "How sturdy do you think this table is?"

Reading her meaning, feeling an instant arousal tightening in his groin, in two great strides he closed the distance between them, whirled her around and crushed her to him. She tilted her head up to his, her mouth twitching slyly. Sliding his hands down her bottom and thighs, he lifted her and set her ass on the table.

"Let's find out, shall we?" he murmured against her mouth.

And they found, after rigorous experimentation, the table was *very* sturdy.

Much later, lying in his bed, Colin was on his back struggling between feeling sated, exhausted and aroused. Sibyl, pressed against his side, was absently drawing soft patterns on his stomach with the tips of her fingers.

"Sibyl?"

She nodded her head against his chest but didn't speak.

"I need to be at the train station tomorrow at six-thirty."

"Okay," she mumbled against his chest but her hand didn't stop.

"And it's relatively important that I have my faculties about me when I arrive in London."

It was more than relatively important, two of his meetings concerned deals that involved millions of pounds.

"Mm," she carried on with her hand distractedly.

He gently took her hand in his and shifted it lower, under the sheet, showing her the unconcealed evidence of what she was doing to him. He felt her cheek move on his chest as she smiled.

He ignored it.

"So, perhaps you'll tell me what's on your mind," he suggested.

She lifted up on her elbow and pulled her hand from his, rested it on his chest and looked him in the eyes. Hers were a thoughtful hazel.

"Colin?"

"Hmm?"

"I just wanted you to know that I . . ." She hesitated and he watched as she struggled with some unknown. When she found it, she finished, "Like you."

He stared at her in incredulity for a moment before he roared with laughter. Shifting her on her back, he covered her body with his.

"You *like* me?" he teased affectionately.

"Yes." She now looked disgruntled as if she regretted her decision to impart this information on him.

"I'm pleased to hear it, darling," he murmured after he bent his head and nuzzled her neck, laughter in his voice.

"No, I mean it."

"I know you do." He lifted his head and cupped her beautiful face in his hands.

"You're a good man," she told him fervently.

"Thank you." He smiled at her, his body beginning to shake with mirth.

Something shifted in her face. "Colin, listen to me," she said forcefully and very somberly. "You *are* a good man."

His amusement fled at the grave look in her eyes. She was telling him something important, her true intent still guarded but he recognized that this moment was profound for her.

"Thank you."

This time, he said it seriously.

"You're welcome."

Her voice was solemn and intense and she was watching him with an entirely new look on her face, a look full of exquisite hope, and he felt, for the very first time in his entire life, humbled. So humbled, if he had been standing, he would have fallen to his knees.

"Jesus, Sibyl," he muttered as he recognized what was so profound about this moment.

It being the fact that she'd let him into her heart.

And knowing that, he did the only thing he knew how to do. He made love to her, slowly. It was not about sex, about passion or about climax.

It was about something else.

It was sweet and wild and beautiful and very nearly, but not quite, everything a coupling should be.

And after it was done Colin found it had moved him deeply, right into his soul.

Falling asleep, his front pressed full-length against the back of her body while his arm was wrapped around her waist, his hand cupping her breast, he did not notice the dim, golden, ethereal shimmer that slid out of the bedroom, waving, undulating and growing as it spread through, around and over the house.

It continued. Covering the grounds of Lacybourne Manor and up into the very atmosphere, going so far as to brighten the moon in the cloudless sky.

THE NEXT TWO days in London, he was luckily so busy he only spent half of his time thinking about Sibyl.

Between meetings, he'd called her on Monday, listening to her shouting into her mobile over the wind, "We're at Tintagel, over the other side of the ruins. Oh Colin! I haven't been here in so long, I forgot how beautiful it is. I wish you were here."

Colin Morgan was not one to go tramping through ruins. Ever. But regardless of that, he found himself wishing it too.

Again, he called her on Tuesday to hear what could only be described as pandemonium behind her.

"Colin, I'm sorry, babe, but I can't talk now. I'm at the Day Centre and Mags suggested a game of strip bingo to the oldies and they've taken her up on it. I'm in Damage Control Mode," she spoke urgently as Colin heard the words "unlucky for some" called in the background. "Dear goddess, they've started!" she groaned into the phone. "I'll call you later."

He didn't care that she couldn't talk. Not only had she called him "babe" in her engaging American accent, he needed her to control the proposed game of Pensioner Strip Bingo. He didn't even want to think about it much less learn it actually occurred.

On Wednesday, after a meeting finished in his conference room, he headed to his office to return some calls when his London secretary stopped him and announced, "Miss Godwin is waiting in your office."

He nodded curtly and lengthened his stride at news of this surprise. The Godwins had come on a shopping and museum expedition to London and they were supposed to meet Colin and his entire family at Claire's house in Kew at six o'clock.

He opened the door to see her standing across the expanse of his office, staring out the window at his unobstructed view of the Thames, Big Ben and the London Eye.

She looked contemplative, standing behind his vast desk lost in thoughts he couldn't fathom.

At her posture, he felt an unusual sense of dread creep through his bones.

He halted and shut the door, and when she heard it her head turned to him with a jerk.

He rested his back against the door, crossed his arms on his chest and waited for her to speak.

She didn't move a muscle as she regarded him.

Finally, she broke the silence.

"I left my family at the Tate," she said in a voice so low he could barely hear her. "I came around, thinking you might have time to join us for lunch."

Even though he was delighted at this news, he didn't answer. Something in the way she was speaking and holding herself stopped him.

She broke his glance and looked back at the view.

After a moment, she spoke again.

"How much money do you have?" she asked the window despondently.

Without hesitation, he answered, "A lot."

He saw her shudder and felt his heart squeeze painfully in response.

"I don't know what to do with that information," she admitted, her voice loaded with a wealth of meaning, none of it good for Colin.

"Does it matter?"

He couldn't believe he was in the position of having to defend his wealth. Women were normally seduced by it, coveted it, went out of their way to the point of demeaning themselves to get it.

Sibyl, however, was not like normal women.

And this made her all the more precious and, he feared in that moment, perhaps the only thing in his life that had ever been out of his reach.

She turned to face him. "There are a lot of people who don't have anything and you have so much."

"I work hard for it," he informed her honestly.

"I know," she whispered, watching him with an expression he could not read as he was too far away to see the color of her eyes.

"Why are you standing over there?" she asked absently, as if noticing for the first time he had not approached her.

"I think, right now, you need to come to me."

Her body froze as she realized what he was asking and the importance of it. And he waited with a great deal of trepidation as she made up her mind.

"Halfway?" she suggested.

"No," Colin stated implacably.

He was who he was, he wasn't going to change.

She was who she was, he had no desire to change her. Perhaps protect her from her own good intentions, but not change her.

She nodded, turned back to the window and sighed. It was in that moment, he thought he'd lost and the very idea of it nearly drove him across the room.

But he stood his ground.

He needed her to accept him as he was.

"Do you have time for lunch?" she asked the window, still not moving toward him, her shoulders held straight and tense.

"No," he answered honestly again.

"I didn't think so," she whispered.

It was then she turned, and without hesitation, she walked straight to him. She put her hands on either side of his waist when she arrived and tilted her head to his.

His relief was so great, his arms closed around her with stunning force and he pulled her to his body. He buried his face in her neck and smelled the same scent of lilies he'd smelled when he first admitted he wanted her that morning in Lacybourne.

"I suppose I should let you get back to work," she murmured.

He lifted his head and she smiled, it was not a full-fledged Sibyl smile but it told him everything he needed to know.

It was then, after all their misunderstandings and distrust and across the great expanse of difference in their personalities and upbringing, that he found, finally, she was truly and completely his.

And Colin felt such an immense satisfaction that it overwhelmed him.

Hiding it from her in order not to frighten her, he brushed her mouth with a light kiss and she laid her hand on his cheek.

"At least I don't feel so guilty about the fifty thousand anymore. Obviously, you can afford it." Her voice was hesitantly teasing.

He was so relieved laughter erupted from him with the force of thunder.

Outside his office, his London secretary lifted and turned her head at the amazing, heretofore unknown sound coming from her boss's office.

She had been told that should a Miss Godwin phone, she was to be put through immediately, no matter what. Apparently, after the many before her, this woman had found her way into Colin Morgan's cold, unyielding heart.

His secretary wasn't at all surprised, she was a beauty (of course), but she also had the sweetest smile.

THE EVENING WAS spent in easy, but loud, camaraderie with the Godwins, Phoebe and Mike, Claire, her husband Jack and their two young children, Colin's brother Tony and his wife, Ellen.

Tony and Ellen found Sibyl and the Godwins just as enchanting as the rest of the family seemed to do.

After, Colin took Sibyl and her family back to Paddington Station to catch the last train to Yatton. Before allowing her through the ticket machines, he engaged her in a full-fledged, back-bending, passionate kiss that granted him a gleaming smile of unadulterated approval from her mother.

THAT HAD BEEN Colin's last two weeks with Sibyl.

Now, he pulled up outside her cottage and alighted from his car, seeing around him the flowers of full spring blooming everywhere. He opened the door and entered, responding to easy calls of greeting from Bertie and Scarlett who were both sitting in the living room.

Scarlett had given him her full blessing somewhere along the way and her behavior was no longer sardonic but almost cheery (or as cheery as Scarlett could get).

Mallory charged him but skidded to a halt at the last moment, planted his bottom on the floor and licked Colin's hand in welcome.

Sibyl walked in from the kitchen, holding Bran upside down in her arms, the cat's feet dangling uselessly up in the air, his tail twitching angrily over her arm. The cat turned a baleful glare at Colin, promising later retribution at this grievous affront to his feline dignity.

Sibyl walked right up to Colin and gave him a brief kiss.

"Hi," she breathed, her eyes warm with happiness and he completely lost himself in them.

"Hi," he returned.

"You're early and I'm running late." With her attention on him, Sibyl lost hold on her cat and Bran took his opportunity at escape and jumped away. Then she leaned further into him and Colin's left hand glided around her waist while his right hand cupped her jaw. "I've got to finish getting ready."

He ran his thumb along her cheekbone, dipping it to slide along her lower lip, watching its progress with fascination the entire time.

He lifted his eyes from her mouth to her gaze and whispered, "I'll wait."

Regardless of what she said, she didn't move and they stood there, pressed against each other next to her father's dining-room table as

Scarlett and Bertie watched with contented glances and Mallory settled to the floor with an exaggerated dog groan.

And in their sweet, close huddle, staring into each other's eyes, no one in the room could know that the two lovers were about to enter a battle for their lives.

Chapter TWENTY-ONE

The Talent Show

Marian Byrne paid her one pound and entered the Community Centre for the talent show.

The huge Hall was packed, music was playing and the hum of conversation was friendly and welcoming.

The minute Marian entered the Hall, she saw the dim, golden aura that glowed in the air and its presence so startled her, her eyes flew searchingly about the enormous room.

She found Colin easily. He was head and shoulders above most people in the room. Definitely head and shoulders above the elderly lady standing beside him, holding his hand in a grip so strong, it looked like she was attempting to leech the youth, power and vitality out of the handsome man.

And when Marian saw him, she saw Colin's golden aura was not as dim as the one that glittered in the air for it shown around him with nearly blinding clarity.

Marian smiled contentedly to herself and approached him as she thought with unsuppressed glee, *Nearly there.*

She was waylaid by the Godwins who were standing in line for tea.

"Mrs. Byrne! What a pleasure. I didn't know you were coming

tonight," Marguerite Godwin greeted and kissed Marian's cheek.

"I wouldn't miss it for the world," Marian informed the delightful woman she found (not surprisingly) she liked very much and accepted greetings from Albert and Scarlett. "I see Colin has an admirer," she noted, her eyes sliding to the tall man.

"Ah yes, she latched on to him the minute we arrived and hasn't left his side," Marguerite explained while Albert placed their tea orders, thoughtfully adding one for Marian.

"How are . . . things?" Marian asked even though she didn't need to after her glance at Colin.

She turned her attention to him again and saw him dip his head politely to listen to whatever the older lady was telling him.

He was relaxed and at ease, seeming in his element casually wearing his expensive suit and standing in the decrepit, old Hall. Colin Morgan seemed to own every space he occupied, she knew, but since Marian met him, he'd always been coiled as tight as a spring. Now he seemed content.

"Things are brilliant," Mags enthused, putting Marian's thoughts into words, adding. "Sibyl's around somewhere but she's crazy busy."

It was then, as if on cue, Sibyl entered the Hall through sliding doors at the side. Wearing a wrap-around, red dress that hugged her generous curves, a pair of open-toed, black high heels, her hair pulled back in a clip at the nape of her neck, she approached Colin.

Her aura was different, astoundingly so. It was golden but shot with white hot sparks some of which glittered nearly blue.

Marian felt the world come closer together.

Sibyl Godwin was in love.

Deeply, truly, completely in love.

She reached Colin and the intensity of her aura, although it seemed impossible, deepened. Marian thought it could almost singe a person if they came too close.

But it didn't affect Colin. He pulled her to him with a strong arm and smiled down at her upturned face with a warmth so unguarded it nearly made him seem boyish.

Marian's heart sang with delight even as she felt almost embarrassed watching them.

Then she accepted her tea and biscuit from Albert and they moved across the Hall toward Colin and Sibyl.

"Mrs. Byrne!" Sibyl cried and detached herself from Colin's arm to give Marian a brief but strong embrace. "I'm so glad you came."

Marian smiled dotingly on the pair.

It would take the force of more than one dark soul to cross these two, in that joyous moment, Marian felt sure of it.

Unfortunately, as her many Great-grandmother Esmeralda was nearly five hundred years before her, Marian didn't know it, but she was terribly wrong.

Sibyl introduced everyone to Mrs. Griffith who, throughout this, did not drop Colin's hand.

"Mrs. Griffith, what a delight," Mags remarked after the introductions.

"Did you get my letters?" Mrs. Griffith barked to Sibyl's mother, a severe tone that mildly surprised Marian but which made Mags grin.

But Sibyl started then stared at her mother. "Letters?"

"All six of them," Mags assured the old lady, ignoring her daughter's question.

"Did you get the letter about this one?" Mrs. Griffith queried abruptly, swinging her cane dangerously to indicate Colin, its unsteady arc coming so close to him he had to swiftly lean back to avoid it smashing into his jaw.

"I did indeed," Mags replied.

"Mrs. Griffith, what did you do?" Sibyl turned her attention to the older woman.

"Well, I approved, of course. And not just because you're both sickeningly good-looking." She turned to confide in Colin, "You are remarkably handsome, my boy, but don't let it go to your head. Nothing's worse than a conceited man." Colin's lips twitched at her blunt advice as Mrs. Griffith turned back to Sibyl and stated, "His minibus tirade was too good not to share."

Sibyl closed her eyes slowly and one could practically hear her mentally counting to ten.

When she opened them, she glowered at her mother. "You could have said something."

"Do I need to tell you everything?" Mags countered.

Marian noted that Colin seemed unaffected by all of this except, perhaps, to look mildly amused.

"Well, I approve too, Mrs. Griffith." Scarlett threw in her lot. "He's a shocking chauvinist and unrepentantly bourgeois but he'll do."

"That's what *I* thought. Not about the chauvy-and-bourgie-whatsit, don't know a thing about that, but he'll do," Mrs. Griffith agreed and suddenly giggled like a schoolgirl.

Sibyl emitted a frustrated noise before she announced, "I need to go backstage."

At this, Mrs. Griffith declared, "And we need to find seats, the good ones are mostly taken, so . . ." she turned to Colin, "*you* might have to throw your weight around." She shifted slowly, indicating her intent to move while proclaiming as if she was bestowing a great honor, "Now, you may escort me to *our* seats."

"Lead the way," Colin murmured politely but stopped and turned when Sibyl's hand landed lightly on his arm.

She went up on her toes to touch her lips against his.

"I'll see you after," she whispered.

He nodded and then allowed himself to be led away by the older woman as Sibyl disappeared between the sliding doors.

"Watching them, you almost feel like a voyeur and she'd barely kissed him," Marian heard Bertie mutter to himself.

Marian didn't respond for at that instant she felt an ice-cold thrill go down her spine and her head shot up.

"No," she whispered, not wishing to believe it.

"What's that?" Bertie asked. He had taken her by the elbow and was showing her to a seat.

She gently pulled her arm away, hid her concern and smiled at Sibyl's father. "I need to see to something. I'll only be away a moment."

Bertie misinterpreted her meaning and inclined his head politely. "I'll save you a seat."

She nodded to him and scanned the crowd as they all began to settle into their chairs.

She felt nothing.

She moved to stand at the back, carefully considering each person as her eyes touched the backs of their heads.

More nothing.

She felt the hairs go up on the back of her neck and she whirled, seeing the dark material swirl about the corner of the doors to the Hall and disappear outside.

On her guard and chanting a swift spell under her breath, she followed.

There was no sight of anyone as she looked this way and that in the now deserted front of the Community Centre.

She thought perhaps she was being silly. The golden aura was dim, yes, Colin had not yet realized his true feelings for Sibyl. But Sibyl's were more than strong enough to protect the pair. She radiated her love for him, true and pure. And Marian was aware enough of their generation (and Colin's reputation) to know, without a doubt, that this love had been consummated.

However, for good measure, she decided to put a protection spell on the Hall. She wasn't going to be caught unawares this time.

She carefully closed the double doors, turned her back to them and walked two steps into the lobby. Then she opened her mouth to start her chant and cast her spell. But before she uttered a noise, a dark figure spirited out of the cloakroom to her left.

With a blinding flash of excruciating light, Marian crumpled to the ground.

And the darkly clad form dragged her limp body, unnoticed, out into the night.

COLIN WAS SURPRISED at how good the talent show was, definitely worth the meager price of admission. It was lovingly, if cheaply, produced and obvious that each child had received a good deal of kindly direction.

Sibyl's "girls" did not win, but came in second place to a young lady who recited a poem so precociously, with her talent and a great deal of luck to get out of her dire surroundings, Colin could see her in the West End.

Throughout the performance, keenly tuned to her, he saw Sibyl slide in and out of the hall. She would tiptoe in to talk to the DJ or stand at the side and gesture to the man who trained the spotlight from the loft in the back. But when her girls performed, Colin noticed she stood to the very edge of the back of the audience and, hilariously, did the entire dance right along with the girls and then hooted and cheered the loudest when they were done.

When the lights came up after the prizes were awarded, people milled about and Mrs. Griffith announced her intention to go to Sibyl's office and call herself a taxi.

"I'll take you home," he informed her as she started to move away.

She turned and, for the first time, awarded him a non-cantankerous smile and in a gentle tone he didn't know she had in her, she said, "You get Sibyl home, luv. She's worked hard tonight and is likely dead on her feet."

On that she patted his forearm affectionately and shuffled away.

The Godwins were all engrossed in conversations with a variety of people, and Colin gave himself time to watch Sibyl in her element.

Although she didn't live in this community, she was obviously a part of it and loved her place just as those around her loved her in it. She knew everyone, not just her "oldies" and the children, but everyone.

Colin himself had been warmly welcomed. It became clear after moments of entering the Hall his "anonymous" donation was no longer anonymous and his other gestures had been gratefully received.

He was not, however, accepted by these proud people, and his class and station meant he would likely never be. Nevertheless, most were courteous and very kind. The ones closest to Sibyl, including Kyle, his wife Tina and their daughter Jemma, were completely accepting of him because of their closeness with Sibyl.

"Do you know where Marian went?" Bertie asked, approaching Colin but looking around the Hall. "She was acting a bit strange and then went to the loos before the performance but never returned. I kept a seat for her the entire time, but she didn't use it, and I looked for her at intermission but couldn't locate her. Now, I still can't find her."

Colin helped Bertie scan the crowd, concerned about Marian's disappearance but also impatient and wanting to get to Sibyl, who was now surrounded by her four girls, all of them jumping around her excitedly.

"I don't see her," Colin informed Sibyl's father. "Perhaps she felt unwell and went home."

"Perhaps," Bertie didn't sound convinced.

"Does anyone have her mobile number?" Colin asked.

Bertie shook his head.

"I don't know. I'll ask Mags and get her to look in the toilets for her." Bertie muttered distractedly and wandered away.

By the time Colin reached Sibyl, it looked like some of the girls' parents were also standing around them.

"Can we keep the outfits?" the girl named Katie asked, her eyes shining up at Sibyl.

"Of course, they're yours," Sibyl replied with a sweet smile and the girls shrieked their delight with such ferocity, Colin winced and feared the glass in the windows would shatter.

"Really, we couldn't—" one of the men was saying and Sibyl turned laughing eyes to him, effectively cutting him off.

"I can hardly wear them, Phil," she responded with a teasing tone to which it would have been impossible to take affront.

"Hey, Mr. Morgan," Katie called, upon noting his arrival.

"Hey, Mr. Morgan," Emma echoed.

"Hey, Mr. Morgan," Cheryl, not to be outdone, repeated.

"Girls," Colin greeted them and this caused another series of shrieks and giggles as Colin finally made it to Sibyl's side.

He dared not kiss her (which he very much wanted to do), the girls' high-pitched screeches might be the final death blow to the rundown building and bring the roof crashing down on their heads.

Sibyl introduced Colin to the girls' parents, and after a brief conversation they all peeled off toward home, taking their loud daughters with them. Except one, who stood alone, no parent behind her. She looked acutely uncomfortable and was trying to put her eyes anywhere but on Colin or Sibyl.

"I'm going to go home now, Miss Sibyl, I'll see you next week," she muttered and started away.

Sibyl put a gentle hand on the girl's shoulder to keep her where she was. "Wait a second, Flower, where's your mother?"

"She's out tonight. My brothers are with Nan. I was supposed to be there too but I talked Nan into letting me come tonight."

"But tonight's the talent show . . . your mother—" Sibyl started.

"She forgot," Flower quickly explained with a deftness borne of practice.

"But, how did you get here?" Sibyl asked.

"I walked," Flower answered.

"By yourself?" Sibyl inquired, the last syllable higher than the others, a tone that showed her irritation.

Flower nodded.

Colin regarded the young, awkward, but pretty, girl. He hid his reaction to her words and the thought of any parent or grandparent not only not remembering a talent show but not being there to witness it.

Sibyl, however, did not hide her reaction. Her lips thinned, she turned angry eyes to Colin and he saw the warning light of emerald fire.

"Sibyl," he murmured as Scarlett approached.

Sibyl whirled back to Flower. "Where are you staying tonight?"

"With Nan."

"Go and get your things, honey. Mr. Morgan and my sister, her name's Scarlett, are going to drive you home. Once you're inside, I want you to go to the window and wave to them that everything is okay. You must remember to go to the window and wave because he's going to be waiting. Can you remember to do that?"

Flower looked uncertainly between Sibyl, Colin and Scarlett and nodded her head slowly, clearly not used to anyone taking care of her.

"Good, honey, now go and get your things," Sibyl urged gently.

The minute the girl ran off, Sibyl turned to Colin and belatedly asked, "Do you mind?"

Her tone, her face, the way she held her body indicated her barely contained fury.

He did the only thing he could do in the face of her oncoming wrath, he shook his head.

Letting some of her anger seep through, she snapped, "What would you say if I told you I was adopting that girl?"

"I'd give you the name and telephone number for one of the solicitors I have on retainer," Colin drawled.

Sibyl's eyes rounded in disbelief but scant seconds later they melted with something else entirely. He took note, for future reference, that his comment made the rage slide out of her.

"She has three brothers," Sibyl said quietly.

"You'll need a bigger house," he informed her drily.

"Luckily, Colin, you have a *huge* house," Scarlett put in, always of assistance.

Scarlett was saved from the edge of Sibyl's tongue by Flower's arrival.

"Let's go, kiddo," Scarlett said, deftly affecting her escape by propelling the girl forward.

Colin took his chance to give Sibyl a quick kiss, "I'll be back to take you home."

She nodded, still lost in her thoughts for Flower. "I can't wait to sit down. I've been on my feet for hours. They're killing me. Are we going to Lacybourne?" she asked distractedly.

"Is that where you want to go?"

She nodded.

"Then that's where we're going."

She gave him a weak smile of gratitude and walked toward her friend Jemma.

Colin walked to a waiting Scarlett and Flower then he escorted them to his car.

Scarlett slid in beside him after she made sure Flower was buckled in the back and they took her to her Nan's, which was further away than he expected. Colin was pleased Sibyl wasn't with them, if she knew the distance the girl had walked alone, she'd likely abduct the child *and* her brothers from their Nan's house.

After receiving their dutiful wave, on the way back to the Hall,

Scarlett spoke, "She's not of the earth, you know?"

"I'm sorry?" Colin asked, surprised at her tone which was sedate and earnest.

Since she shined the light of her approval on his union with her sister, Scarlett had been her usual drily humorous self, just not caustic.

He'd never heard her serious before.

Still, he had no idea what she was talking about.

"Sibyl, she's not of the earth but of the air. She's like a kite, all her life, darting about in the wind with no one holding on to her string."

Colin remained silent, patiently waiting for further explanation.

"You're of the earth," she carried on. "You have your feet firmly planted on the ground. She's lucky to find someone like that, like you, willing to let her dart about happily in the wind but still keeping her tethered to the ground."

Colin couldn't help but be moved by her compliment, especially coming from Scarlett.

However, she wasn't finished.

Quietly, she said in a near whisper, "All my life, I thought she'd get swept away. Get herself helplessly tangled in some trees and be torn to shreds when someone yanked her free. It was terrifying."

"I can imagine," Colin murmured and he could.

"Please protect her, Colin." It was now a whisper and even though he barely knew her, Colin knew how much it cost her to make this request.

"I will."

"You must promise," she pushed.

He pulled up outside the front doors of the Community Centre, fixed the emergency brake, turned to Sibyl's sister and promised, "I'll protect her."

It was a vow and she knew it, and for the first time of their acquaintance, she gave him one of *her* spectacular smiles.

Then she whispered, "I believe you."

And without another word she turned to her door so Colin did the same.

They walked, both lost in their own thoughts, into the Hall together where they saw volunteers were cleaning up, Sibyl's mother and father helping to stack chairs against the walls.

"Where's Sibyl?" Colin asked Tina who was tidying the small kitchen to the side.

"She went to her office to get her handbag," Tina responded. "I'm doing cuppas for everyone. Would you two like one?" Her kind gaze drifted from Colin to Scarlett.

"I'd love one and I'll help," Scarlett replied but Colin moved toward Sibyl's office just as a young boy came flying into the Hall and slid to a halt beside Jemma.

"Mum, there's an old lady lying out back in the grass. She isn't moving." His words were rushed with panic and his brown eyes were filled with fear.

Colin froze and caught Bertie's frightened eye.

Bertie made a dash out the front door.

Colin went in the opposite direction, to Sibyl's office.

He threw back the sliding doors and immediately heard the muffled noises coming from behind the office's closed door. He ran to the room, threw open the door and was momentarily stunned motionless by what he saw.

A black-clad figure wearing a ski mask was holding a struggling Sibyl in the corner of the room, one arm gripping her about the waist, one hand held over her mouth.

Another figure wearing the same outfit was being pounded violently by the end of Mrs. Griffith's cane, each blow causing an angry, pained grunt to come out of him.

"Let her go, I tell you!" Mrs. Griffith shouted.

Colin jerked out of his shock and exploded into the room, wresting the cane out of Mrs. Griffith's hand and swinging it with far more force on the cowering figure. With furious pleasure, he heard it connect with a hideous noise of cracking bone at the same time the cane split in half and a stifled howl came from his victim.

Wasting no time, the figure shoved Mrs. Griffith aside, and holding his injured arm in his healthy one he ran from the small office.

Colin whirled on the other figure, raising the remains of the cane threateningly.

The figure let go of Sibyl's waist, his arm went around his back and Sibyl took her opportunity to break free. She took one step forward but was yanked back as the man grabbed her hair. She gave a startled, pained cry and Colin took two quick, menacing steps forward when the figure's arm whipped back around and Colin saw the glint on the blade of a knife.

"Call nine nine nine! Call nine nine nine!" Mrs. Griffith shouted repeatedly as she rushed (slowly) out of the office.

"Drop the cane," the figure demanded, his voice rough and threatening.

He raised the knife to Sibyl's throat and Colin froze.

The dream seared through his brain, visions of her blood pouring freely from her throat and Colin felt fear spread through him like a virus.

"Drop the fucking cane!" the figure shouted.

Colin dropped the cane and held his hands up in front of him, his eyes never leaving the blade.

"Let her go," Colin ordered, his words crackling with authority.

The figure yanked Sibyl's hair again and she made another noise filled with pain and Colin's body tensed in fury. He welcomed it as it fought away the fear.

Colin didn't take his eyes off the pair and didn't move. He thought, in an instant, if that blade slit her throat, he'd charge the man regardless, he didn't care if it next penetrated his gut.

He was weaponless, powerless, and if they came out of this unscathed he was going to track this man down and take great satisfaction in wringing the air out of his body with his own two hands.

"Let her go," Colin repeated and with a swiftness that surprised him, Sibyl was thrown forward. Colin caught her in his arms and wasted no time in whirling her behind the protection of his body.

As he did this, the figure ran by Colin and Sibyl.

Colin immediately gave chase.

"Get to the Hall," he ordered Sibyl, not breaking stride, *"now!"*

The man was out the Day Centre door, into the night and Colin followed him, running through the grass toward the church that was next to the Centre.

Then Colin heard a strange noise and felt a piercing, unexplainable pain in his shoulder but he was too intent on his pursuit to pay it any heed.

The man was fit, Colin realized, but Colin was also fit, swift and tall. He covered twice the distance with one stride as the other man could and he was soon gaining on him.

He was nearly upon him when he started to feel a penetrating sluggishness permeate his body. He reached his arm out to grasp the figure's collar and found he could barely hold that arm up.

Colin shook his head to clear his rapidly blurring vision and saw the man pull out in front, doubling then trebling the distance as Colin fought the overwhelming, unusual, unexplainable lethargy stealing over him.

He struggled against it, wondering vaguely why he felt it at all but within moments he slowed to a halt, breathing heavily.

Within minutes, Colin lost his battle and collapsed to the ground.

Chapter TWENTY-TWO

Fear

Sibyl sat next to Marian's hospital bed, leaning forward on the side of it.

Exhausted and stressed she rested her forehead on her crossed arms.

The older woman lay sleeping now and, for the first time, Marian Byrne looked every one of her advanced years. She'd regained consciousness at the Centre, muttering strange, dire warnings about "dark souls" and vehemently lamenting "letting Granny Esmeralda down."

Sibyl and Bertie, witnessing her ranting, feared she'd sustained a terrible head injury as Scarlett carefully tended to her.

Marian had calmed by the time the paramedics arrived but Sibyl's panic had increased when Colin hadn't returned then escalated to sheer terror when she heard the police found his motionless body.

Luckily (*they* thought), in their hunt for him, they discovered the tranquillizer dart that brought him low, a great deal of the tranquillizer still in the shaft.

Sibyl did not consider this lucky at all, she was becoming far too acquainted with the awful effects of tranquillizer darts and couldn't comprehend for the life of her why someone kept shooting beings she cared about with them.

In all the heartbreak and despair to which Sibyl's professional life had forced her to bear witness, nothing affected her quite so profoundly as seeing her charismatic, powerful, rugged Colin taken, unconscious, into an ambulance. If Mags hadn't been holding on to her whispering soothing words, Sibyl knew her body would have collapsed.

And she knew in that instant that she loved Colin.

She was in love with Colin and loved him with all her heart, through her blood, veins and muscles, down through to the marrow of her bones.

She'd finally found him.

Colin was *him*.

Her soulmate, the one she'd been waiting for, just plain *hers*.

There was no reason for it. He didn't suit her, not in the slightest. He was autocratic, possessive, dictatorial and had far more money than one person with good conscience should. He was nothing like she expected her true love would be and somehow everything she wanted. She didn't think it even had anything to do with reincarnated souls of dead lovers. They could have been entirely different people altogether and they would have found each other.

He wasn't Royce but now Colin looked at her the same way. As if she was the center of his universe and nothing else existed or mattered beyond her.

Not to mention, he was a good man. He didn't like to let on to that sweet, simple fact but he was.

So, there was nothing she could do. She let him into her heart.

Or more to the point clicked him into the place that had been waiting for him since the day she was born.

And she thought he fit perfectly.

Colin had regained consciousness in accident and emergency not half an hour before, groggy for approximately five minutes, he shifted quickly to icy fury. Knowing with relief that he was going to be all right, Sibyl escaped to check on Mrs. Byrne and left Colin to talk privately to the police.

Sibyl had already given the police her account of the evening, of the two masked men who came stealthily into her office, demanding to know where Colin was and for her to take them to him.

Neither Sibyl nor her attackers saw Mrs. Griffith, who was waiting for her taxi while dozing on the couch, hidden by a precarious pile of talent show costumes and props.

Sibyl had backed away, telling them Colin had already left and it was then they grabbed her.

At that action, Mrs. Griffith rose, like the Eternal Wrath of the Pensioners, wielding her cane and making imperious demands.

Moments later, Colin had burst into the room.

As she sat by Marian's hospital bed, Sibyl struggled to sort through her rampaging thoughts of tranquillizer darts, knives, Mrs. Griffith avenging her and, most terrifyingly, Colin's savage display of violence. He was like a Warrior God and she could easily transpose him on an ancient battlefield, swinging a broadsword with deadly intent rather than an old lady's cane.

She could still hear the sickening crunch of bone mingled with splitting wood.

She shuddered at the memory.

She felt a light touch on her hair and her thoughts skittered away as she lifted her head to gaze into the faded, opened eyes of her friend.

"Will you call my daughter?" Marian asked weakly.

Sibyl nodded, her heart breaking at the feeble sound of Marian's usually strong voice. She took the number down on a scrap of paper from her purse.

"They say you're going to be all right," she assured Marian after she'd taken her daughter's telephone number. "You'll need to stay here a day or two—"

"It's the dark soul," Marian broke in fervently, her eyes growing bright with intensity. "They want to keep you and Colin apart. Sibyl you must listen to me, believe me."

Her words were fierce, frightened, and Sibyl nodded her head even though she didn't know what the older lady meant.

"Sibyl, you must—" Marian went on.

"Marian, please rest now," Sibyl interrupted her gently. "Don't get excited, we'll talk later."

"It's crucial that you know—"

Sibyl squeezed Marian's hand. "I promise I'll come back tomorrow. You can tell me all about it then and I'll listen."

Mrs. Byrne closed her eyes and there was pain in her expression that had nothing to do with the blow to her head.

When she opened them, she nodded.

"Please, my dear, take the utmost care," she whispered.

"I will."

Sibyl went to the front of the hospital and stood outside to make the awful call to Marian's daughter, Angie.

After Angie expressed her shock and horror, she asked, "What did you say your name was again?"

"Sibyl Godwin."

"Oh my *God,*" Angie breathed then rushed on, "I'll leave right away."

Understanding that likely Marian's daughter knew the whole story of Royce and Beatrice and even Sibyl and Colin, Sibyl didn't react to her urgency and quietly ended the call with a promise to meet Angie the next day.

She walked to the A&E and found Colin, her family, and a variety of police officers standing in the middle of the bustling department. Colin seemed to be tearing into one of the officers but she could tell it was in his supremely-controlled, still-very-frightening way by how he held his body and the fact that he wasn't shouting the roof down.

Sibyl noted absently that Colin, surprisingly, was suffering no visible ill effects to the dart. Indeed he seemed fully awake, alert, emanating his usual power with his face a mask of rage.

He saw her approaching and he turned blazing eyes on her.

"*Where the bloody hell have you been?*" he barked, his voice cracking like a whip.

She jumped at his tone. "I went to see Mrs. Byrne."

"Don't you fucking leave without telling someone where you're going and taking someone with you, do you understand me?" he demanded angrily.

"Colin," she murmured soothingly, shaken by his tone and his words.

He was not to be soothed.

She knew this when he thundered, *"Do you understand me?"*

She nodded mutely.

She *had* left without saying anything to anyone, it just hadn't crossed her mind. Realizing he was worried rather than truly angry with her, she sidled up to his side in an additional effort to soothe him. Gently, she pushed under his arm and slid both of hers around his middle. Without hesitation, he lifted his arm to rest tightly around her shoulders and she felt the tension ease slowly out of him.

"I'm sorry, it was thoughtless," she told him quietly when she'd lifted her head to gaze at him. "I just had to see Mrs. Byrne. I promise, babe, I won't do it again."

She saw her family watching this, all with identical expressions of relief and wisely they did not utter a word.

"We're going home," Colin announced and didn't allow her family or the police to protest. He simply guided her out the door with his arm still around her shoulders, one of hers around his waist.

Bertie had driven the BMW to the hospital, and without argument Colin allowed Bertie to slide in the driver's seat. Colin courteously helped Mags (and for once, at this gallant show, she didn't utter a feminist quibble) in the front and Sibyl sat between Scarlett and Colin in the back.

"Albert, take us to Brightrose, everyone will pack a bag, we'll get the animals and we're all going to Lacybourne," Colin ordered.

No one made a sound and, as it wasn't a suggestion that invited discourse, Bertie did as he was told.

Her family was set to leave from Heathrow on Sunday, two days . . . Sibyl glanced unseeing in the darkness at her watch and suspected it was now only one day away. She hadn't even approached the topic of this latest misadventure with Colin to her family and she didn't relish the idea. They knew about Mallory and the vandalism at Brightrose but everyone thought that was relatively harmless.

This was not harmless at all and everyone knew it.

They all trooped into Brightrose, made swift work of packing while Sibyl saw to her own and sorted out her pets. Scarlett loaded Mallory in the MG and followed the BMW to Lacybourne.

Exhausted, bidding goodnight to everyone, Bertie and Mags made their bed in one of the six bedrooms with sheets Sibyl uncovered in a linen closet while Sibyl helped her sister with her bed.

"You okay, Billie?" Scarlett inquired softly as they went about their task.

Sibyl shook her head.

As usual, she wasn't going to lie to her sister. "I was held at knifepoint, Scarlett, and someone shot my boyfriend with a tranquil-lizer dart." She lifted her head and her eyes hit her sister before she finished, "I'm scared out of my mind."

Scarlett twitched the coverlet into place, rounded the bed, took Sibyl in her arms and gave her a fierce hug.

"I think Colin would die before he'd let anyone put a scratch on you," Scarlett whispered in her ear.

Sibyl shuddered.

"That's what I'm afraid of," she admitted with a force of feeling and a terrible premonition that she had to keep under complete control or it would overwhelm her.

Scarlett's embrace tightened.

Her sister knew about the dream, *everyone* knew about the dream. They also knew that Sibyl had visions like this before, visions that came true. Scarlett was likely just as terrified as her sister but too proud, and too protective, to show it.

Sibyl kissed Scarlett's cheek and went to find Colin.

He was standing in his bedroom, staring out the window holding a cut crystal tumbler that contained something that was the color of his beautiful eyes. Mallory lay at his feet and Bran was already curled contentedly at the foot of the bed.

When she entered, he glanced at her, put the tumbler to his lips, threw back the entire contents of the glass and set it down on the dresser.

With his long-legged strides, he approached her and without a word, he tugged on the belt that kept her wraparound dress in place. It immediately loosened and fell apart at the front. The look on his face was carefully controlled and try as she might she couldn't read a single thought on it.

"Colin, we need to talk," she whispered carefully.

His hands went to her shoulders, slid the dress off her shoulders and it fell in a pool at her feet.

"We need to go to bed," he contradicted, his fingers finding the clasp at the back of her bra and freed it with an astonishing deftness.

This he slid off her shoulders and dropped to the floor too.

"Colin—"

"Sibyl," he interrupted her and slid his hands into her hair on either side of her face, holding her head tilted to peer at him, "I'm exhausted, we'll talk tomorrow."

He released her abruptly and turned away, his hands going to the buttons of his midnight-blue shirt. She flipped off her shoes, walked to one of his dressers, pulled open a drawer and snatched out one of his T-shirts.

And she didn't give up.

"We need to let it out, talk about it. We shouldn't bottle it in. It isn't healthy." She tugged his shirt over her head, pulled her hair free of the collar and turned to him, her eyes on his back.

He yanked the shirt off his broad shoulders, keeping his back to her. "We'll talk about it tomorrow."

"Colin!" she protested, her composure slipping. "I'm scared half out of my wits! I *have* to talk about it. Someone held a knife to my throat and we *both* know what that means."

He turned to her slowly and when she saw the look in his eyes, she pulled in her breath and held it.

He looked primitive, even elemental, and very, *very* frightening.

"Nothing's going to happen to you."

He enunciated every word carefully, nearly brutally.

She opened her mouth, and before a single sound came out, he repeated, more forcefully than before (if it could be credited), "Nothing's going to happen to you."

"What if something happens to *you*?" she cried. "They wanted *you*, not me. They asked for *you*!"

"I'll handle it." He divested himself of the rest of his clothes while Sibyl stood in his bedroom and stared. When he was done, standing there in his naked glory, he commanded, "Darling, get in bed.

He may be done talking but she damned well wasn't.

"Who are those people?" she demanded.

"Get in bed, Sibyl, we'll talk about it tomorrow."

"We'll bloody well talk about it now!" she yelled, letting her temper get the better of her.

She'd had enough. She'd had a knife at her throat and seen his seemingly lifeless body loaded into an ambulance. She couldn't just go to sleep, not with her mind racing as it was.

"Who are those people, were they the ones who hurt Marian?" she pushed.

He closed the distance in two quick strides, hooked her around the waist and swung her up in his arms then stalked to the bed and threw her on it. Mallory lumbered to his feet at this unprecedented flurry of action at such a late hour and Bran flew off the bed.

"Colin, don't manhandle me!" she snapped.

He stood by the bed and scowled at her. The muscles in his body visibly taut, she could see the ones in his upper arms bunching reflexively as he clenched his fists.

"Sibyl, I've been shot by a fucking tranquillizer dart, watched, powerless, while someone held you at knifepoint, you disappeared for what seemed an endless period of time at the hospital and I didn't know where the hell you were. I'm bloody tired. I don't know what *the fuck* is going on and, right now, can't do anything about it. Talking is not going to help. It's late. I need sleep. You need sleep. So for Christ's sake, be quiet and stop arguing with me."

She realized then he was just as frightened as she was but too damned much of a man to admit it, and her heart, as was Sibyl's wont, went out to him.

She got up on her knees, walking on them across the top of the bed until she reached him, wrapped her arms around him, pressed in close and rested her cheek on his chest.

Then she said softly into his chest, "Okay."

And at her soft word, Sibyl felt his anger drift out of him and his arms wrap around her tight.

"You're the most annoying woman alive," he mumbled this familiar refrain into the hair at the top of her head but there was affection in his tone that obliterated any sting to his words.

"Come to bed," she beckoned.

He did and they did nothing but sleep, nestled together, her back to his front. The warmth of his body and protective arm he wrapped around her comforted her, and she surprisingly found herself giving in to her exhaustion and drifting to sleep almost the moment they settled.

SIBYL WOKE TOO early, feeling like she hadn't slept. She was lethargic, headachy and most definitely cranky. And that was *before* she opened her eyes and saw she was alone in Colin's gigantic bed.

Colin never left her in bed without an embrace, a kiss, a caress or some loving gesture.

Never.

Fear coursed through her and she catapulted from the bed and ran to the bathroom looking for him. He wasn't there and she noticed both Mallory and Bran were gone as well.

Panic seized her and she flew from the room and down the hall. Visions of blood and knives and broken canes stampeded through her brain.

She still had not had her tour of Lacybourne, she and Colin always too busy with other things, but she was becoming familiar with it all the same. She ran down the stairs to the Great Hall, her glance sliding past Beatrice and Royce on her way down.

He wasn't in the Great Hall either.

Watery light was coming through the windows and the day was gray with drizzle. She searched the library, frantically paused in the dining room and then heard a deep man's voice in the study.

She threw open the door and burst in.

Colin was standing behind the desk talking on the phone wearing faded jeans and a maroon, long-sleeved T-shirt that hugged the muscles of his chest and stomach tightly. His dark hair was still damp from a shower and he looked refreshed and nonchalant and, she vaguely noted, unbearably sexy.

Mallory was lying flat out in front of his desk and Bran was picking a trail delicately across the scattered papers on the top.

Colin's head shot up at her entry.

Mallory's body jerked, he glanced over his doggie shoulder at her, gave her a soft welcoming "woof" and then settled contentedly back into to his usual morning-after-a-night's-sleep nap.

Bran rested his bottom on a bunch of papers and blinked at her with a twitch of his tail.

"You scared me half to death!" Her voice was sharp and frenzied and she glowered at Colin.

"I'll call you back," he muttered into the phone and pressed a button to disconnect without saying goodbye.

"You scared me half to death," she repeated when he'd tossed the cordless on his desk.

"I—" he began.

She quickly interrupted him by slamming the door behind her and whirling back around. "I woke up and you were gone, Mallory was gone, Bran was gone, everyone was gone!" she shouted.

"Calm down, sweetheart," Colin said gently, completely calm himself, and in the face of it she went from irrational to insane.

"Don't tell me to calm down! You *never* leave me in bed without—"

She stopped abruptly and lifted her hands to the sides of her hair, shifting the heavy masses away from her face and holding them up.

"I thought something happened to you."

This came out as an accusation and after she voiced it, Sibyl glared at him as if it was entirely his fault.

"I didn't want to wake you," Colin explained.

"Well, I'd rather you wake me than have the living daylights frightened out of me first thing in the goddess-damned morning," she snapped.

His gaze dropped lazily to her thighs and she looked down, realizing her hands in her hair brought the T-shirt up to show a hint of the lacy, lilac underwear her sister had cajoled her into buying.

She dropped her arms instantly.

"Come here." Now his voice was pure silk, his eyes were warm and her bones showed signs of beginning to melt.

Regardless of all that, it was still morning and she was still very grumpy.

"No. My head's pounding and I'm in a very bad mood."

He gave her one of his lazy smiles while noting, "You're *always* in a bad mood in the morning."

"Stop being all teasing and sweet. I'm telling you, I'm not in the mood," she warned.

"Am I being teasing and sweet?" he asked, while, she noted, being teasing and sweet.

In answer, she growled.

"Sibyl, come here," he ordered.

"Why?" she shot back.

"So I can help with your mood," he tempted, his eyes, if possible, growing warmer.

"How are you going to do that?" she queried warily, even as she moved forward. She didn't allow him to answer because she knew by the look in his eye what the answer was. She tried to change the subject. "And who were you talking to on the phone?"

"A private investigator." Colin's arms stole around her when she arrived within reaching distance and she lifted her hands to rest on his upper arms.

At her wide-eyed look at his statement, he continued, "I've engaged him to put a team together to find the men from last night."

"The police—" she started.

"I want them first," Colin stated, the warmth in his eyes gone in a flash, they were glittering like shards of ice.

"Colin."

"Quiet Sibyl, we're not discussing this. I'm handling it. You're not to interfere."

This was not what Sibyl wished to hear at the best of times but certainly not in the morning.

Therefore her eyes narrowed dangerously. "I beg your pardon?"

"They held a knife to your throat," he reminded her curtly, clearly not used to explaining himself and only doing so because he knew she'd rocket to the moon on the fuel of her anger if he didn't.

"You can't circumvent justice," Sibyl pointed out impatiently. "The police will deal with them."

"The police can have them after I'm done with them."

Her eyes widened before she asked, "What do you mean to do?"

"It's none of your concern."

Sibyl stiffened to the approximate pliability of a two by four.

"Excuse me?" she whispered angrily. "But my rich and powerful boyfriend is threatening vigilante justice and it's none of my concern? I beg to differ."

His hands tightened on her waist and the ice shards in his eyes polarized.

"One of them stood in front of me and held a knife to your throat while I was powerless to do a thing. He touched you, and *no one* touches you, *no one* but *me*. He yanked your goddamned hair, the most beautiful hair I've seen in my life, using it to cause you pain." He was using his low, even voice and she knew he was very close to losing control.

Sibyl also knew every minute, every sound, every word, everything he saw and experienced last night was seared into his memory. She knew it at his words. And last night for brief moments in time, Colin Morgan had been powerless.

Men like Colin were not used to being powerless and it dawned on Sibyl, belatedly, that he did not like it.

At all.

He continued, "I'm going to find them, have a chat with them to express how *unhappy* the events of last night made me, and then I'll turn them over to the proper authorities."

"You won't hurt them?" Sibyl asked quietly, hoping the lowering of her tone would soothe him.

It didn't.

"Are you asking for mercy for a man who put a knife to your throat and has you wound up so tight you fly through the house in a panic when I do something innocent and absolutely normal, like leave you alone in bed?" he demanded in exasperation.

Putting it that way, she had to admit, it sounded rather silly.

She decided she better stop talking.

He sighed an enormously patient sigh before saying, "I promise I won't hurt them . . ." She began to smile, "unduly."

Her smile turned to a frown.

"You frighten me when you're like this," she told him and his face shifted but he did not relent.

"I'm trying to make it so you'll never be frightened again," Colin explained.

"But—"

He cut her off to inform her, "I'm going to do this, Sibyl, whether you like it or not, so I suggest you accept it because it's going to happen."

She blinked at his words and his tone then muttered, "You're ruthless."

At her comment, he leaned closer and his hands slid over her bottom and then suddenly down to grasp the backs of her thighs, lifting her up. She gave a shocked gasp and had to clamp her thighs around his hips and hastily grab his shoulders for support as he carried her to the desk.

"Yes," he agreed amiably, all *his* mood gone, "I am."

He settled her bottom on the desk and Bran scattered. Colin kept himself determinedly positioned between her legs as he tilted her chin up with one hand and his other hand drew lazy circle on the top of her thigh.

"Now, what shall I do about your morning mood?" he asked conversationally, gently rubbing his thumb across her lower lip.

"I take it we're done talking," she guessed.

"Oh, we're definitely done talking," he stated, his voice sexy low and she knew what that meant, and she also knew acutely how it made her belly feel.

"My family—" she started to say but his lips took hers in a slow, soft, mind-numbing kiss.

When he was done, against her lips he murmured, "For a daughter born of Mags, you're amazingly prissy."

Her eyes flared. "I am *not* prissy."

"Prove it," he dared on a whisper.

"You aren't going to goad me into—"

He moved into her and she was forced to lean back, resting her hands behind her on his desk as his hands slid inside the T-shirt and up the skin of her back, sending shivers through her against her will and he quieted her by kissing her. This was not soft or slow but hard and demanding and she couldn't help but respond.

So she did.

Many minutes later, her breath coming fast, her hands buried in his hair, his lips at her neck, her body throbbing, his hands spread her legs further apart and his fingers expertly delved inside her panties.

Her head rolled back.

And there was a knock on the door.

Her head snapped up.

"Breakfast in five minutes," Scarlett called jovially through the door.

Sibyl made a trapped noise that, mid-way out of her throat, changed to a loud moan as Colin's finger slid inside her just as his thumb hit her in a *very* good spot.

"Colin," she whispered, caught between mortification and desire.

His head came up and he looked at her.

"Hurry up, darling, breakfast is nearly ready." He grinned wickedly but his eyes were dark and his voice was husky.

"Aren't you going to—"

"I'm going to watch."

"But—"

"I *like* to watch. You're beautiful always but you're fucking breathtaking when you come."

She couldn't help it, she melted at his words and his thumb, still at the right spot, starting pressing and rolling in circles as his finger inside moved out and was joined, delightfully when it returned, with another one. At their skillful maneuvering, the throbs turned to jolts and she bucked against his hand as the incredible heat shot through her.

"That's it, sweetheart," he encouraged when he knew she was close, his deep voice beyond husky straight to throaty.

The sound of it undid her, her neck arched back again, she pulled in a ragged breath and let go.

Still in the throes of her resplendent climax, he slid her off the desk and sat in his chair, pulling her into his lap so her legs were over the arm of the chair. Then, with his hand cupping the back of her head, Colin buried her face in his neck and she clutched his shoulders as he held her trembling body and stroked the soft skin at the side of her breast with the other.

"You're ruthless," Sibyl whispered again when she had the strength to speak and anyone could tell she didn't really care.

"Yes," Colin agreed roughly, "I am."

Chapter TWENTY-THREE

Sibyl Bares Her Soul

After breakfast, they all went to the hospital to visit Mrs. Byrne. They met her exhausted-from-her-all-night-drive daughter, Angie, who shrugged off her fatigue at meeting the entirety of the legendary Godwin clan *and* the fabled Mr. Colin Morgan, the vision of the dead warrior, Royce.

They were all delighted to hear that Mrs. Byrne was to be released that afternoon. She had a concussion but was told she was fine to go home if she rested, took it easy and had someone to watch over her.

Sibyl thought she looked far better and much more herself than the night before. Scarlett read her chart and agreed, promising to stop in and check on her that evening and the next morning before going to Heathrow.

Marian asked to talk to Sibyl privately and allowed (because she was given no choice) Colin to sit in on their discussion.

When they were alone, Marian wasted no time and began her recitation of the "dark soul," the name given by Esmeralda Crane to the unknown and never discovered murderer of Royce and Beatrice. Marian spoke of unconsummated true love, the power of consummation (which was the only comment she uttered that made Colin grin), protection spells and other powerful binding magic.

Marian told them that just their being together put them in danger. That the dark soul could not countenance their relationship and certainly not their happiness and would stop at nothing, even murder, to drive them apart.

She spoke of how the line of Crane Witches had known that the dark soul would follow Royce and Beatrice's line and eventually threaten the reincarnated lovers once they found each other again. She was adamant that this was the person who nearly ran over them with the car outside the restaurant, shot Mallory, vandalized Sibyl's cottage and attacked the three of them the night before.

She did not know who it was but Marian *felt* them and knew they were there.

The only way to break the curse was to consummate true love, and if Sibyl and Colin didn't do it then there would be two lovers down their line to whom this task would fall. It was fate, it was destiny and their story would be told again and again until the curse was lifted.

It all came down to love.

At this fervid pronouncement, she felt Colin glance her way but Sibyl kept her eyes carefully averted. She hadn't shared her feelings for Colin *with* Colin mainly because she had no clue as to his. He certainly *acted* loving but being loving and being *in love* were two different things. With everything else going on, she couldn't cope with being in love with a man, a wonderful (albeit hopelessly irritating) man, her soulmate, the one she'd been searching for a lifetime and having that love be one-sided.

When no immediate assertion that true love was glimmering in the very air was made by either Colin or Sibyl, Marian demanded to settle protection spells on them the minute she felt up to it, which by her estimation was the very next afternoon when they arrived back from Heathrow.

Sibyl dutifully promised to be at her house as Colin gazed at the two women, making no promises of his own, his expression carefully blank.

After she'd given Marian's cheek a kiss, Sibyl left with Colin to find her family.

They walked down the hall together and she tried to act casual and steady her rapidly beating heart when Colin laced his fingers in hers.

"You don't believe her," Sibyl noted as she watched him out of the corner of her eye.

"It's nonsense," Colin stated firmly.

She stopped, tugging at his hand to halt him too as she saw her family with Angie at the end of hall.

"It makes sense," she defended her friend.

He shook his head slowly but his lips were twitching. "You think it makes sense that some unknown entity is stalking Beatrice and Royce's souls through eternity?"

"What do *you* think it is?" she demanded in exasperation.

Before he spoke, Colin turned so that his back was to her waiting family and hiding her from them.

"I don't know what to think. I'm prepared to believe, just barely and only because of the dreams, that we've been drawn together by something that goes beyond lucky coincidence but not that some unknown person has murderous intent simply due to a longstanding curse."

She felt her stomach lurch hopefully at the words "lucky coincidence" but she hid it by querying, "Okay then, *who* do you think it is?"

His shoulders stiffened and all humor fled.

"Sibyl, you haven't . . ." He stopped and dragged his hand through his hair in agitation, and she saw with some surprise it was because he was trying to find the right words. After some thought, he continued, "I've not exactly led the life of a choirboy. My family is wealthy but the kind of wealth I have comes from . . ." He stopped again and finished shortly, "I've made enemies."

"You think it's someone you've wronged who's doing this? And, if so, why would they shoot Mallory and attack my toss pillows?" she asked.

"Not someone I've *wronged*. I wouldn't say I wronged anyone, though they might not think of it that way," Colin answered.

Losing patience, Sibyl cried, "You're talking semantics and I'm talking decimated toss pillows!"

His amusement came back as quickly as it faded.

He put his hand to her jaw and muttered, "Sometimes, you're too adorable for words."

Her eyes narrowed on him as she grumbled, "You can't distract me with flattery."

"At least I tried," he replied, still in fine humor and she glared as he turned around again, and, with a gentle pull on her hand, they headed back down the hall.

She noted, later, that he never answered her.

Apparently, she thought with disgust, he *could* distract her with flattery.

Promising to see Angie the next afternoon, if not sooner when Scarlett checked on Marian, they all left. They went to Brightrose where Colin instructed everyone to pack in preparation for Heathrow the next day. He also demanded that Sibyl pack much more than an overnight bag.

"Why?" she asked.

"You're moving into Lacybourne," he answered, completely calmly.

At his words, Sibyl's eyes bugged out as her family drifted around them to take in what would undoubtedly be a fiery show.

"I'm not," she defied.

"You are," Colin stated.

"I am *not*." She nearly stamped her foot.

"Until these men are caught, you're staying at Lacybourne. The alarm hasn't been installed at Brightrose, and even if it were I don't want you here by yourself . . . at all."

"I have a business here," Sibyl pointed out.

"We'll move that to Lacybourne as well."

As her eyes were as wide as they could open, her brows shot up.

"You're . . . you can't . . . I . . ." she spluttered then immediately digressed to an eight-year-old and turned her eyes to her father and whined, "Dad!"

"He has a point," Bertie said quietly.

This time, her mouth dropped open.

"Pack your bags Sibyl," Colin ordered.

She swung from Colin back to her father and tried again by repeating, "Dad!"

"Pack them, Sibyl," Bertie stated in the fatherly tone that, all her life, she could never oppose.

"Bertie, I don't think—" Mags decided to wade into the fray.

"Quiet, Marguerite," Bertie demanded.

At that, all three women's mouths dropped open (or, more to the point, two as Sibyl's was already gaping).

Even so, they stomped up the stairs with dire mutterings that consisted of such words as "overbearing," "chauvinistic" and "tyrannical" but still, they packed.

None of this affected Colin or Bertie in the slightest.

Colin went to Lacybourne while they packed, taking Bertie with him and coming back with the BMW and the Mercedes. They packed the cars to the brim with bags, pet supplies, the food that might spoil in the fridge and all were hauled to Lacybourne.

Then, as if the day couldn't get worse, they arrived at Lacybourne to see it crowded with cars.

It was National Trust Saturday.

They dragged in their bags without incident, putting away the food and leaving the other luggage in the study, which, since it was Colin's personal office, was off-limits to National Trust visitors. Upon leaving again to head out to a late lunch, some of the tourists who'd been in the house stopped and gawked.

"Oh my *gawd*!" a large American woman with dyed-black hair and nicely tailored clothing shrieked. "It's the couple from the portraits."

"Brilliant," Colin muttered, starting to assist Sibyl into the BMW and his tone stated he didn't find it brilliant at all.

"I thought you were dead!" the woman yelled, striding forward quickly. "Inside, they said you were murdered . . . oh . . . my . . . *gawd*!" Her voice rose even further as she turned to a harried, embarrassed-looking man beside her. "They said they'd come back to life. Oh . . . my . . . *gawd*, Harold, look at them. They've been *reincarnated*!"

More people were now peering at them, some of them curiously, others, who had also been inside the house and seen the portraits, excitedly.

"Did you come to visit the portraits?" the woman asked.

"They *live* here," Mags offered proudly.

Colin cursed eloquently under his breath and Sibyl's eyes sent icicles shafting toward her mother.

"Oh . . . my . . . *gawd*," the American woman breathed before shouting, *"It's magic!"*

Colin practically shoved Sibyl into the BMW, and once her feet cleared the door he closed it cleanly and prowled to the other side while Mags, Bertie and Scarlett slid into the back.

Colin took them to the village next to Clevedon, to a lovely, small café nestled into pretty woods at the back of a garden center. As the day stayed cold and misty, they were forced inside to sit amongst the brightly painted tables and gaily blinking fairy lights. The food there was delicious, and after they'd finished Bertie cleared his throat.

"We've been talking and we've come to some decisions," he announced and everyone's eyes turned to him. "Scarlett and I have to get back but seeing as things are . . . well, the way they are," he paused hesitantly before he let the bomb drop, "Mags feels she ought to stay."

Sibyl looked at Colin who, she was surprised to see after the recent incident at Lacybourne, had no reaction whatsoever to this news.

Her gaze slid away from Colin and the rest of the family glanced at each other then finally Bertie asked, "If that's all right with you, Colin."

Colin looked first at Bertie then directly at Mags. "You're welcome at Lacybourne for as long as you wish to stay."

Mags beamed then instantly offered, "I'll take the bedroom the *farthest* away. Give you both some privacy."

Sibyl glanced at the ceiling, praying to the goddess for patience which, luckily, the goddess bestowed on her and the rest of the day went without incident.

LATE IN THE evening, after their visit to Mrs. Byrne and Angie, dinner and everyone was in bed, Sibyl found (not surprisingly) she was unable to sleep.

Listening to Colin's even breathing, she gently slid out of his arms, out of bed and pulled on the plaid dressing gown her father had discarded years before but she'd saved from the Goodwill bag and she'd used ever since.

She stepped over Mallory, whose body was twitching, running after something in his sleep that he would never chase when he was awake, and went to stand by the window. In order to be quiet and not disturb Colin, she carefully opened the drapes and stared out into the moonless night. Her eyes adjusted to the dim light from the streetlamps that barely filtered through the heavy tree line and tall shrubbery at the edge of the estate.

She could see the outlines of the trees and thought of Royce and Beatrice dying hideous, bloody deaths somewhere out there hundreds of years ago.

She hadn't been back to see Royce in her dreams in weeks. Now, she wished to go back, was desperate to go back so she could talk to him, warn him, tell him what awaited him and Beatrice. If she was able to convince him, she could stop the curse before it started.

But even though she wanted it, her nights were dreamless, and it seemed, she realized with a heavy heart, Royce was lost to her.

"Sibyl, get away from the window." Colin's low voice startled her, she jumped and turned toward the bed.

"I didn't know you were awake," she whispered as if he was still asleep.

The covers snapped back, he knifed out of bed, took a great stride toward her (a distance that would take her at least three), snatched her wrist and yanked her back to the side of the bed. He then went to the window and slapped the curtains shut.

"What are you doing?" she asked, watching him.

"Has it occurred to you that someone out there wants to hurt you, me or both of us and standing by the window in the dead of night gives them a clean shot?" he asked in return, his tone sharp.

The thought jarred her to her senses and she replied quietly, "I didn't think."

"Sometimes you don't," he muttered this on a weary sigh and she was stunned to hear that this was said non-judgmentally, devoid of insult or even mild annoyance (well, perhaps there was mild annoyance but it was *very* mild annoyance).

And, because of that, because he understood that failing of hers and accepted it (with only *very* mild annoyance), Sibyl very nearly blurted out right then and there that she loved him.

But, luckily, before she could, Colin pulled her back into bed with him and settled himself behind her, his arm wrapped around her and his body pressed down her length.

Then he asked, "Why were you up?"

His deep, velvet voice rumbled through her and she decided she loved that too.

"I couldn't sleep," she explained.

"I gathered that," he muttered drily in return.

She smiled and she decided she loved that about him too and she didn't even know what *that* was.

Then she whispered, "My family is leaving tomorrow and it makes me sad."

"Your mother is staying," Colin offered in consolation but his arm tightened comfortingly and his breath stirred her hair and her love bloomed even more. That thing inside her she thought was long since ash, she knew now, was alive and flourishing.

"My mother is staying tomorrow and that makes me worried," she replied.

She felt his body shake gently with his chuckle and her smile deepened at the thought that she was able to make him laugh and she decided she loved that too.

"At least things will be more interesting with her around," Colin remarked.

He had *that* right and he likely didn't even know how right he was.

But he would find out.

"I think we can barely cope with things getting much more interesting," Sibyl countered.

Colin made no response.

With his silence, she settled deeper into him and nestled her bottom into his groin. When she'd done this, finally, she relaxed.

But when he next spoke, all relaxation fled.

"Now, why don't you tell me why you really couldn't sleep?"

Her eyes grew round in the dark.

"How did you . . . ?" she started.

He cut her off before she could finish. "You're an immensely bad liar."

She tensed for a moment then heaved a sigh but kept her silence.

Maybe (she hoped) she could wait him out.

"I asked you a question," he reminded her.

Apparently, she couldn't wait him out.

Sibyl remained silent. She'd avoided the "Royce Discussion" so far, she wasn't going to court it now.

His hand shifted to cup her breast.

"Do I need to make you talk?" His voice was silky smooth and utterly dangerous.

She felt whirls of desire, and dread, spread through her, both at the same time.

The last time he did that . . . well, she didn't want to think of that.

"No."

"Then let's have it."

She hesitated before she said quietly, "I was thinking of Royce."

It was his turn to tense but he did it better than her, mainly because his hand was still cupping her breast and the reflexive action caused his grip to tighten splendidly.

It didn't last long before he released her, moved and turned away. She felt some confusion at his retreat before the dim light on the bedside table came on.

By the time Colin came back to her, she'd rolled onto her back and he looked down at her from his position on his elbow.

"Why did you do that?" she queried.

"I want to see your eyes," he answered simply.

"I'd rather talk in the dark," she informed him honestly.

Actually, Sibyl didn't want to talk at all but, since apparently she couldn't avoid it, she would *vastly* have preferred to say what she had to say in the dark.

"I don't particularly care," Colin returned.

She gasped at his words.

His face was hard and unyielding and she couldn't understand it.

"I don't know why this is such a big deal to you," she grumbled, feeling her anger build and trying to control it.

"You don't?"

"No, I don't."

"You kissed him."

"It was you."

His face went from hard to stony and his voice was a dangerous rumble when he reminded her, "It *wasn't* me."

"Okay, then, it wasn't you but I didn't kiss him," she tried and his eyebrows shot up so she finished, "*He* kissed *me*."

"It made you cry." It was an accusation and somehow she was stung by it.

Because of that, she retaliated, "Well, it was beautiful. Beautiful enough to . . ." She saw his jaw clamp and the now-familiar, telltale muscle leap. "Colin, it was you . . ."

"It *wasn't* me and we both bloody well know it," he bit out.

She stared at him and then brought her hands up to her face, pressing her fingers into her forehead and beginning to count to ten.

He interrupted her at three.

"Put your hands down, Sibyl."

She did, quickly, and just as quickly she shot upright, making him rear back to avoid her smashing into him. She hauled the sheet up to her chest, even though she was still wearing her father's robe but somehow she felt vulnerable and needed its protection.

She wasn't comfortable and she wasn't happy.

She was scared.

More scared than when she walked to her front door and saw Mallory's motionless body, more scared than when the knife was at her throat, more scared than any time in her life.

Part anger and part desire to have her cards on the table and find out what he felt for her drove her to say, "Okay, Colin, you want to know, I'll tell you."

She turned to him and found that he'd sat up in the bed as well and she had to tilt her head up to look at him. Something made her pause, something that was missing, something that made her fear she couldn't trust him with this, her deepest secret.

But she'd started and now, she couldn't stop.

"All my life," she began, her voice soft, "I knew in my heart, knew without a doubt, that I was destined to be with someone. That some great force, bigger than any human or deity, was going to guide me to that man. I told my family and all my friends. I had boyfriends but I knew none of them was him so I didn't get attached, couldn't, because I had to be free when he found me or when I found him."

She took in a ragged breath and realized she was having trouble breathing. She pulled in all her courage and forged ahead.

"The years passed and he never came. Then I realized he probably wouldn't. Every day he didn't come, it broke my heart a little more. That's why I moved to England. Because I was always at peace here, at Brightrose especially, I knew somewhere deep inside me that this was my place. And if I couldn't have him at least I'd be *home*."

She realized she was relating all of this to Colin's bare chest and she glanced at him and saw he was utterly still, and even at her glance he remained completely silent.

His eyes, however, were very alive, so active she felt they were reaching out absorbing her.

She tried to ignore it, shifted her gaze to the bed and continued.

"A part of me still believed but I was beginning to lose faith."

She stopped.

This was the hard part. Her breath was coming rapidly and she pulled one in deeply and let it out through her nose.

"Go on," Colin urged, his voice back to velvet and her eyes flew to his to find them warm and searching.

"Then I dreamed of you."

His eyes darkened and his hand instantly lifted to cup her jaw tenderly.

"Sibyl," he murmured.

She shook her head but didn't dislodge his hand as it slid into her hair, lifting some of its massive weight away from her shoulder.

"I was sure, after that dream, that you were the man I'd been looking for all my life, even though I'd never met you. But it was terrifying because, Colin, in *my* dream, *your* throat is slit."

His hand gently fisted in her hair, he leaned into her and rested his forehead against hers. "You never told me that."

"It's true," she whispered. "I called Mags the minute I dreamed it. *She* thought it meant I desperately needed a lover."

She watched his lips turn up.

"Then I met you, Colin, and you were so angry with me, you hated me and I didn't know why, all I wanted to do was see your house."

His lips turned down, his hand moved from her hair to glide down her back and pull her to him but she resisted. Leaning slightly away, she tilted her head further back to look at him.

"The next time I saw you, you were lovely, you were . . . *wonderful*."

The smile came back but froze at her next words. "Then you offered me fifty thousand pounds to sleep with you and I lost all faith that I'd ever find that man."

"God, Sibyl," he groaned, his voice full of regret and she felt tears begin to prick the backs of her eyes.

"And all that time and after, I dreamed of Royce. *He* was Beatrice's true love, her soulmate, he looked at her as if the world shined through her. I wanted that for me and, in the dreams, I had it. And in the summer house that afternoon, I saw it in his eyes as he looked at me."

This time, his whole body froze, as did the hand at the small of her back. Then, she felt it clench into a fist.

Still, she kept speaking.

"It was our private moment, his and mine, the only one we'd ever have and, even though he wasn't kissing *me* but the memory of Beatrice, it was still the most beautiful thing I'd ever experienced and I was happy to have that fleeting moment than nothing at all. And *that's* why I didn't share it with you, because it was mine . . . his and mine."

He stared at her, his face and frame barely controlling some emotion she couldn't fathom, and then he looked away as if he couldn't bear the sight of her anymore. His arm moved away from her and she felt his awful retreat and the first hint of panic.

And she realized that now was the time, perhaps the only time, and no matter what his response, she had to take it. Anything but have him pull away.

Her voice so low, so quiet, it was hardly even a whisper, she said, "Then I fell in love with you."

His head snapped back around and she took a fragmented breath and looked him in the eye.

"If you can believe, it was that damned minibus," she said on a shaky grin. "I watched you dealing with the driver and your . . . you . . . it was just magnificent. Maybe it was before then. I know it *started* before then but it was then when I knew. And everything since clicked into place, piece by piece. I realized after every moment I spent with you, *you* were the one I've been waiting for my whole life, not some long-dead warrior."

When she told him he was the one she'd been waiting for, the rest of her words were said through his swift, gentle, violent snatching of her into his arms. A movement that nearly stole her breath, and as she finished speaking he shoved her roughly back on the bed.

And then, Colin made love to her and it was like nothing they'd ever shared. It was full of fierceness and pounding intensity as if he wanted to use his hands, mouth and body to brand her as his, as if, since he couldn't make a physical mark on her body, then he'd make one on her soul.

And he did.

Proving her right, moments before they both climaxed, he growled, "You're mine."

She nodded, lost in her love for him and the desire throbbing through her body.

"You belong to me." His body pounded deeper inside her than he'd ever been and tears of love sprang to her eyes.

She nodded.

"Yes," she breathed then she said it again as the pleasure he was giving her washed over her, crying it into his ear as she heard him topple over the edge with her. "Yes, Colin, I'm yours."

After they both came down and she felt Colin's breath against her neck, the weight and warmth of his body on hers, him still planted deep inside her, she knew she loved all of that too.

LATER, WHEN HE'D pulled her to his side, his arm came around her like a steel band, she realized he didn't tell her he loved her in return.

He made love to her with a ferocity they'd never experienced but he hadn't said the words.

She wanted to slide away, to find some privacy on the other side of the bed because she felt certain his not saying it meant he didn't feel it. As she was preparing to do so, Bran delicately walked up the length of them, zigzagging across their bodies, his little kitty feet remarkably weighty. The cat jumped to the small of her back and curled there, his warm, furry body keeping her imprisoned in Colin's arm.

That was when the depth of Sibyl's emotions and her lovemaking with Colin finally stole over her and she relaxed against him, letting sleep take her.

And she didn't notice before she fell into slumber, Colin's iron arm had not loosened.

COLIN LAY AWAKE and stared at the dark ceiling, listening to Sibyl's soft breathing.

Having all of Sibyl now laid bare to him and the additional gift of her love drove all ideas of peace and rest out of his mind.

Her love was by far the finest possession he owned.

And someone was trying to kill her.

He felt an insidious, hated sense of fear steal over him and realized that, above all else, he had to focus all of his considerable energy on making certain that didn't happen.

Or die trying.

Chapter TWENTY-FOUR

Magic Dust

Colin glanced out the rearview mirror and saw the familiar car following them.

The car had slid out behind them when they left Lacybourne that morning, stayed with them after their brief visit for Scarlett to check Mrs. Byrne and continued behind them all the way to Heathrow.

And now, coming back to Clevedon, it was still there.

Colin could see the black hair and alabaster face behind the wheel.

Tamara Adams.

No, a clearly not very clever, in fact, enormously *stupid* Tamara Adams.

Colin was relatively certain it was also the car that nearly ran them down outside the restaurant.

He ground his teeth.

Sibyl had been desolate upon seeing her father and sister moving through the security area at Heathrow, but Mags had swiftly cheered her spirits with chatter on the way home, and for this alone Colin was grateful for Mags's company. Even though Sibyl and her mother had an odd relationship that was based half on exasperation, half on adoration,

Mags knew exactly how to manipulate her daughter's feelings, giving her a needed uplift.

Slowly, the BMW's smooth ride and her interrupted sleep last night came over her and Sibyl fell asleep with her head against the window.

This, Mags (as any good mother would) noticed immediately and all chatter stopped. For fifteen minutes, Mags was surprisingly silent.

Then she asked quietly, "Who's that following us? Do you know her?"

Startled, Colin's eyes shot to the rearview mirror to take in her knowing face. Mags was free-spirited and flighty but, Colin realized just then, she was also no fool.

"Yes," he answered brusquely.

"Spurned lover?" Mags guessed correctly.

Colin nodded and found himself saying, "The one I was with when I met Sibyl."

She immediately returned, "The one who was *there* when you met Billie?"

He nodded again marking, for future reference, how much Sibyl told her mother.

"Oh dear," Mags sighed. "Well," she brightened, "at least we know who and why. Now you just need to stop her." She paused and glanced out of the window and said distractedly but with such certainty Colin was momentarily stunned, "I have every faith."

Colin watched as she settled back into her seat contentedly.

Half an hour later, he pulled into Lacybourne only to see his mother's blue Audi.

"What in bloody hell?" he muttered under his breath.

The change in speed coming off the motorway and maneuvering of roundabouts had caused Sibyl to awaken, but all the while she kept a still sleepy silence.

Now she spoke.

"Who's that?" she asked, her voice husky with sleep.

"My mother," Colin answered impatiently.

"What's she doing here?" The sweet sound of sleep was quickly leaving her voice and suspicion was edging in.

"I, um, might have called her," Mags said hesitantly from the back.

Colin again swore under his breath.

Sibyl's head snapped around to scowl at her mother.

"Why on the goddess's green earth would you do a fool thing like that?" she cried, her sleepy voice a distant memory.

Colin parked in the garage as mother and daughter squared off.

"Colin was shot with a tranquillizer dart!" Mags defended herself. "She's his mother. I thought she had the right to know!"

"Don't you think Colin should be the judge of that?" Sibyl returned angrily, and if she hadn't been so adorably peeved on his behalf he might have kissed her for defending him.

Before Sibyl's temper could explode in a car that was much too small for the force of it, Colin broke in.

"It's done. There's no sense arguing about it now." Colin felt a bit more of Bertie's lifetime of pain when both pairs of angry eyes moved to him and both women's mouths opened to blast him with their wrath when he smoothly continued, "If anyone has the right to be upset it's me and I'm not so that's the end of it."

Both mouths snapped shut and Mags's face instantly settled happily while Sibyl's suffused with mutiny.

"We'll talk about this later," she warned her mother as she alighted from the car.

"Okay," Mags agreed, unaffected by the threat, and she walked to the house.

Colin surreptitiously glanced down the lane, didn't see any sign of Tamara or her car and he put his hand in the back pocket of his jeans to grab his mobile.

Sibyl stopped, waiting for him to walk to the house with her.

"Go in, sweetheart, I need to make a call," he directed her gently. "Tell Mum I'll be in in a few minutes."

She looked at him closely then turned, and, with no small amount of absorption, he watched her generous hips sway as she walked to the house.

He did this while he called Robert Fitzwilliam.

"Look into Tamara Adams. She's been following us the entire day, all the way to Heathrow and back," Colin ordered.

"Got it. You still need Rick tomorrow?" Robert asked about the bodyguard Colin had engaged to watch Sibyl and now her mother and, much more recently, *his* mother.

"Yes," Colin answered.

"Fine, he'll be at your house at seven."

Colin ended the call, not looking forward to the upcoming conversation with Sibyl about her future bodyguard.

With resignation, Colin went in to greet his mother.

SIBYL SAT NEXT to Colin in Mrs. Byrne's magic room.

Across from them, Mrs. Byrne, who was still not her usual, vital self, was moving around carefully as if her body was a fragile thing. Still, she was muttering chants as she clinked and clacked amongst a plethora of vials, shakers, mortars and pestles, and other extraordinary flotsam and jetsam of witch paraphernalia she kept in her magic room.

A room, done up in plums and roses, tassels and velvets, shelves and spindly tables carrying strange and fascinating objects, it looked like a set right out of a movie.

Phoebe, who had come into the story late and was still processing it, sat silently across the room, staring stupefied at Marian's activity.

Angie, Mrs. Byrne's daughter, was assisting her mother as if they did this kind of thing every day.

Mags was sitting next to Phoebe barely able to hold herself still, alight with glee.

Sibyl slid a cautious glance toward Colin who was not happy at all. He was obviously dubious and it was just as obvious he wished to be somewhere else. He was sitting with one ankle casually resting on his other knee, slouched arrogantly and one of his arms was lying across the back of Sibyl's chair.

Regardless of his nonchalant position, he seemed wired, ready to pounce.

Since returning from Heathrow, Sibyl noticed that something had changed in him. He seemed impatient and energetic, like a big cat prowling back and forth in front of its cage in a zoo, desperate to get out.

Sibyl thought, looking at him, that perhaps it hadn't been wise to push this magical protection spell thing that afternoon. He hadn't wanted to come and now that he was there, it was blindingly obvious he very much didn't want to be.

However, Sibyl had a plan. In fact she had two plans, and she needed to talk to Marian about them because she needed the older woman's help.

She'd been thinking about it in an effort not to think about her confession of love last night and the fact that it was not returned.

Sibyl believed this was all more than lucky coincidence. That it all fit together. That there was magic and mayhem in the air and Sibyl had to find a way to stop it.

As crazy as it all seemed, Sibyl believed Mrs. Byrne.

Colin could hire dozens of private investigators if he wanted to but Sibyl was going to investigate the magical side.

"Now!" Mrs. Byrne announced happily, turning toward Sibyl and Colin and taking Sibyl from her thoughts.

Phoebe jumped nervously as Mags leaned forward in excitement.

"I started this weeks ago, so it's been fermenting nicely," Mrs. Byrne explained. "I've added a few of my own, personal touches and left it to marinade this morning. It should do the trick."

She sounded like she was talking about a recipe for chicken.

"She's very good," Angie stated proudly, her eyes on her mother.

Mrs. Byrne moved forward with a glass vial in one hand that had a powder in it that looked like cinnamon, a common kitchen strainer in the other.

Marian moved directly toward Colin.

"This won't hurt a bit," she assured and lifted the vial and strainer over his head.

"What," his voice was low and even and very, very frightening but not nearly as frightening as the hard, cold look on his face—a look and tone that froze Marian's hands in mid-air, "do you think you're going to do with *that*?"

"Why, pour it over your head," Marian explained as if it was the most normal thing in the world.

He lithely slid out of his chair, out from under the strainer and towered over her. "I think not."

Marian's face set resolutely. "My dear man—"

"Do me!" Sibyl interjected, finding herself in the role of peacemaker. If she didn't step in, by the look on his face, Colin was likely to explode. "You can do me first, I don't mind."

Marian turned to Sibyl. "The most potent effects of the charm come in the first few sprinkles," Marian explained, "and Colin—"

"By all means, shower away on Sibyl, *especially* if they are the most potent," Colin cut in.

He'd crossed his arms on his chest and now, instead of looking furious, he looked amused.

Sibyl made a face at him that caused him, to her great distress, to let out a sharp bark of laughter.

Marian sagely ignored him and muttered to Sibyl, "This won't take even a minute, dear."

And then she lifted the strainer over Sibyl's head and poured the cinnamon concoction in and Sibyl waited to be dusted with its rusty, brown contents.

Instead, to her utter amazement, the minute the brown powder sifted through the strainer, it sparkled and glittered brightly, raining down on her like fairy dust, disappearing altogether the minute it touched her hair, her skin, her clothes.

"Oh . . . my . . . *goddess*," Mags breathed.

Phoebe's mouth gaped open and stayed that way.

Colin's eyes narrowed.

"That'll do." Marian swiftly pulled the strainer and vial way.

"You see!" Sibyl, feeling hope for the first time, a witness to obvious magic (with pixie dust and all!), she shot out of her chair with excitement. "Oh Colin, this might possibly work!"

"Of course it'll work," Angie grumbled.

Colin did not appear, in any way, to be convinced.

"I fail to see—" he began but she ran to him.

Flattening her palms against his abdomen, she leaned into him.

"Please do it, for me?" she begged, looking beseechingly into his doubting eyes.

He stared at her a moment and then, to her delight, gave in, though not at all gracefully.

And he did this by muttering, "For Christ's sake," before he sat down to get his sprinkling.

When all was done, Colin announced, "I need to make a few calls, I'll be out front." And he marched out of the magic room, the very picture of affronted male dignity and, if possible, Sibyl's love for him deepened.

Oblivious to all of this, Angie chimed in happily, "Time for a cuppa," and she herded a still stunned Phoebe and an excitedly chattering Mags into the kitchen.

Sibyl hung back with Mrs. Byrne who was cleaning her magical implements.

"Mrs. Byrne. You've done so much and at great personal cost—" Sibyl charged right in to begin work on her plan.

Time was of the essence.

"No cost at all, dear, it's my pleasure, it's my *destiny*." Although still not fully back to herself, Mrs. Byrne was obviously in her element, enjoying every second of this.

Sibyl approached her and watched her working, "I need to ask you a favor."

Marian threw her a smile and immediately replied, "Anything."

Sibyl smiled back at her before she she asked, "If you can bring Royce forward, could you send me back?"

Marian's hands stopped what they were doing and she turned to Sibyl with questioning eyes. "Of course, dear, it's very basic magic, though a costly endeavor in time and energy, but why would you want to do that?"

Sibyl quickly explained.

"I've been waiting to have another dream memory but I haven't had one in ages. I think now, if I went back, maybe he would recall me or I could get him to listen to me. If I go back, I can tell him what's going to happen and he can be prepared for it, fight it, keep himself and

Beatrice alive and . . ."

She trailed off when Mrs. Byrne turned back to her task while shaking her head.

"No, no. As much as I'd like to, you don't mess with time. Never." She paused thoughtfully, as if considering it. Then shook her head again, sadly, and finished, "Ever."

"But Marian, don't you see? If we stop the curse before it starts—"

Marian set down the strainer, which had been cleaned with some clear fluid in an oddly shaped, cork-topped bottle, and she turned to Sibyl.

"Sibyl, as lovely as it would be to allow their love to blossom and grow, if we change time and Royce and Beatrice lived, then the whole world could change. It could be good or it could be bad. We don't know. We'd have no way of ever knowing. It could be that you or Colin, or the both of you would never exist. Or me. Or my children. Or Japan could fall into the ocean. Anything could happen."

"It couldn't be that bad and if—"

Marian put her hand out to touch Sibyl's cheek.

"No," she said in a quiet voice, trying to soften the blow of her refusal.

Sibyl closed her eyes.

So much for Plan A, now she had to try Plan B.

"Okay, I have another idea."

"I'm all ears," Marian informed her and moved to sit down in a plush, worn, plum-colored, velvet chair with a doily hanging on the back of it.

Sibyl took a seat beside her, took a deep breath, pinned her hopes on her words and plunged ahead.

"You can give me the potion you gave Colin and give some to him. But more this time, so that Royce and Beatrice could come forward for long enough to consummate their love using our bodies."

Marian's eyes widened and she pulled in a swift breath.

Sibyl found this encouraging and she forged ahead.

"The time before, it didn't last long so it would have to last long enough for them to have time to, um . . . *do it*. They'd know each other immediately, I know it. Even though the time has changed, the place has changed and our hair has changed. I know they'd recognize each other. We could . . ." She stopped because she was making up the entirety of the plan as she went along then she hit on it, "Write them a note! Tell them what to do. Then *they* could stop the curse and give Colin and me time, without this hanging over our heads, to . . ."

Again, she trailed to a stop when Mrs. Byrne shook her head.

"Sibyl, my dear, that is a very volatile potion. *Anything* could go wrong with that. I took a grave risk the last time and was very lucky with the outcome. And, it cannot be taken in large doses under any circumstances. It could be catastrophic."

"But why?" Sibyl cried.

She needed either Plan A or Plan B because Plan C was unthinkable.

Plan C meant that in order to save Colin, she'd have to leave him.

It was all about them being together, Marian had told them that and she knew it was true in her heart. The minute she left, he'd be safe again.

"One of the souls could get stuck, forever, in the present, leaving either you or Colin in some horrible limbo for eternity. Obviously, I either hit it right or Colin has no other incarnations, but you could have. What if I brought forward someone else, some*thing* else? A bee, for example. A samurai. No, it doesn't bear contemplating." Looking at Sibyl's dejected expression she leaned forward and patted her hand. "I'm sorry, my dear. They are clever ideas but you're just going to have to tell him you love him."

She smiled at Sibyl with knowing eyes and Sibyl's heart sank.

"I already did," Sibyl whispered.

Marian's face glowed. "Well done! And?"

"And nothing." Sibyl answered, "He doesn't love me back."

It was Marian's turn to give a hoot of laughter (a hoot that lasted a good while). When she had her mirth under control she actually wiped her eyes.

Then she said, still chuckling, "Oh, my dear, that's too much. Do you think Colin Morgan would sit and be sprinkled with magic dust for just *anyone*?"

Sibyl bit her lip but replied, "He cares about me. I know he does. He wants to keep me safe. He's very patient with me but if he loved me, he'd tell me." Marian smiled kindly but Sibyl shook her head, feeling tears stinging the backs of her eyes, tears she refused to shed, for now. "No, Marian, I told him last night and he could have . . . there's no reason why he didn't tell me so he must not feel it. Maybe one day, I can hope, but we need *time* and someone's trying to kill him."

"They're trying to kill you both, you must remember that," Marian warned softly. "You are in just as much danger as Colin is."

"I had a dream where his throat is slit, *his*, not mine. And I have these dreams—"

"I know, my dear Sibyl. You're clairvoyant." Marian waved that strange fact away as if it meant nothing. "But we can change what you saw."

Sibyl felt all hope leave her. They couldn't change it, she knew it, she *felt* it.

So she had to leave even if it meant going back to America.

She had to keep Colin safe.

And even though she'd been waiting her whole life for him, in order to save *his* life, she had to leave him.

It was the only way.

If he loved her then they'd surely consummated it so many times that they'd have an ironclad shield around them so strong a nuclear bomb would have left them unscathed.

But they were obviously still vulnerable.

"Thank you for everything, Marian," Sibyl muttered with finality trying to hide her dejection but she couldn't.

Marian tried to reassure her. "It will all work out. I feel it. Stick in there, dear, we'll get them this time."

Sibyl nodded but she wasn't convinced.

And she certainly was not going to risk Colin's life, stand aside and see his motionless *and* lifeless body loaded into an ambulance.

PHOEBE AND MAGS were happily preparing dinner in the kitchen and Colin was working in the study, so Sibyl took her chance and crept up to the bedroom with Mallory and Bran.

With tears silently rolling down her cheeks and a heart so heavy it felt like a load of bricks weighing down her entire body, Sibyl pulled out her suitcase and started to pack.

If she was quick, she could get out without anyone noticing.

Colin nearly always worked the weekends and he hadn't had a moment to spare, what with being shot with a tranquillizer dart, a visit to the A&E, being outed publicly as a reincarnated knight, getting saddled with Mags, having Mags ask Phoebe along for their roller coaster ride and being sprinkled with magic dust, so she figured he'd be occupied for at least several hours.

And who knew how long it would take Phoebe and Mags to make dinner? It took Mags forty-five minutes to make toast, dinner would definitely be delayed.

So she had time to pack her things, pack her animals and she would leave a note.

She had no idea what she was going to do, where she was going to go.

She could stay with Jemma tonight or find a B&B that took pets. She might be able to lose herself in Bristol. Colin might try to find her, he might not. She didn't know and the fact that she *didn't* know made each piece of her shattered heart break into tinier pieces.

Quickly she shoved clothes into the suitcase willy-nilly, not bothering to fold them (which was a mistake because they were certainly not all going to fit in a jumble). She decided that she'd have to leave some things behind and swiftly sorted through what was essential and what was not.

"What are you doing?"

She yelped, jumped and whirled, all at the same time.

Colin was leaning in the doorway, his arms folded on his chest, one foot crossed at the ankle clay-colored eyes narrowed on her. Mallory gave a woof of greeting but didn't move when Colin sliced a warning glance at him before his gaze snapped back to Sibyl's face.

"I thought you were working," Sibyl whispered.

"I was."

His face was blank, his voice was smooth, his eyes never left her.

"Why . . ." she swallowed, "why did you stop?"

Without delay, Colin answered, "It occurred to me that I hadn't made love to you yet today and as our mothers are systematically destroying the kitchen by the sounds of it, I thought I'd take the opportunity when we have the upstairs to ourselves."

She just stared at him, those tiny pieces of her heart broke another time. Soon, they'd be grains of sand.

"You've been crying," he noted blandly.

"I stubbed my toe," she lied.

This, for some reason, made him smile. Then he pushed away from the door and strode into the room.

"I would ask why you would lie about stubbing your toe but you've already left one of my questions unanswered and I'd much prefer to have a response to that."

He seemed to be heading for her so she backed away. The backs of her thighs hit the bed so she changed direction and scuttled around it.

"I'm sorry," she started and then fibbed again (as she knew perfectly well) by asking, "What question is that?"

He was still stalking her. Definitely the big cat had gotten out of the cage and she was his first victim. She felt her heart skip a few beats before beginning to pound.

"What are you doing?" he repeated patiently.

Her glance flew to the semi-packed suitcase on the bed and then back to him. She was close to the wall, she knew, so she changed directions and headed toward the fireplace.

"Doing?" She needed to stall and decided to act stupid, it shouldn't be that hard.

Colin, however, was losing patience.

"Sibyl," was all he said and her name was loaded with meaning.

"I was packing." She pointed out the obvious and rounded a chair.

He stopped at her new direction, changed his and she realized why even if she hadn't noted it before. If she had, she might have been able to make a getaway, but, alas, her flighty mind worked against her, again.

With quick strides, he made short work of heading for the door. Upon arrival he closed it, walked calmly to a dresser by the door, opened one of the drawers and took something out. Then he walked back to the door and she watched him turn a key in the lock.

Her eyes rounded in alarm.

He turned back to her, rested his shoulders against the door and slid the key in his pocket.

Then he asked, "Why were you packing?"

His voice stayed bland, casual, as if they were having a friendly conversation over coffee and he hadn't just locked her in his bedroom.

She'd stopped behind a chair. She decided, vaguely, lost in the intensity of his eyes, it was not nearly enough protection.

Her mind whirled and she tried to read the situation.

He *seemed* quite unaffected by the sight of her packing. That, in a way, was good.

He also *seemed* not to care much that she'd been crying. That wasn't *really* good, but for her current purpose she'd count it as good.

Regardless of this, he'd locked them in the room.

That was very, *very* bad.

When she didn't speak, he did. "Have you decided to go on holiday?"

She pulled both her lips between her teeth, wondering if she should say yes or no.

He didn't give her a chance to say either.

"I think that's an excellent idea, where are we going?" He pushed his shoulders off the door and started after her again.

She couldn't take much more of this.

"Colin, stay where you are," she demanded, unfortunately in a shaky voice that made it sound more like a plea.

"I've a friend who owns an island. No way on or off without us knowing about it. It would be hard to find us, let alone kill us. You've hit on the perfect solution."

Maybe she had misread the situation. He no longer seemed unaffected by her packing.

At all.

"I'm leaving," she blurted out when he was not two of his great strides away. She lifted up her hand, palm out, "Colin, please stop."

To her surprise, he did.

"Where are you going?" His voice was low and even and she forgot how much it scared her when he used it on her.

"I don't know. I haven't figured that out yet."

He nodded, once, sharply, then asked, "For curiosity's sake, *why* are you going?"

She blinked.

"For curiosity's sake?" she echoed.

"Since you aren't going anywhere, it's a moot point. However, I'm curious so humor me."

She squared her shoulders and announced, "I'm leaving." And she was pleased to hear her voice sounded stronger.

"Tell me why," Colin demanded.

She shrugged, trying to seem unconcerned, "Things aren't working out between us."

Without hesitation, he immediately fired back, "That's an interesting assessment of our situation. Would you care to elaborate?"

She was beginning to realize why he was so successful. He wasn't just ruthless, he was merciless.

"I . . ." she began, her mind trying to find a lie he'd actually believe, "well . . ."

He smiled but instead of being cruel or belittling, it was magnetic and her stomach lurched pleasantly.

He settled into his stance and crossed his arms on his chest.

"Take all the time you need," he offered magnanimously. "I'm sure you'll think of something."

In an instant, she did.

"We don't suit," she informed him, tossing her hair mutinously because he was beginning to make her mad.

His brows lifted. "And how's that?"

"You are . . . well . . . *you*."

His smile returned, deeper, more electric, and her stomach pitched then melted with warmth.

"Indeed I am."

"And I'm me!" she snapped when she saw that he was very close to laughing at her. "We're from entirely different worlds, have different viewpoints. You're probably a . . . a . . . *Tory*!" she burst out, making the word "Tory" sound like the words "ax murderer."

"Actually I am," he admitted without apology.

She threw her hands up. "That in itself makes us impossible," she announced dramatically.

He shook his head. "You're forgetting a few very crucial things."

She didn't want to know so she didn't ask. She started to slide away from him to put more space between them but she, of course, had nowhere to go. At least it gave her something to do.

He didn't wait for her request to elucidate. "There is the fact that we're spectacular in bed together."

"I—" she started to lie.

He chuckled and she could have thrown something at him. "If you tell me you've had better, you're lying. I know you haven't and neither have I."

She stopped creeping around the chairs and stared at him in wonder.

She could not imagine she was the best Colin had ever had and the very thought made her stomach do a cartwheel of happiness.

She shook off the result of what *that* tidbit did to her stomach and she said, "That isn't enough."

"No?" he asked as she began creeping again. "Then, sweetheart, you force me to play my trump, so I'll have to remind you that you're in love with me."

She halted.

Bloody hell.

Bloody, *bloody* hell.

She was stupid, definitely stupid, stupid, *stupid*. She'd led him straight to throwing that in her face and she had no retort. She couldn't exactly force him to declare his love for her, especially if there was no love to declare.

So she did the only thing she could do, she kept silent.

Colin didn't.

"That fact makes you mine and I don't let go of what's mine."

She noted he didn't mention love but possession. Her heart ground to dust as the tears pricked her eyes. She told herself not to cry but she felt the wetness balancing on her lower lids and then sliding down her cheeks.

"You don't own me," she said quietly.

"Yes I do, sweetheart, and you know I do." His tone was gentle and she found it far more difficult to handle than the game they'd been playing. "Why were you packing?" he asked softly.

She could no longer bear up so she gave in.

"I don't want you to die," she whispered, her voice broken and small. "If I leave, they'll let you alone and I'd rather have you alive without me than dead . . ." She lost her train of thought but soldiered on. "Than just plain dead," she finished lamely.

It was then he leaped out of his casual stance, and with another surprised yelp she backed away, all the way to the wall. She slammed against it and before she could flee in another direction, his hard body was pressed against her.

"Colin, I have to go," she begged, staring at his throat.

"You're not going." His voice was uncompromising.

"I have to!" she cried and his hands came up to either side of her face, forcing it to tilt back to see his.

"Darling, I'm going to ask you this once and you have to answer me and then stick by your answer no matter what happens in the coming weeks." His voice was both sweet and grave, and her eyes riveted on his beautiful face, "Do you trust me?"

She gawped. "Of course I trust you. I mean, how could you even think . . . ?"

She stopped when she felt the tension ease out of him and realized what he was asking and how, exactly, what she had been doing appeared to him.

She closed her eyes and all the fight left her.

"I'm an idiot," she whispered.

"Yes," he agreed, "but you're *my* idiot." His voice was full of humor, her eyes flew open and all the fight came back into her.

"You think I'm an idiot?" she snapped.

"You're just spoiling for a fight, aren't you?" His eyes were dancing and she let out a huffy breath.

"Well, pardon me. No one gave me the etiquette book on how to behave when you're the reincarnated soul of one of a pair of dead lovers, you're living under a five hundred-year-old curse and have lunatics with knives and tranquillizer guns chasing after you with deadly intent. Perhaps I'm not thinking too clearly. Perhaps I'm just a wee bit *stressed*."

His hands slid from her jaw to lift her hair at the back of her head, and as he did this Sibyl noted his eyes were so intense, they were liquid.

His gaze on her mouth, he murmured, "I know a *much* better way to deal with stress."

"I'm sure you do," she noted crisply. "You know everything."

Colin's head dipped and he smiled against her lips and there he whispered, "Just remember that."

Then he kissed her.

Then he helped her work out her stress.

Succeeding spectacularly.

Chapter TWENTY-FIVE

Settling In

The next week and a half with Sibyl was eventfully uneventful. Although they had no attempts on their lives, Colin found his turned upside down.

Lacybourne was an enormous manor house that, since he'd moved in, had always seemed empty, even when he was occupying it.

Now, every corner seemed filled with Sibyl, her pets, her mother, his mother and anyone else the trio deemed fit to add to the mix.

Sibyl had taken the news of a bodyguard watching after her very well. Colin inadvertently hit on the perfect way to break news that she may not like and avoid her formidable temper in the process.

After her rather endearing yet entirely unacceptable bid to save his life by leaving him, he'd punished her.

For anyone else but Colin Morgan, inflicting punishment for such a selfless act would seem a strange reaction. However, he didn't particularly like how he felt when he'd walked to their bedroom with the purpose of making love to her only to find her packing a suitcase. Therefore, when he'd finally subdued her impulsive, hilarious and ill-conceived flight and taken her to bed, he'd spent a good deal of time using most of the weapons in his rather honed sexual arsenal to drive her mad with desire.

When he had her wrists imprisoned over her head and after he'd lavished a goodly amount of attention on her lovely, responsive breasts, he surged over her. Thinking, finally, she was going to get what she'd been begging him to give her for at least fifteen minutes, she opened her legs to receive him.

"By the way," he muttered against her mouth and felt her hips tilt upward in invitation. At this act, his control slipped and he finished through gritted teeth, "I've hired a bodyguard for you. Starting tomorrow morning, he'll be with you every minute when I'm not."

Sibyl's eyes focused on him but Colin realized by their dazed quality she wasn't hearing a word he said. Her mind was definitely elsewhere.

"Okay," she mumbled without hint of protest and wrapped one long leg around his hip.

Ever the practiced negotiator, he decided to stop while he was ahead and slid slowly, deeply inside her and then his mind went elsewhere as well.

Later, he was sitting at the head of the dining-room table, Sibyl to his left. They were all eating her mother's vegetarian lasagna, homemade garlic bread and a salad that was so big it had to be served in two bowls.

Colin turned to Sibyl. "About Rick."

Absorbed in eating her mother's admittedly delicious meal, she munched a piece of bread and asked, "Who's Rick?"

"Your bodyguard."

Her head didn't move but her eyes shifted swiftly to the side to stare at him and her mouth froze mid-crunch.

Unaffected by her response, he carried on, "He's being paid to protect you, not to be your friend, not to be your project. This is a professional relationship. He drives you, watches you, guards you, keeps you safe. If he has a girlfriend he isn't getting along with, that's none of your concern. If his mother has terminal brain cancer, you don't bake her cookies and hold her hand during chemotherapy."

Her head snapped around to glare at him and she gulped down the bread before snapping, "Colin!"

"Is that understood?" he asked the question but didn't expect an answer, he simply expected to be obeyed.

"I can hardly ignore it if his mother has a brain tumor," she retorted angrily, hilariously defending her right to be the guardian angel for a fictional unfortunate.

"Then I suggest you don't even talk to him so you won't find out."

"I can hardly not talk to him if he spends every minute of the day with me."

"Sibyl," he said warningly.

"Colin." She used his tone against him.

"You befriend him and he loses focus, he's gone."

"I cannot believe—" she hissed.

"You do it with the next one then *he's* gone," Colin went on and finished, "Do you catch my meaning?"

Her rebellious gaze slid to Phoebe and Mags who were sitting across from her. Phoebe was trying very hard (but failing as her lips were twitching) to keep her face impassive. Mags wasn't even trying to hide her smile but at least she dropped her head so she smiled at her plate of lasagna.

Finding no reinforcements at the table, Sibyl bit out, "Fine."

Monday, he had barely sat behind his desk in his office when Mandy came rushing in with his coffee.

"There's a man out there named Kyle James. He says he needs to talk to you. He says you know him from what he calls 'The Centre.'" Mandy's wide eyes got wider as she finished, "He mentioned something about a tranquillizer dart!"

When she finished, her eyes were round as saucers.

Calmly, Colin told her to send him in.

Sibyl's friend strolled in, taking a good look around him as he did and then put out his hand for a friendly handshake. "All right, mate?"

"Kyle," Colin responded to the familiar West Country greeting.

"Like the office," he remarked. "Is Billie's going to be this nice when you finish building it?"

When he stopped speaking, he had a twinkle in his eye.

"I think something like this may clash with the current décor of The Centre." Colin grinned at him and gestured to a black leather chair in front of his enormous desk. Kyle sat and waited as Colin took his seat behind his desk. Then Colin inquired politely, "Do you want some coffee?"

"That's nice of you but I don't want to take up too much of your time. Need to be on my way soon anyhow."

Colin sat back and regarded him carefully, wondering why he was there, before he asked, "What's on your mind?"

Kyle shifted and looked out the window behind Colin's head, and Colin saw, with interest, Kyle's normal amiability slowly fade.

"Been asking around. Not good what happened to you and Billie last Friday." His eyes moved back to Colin, the twinkle was gone and it was replaced by something very serious. "Got a boy on the estate, not a bad kid but he doesn't hang around with a good crowd. Heard word he was talking about a friend of his who showed up at his place Friday night, arm busted."

That got Colin's attention and his back straightened.

"Yes?" he prompted.

"Me and a couple of . . ." He hesitated and stared at Colin assessingly. Deciding he trusted what he saw, he continued, "My boys paid him a visit. Seems this kid's friend didn't want to go to hospital. Eventually he passed out with the pain so the kid loaded him up, meaning to take him to Weston Hospital anyway. On the way there, his friend woke up and demanded he take him somewhere, anywhere, but Weston or Bristol. The kid took him down to some place in Exeter. His friend slipped away after getting treated. Our boy doesn't know where he went."

Colin clenched his teeth but nodded his head. He realized in that moment he'd vastly underrated the even-tempered Kyle.

"Another thing," Kyle carried on, "kid told us his friend said some woman owed him more considering his arm was broken. He said he was paid a load but not enough to get his arm busted." He stopped and watched the muscle working in Colin's jaw. "Thought you'd want to know."

"Thank you," was all Colin could manage to get out.

It was Tamara, he knew and he was pleasantly contemplating wringing her skinny, alabaster neck.

"Haven't told the police yet, figured you might want to do that, er . . . anonymous-like."

Colin nodded again, easily catching his meaning. Kyle and "his boys" part in this drama was to remain a secret.

Obviously done with his errand, Kyle slapped his thighs, morphing straight back to his old, friendly self. "Well, that's it. Got things to do."

He stood and Colin joined him around the desk for another handshake but when it should have ended, Kyle's hand tightened.

"We take care of our own," he said in a low voice, staring Colin in the eye and the older man's were sober. He dropped Colin's hand. "We're still lookin'," Kyle told Colin. "We find out any more, we'll let you know."

Colin wrote his mobile and home numbers on the back of a business card and handed it to Kyle, making his meaning clear as he said quietly, "Please do that."

The minute the door closed behind Kyle, Colin called Robert Fitzwilliam to relate the news.

Later in the afternoon, he called the alarm company ordering them to increase security at Lacybourne, including putting a panic button and warning light in his and Sibyl's bedroom. He then called his housekeeper, Mrs. Manning, to tell her that he was changing all the codes and that he had guests who would be staying for an indefinite period of time.

She asked for the new codes but he told her he would tell her in person when he next saw her. He wasn't even going to trust his own damned phone line. She, strangely, pressed him but he flatly refused to divulge the information over the phone. He explained she'd have to wait, for the time being, to be let in by him, Sibyl or whoever else his mother or Mags dragged into their drama.

That evening he changed all the alarm codes and explained them and how to work the complicated system to the three women currently occupying Lacybourne.

On seeing three uncomprehending faces, he explained them again. Then, when his mother bit her lip and Mags's eyes shifted uneasily this way and that, he patiently explained it again.

He did not even want to consider what would happen when the new system he'd ordered was installed.

Preparing for bed, he exited the bathroom after brushing his teeth to see Sibyl sitting cross-legged on the bed wearing another one of his T-shirts.

Apart from the fact that she loved him, which he found a vastly pleasurable experience the like of which he'd never known, the second thing he liked best about her was her new habit of wearing his T-shirts to bed. Not just that she did it, but the casual intimacy it evoked that she did.

Not to mention she looked utterly adorable sitting cross-legged close to the end of their bed, her face free of makeup, her fantastic, gleaming hair loose around her shoulders.

She broke him out of his reverie by saying, "Um . . . Colin?"

The hesitant somewhat guilty tone of her voice tore all pleasant thoughts of Sibyl's love and how adorable she was in his T-shirt out of his head.

He just looked at her, mentally preparing for the worst.

"I have something to tell you," she continued.

He stopped at the foot of the bed and stared down at her.

"Let me guess," he drawled, "you discovered your bodyguard's sister has diabetes and you've decided to give her your kidney."

Her head jerked slightly and then her face lit up in a magnificent smile before she burst into deep, musical laughter. His body jolted at the sound and it occurred to him that this was the first time he'd ever made her laugh.

And doing it he felt, oddly, like he'd conquered the world.

Once she had herself under control she shook her head, her hair shifting beautifully around her face, and said, "No."

"What is it?" he asked and then leaned forward.

Unable to prevent himself even if it meant losing the millions he'd worked so hard for, he placed his hands on the bed on either side of her hips and kissed the smile on her face.

When he lifted his head she said, "It was National Trust day today at Lacybourne."

"I know." He put his knee on the bed and she had no choice but to grab his shoulders as he loomed over her and she had to lean back to allow his body into the space where hers had just been.

"Well, word is getting out about you and me, Royce and Beatrice."

He froze then he narrowed his eyes at her.

"How's that happening . . ." he paused, "exactly?"

She pulled her lips between her teeth for a moment before releasing them and saying, "Well . . ." and that was all she said but she drew the word out so it lasted several seconds.

"Sibyl."

"They already knew about you, of course," she started quickly. "But some of the tourists told some of the Trust volunteers last Saturday after they'd seen us, I mean *me* . . . with, er, *you*, outside and then today the volunteers and tourists kind of saw me—"

He moved forward more, this time menacingly and she clutched his shoulders and her legs uncrossed as he settled her back, dropping his weight on her. She didn't have a chance to close her legs and he pressed himself between them.

"Kind of saw you?" he asked as he lifted himself up with his elbows in the bed at her sides in order to look down on her.

"Yes . . . well, I was kind of, er . . . *mingling* amongst the tourists."

He closed his eyes and silently asked whatever deity, God or her goddess, to grant him patience.

She went on hurriedly, "Well, it was Mags's fault. She went down into the Great Hall first and was shooting off her mouth. Then *your* mother joined her and I can't really say anything to her, because I don't know her very well and it isn't my place. I just went in to try to get them *out* and then things got a bit out of control—"

He opened his eyes. "*How* out of control?"

"I think there might have been reporters," she whispered, her eyes wide.

He dropped his forehead to hers and sighed, "Sibyl, you truly are the most an—"

Before he could finish, she burst out, "Mags started it!"

He lifted then shook his head. "What am I going to do with you?"

Her mouth twisted into an adorable pout before she grumbled, "It wasn't my fault."

"Darling, do me a favor," Colin muttered.

She nodded.

"While I'm trying to save our lives, could you please try not to further endanger yours?"

She heaved a great breath and then said, "I'll try."

But he knew, and she knew, that she most likely wouldn't be very successful.

The next morning, he'd barely sat behind his desk when Mandy rushed in with his morning coffee and slapped a newspaper down on his blotter.

"I thought I'd show you that first thing, before anyone said anything," she declared in a dire voice, her eyes so big Colin was concerned they'd pop out of her head. "I'll hold your calls," she mumbled ominously and quickly exited the room.

He flipped open the paper to where Mandy had helpfully folded it back to a page. There he saw a stock photo of himself, a picture of Sibyl standing in the Great Hall smiling winningly at two poorly dressed tourists and replicated photos of the portraits of Beatrice and Royce.

The title of the article read, Tycoon and Social Worker are Cursed Lovers Reincarnated.

He swore under his breath.

By the time he left that evening Mandy reported, in an extremely harassed way, she'd taken more calls that day than she usually took in a month.

He decided he'd better give her a raise in the morning or he'd be hiring a new secretary and that was a headache he didn't need at the present time.

And anyway, he liked Mandy.

The three women he was currently accommodating were saved from his wrath that evening by the addition of a fourth. Sibyl had brought her elderly friend Meg over for dinner.

Meg was still in a wheelchair but recovered enough to get out and about. Sibyl, blatantly ignoring his orders, arranged it so Rick, her bodyguard, who lived in Weston (close to Meg), would stay for dinner and afterward take Meg home.

Meg was a lovely older lady with a kindly face and clearly a close relationship with Sibyl.

Rick was two inches shorter than Sibyl but twice her body weight in pure muscle. He had short-cropped, blond hair and an expression that looked like it would fell a tree if he just glanced at it with mild irritation. Rick also had no intention of having a nice, friendly supper with his employer and pointedly picked up his filled plate and cutlery and carried it out of the room when dinner was served.

Colin decided he liked Rick.

Later that evening, he managed to snare his mother when they were following Meg and the others out to the car. He fully intended to tell her how he felt about her behavior with the tourists the day before.

"About yesterday—" he began.

"I know!" Phoebe beamed with happy excitement. "It was in the papers. Did you see it?"

"Yes," he ground out.

"You should have seen her. She was an absolute darling to all those people. The National Trust volunteers were all gushing about her. She even talked to some Spanish tourists in *Spanish*." She said this last as if it was a feat parallel to solving the puzzle of the meaning of life.

His mother put her hand on his arm and her eyes were aglow. "Colin, I'm just so pleased for you, my darling. Sibyl is a delight!"

With that she rushed away to say goodbye to Meg, leaving Colin unable and strangely unwilling to remonstrate her about that day's papers.

When Colin arrived at Rick's car, Sibyl and Rick were having a low-voiced argument.

"You have to watch what I do," she hissed.

"I can put an old lady in a car," Rick muttered, clearly aggrieved.

"You can't manhandle her, you have to do it carefully. Just watch what I do."

Rick gave Colin a long-suffering look and Colin wondered how

Rick would look on his *third* day with Sibyl.

Colin watched as Sibyl positioned Meg's wheelchair between the car and the door and then he surged forward and clipped, "Hold on . . ." when she reached in to take on the older woman's considerable weight.

With astounding agility, she grabbed on to a belt at the woman's waist, hauled her up, pivoted with her and then, with control, gently settled her into the car. She did it all as if Meg weighed no more than a feather.

Colin halted and stared incredulously as Mags said beside him, "She's done this before, you know."

Colin found himself thinking the wonders of Sibyl never ceased.

And also hoping they never would.

After she'd said her goodbyes and closed the door she turned to Rick. "Do I need to go with you?"

"No!" Rick snapped and stomped to the driver's side.

Mags and Phoebe went into the house while Sibyl waved the car out of sight. She turned to him, grabbed his arm in both of her hands and leaned into him, her head pressed to his shoulder. They walked together that way into the house, and Colin wished he could enjoy her casual affection rather than worrying that a tranquillizer gun, or worse, was trained on one of them.

The minute he closed and locked the door and turned to go into the Great Hall, she slid her arms around his neck, pressed her soft body against his and gave him a quick, sweet kiss.

When her lips moved away, she smiled up at him and he felt his gut clench when he saw her face was awash with an extraordinary light, and he realized that she was happy.

Blindingly, beautifully, glamorously, unbelievably happy.

Moved by this in a profound way that was nearly raw, his hand went to the side of her neck and he positioned his thumb under her chin to keep her radiant face tilted to his.

"You're in a rare mood tonight," he commented lightly in an effort to hide how her happiness affected him.

If it was possible, her smile brightened.

"She's going to be all right, Colin. You saw her! She's nearly back to the same old Meg." Her arms tightened with delight around his neck.

He could do nothing but smile back.

In the middle of the night, with Sibyl's naked body pressed heavily against his side as she slept, his own sleep eluded him.

His thoughts were about finding a way to make Sibyl that happy always. He wanted her constantly radiating happiness, peace, warmth and affection and never again worried.

Never.

And what Colin wanted, Colin found a way to get. The problem was, he was beginning to be impatient.

On Wednesday, Colin learned that Tamara Adams had disappeared and no one had seen her for weeks. She had not taken Colin's breaking things with her very well and had said as much to family and friends, rather vociferously, according to Fitzwilliam's phoned-in report. Then she told people she was going on holiday but didn't return. Everyone, reportedly, was concerned.

Colin obviously wasn't concerned, he just wanted her found and soon.

He arrived at Lacybourne early on Wednesday, thinking to work at home and immediately went in search of Sibyl. He found her in the buttery, which had been, the day before, turned into her makeshift "laboratory."

She was standing in front of the window, her back to him, one of the gray, misty days that had been the incessant weather of late providing weak light for her work. She was wearing her torn jeans and a fitted, white T-shirt and her hair pulled up in a messy ponytail at the top back of her head.

Without a word, he silently walked up behind her and slid his arms around her waist. She jumped in surprise but when his lips touched her neck, she relaxed against him.

"Hi," she whispered and he felt a thrill down his spine at her utterance of that single word.

He lifted his mouth from her neck and caught sight of her hands encased in gloves that went up to her elbows, immersed in a huge bowl of glistening, white goo.

"What is that?" he asked.

She laughed softly before saying, "That is an experiment. A new face mask. As I don't do animal testing and Mallory would likely eat it anyway, Mags and Phoebe are going to test it for me."

He was powerless against her warm voice and soft laugh and he allowed his hands to slide under her T-shirt and crisscross on the skin of her midriff. He felt her muscles tense there but the rest of her body relaxed further into him.

"Would you be a test subject?" she teased for she knew the answer to that would be a resounding *no*.

His mouth descended to her neck again.

"No," Colin gave her the answer she knew she'd get and he said it against her skin then parried her teasing by drifting his hand up her midriff to cover her breast. His thumb found her nipple and dragged against it, feeling it immediately harden.

"Colin," she admonished softly without really meaning it, "I'm working."

His arm at her middle tightened and his fingers moved to trace the lace at the top of her bra just as his mouth slid up her neck to behind her ear.

"Carry on," he murmured and his fingers closed around the lace and pulled it sharply down under her breast.

Sibyl gasped.

"Colin!" This was half-admonishment, half-whimper.

He smiled against her ear and then touched his tongue there. She smelled of flowers and musk and he felt his groin tighten. He found her nipple with his thumb and forefinger and tugged at it sharply in a rough, gentle demand.

Her head fell back on his shoulder and she shuddered, her body's movement absorbed by his.

"That's nice," she breathed and all admonishment was gone from her tone.

To reward her, he did it again and her response was so intense, his arm had to tighten around her waist to catch her as her legs buckled beneath her.

He nipped her ear with his teeth.

"You're not working," he informed her helpfully.

She didn't respond, she simply trembled and he knew she was ready for him.

As he had her exactly where wanted her, he pulled the lace back over her breast and slid his hand down and out from under the T-shirt. He removed his mouth from the sensitive area of her ear and kissed her neck chastely.

"I'll let you get on with it."

"Colin!" she cried and whirled, white goo flying everywhere.

He grinned at her.

"Don't give me one of those devilish grins, get back here!" she demanded.

He walked away and heard her growl with frustration.

As he understood when he started it, he knew he'd pay for that episode later that night and he was very much looking forward to it.

Later, while he could smell one of Mags's vegetarian feasts cooking in the kitchen, he snagged Mallory's lead and commandeered the recalcitrant dog to take a walk. He and Mallory were passing the library when he heard feminine voices.

He glanced in while walking by and heard his mother exclaim, "Mine's tingling!"

He stopped and stared at the three women sitting side by side on the couch, all of their faces covered in white goo, their legs stretched out before them, their heads resting on the back of the couch.

"Is it a good tingle or a bad tingle?" Sibyl asked with concern.

"Oh, a good tingle, dear."

"Mine's not tingling but it smells good enough to eat," Mags put in.

"*Don't* eat it, Mother," Sibyl warned.

"I wasn't going to eat it. I was just saying it smells good enough to eat."

Colin decided to escape before the oncoming escalation and he walked the dog.

All the days that followed were more of the same.

Mandy was taking reporters' phone calls by the dozens and they'd even found the number to Lacybourne and were ringing there wanting pictures and interviews of the reincarnated lovers.

The next two National Trust days were so crowded, the Trust had to arrange for timed viewings and had phoned Colin telling him that, if this persisted, they would have to do visits by booking only. They also asked if he and Sibyl wouldn't mind being part of a new pamphlet and helping with a fundraiser.

This he refused, of course, and didn't even bother to mention it to Sibyl for she would definitely *not* have refused and the last thing he needed was for her to be gunned down at a National Trust Ball.

Marian Byrne's daughter had left after Marian had sufficiently recovered, so in order for Sibyl to watch over her she became a regular guest at dinner. Colin had come home on Friday evening to catch Marian and Mags in the kitchen, leaning expectantly over a large pot that was emitting a foul odor that was (he hoped) not food while his mother sat at a stool by the counter calmly reading a woman's magazine.

"Just experimenting with—" Mags began to explain upon his entry.

He lifted up his hand and didn't break stride as he continued to walk through the kitchen. "I don't want to know."

He'd encountered Sibyl in the hall.

"Hi, babe." She brushed her lips softly against his in greeting and he vastly preferred her welcome to the dastardly trio in the kitchen. "Enchiladas tonight," she informed him.

He was relatively certain enchiladas did not smell like what was in the kitchen and if it did, he wanted no part of it.

"Is Mags cooking?"

She knew exactly to what he was referring and her body started to shake with silent laughter.

"Yes, but I've made ones especially for you *and* they contain meat."

His kiss of greeting was heavily weighted with relief.

They had a relatively peaceful weekend.

This was, of course, if one didn't count Sibyl's extraordinary tirade when he'd had the MG towed back to Brightrose and presented her with an Aston Martin. She categorically refused to accept the car and a reluctant compromise was only reached when his mother suggested Colin take the Aston and Sibyl use the BMW. The Mercedes was offered on the Alter of Environmental Correctness and this last he agreed to but carefully made no promise as he had no intention of getting rid of his car, mainly because he *liked* the Mercedes.

Tuesday night, Sibyl was tucked against his side while Colin was staring at the ceiling and contemplating the unacceptable lack of progress his investigation team was making in finding Tamara Adams.

She was a socialite, not a super sleuth. How she could be evading a ten-man team was beyond him and Colin wanted answers *and* results.

As the days went by, Sibyl seemed to be settling in quite contentedly at Lacybourne, almost as if she'd forgotten someone wanted to harm them. She went about her busy schedule, radiating happiness and warmth with unflagging energy.

Even though Colin was pleased that she obviously trusted him and was happily getting on with her life, especially as that life included him, he was becoming more and more impatient. He wanted this business complete so he and Sibyl could move on. He wanted to come home to her (and even her many and varied escapades) every night, his ring on her finger and her carrying his name, and he wanted all of this without death threats hanging over their heads.

"Do you think we have too much sex?" Sibyl asked musingly, interrupting his unhappy reverie with her mystifying question.

"What?" he asked back, thrown.

She came up on her elbow and leaned over him.

"We have a lot of sex. Of course, it's normal to have a lot of sex when you start a relationship but we have *a lot*, a lot."

He couldn't answer her, his unhappy thoughts shifted to even unhappier thoughts, including the fact that she'd had lots of sex at the start of relationships with other men.

Furthermore, she was right. He had a very healthy sexual appetite but he'd never been as hungry for a woman—carrying a constant, overwhelming desire—as he was for her. He found himself wanting her more even when he was embedded inside her.

She was an obsession, even an addiction.

Upon brief consideration, he found this didn't bother him in the slightest.

"I think it's the curse," she continued, either ignoring or not noticing his lack of response. "Royce and Beatrice didn't . . . um, get any and so we're making up for it."

"I don't care why I want you, I just know I do, there's no purpose in evaluating it," Colin replied.

"Yes, but don't you think it's *weird*?" Sibyl pressed.

"I hardly think it's 'weird' for any man to have an irrational craving for you. You're quite simply the most desirable woman I've known."

Her mouth dropped open and, to his surprise, she clamped it shut on a disbelieving, very unladylike, snort.

"Sibyl," he remonstrated softly, "it doesn't suit you to fish for compliments."

"Fish for . . . !" She started then burst out laughing and he felt its beauty seep into his bones. When she was done, she laid her hand on his cheek and smiled at him. "Colin, you like me, we're good together." Her smile deepened. "Of course you think I'm desirable but that doesn't mean every man does." She carried on, as if he hadn't even spoken, "Personally, I still think it's the curse."

He stared at her assessingly and realized she didn't comprehend her incredible allure.

"You aren't to be believed," he mumbled.

She tilted her head, the smile still tugging at her lips. "What's that?"

He pulled her weight on top of his body, his arms stole around her and he studied her beautiful face for long moments.

Then he muttered, "Christ, you have no idea."

Something about that knowledge awed him.

"Okay, I get it, you don't think it's the curse but—"

"Sibyl, listen to me," he interrupted her. "You are beautiful."

Her eyes sparkled. "And you're very handsome," she returned, completely unfazed by his words. "But then again, I love you so of course I'd think you're handsome, to others, you're probably very ugly."

He found himself biting back laughter at the same time growling with frustration and something infinitely deeper. She lifted her knees so she was straddling him and bent her head to kiss the base of his throat, her hair sliding across his chest.

"Likely extremely ugly," she muttered as she moved lower and kissed his stomach and his muscles tensed as he understood her intent. "Hideous," she whispered as she moved lower.

He let go of his unhappy thoughts and moved his hands into her hair to pull it away so he could watch.

Later, after he'd yanked her back on top of him to finish what she started with her mouth in an entirely different but infinitely pleasurable way, he rolled them to their sides and her arms tightened around him.

"That was nice." She spoke what he considered the understatement of the year and he chuckled.

He felt her body settle and her breathing even out and he remembered a phone call he'd had that day.

"Sibyl?"

"Mm?" she murmured against his neck.

"Mrs. Manning called today."

"Who?"

"My housekeeper, she requests that you not make the bed. She says it's her job. Since I pay her to do it, there's no reason you should."

"The invisible housekeeper," Sibyl said quietly. "Now *that's* weird. She's here but you never see her."

He found that rather surprising as he wasn't letting Mrs. Manning in. He wondered who was. Nevertheless, with other weighty things on his mind, he didn't spend any time thinking about it.

"I'd rather not hire a new one—" he started but she cut him off.

She did this by declaring on a yawn, "There are lots of things in life worth fighting for, Colin, my right to make a bed is not one of them."

And then she promptly fell asleep.

And, as with nearly every night since Meg had dinner with them, Colin did not.

Chapter TWENTY-SIX

Pensioner Posse

Sibyl stood in the doorway of her office at the Community Centre. She watched as Mags, Marian and Phoebe all concentrated very carefully on their bingo cards as Marianne's scratchy voice called out the numbers.

Sibyl was allowing herself the luxury of contemplating her new life and further allowing herself to decide it was, quite simply, wonderful.

Colin may not love her but she'd come to the conclusion that, from Colin, she would take what she could get. Furthermore, what she was getting was pretty heady stuff so she felt it would show extreme ill grace to complain.

It was clear to Sibyl that even if he didn't return her love she loved him enough for the both of them. Threat or no threat, curse or no curse, she felt invulnerable and strong, as if nothing could harm them. Her love and Marian's protection would be enough. Sibyl was certain of it.

So, Sibyl ceased worrying.

Colin, however, had not.

She tried to make him feel some of her calm but no matter how she tried to soothe him, it didn't work. As the days went by, he became more and more impatient and tense.

And Colin could get *very* impatient and Colin's tense was a little scary.

She decided she loved this about him (as she loved pretty much everything about him). He was not impatient and tense worrying about himself, he was so because he worried about *her*. If she didn't have his love then she was definitely certain she had his care, his concern, his affection and his protection.

And that would be enough.

For now.

She'd worry about the rest later, when all this troublesome business was concluded.

She moved out of the doorway and sat down beside Meg who had come back to the Pensioners' Lunch Club that week, nearly fully-restored. Meg was now resting comfortably in one of Colin's new, plush chairs, watching but as usual not participating in the bingo action.

When Sibyl had settled, Meg patted her hand then her fingers closed around it to hold it lightly.

"It's good to see you so happy, Billie," she whispered for it was a *very* bad thing to make too much noise when bingo was under way, the players got somewhat irate if their concentration was disturbed.

"Is it so obvious?" Sibyl smiled, completely unaware that her glorious smile said it all.

"Oh yes, it's very obvious." Meg's faced collapsed happily and Sibyl gave her hand a soft, affectionate squeeze.

Sibyl caught sight of Rick prowling through the Day Centre, glowering at the pensioners as if one of them was, at any moment, intending to pull an Uzi out of their carrier bag and go on a killing spree.

"He needs a girlfriend," Meg noted sagely, eyeing Rick.

"He needs a lot more than that," Sibyl agreed.

"All right folks, last game. The minibus leaves in fifteen minutes," Kyle announced, striding through the room, completely unmoved by the glares he was receiving.

The only thing worse than interrupting a bingo game with unnecessary noise was announcing it was concluding.

Kyle had finished his training course the week before and now the minibus, Colin's minibus, was in full use.

Sibyl thought that finally all was (nearly) right with the world.

And she'd never been happier.

Never.

In her whole life.

As Sibyl began to assist some of the folks who'd started quietly to pack up, she didn't catch Rick's head snap around or his eyes narrowing as he focused on something outside the window. She also didn't notice him have a quick word with Kyle before they both exited the Day Centre's side door, splitting outside the door—Kyle going right, Rick going left.

"Bingo!" Phoebe shouted, waving her hands in the air and everyone groaned. She jumped out of her seat and gave a whoop of joy. "I never win, *ever*. Hurrah!" she gloated and groans turned into grumbles.

At Phoebe's victory, Sibyl could help the oldies without having to be quiet, and she started to do so at the same time she began to clear up the bingo paraphernalia and collect ashtrays.

She was eager to get back home. Colin may decide to work from home and she liked to be there when he was there.

Mentally she made a list of what she needed to do before going to Lacybourne.

Put bingo supplies away.

Get Meg into her wheelchair.

Get oldies out to the bus.

Clean out ashtrays.

Collect tea mugs and stack in dishwasher.

Her mind occupied, she was completely unprepared (though nothing would actually have prepared her) for the sliding doors to the hall being thrown open with such force that they crashed loudly in their pocket frames.

She distractedly heard some stifled and some not-so-stifled screams but definitely saw, clear as day, Colin's ex-girlfriend, Queen of Icicles and All Things Frozen, Tamara, standing between the opened doors, her arm raised, a gun clenched in her hand.

A gun that was pointed at Sibyl.

Before Sibyl could react, say a word, lift a finger, Tamara shouted, "I've had enough of *you!*"

Then without further ado, she pulled the trigger.

Sibyl's heart stopped. She thought she could actually see the tranquillizer dart in the scant seconds it took to zoom toward her. What she most certainly and astonishingly *did* see was the dart ping off some hidden barrier an inch away from her shoulder emitting a small burst of white light, like a sparkler, and then fall useless to the ground.

This remarkable occurrence was met with absolute silence as everyone stared at the tranquillizer dart on the ground.

Then their eyes shifted and they stared at Sibyl.

Finally their eyes swung to Tamara.

Tamara seemed just as stunned by what happened as anyone because, indeed, it *was* stunning and this was because it was *magic*.

She shook off her surprise and screamed, "*What?*"

"Told you it would work," Marian whispered somewhat smugly to Phoebe and Mags.

It was at this point that Tamara charged forward.

And her intent was clear.

It was going to be a catfight.

Sibyl had never been in a fight in her life (if you didn't count the hair-pulling fights she had with Scarlett as a child . . . and as a teenager . . . and once in their twenties).

There was no way to avoid it, Sibyl knew, and with nothing for it she braced for impact.

Except the oldies had been in preparation for leaving so some of them were upright and most of them had carrier bags.

To the unpracticed eye, these facts would seem harmless.

And therefore Tamara vastly underestimated her adversary's allies.

Two steps into the room, Mrs. Griffith put out her new (steel) cane, tripping Tamara.

This would have been enough and Tamara would have gone (and actually did start to go) flying.

However, at the same time Marianne heaved out her carrier bag, losing hold of it as its momentum grew with its weight so it went flying toward Tamara, hitting her smack in the chest.

With an awful grunt of pain and surprise, Tamara fell backwards instead, completely stunned and unable to catch herself, landing flat on her back.

To this, Gilbert forged (slowly) into action and threw himself on Tamara to hold her down (or actually, gingerly got down on his knees and then fell forward on top of her).

In an effort to pin her on the ground and also not be outdone, one of the other oldies dropped her carrier bag on Tamara's right leg, another on her left, and slowly but surely Tamara (and Gilbert) were being buried under the considerable weight of carrier bags.

"Jesus," Rick breathed from behind Sibyl, finally arriving on the scene and watching the Attack of the Old Age Pensioners as Kyle jogged in through the sliding doors the other way, skidding to a halt at the sight.

"Stop!" Kyle shouted, and immediately all the pensioners ceased their vengeful activities and moved back.

"I'll call the police." Phoebe fumbled in her bag for her mobile.

"I've already done it," Tina murmured from her new place beside Sibyl.

Mags, Phoebe and Marian joined Sibyl and Tina and they stood watching as Kyle helped Gilbert up. Tamara, who was struggling to pull herself out from under the carrier bags, was hauled out none-too-gently by a stony-faced Rick. Rick ripped the gun viciously from her hand and rather alarmingly (in Sibyl's opinion), handed it to Mrs. Griffith. Luckily, Mrs. Griffith took it between thumb and forefinger, a look of distaste wrinkling her nose and hurled it into the seat of one of Colin's plush, new chairs.

This, Rick knew, he would never live down: to have the person he was supposed to be protecting defended by a slew of oldies was just too much. He found himself, not for the first time, lamenting the day he took this job.

Unfortunately, now Tamara was angry *and* humiliated and this was not a good combination. Once she got to her feet, with Rick's strong hand holding her exactly where she was, she whirled (as best she could, nearly pinned to the spot) woodenly toward Sibyl.

"Why wouldn't you just *go away*?" she shouted madly, scowling at Sibyl. "Colin is mine!"

"Colin?" Marianne hacked.

"Sibyl's man," Mrs. Griffith answered.

"Oh yes." Marianne nodded. "I remember him, he's tall."

"He is *not* her man," Tamara stormed. "He's *mine*." She struggled (unsuccessfully) against Rick's hold on her with her glare steadfastly aimed at Sibyl. "I waited years for him to notice me. *Years!* And when he finally did, it took me ages to get him where I wanted him. I was so close. I worked so hard and then you stroll in and he instantly forgot me. It was like I never even existed!"

"I wish I could forget her but I don't think I ever will," Tina mumbled.

Tamara kept ranting. "I kept warning you. I shot your dog, tore up your house, made threatening phone calls. But you just would . . . not . . . go . . . *away*!"

"Of course she wouldn't just go away," Gilbert put in at this juncture. "They're supposed to be together. Don't you read the papers?"

"You *shot* her *dog*?" Mrs. Griffith's eyes had narrowed ominously at the very idea of anyone hurting an animal.

"He was okay, Mrs. Griffith," Sibyl assured the older lady quickly before her cane had a chance to be put back into action.

"Enough," Rick growled, his patience at an end.

He dragged Tamara without apparent effort kicking and spitting down the length of the Day Centre. Without another word, he threw Tamara into Sibyl's office, followed her and slammed the door.

Everyone stared at the door for several moments and then jumped when they heard Mags.

"Well! I guess that's that," Mags stated with a sliding clap as if she was cleaning off her hands after a messy task even though she hadn't done a thing. Then, as if they had all not just witnessed something *entirely* out of the ordinary, she suggested, "Let's get these carrier bags sorted," and she bustled forward with Phoebe to help the oldies claim their bags.

Marian did not go to help Mags, Phoebe and the oldies. Instead, she placed her hand on Sibyl's forearm and peered closely into the younger woman's eyes.

"Are you all right, dear?"

Sibyl turned dazedly to Marian.

"I think so," she whispered and continued incredulously, "Did you *see* that?" Her eyes cleared and they were shining brightly. "The dart didn't even touch me just . . ." She made a loud *ping* noise, combining it with a quick slap of her fingers against her thumbs and an endearing blink and she carried on, "like I was encased in invisible armor. Marian, you are the greatest witch ever! I cannot believe it's all over!"

Sibyl pulled Marian to her for a fierce hug and kissed her cheek.

"I can't wait to tell Colin," she enthused, and then her attention was turned and she rushed forward to mediate the carrier bag organization as it appeared to be becoming somewhat confused, with the situation escalating rapidly as oldies confusedly claimed other oldie's bags or, at least, what the others *thought* were their bags.

MARIAN WATCHED AS Sibyl, her mother and Colin's mother sorted out Sibyl's charges.

That was too easy, she thought as she heard the police sirens approaching the Centre.

Something wasn't right, Marian knew. She would have sensed the dark soul in the young woman the moment she met her the night Sibyl and Colin started their challenging journey.

She felt a sense of disquiet, knowing, somehow, it was not over.

"Are you all right, Mrs. Byrne?" Tina asked her, still standing quietly at Marian's side, wisely choosing not to enter what had now become a carrier bag melee.

"Yes, dear, fine," Marian answered distractedly but Tina kept watching her, not believing a word she said.

COLIN SAT AT the head of the dining-room table. He had pushed his chair back with a slight tilt to the left, put an ankle on his opposite knee and he was now resting his elbows against his abdomen, his fingers linked and his chin resting thoughtfully against them. The dishes carrying the remains of his mother's heavy treacle pudding with custard littered the tabletop.

Sibyl sat to his left, her bowl pushed forward, her forearms bent at the elbows and resting on the edge of the table, her head on them. Her face was hidden from view, buried in her arms and her hair, partially (but not competently) held up in a clip, fell all over her shoulders and down her back.

And those shoulders were shaking uncontrollably with hilarity.

Phoebe and Mags sat opposite her. His mother's whole body was bouncing up and down in her chair with the force of her uncontained laughter.

Marian, Colin noted with interest, sat next to Sibyl and her face was oddly blank.

"And then Gilbert dropped to his knees, although I wouldn't call it a 'drop' so much as a 'cautious descent.' Then he . . . he . . ." Although Colin had heard it earlier from Rick, Mags was relating the story about what happened at the Day Centre and found, not for the first time, she could no longer continue as her cackling got the better of her.

These last words sent both Phoebe and Sibyl into fresh shouts of laughter.

Although all three women thought this was the height of entertainment, Colin did not find it the least bit amusing. In fact, he found it supremely annoying; not their amusement but that afternoon's escapade.

His eyes slid to Marian who, feeling his gaze, moved hers to him. She shook her head and offered him a weak smile.

With a great jolt, Sibyl flew upright.

"I can't take anymore." Tears of mirth were streaming down her face. "I'm going to do the dishes."

She collected the dishes while Phoebe offered help and scurried out of the dining room behind Sibyl.

"Oh, Colin," Mags wiped under her eyes as she stood, "I wish you were there." Then she followed the other two out of the room.

Colin leaned further back into his chair, dropping his hands, and turned to Marian.

"You seem not to share in their enjoyment of the events of the afternoon."

Marian shook her head slowly.

"Why?" he pressed.

She seemed to weigh her answer and finally said, "They find it so amusing because, for weeks, they've lived on fear and nerves. They're feeling a release. What I saw today was a number of people who adore Sibyl and would do anything for her. I don't find that funny at all. I find it deeply touching."

Colin agreed silently but knew she was not done therefore he prompted, "And?"

She regarded him warily before she said on a heavy sigh, "I know you won't believe me, didn't believe me in the first place, but that woman they caught today was not the dark soul. I still think you need to be careful. I think the dark soul is still out there and wants to hurt you and Sibyl."

Colin studied the woman a moment, nodded gravely then stood.

She was correct. He didn't believe her.

What he knew, however, was that she believed. Even though he did not want her to be concerned further, he had enough respect for her to allow her that.

And, there was something so deadly serious, so intent, rather than dramatic and overblown, about the way she spoke, that it gave him pause.

"I believe I need a drink, something a hell of a lot stronger than wine. Would you care to join me?" he asked politely.

Marian stood too, he offered her his arm and with a startled smile at his gallant gesture, she took it.

They walked to the library and as they went she kept talking, "Even if you don't believe me, if you think it's over, will you promise to still be careful, still—"

"I'll always be careful when it comes Sibyl, nothing's going to harm her," Colin assured the older woman. "Not even the messes she gets herself into."

This, finally, made Mrs. Byrne laugh and they entered the library.

COLIN WAS QUIETLY furious and trying very hard not to show it.

He had spent thousands of pounds on a small army of investigators and security experts, as well as a bodyguard, only to have Tamara felled by Sibyl's Pensioner Posse.

And this was *after* Tamara had shot a tranquillizer dart at Sibyl. One that, reportedly magically, glanced off Sibyl and fell to the ground.

What Sibyl, their mothers and Mrs. Byrne did not know was that the police had informed Colin that the dart was loaded with enough tranquillizer that, if it had penetrated, for Sibyl's height and weight, it could have killed her with an overdose.

This fact, fortunately, would mean Tamara was facing a prison sentence. She wouldn't merely get a slap on the wrist for vandalism or stalking.

This fact also meant that today, if things had gone any differently, he would not have been watching Sibyl struggling with mirth at the dining-room table. Instead, he would have been dealing with her grieving mother, his grieving mother and the certainty of a life yawning before him without Sibyl in it.

No, Colin didn't feel that anything about that day's events was the least bit humorous.

Much later, after several whiskies had soothed his nerves if not his temper, he lay on top of the coverlet on the bed, propped up on his elbow and watched as Sibyl brushed her hair. Mallory had long since collapsed with the effort of sleeping all day and was sprawled out on the floor by Colin's side of the bed. The cat was somewhere in the house, probably stalking mice or shadows or whatever cats did when their humans weren't around. Sibyl stood in the center of the room wearing one of his T-shirts and babbling.

"I cannot *believe* it's all over. You would not *believe* how relieved I am." She tossed her brush on a dresser and whirled toward him then walked to the bed. "Mags is going home. She's responsible for refreshments at her next coven meeting and she's in a bit of a finger-food-feud with one of the other members. She's got the whole menu planned. It's going to take her *days*! Not to mention, she simply cannot *wait* to tell them about what's happened here. She'll be the belle of the coven."

Sibyl threw herself on the bed and he watched as she bounced then came up on both her elbows and awarded him with a dazzling smile as she settled on her belly.

"I'll move back to Brightrose at the weekend after she's gone," she told him, clearly (and inaccurately) having it all planned out.

"No," he stated firmly.

She blinked in adorable confusion and her smile faded before she asked, "What?"

"You're not moving back to Brightrose."

Her relaxed and happy body froze a moment before she pushed herself up to her knees, resting her bottom on her calves and stared down at him.

"It's safe now, she's been caught. I can go home and you and I can, well . . . do things normally, like normal couples do. Like go out on normal dates and—"

She stopped because finally, after all the events of the day, *that* he found hilarious and he threw back his head and let out a sharp bark of laughter.

"What's funny?" she asked over his hilarity, her brow furrowed and her eyes beginning to move from hazel to green.

"You want to *date*?" His voice was dripping with amused incredulity.

She pulled in both of her lips.

Then said quietly, "Don't you?"

He thought about pushing himself up to be eye to eye with her but decided against it and his hand snaked out and grasped her wrist, giving it a gentle yank and pulling her down. He rolled on his back and positioned her on top of him.

"I think we're beyond dating," he noted.

"What's 'beyond dating?'" She looked confused and very wary.

He gathered her hair away from her face and held it in a tumbled bunch behind her head in one hand while his other went to rest on her lovely, rounded bottom.

"You're moving into Lacybourne, permanently."

Colin, too, had it all planned out.

However *his* plan was the *only* plan.

Her head shifted slightly to the side and she watched him out of the corners of her eyes as her lips puckered before she whispered, "I don't think so."

"I don't think you have a choice," Colin returned.

Her body started and her eyes definitely switched, blazing an emerald green. "You can't just order me to move in with you!"

"I just did."

She put her hands on either side of his chest on the bed and pressed herself upwards but he came up with her and flipped her on her back, resting his weight on her.

"You're . . . I don't even *know* what you are!" Sibyl snapped, her temper hitting altitude.

"Sibyl, can you please tell me why everything has to be a struggle with you?" Colin asked, what he thought was patiently.

Her eyes rounded. "I have a home, a business, a life. I . . . you . . . you and I—"

"Yes?"

She clamped her mouth shut, unable to find any feasible reason why she shouldn't move in with him.

"I didn't think so," he drawled knowingly and he couldn't help but grin when she made a grumpy, frustrated noise in the back of her throat.

His knee pressed between her legs and they parted (even her legs moved mutinously, but they still moved). He slid his hands slowly down the backs of her thighs to pull them up at the knees.

"Give me one good reason to move in with you," she demanded, and if his chest wasn't pressed against hers he had no doubt she would have crossed her arms.

"I like you in my house."

"That's—" she began to interrupt him.

"I like you in my bed," he continued and she closed her mouth and glared at him. "I like the way your laboratory makes the house smell like fruit and flowers. I like walking your damned dog. I like seeing your clothes in the wardrobe. I like you wearing my T-shirts to bed. I like coming home to you."

As he spoke, her face shifted and relaxed, the emerald melted and the sherry took its place.

She regarded him a moment with her face soft, her eyes warm then she whispered, "Okay, Colin."

"Okay, what?"

"I get it," she answered softly but somehow uncertainly. "I'll move into Lacybourne."

"I wasn't asking." He felt it necessary to remind her.

Finally, she let go of whatever was troubling her and her lips twitched.

"I know. You're very bossy. I've decided that it's better if I move in with you. If I live at Lacybourne, I'll have more time to break you of that bad habit."

He smiled at her before he warned, his head descending, "I wouldn't count on it."

HE HAD ANOTHER good reason for her moving into Lacybourne.

He could not shake his unease that Mrs. Byrne was right.

And he didn't want Sibyl going anywhere until he was certain she was safe.

Chapter TWENTY-SEVEN

The Good Kind. And the Bad.

Sibyl woke in a bed that felt strange beneath her. It was feather soft, had no firmness and the sheets were slightly scratchy.

Her eyes flew open and she realized she wasn't in Colin's bed. She wasn't in any bed she'd ever seen before.

And Colin wasn't there.

She jumped out of the bed thinking to see Bran or Mallory but neither was in sight. There was also no elegant furniture in the room. Indeed, although the room was grand, it looked slightly rough and definitely strange.

She was someplace she'd never been.

Even though she knew, somehow, she was in Lacybourne.

Her hands went to her hair, which she found was plaited in a thick braid down her back.

She flipped the braid around to the front and stared at it.

Colin's hair, nearly dark as black.

She stared down at her nightgown and it was old-fashioned and prim.

She was in a different time.

She was in Royce's time.

"Oh my goddess," she murmured.

Her eyes frantically searched the room and she found a soft, blue wrapper thrown across the back of a chair. She grabbed it and shoved her arms into the sleeves as she ran from the room and down the hall toward Colin's room, which she prayed silently to the goddess had also been Royce's room.

She threw open the door and startled a maid who was making the bed.

The maid's eyes rounded in surprise and she stared.

"Miss Beatrice," she breathed.

Sibyl didn't know what to say. Goddess, she wished she'd listened to her father more closely. How did one talk medieval?

There was nothing for it, Sibyl would have to bluff it.

"Where's your master?"

She must have said the right thing because the woman's face melted knowingly. "He's . . ." Her eyes dropped to Sibyl's body. "But you're not dressed."

Sibyl looked down at herself knowing it was most likely not seemly that she was running around in her nightclothes but she didn't care. Time was of the essence.

"I need to see, um . . . Sir Royce right away."

She felt like an idiot but she didn't care about that either. At any moment, she could wake up.

"But Miss Beatrice . . ."

"*Where is he?*" she cried desperately.

The woman jumped at her tone, which was obviously something with which, coming from Beatrice, she was not familiar.

Then she spoke. "He's at his meal in the Hall."

She said more but Sibyl didn't hear her. She flew down the corridor like the very devil was at her heels and then bounded down the stairs. Finally, she skidded to a halt, seeing the used dishes on the table . . . but no Royce.

She stomped her foot.

"Blooming hell!" she said in more than mild exasperation.

"Beatrice?"

His deep, smooth, velvet voice came from her right and she whirled.

Royce, standing straight and beautiful in one of the two semi-circular windows, was watching her with obvious amusement. His hair shone gold, was breathtaking in the sun pouring in from the window, and she wondered if her own looked like that when hit by the sun's rays.

"Royce," she whispered. She flew right to him, and regardless of her relief at finding him, she stopped a foot away and exploded, "I've been looking everywhere for you!"

He grinned down at her. Without giving any sign he noticed she'd just yelled in his face, he lifted a hand and traced his finger lightly down her jaw.

"I see, no matter that we will be wed this day, you are still not capable of a pleasing morning humor."

Her eyes widened *and* her brows shot up. "We're getting married today?"

His grin immediately turned teasing. "You forgot?"

"No, yes . . . I . . ." she stammered and his grin broadened into a knowing smile.

"I should not be surprised you would forget. You forget many things, my Beatrice, but our wedding day? You wound me," he joked, taking his finger from her jaw to put his hand to his heart in mock injury.

This was just *too* weird and he was being *too* sweet.

But Sibyl didn't have time to process Royce's effective teasing, she had things to say, things to *do* so she charged on.

"We don't have time for this, we have to . . ."

She stopped speaking when he leaned forward unexpectedly and reached around her then she felt a soft, deft yank at the back of her head.

"I do not like this," he muttered, his hand coming back around and he held a pale-blue ribbon in front of her face. He dropped it and she had to swiftly throw up her hands to catch it as his reached back around and she felt him uncoiling her braid.

Good goddess, just like Colin.

Her knees went weak.

"Royce," she whispered.

His eyes, which were looking over her shoulder, moved to hers and at the look in them she felt herself holding her breath. "Beatrice?"

She didn't know what to do, what to say. Would he remember her from the future?

She couldn't count on that.

She had to pretend to be Beatrice.

And she had to work fast.

As he arranged her heavy hair around her shoulders, he murmured, "Better," as if to himself.

"We have to go upstairs," she whispered because his eyes had warmed and she *definitely* knew what that meant and she thought it best to press her advantage while she had one.

His grin turned wicked but his hand dropped and took hers, lifting it to his mouth, he pressed a kiss against her fingers. Through this, never once did his eyes leave hers.

"You are very impatient, my sweet," he murmured. "We can wait. It will only be a few . . ."

"No!" she cried. "We have to go now, upstairs, you and me, *now*. There isn't much time."

And suddenly, she felt like bursting into tears.

She had to make him go upstairs, she had to—she gulped—she had to cheat (essentially) on Colin in order to save Royce and Beatrice. Or, she hoped, get the ball rolling then wake up in her time and in this time Beatrice could take over. And hopefully Beatrice wouldn't come back from wherever she went when Sibyl was in her body and not be too freaked out.

She didn't care if it messed with time (although she really didn't want Japan to fall into the sea). She felt, believed to the bottom of her heart, that she and Colin would find each other, even if she *did* save Beatrice and Royce.

And she was going to do it, if there was time.

She'd forgotten that Royce was a seasoned warrior and he knew the kind of fear he saw in her eyes. Therefore the warmth went out of his, his body stiffened and he stared at her with concern.

"Speak to me," he demanded.

"Royce." She stepped closer and his arms instantly moved around her, pulling her protectively, lovingly against his hard body. She nearly came undone at the strange, casual beauty of his light embrace. "We have to go upstairs, Royce, tonight it will be too late because tonight . . ."

Then it happened. She was slipping away, she could feel it. She was waking from her dream and Beatrice was coming back. She had to change tactics. There wasn't enough time, she simply had to warn him that tonight they would be murdered even if he thought she (or Beatrice) was crazy.

"Tonight? Beatrice, what do you fear happens this night?"

"Royce." She could have sworn she shouted his name but it came out less than a whisper.

And then he was gone or she was gone and instead she was on her side in Colin's bed, Bran curled up in the warm space made by her belly and her bent legs. She felt a hand smooth over her shoulder and she turned her head to see Colin's dark one descending to kiss the place where his hand had been.

She wanted to burst into tears.

Instead she hid her rampaging emotions with a sleepy, "Morning," and she closed her eyes to hide her feelings from Colin.

She felt his finger run down her cheekbone. "Go back to sleep, darling."

And then he was gone, settling back in behind her.

And when he did, she finally allowed the tears to come.

For she knew somewhere in the bottom of her heart that was her last chance.

And she had failed.

FIRST THING THAT morning, Mandy walked into Colin's office with his coffee and whispered, "Mr. Fitzwilliam is here to see you."

She was privy to who Mr. Fitzwilliam was and perhaps, considering she opened his mail and had access to his desk, what some of his reports contained.

She also was well aware of Colin's impatience with any kind of lack of progress.

She took one look at the restrained fury on Colin's face, set the cup down at the far, outer corner of his desk as if she feared for her very life if she came within close proximity to him.

Then she slid the newspaper cautiously beside his coffee.

"And you might want to have a look at that . . ." she paused then finished warningly, *"later."*

With that, she ran-walked out of the room.

Robert Fitzwilliam entered seconds after.

Colin did not rise. He sat back in his chair and watched as Robert came into the room, stopped at the other side of the desk and looked, Colin was further infuriated to see, not the least bit ill-at-ease.

Before Colin could say a word, Robert announced, "We caught the boy."

"I beg your pardon?" Colin asked quietly.

"The boy whose arm you broke, we caught him," Robert answered. "We have him. We're holding him not far from here."

Colin took in a breath, trying for patience.

Fitzwilliam continued, "He's been talking. We expect to have the other one within the hour."

Colin regarded him carefully and when he spoke his voice was dangerous. "At this point, I'm not certain how relevant that is. Considering, of course, that the socialite and apparent villainous mastermind who orchestrated this entire lark is now in jail. Brought low, I might add, by a bevy of OAPs."

Finally, the investigator looked a touch ill-at-ease. "Mr. Morgan, if you would allow me to explain."

"This," Colin said, his tone reaching stratospheric levels of ominous, "had better be good."

Fitzwilliam, quite bravely since he was not invited to do so, took a seat.

Then he started. "We knew Tamara Adams was following you. I did not report this to you because there seemed to be matters of weightier concern and, quite honestly, I had enough on my hands that I didn't have the time to write reports or make phone calls about a common stalker. You, sir, are a man who can protect himself."

Colin's lips tightened at what he considered empty and overly respectful cajolery.

"Might I remind you, Robert, that I wasn't concerned about *me*."

"Of course, I know that. But Miss Adams was not following Miss Godwin, she was always following *you*. More to the point, my men were seeing quite an alarming number of tails. You had yours and not just Miss Adams, but these other tails seemed especially devoted to Miss Godwin. Yet, when my men would investigate, there was no one there. No one in the cars they saw following, no one in the bushes they'd seen rustling, the shadows they saw lurking at windows seemed to simply disappear, it was like whoever he was, he was invisible."

Colin raised his brows and Robert went on speaking.

"Or at the very least slippery. We found this telling and went on high alert, obviously, because this was the work of a professional, or several, as these tails could be on both you and Miss Godwin at the same time. Not to mention, I had to set a man on each of your houses in case something was rigged while you were away. And, I'm afraid, as your home is open to National Trust visitors, I also had to have several men available on those days mingling with the tourists and watching for suspicious activity. Miss Godwin and her family are a highly active bunch. Shopping, walks, day trips, playing Frisbee out in the open on the seafront, they were everywhere and very exposed and being so made our task very difficult."

"You were paid well to deliver on a difficult task," Colin reminded him. "Furthermore, I'd like you to explain why now is the first time I'm hearing all of this."

For the first time appearing frustrated, Robert raked a hand through his hair and he looked at the floor. "We didn't have anything concrete. I didn't want to alarm you *or* Miss Godwin if it turned out to be nothing. And every time we approached, it was exactly that, nothing."

Colin said not a word and Robert shifted nervously in his chair.

Then Robert pulled himself together and carried on, "We investigated Tamara Adams, of course. And the police have been talking to her. I know a few blokes with the police and they tell me she admits to the vandalism of the house, asking a friend to make the threatening phone call and, of course, the tranquillizer darts. She *does not* and adamantly refuses to acknowledge any part in trying to run you and Miss Godwin down with a car. Further, outside of shooting you with a tranquillizer that night, she refuses any knowledge of what happened in Miss Godwin's office at the Centre with the two boys and the knife."

He held Colin's eyes, eyes that were regarding him with disbelief.

"She would of course deny some of the more serious allegations," Colin pointed out. "She loaded the tranquillizer dart with enough drug to kill Sibyl, she's facing grievous bodily harm at the least—"

Colin didn't finish, Robert cut in.

"She swears she didn't know that either. Just loaded it as the instructions she found on the Internet told her. Unfortunately, the instructions were for a very large animal, not a person of Miss Godwin's weight. Apparently, she used the same load on you but it didn't all release. She's using the excuse that it was a mistake."

"Mistake or not, it could have killed Sibyl." Colin bit out.

"Mr. Morgan, you're failing to hear what I'm trying to tell you," Robert was losing his patience and Colin's eyes narrowed, but in his zeal to get his point across the investigator didn't notice. "Miss Adams is not our concern, not now and not ever. She, unfortunately, wasn't harmless but only due to ineptitude. There were no large sums of money drawn from her account, her trust fund or her investment accounts. We've been searching but have not found any evidence that she sold anything of value or even several things or borrowed money from anyone to pay the boys who attacked Miss Godwin. And they were paid plenty, enough money that it couldn't have been just laying around, she would have had to withdraw it or find it one way or the other. We've been talking to the boy all night and he says the woman's voice on the phone was old, not young or posh as Miss Adams's is. He tells us the voice was female, old and scratchy as if she had something wrong with her throat. They never met her. When she paid, she did a drop with the money."

"Tamara might not have made the call," Colin noted.

"We thought of that but we questioned him about the other

events and he says he knows nothing of tranquillizer darts or vandalism and . . . well, the way we've been questioning him, he would have admitted it by now. And I believe he's not lying because he *has* admitted that he was paid to kill you. He has also admitted to striking Marian Byrne on the head and dragging her body behind the Community Centre. He's explained that the terms of the agreement were that he and his partner neutralize Mrs. Byrne, grab you both and slit both of your throats. Not stab you, shoot you, poison you, give you an overdose with a tranquillizer dart but quite clearly and emphatically *slit your throats*. And under no circumstances were they to do it while you were apart, but together, so you could both watch while it was happening."

Colin's entire body seized and his stomach felt like it had been kicked hard.

Tamara may have been angry at being jilted, angry enough to do something immensely stupid, but Colin could not believe she was capable of that.

And the specific instructions that would make Sibyl and Colin's nightmare come true with the addition of Mrs. Byrne being targeted for "neutralization" in this heinous plot were chilling.

He made an instant decision and rose from his chair. "I'll have a word with him."

Robert flew out of his. "Mr. Morgan, there is no need."

Colin rounded his desk but stopped by his investigator. "I said, I'll have a word to him."

When Robert hesitated Colin said one more word.

"Now."

Robert Fitzwilliam looked in his employer's eyes and what he saw sent a shiver down his spine.

Then, without further delay, he led the way.

COLIN LEARNED NOTHING from the frighteningly young man whose arm he'd broken weeks before.

Nor did he learn anything from his friend who was also frighteningly young but had a malevolent gleam in his eye that did not in any way match his age.

With a great deal of patience, he did try to get further information and he did so without harming either of them (unduly) as he'd promised Sibyl. He, however, allowed himself the satisfaction of watching the malevolent gleam in the eyes of the boy who held a knife to Sibyl's throat turn to genuine fear.

Once he'd finished, he'd instructed Robert to turn them over to the police.

Without giving them a thought (as he had a great many other thoughts on his mind), he'd gone back to his office and walked by his harried secretary who was saying into the phone, "I already explained to you, Mr. Morgan has *no comment*." She paused and said far more fiercely and disturbingly, "Neither does Miss Godwin, no matter what you heard." Then she slammed down the phone.

Once inside his office, he picked up the newspaper that Mandy had put on his desk and opened it to the page to which she'd folded it back.

Cursed Reincarnated Lovers Stalked by Evil Socialite, read the headline.

He skimmed the article and his eyes narrowed on the words.

He didn't bother to finish it and threw the newspaper in the rubbish bin.

He barely settled into his chair when Mandy positively stomped into his office.

"Mr. Morgan . . ." she said threateningly and he knew her resignation was nigh.

"Mandy," he cut her off, again coming to an instant decision and putting it into action. "I need you to run an errand for me."

"Mr. *Morgan*," she said more forcefully, not wishing to be denied her moment.

He interrupted her again.

"I want you to find the best jeweler in Bristol or Bath or Cheltenham, I don't care where it is. Go to London if you need to. Take a company car, and when you get wherever you're going, chose an engagement ring for Miss Godwin."

Mandy's mouth snapped shut with an audible clatter of teeth and her eyes bugged out.

Colin carried on, "It has to be something . . . unique. I don't want her to see her ring on someone else's finger. It has to be quality but should not be ostentatious. However, I don't care what it costs. Can you do that?"

His secretary stared at him and gone from her face and frame were the frustrated anger with which she'd stomped into his office.

"I . . . I've never met her," she stammered. "How can I possibly choose a ring for her?"

Colin looked her directly in the eye. "It will be from *me* and for that reason I have every faith in you."

Her eyes slid back into her head, no longer popping out in an alarming fashion and then they filled with tears. "Oh, *Mr. Morgan.* I would be delighted . . . honored . . . *thrilled.*" Then her body jumped and she whirled. "I'll go now," she announced to the other side of the room and rushed across it then stopped and whirled around again. "The phone is ringing off the hook."

"Let it, you've more important things to do than talk to reporters."

She nodded in happy agreement and ran out of the room.

The minute the door clicked behind her, Colin wasted no time, picked up his phone and called Sibyl.

"Colin!" she cried out his name as greeting. "You would just not *believe* what's happening here. Rick has barricaded us in the house. The reporters are storming the door as we speak!"

Colin mentally added something else to his to do list.

"Don't talk to anyone," he ordered.

"I can't," she told him. "Rick won't let me, he's been entirely obnoxious. He's bossier than *you*. I thought, after yesterday, that he'd . . ."

Colin cut in to her tirade. "Let me talk to your mother."

"Mags?"

Colin was silent for he needn't answer, Mags was, indeed, her mother.

There was a pregnant pause and then, "What has she done now?"

Sibyl's voice was leery and more than slightly annoyed.

"Pass the phone to her," Colin ordered.

Surprisingly without further comment, Sibyl did as she was told.

He heard a rustle and then a quiet, "Mother, what *have* you done?"

Without answering her daughter, Mags came on the line. "Colin! It's all adventure here. I must say, you live an exciting life."

"Marguerite, have you been talking to the reporters?"

"Me? No siree. Especially not today. Your beefcake bodyguard will only allow us out of the library for bathroom breaks and even then, he's escorting us. I tried to shock him during my last one but he's unshockable."

Colin mentally added a rise to Rick's salary to his to do list. He thought, vaguely, that this feminine trio was going to bankrupt him.

However, he'd heard Mags say something damning.

"What about yesterday?"

"Sorry?"

Colin prayed for patience. "Yesterday. Did you talk to the reporters yesterday?"

"Me?"

Colin's prayers went unanswered.

"Yes, you."

"No, no, er . . . not me. I didn't talk to the reporters yesterday. They came to the Centre, after the police, but I didn't talk to them and I know Sibyl didn't and . . . well it was all a big hustle and bustle about the carrier bags and . . ."

She'd left someone out.

And she was a worse liar than her daughter.

"Put my mother on the phone," Colin ordered.

"Phoebe?"

He ground his teeth.

Through them, he remarked, "Yes, Phoebe does happen to be my mother."

"I can't imagine why you'd want to talk to Phoebe," she declared with sham innocence.

"Put her on the phone."

"I think she needs a bathroom break," Mags stalled.

"Put her on the phone."

There was a pause and then a grumbled, "Oh, all right."

He heard another rustle before, "It's your son," and then more in the background as the phone was passed, "You're right, Billie, he *is* ruthless."

Colin again gritted his teeth.

"Hello, Colin," his mother greeted him. "How's your day?" Before he could answer, she nervously continued, "We're in the library because Rick thinks one of the reporters could be a murderer in disguise. It's like he wasn't even *there* yesterday and doesn't know we have the all clear. He's instructed us not to stand by the windows and . . ."

He cut her off, his patience at an end.

"Mum, did you talk to the reporters yesterday?"

"Why, yes. I do believe I had a word," she said lightly, *too* lightly.

"Don't do that again," he commanded.

"Colin, you shouldn't talk to your mother that way," she courageously scolded, looking into the eye of the tiger and thinking he was a pussycat. "There's certainly no reason why your extraordinary story shouldn't be told. It's beautiful and I'm so happy for you, I want the world to know it. True love reigns . . ."

"We aren't out of danger. The person who ordered the man to hold a knife to Sibyl's throat is still out there. We don't need to be goading them with stories of true love, exposing our defenses or making them think our defenses are down so they'll act before we've caught them. I'm asking you, don't do it again."

She was silent.

Then she said a shaky, "Okay."

"I don't want Sibyl to know that she's not out of danger."

"You have to . . ."

"Don't say a word. I'll speak to her when I get home."

She was again silent.

Then she let out a breathy, "Okay."

"There will be someone there to clear the reporters within half an hour and they will remain there to watch the house. If Sibyl sees them, make something up but carry on as normal."

"Oh . . . kay." This was even shakier.

"Give the phone to Rick."

She didn't hand the phone to Rick.

Instead she asked nonsensically, "Colin, are *you*, I mean, are they . . . and are *you*?"

But Colin understood her. "Nothing is going to happen to Sibyl or me," and when he said this his voice was far quieter and definitely gentler.

Hers was no less tremulous. "Okay."

"I'm asking her to marry me," Colin found himself saying, simply for the sake of giving his mother a happy thought instead of leaving her with images of possible murder and despair.

There was more silence before, "Okay." This time he heard tears in her voice.

"Don't tell her that either."

A sharp gasp and, "I wouldn't dream of . . ."

"Put Rick on the phone."

"Colin?"

"Yes?"

"I'm so proud of you, my darling. You're a good man."

He'd heard that before recently from Sibyl and he feared his carefully cultivated reputation as a unfeeling bastard was soon to be in tatters.

She gave the phone to Rick. Colin related the current situation and gave him his instructions. Then Colin rang off, called Robert and ordered men to oust the reporters and watch the house.

When the clock hands approached noon, with an immense effort of will, he set all of his current situation aside and set about making *back* some of the money he was losing in this travesty.

At a quarter to four, Rick phoned and without preamble announced, "She's having a barbeque."

Colin couldn't believe his ears. "What did you say?"

"I should have confiscated her mobile," Rick muttered under his breath. "I thought she might need it in case of emergency. I should have—"

"Tell me what's happening," Colin demanded.

Rick didn't delay. "Ten minutes ago, a minibus loaded with old people and kids drove up and unloaded. They all carried in a mass of grocery bags and even a charcoal grill, and now they're in your back garden preparing for a goddamned barbeque."

"Is the team there?"

"Yes."

Colin took in a steadying breath and ordered, "Just watch them."

"Mr. Morgan, I know this'll get me sacked but I gotta tell you that your girlfriend is the most annoy—"

Colin felt Rick's pain acutely, but he interrupted him before he said something Colin could not ignore. "I know."

With that he again rang off from Rick and went back to work.

At ten to five, displaying an amazing swiftness he'd never have expected when a woman was shopping and had a great deal of money to spend, Mandy came back to his office.

She set a small, glossy, burgundy bag with expensively corded handles in the middle of his blotter and stood back with her hands clenched in front of her.

When he just stared at it, she jumped forward and grabbed the bag, upended it and carefully, even reverently, placed a small, burgundy, velvet box in front of him. Then she resumed her position of hand clenching.

He opened the box. He stared at the ring.

And it was perfect.

He looked his secretary directly in the eyes. "Well done, Mandy. I knew you could do it."

Mandy beamed.

And then Colin did something that he did not know and likely would never know (or even understand) that assured his secretary's employ for the next twenty years.

He snapped the case shut, stood and rounded the desk to her. He then wrapped his hand gently around the back of her head, and bending low (because she was quite petite) he kissed her forehead like a loving older brother.

He went back around his desk, grabbed his suit jacket off the back of his chair and walked out of his office.

And Mandy thought, watching him go, that no matter what

everyone else said, Colin Morgan really was a good man.

NEARLY FIVE HUNDRED years earlier, at exactly ten to five in the evening, while Royce and Beatrice danced at their wedding feast, the dark soul sharpened the blade of a knife against a whetstone.

MEANWHILE, ROYCE WATCHED Beatrice's smiling face as she beamed at her father and mother (then mock-scowled at her younger sister) as he whirled her in a dance.

She'd done the change again this morning, turning into a different person, yet the same. He could not put his finger on how he knew she was not her, she just was *not*. She had done it before dozens of times but this time, instead of being oddly not the same, she was both not the same and completely terrified.

For him, for them and because of tonight.

One second she was so afraid, she was nearly in tears, the next second she was confused and blushing at standing before him in her dressing gown, having no idea how she got from her bed to the Hall, standing in his arms.

Something was amiss and, as usual when he felt something was amiss, Royce Morgan was on his guard.

IT SHOULD BE noted at this juncture, there was some pretty hefty magic flying back and forth across nearly five hundred years.

The good kind.

And the bad.

Chapter TWENTY-EIGHT

Proposal

As instructed, at five thirty, Colin met Rick in the Great Hall.

"What's happening?" Colin asked, throwing his suit jacket over a four hundred and fifty-year-old chair with a dry, preserved oak leaf sitting in its seat, The National Trust's indication that tourists were not permitted to sit there.

"They're barbequing sticks with vegetables on them. No meat, just vegetables. Vegetable sticks. On the barbeque. Who does that?" Rick answered, completely at a loss.

Colin speared Rick with a glance. "I was referring to the imminent threat on my girlfriend's life," he drawled.

"Oh right. That." Rick said with a jerk of his chin. "No activity. We've got a bloke doing the perimeter just in the woods beyond the cleared grounds and garden. Got another bloke patrolling in the wood, another at the gatehouse. I've got the house. Someone's relieving me at eight."

Colin nodded.

Rick kept speaking.

"Your alarm men started yesterday. As you instructed me, I told them to install the warning light and panic button first. They did that yesterday and tested it today. All is a go. Left side of the bed, like you asked. That is, left side when you're lying in it."

"Good," Colin muttered.

He turned to go and change his clothes so he could join his guests at the impromptu vegetable barbeque, but Rick stalled him by continuing.

"Mr. Morgan, you should know, what I said earlier . . ." He stopped, searching for the right words. "Any other time and I'd think your bird was . . ." He stopped again then shrugged. "Whatever, she's a little mad but she's all right."

Colin nodded again, indicating he held no ill will against Rick's unsuitable but understandable statement about Sibyl earlier.

He then went to his bedroom to check the work of the alarm company. While there, he changed into jeans and a gray, lightweight, V-necked sweater and walked down to the Great Hall. He heard laughter and the drone of happy, relaxed conversation drifting in from outside and he found it strange that he'd lived at Lacybourne for over a year and that was the first he'd ever heard those sounds in the house.

Because of that, before he joined his guests, with curiosity, he went to one of the two semi-circular windows on the outer wall and looked into the terraced garden.

At the paved area close to the house, chairs and tables had been set up. Kyle was manning the barbeque and Jemma stood beside him, holding a basting brush.

Meg, Mrs. Griffith and Annie were all seated together with Mags, and just watching them, Colin could not tell which ones were talking and which ones were listening as all their mouths were moving. Mrs. Griffith had Bran curled in her lap and Mallory was lying at her feet. His mother, Tina and Marian were in another group of chairs and Tina was relating some story that made the other two women smile.

Colin searched for Sibyl and found her two terraces up racing in a patch of lawn with Flower, three younger boys and Jemma's two children. They were kicking a football in a rag tag game of soccer.

Sibyl nearly collided with one of the younger boys, and instead of falling on him she threw her body forward in a graceful dive to avoid him. Correcting herself swiftly, she burst up from her reclining position and grasped him at his waist, pulling him down to the turf to tickle him.

The other children took this as an invitation to pile on top of Sibyl, a huge wrestling match ensued and Colin could hear the giggles and high-pitched screams through the window.

And then, right before his eyes, the scene melted.

It was the same garden but the colors of the flowers were different, the garden was less formal, it looked wilder and immensely more beautiful.

There were fewer children, only four.

One boy, perhaps eight years old, tall and straight with leonine hair, but aside from his hair he was a replica of Colin at that age. He was standing partially away from the mess with an expression on his face that clearly showed it was beneath him but regardless of that fact, he still wished to join in.

Colin also saw two girls, both rolling all over Sibyl. One had dark, nearly black hair and Sibyl's features, another had leonine hair and a pleasing mixture of both Colin and Sibyl in her face.

And the last was a very young lad of about two with dark hair and a face that nearly matched his older, blonde sister. He was partially cradled in Sibyl's arms but struggling against her hold and her fingers at his sides.

Sibyl giggled, tickled and was tickled in return, and then for no apparent reason she stopped abruptly, her head turned and she stared at Colin straight through the window.

Then she smiled at him with all the love of the world shining clearly in her eyes.

He saw it as distinctly as if she had been standing right in front of him.

And he felt it like it was a physical touch.

And then the scene melted back to the present time and Colin found himself shaken so deeply he had to put his hand to the window to steady himself.

He was in love with her.

Christ, he was in love with her.

He had no idea what just happened and he blinked to try and clear the vision from his mind.

But he couldn't.

He was in love with Sibyl.

He had been in love with her since he saw her that first night under the copse of the trees with Mallory at her side and Bran in her arms.

And he would be in love with her until the day she died.

If he was a different type of man and believed in things like magic or destiny, he might have believed he loved her since before he was born.

For Colin Morgan had been born with a broken heart, the broken heart of a long-dead warrior, a warrior who lost his love and his life at near the same exact time.

Though Colin didn't know that and wouldn't believe it if someone told him.

Colin turned from the window and walked into the Great Hall, looking up at the portraits and seeing Royce and Beatrice with new eyes.

He had been avoiding this knowledge for weeks, with the pursuit of Sibyl and then her safety uppermost in his mind. If he had allowed himself to think about how he felt about her, it would have made him vulnerable.

Which he was now.

And he decided, since he'd never felt it before in all of his years, that he absolutely detested the feeling.

There was someone out there who wanted to slit their throats, wanted them to watch while it happened, just like the dream.

Colin stared at Royce and Beatrice, wondering if that was how they died.

Bile rose up in his throat as it hit him and he believed, for the first time, that something so vile could live for centuries and curse anyone involved in it.

And he couldn't, *wouldn't* allow it to happen again.

AT FIVE FORTY five, nearly five hundred years earlier, the dark soul let the accomplices into the kitchen at Lacybourne.

Much coin changed hands.

And together, they went over the plan.

AND AT THE same time, in William Godwin's hall, Royce Morgan's mother sat next to Beatrice Godwin's mother.

"I congratulate you, Penelope," Beatrice's mother, Mary, stated.

"On what, Mary?" Royce's mother, Penelope, asked.

"Fine meddling, that." Mary nodded at the beautiful couple whirling before them, the dark-haired lass smiling so brightly up at her golden-haired warrior, it veritably lit the room.

"I congratulate you in return," Penelope said generously for she secretly thought it was mostly her doing.

"Thank you," Mary murmured with humble dignity, even though she wasn't humble at all, as she thought it was mostly her doing.

"They'll have fine children," they said at the very same time, turned to look at each other and then burst out laughing.

Their laughter died when they saw Old Lady Griffin tap her cane none-too-gently on a young lad's shoulder and said loudly, "I say, I would like *to dance*."

The two happy mothers burst out laughing again.

IT'S NOT ONLY star-crossed lovers who are reincarnated, you know.

"FOOD'S READY!" KYLE shouted and the children tore away from Sibyl and rushed down the garden's terraced steps in such wild abandon, she feared for a moment they'd all end up in a heap of broken bones at the bottom.

Luckily, fate was smiling down on them and this did not happen.

Sibyl followed at a much slower pace and then, as if by magic, she felt Colin's eyes on her. She actually felt them before she even knew he was there.

And halfway down the steps, she turned and saw him striding out of the back door from the kitchen, striding purposefully with all his masculine grace, all the while looking at her.

Without hesitation, she ran down the steps, across the paved slabs and threw herself into his arms.

He also didn't hesitate and those arms closed fiercely around her.

"We're free!" She smiled as she turned her face up to his. "Rick's no longer holding us captive in the library, the sun is shining, a bunch of people I love are sitting in the garden and the shish kebabs are ready."

He was staring down at her, a peculiar look on his face, and his hand came up to the side of her neck, his thumb at the soft skin under her chin.

Something in his eyes made her toes curl.

And her stomach pitch.

And, if that wasn't enough, her heart skipped three beats.

Then it started racing.

"Are you all right?" she whispered.

"I love you," he said quietly in return.

And then the world fell away and there was only the two of them, alone together, and all time and place faded.

MARIAN WAS NOT the only one to notice the gold shimmer in the air intensify to the point that it seemed as thick as treacle.

Mags noticed it too.

As did Phoebe.

And Jemma.

And, of course, Tina and Kyle.

The kids didn't notice anything.

Annie murmured, 'I'm finding it a bit hard to breathe,' as the golden air caught in her lungs.

This, somehow, caused her no fear. She thought it felt rather pleasant actually.

Meg's face collapsed in a smile for she was looking to her left and seeing Colin holding Billie in a way so tender and true, it could only be love.

Mrs. Griffith missed it all. She was looking around on the ground by her chair.

She couldn't find her cane.

This was because Mallory was lying on it.

"OH MY GODDESS."

Colin smiled.

Sibyl's eyes were wide. The color drained from her face and then just her cheeks suffused with warmth.

"Oh my *goddess*."

Colin's arms tightened.

"Say it again," she demanded.

"You heard me," he growled low.

"Oh . . . my . . . *goddess*!"

Colin's smile widened before he asked, "Is that all you have to say?"

She pulled her lips between her teeth and then let them out. "No."

His eyebrows rose arrogantly.

"I love you, too."

And then her face split into a smile that—if she had known, she would have been devastated but still wouldn't have been able to stop herself—had an ever-so-slight negative effect on the ozone layer.

And just as incapable of stopping himself, Colin kissed her.

It was sweet and wild and beautiful and absolutely everything a kiss should be.

When he lifted his head, he was shaken to his soul.

"Oh my goddess," Sibyl whispered reverently.

Apparently, so was Sibyl.

She blinked and then tore out of his arms but not away. She grabbed his hand and with all her strength, started pulling him towards the house.

He followed for three steps and with a slight tug of his hand in hers, brought her to a halt and she whirled back.

"Colin! We have to go inside."

"Why?"

She walked back to him, closing the short space between them, grabbed his other hand and exerted pressure on both, trying to walk backwards and pull him with her.

"We have to . . ." she explained, "you know . . . *do it*. Break the curse. Like . . . *now*!"

He grinned again and she felt her heart skip three more beats and her legs start to wobble.

"Darling, we have guests," Colin pointed out.

She glanced quickly at their audience, caught their knowing smiles, then she looked back to Colin.

"They won't mind," she assured him.

His grin broadened to a wicked smile but he didn't move.

"It'll only take ten minutes," she cajoled.

His eyebrows rose again.

"Okay . . . fifteen," she amended.

The smile turned lethal, her stomach did a somersault as his head tilted.

"Twenty?" she tried.

He shook his head and she stomped her foot.

"Colin!"

He lifted one of her hands up, brushing his lips on her knuckles, and as he did this, never once did his eyes leave hers.

She stared at him, mesmerized.

Just that morning, Royce had done the same thing.

"Colin," she said far more quietly.

"Marry me, Sibyl."

Her breath caught.

Her mind stilled.

All thoughts of Royce flew into the atmosphere.

She couldn't have uttered a word if she'd learned at that moment that the World Health Organization had been given a gazillion dollars to socialize healthcare globally.

He didn't wait for an answer, just dropped her hand and put one of his in his pocket. Then there was an extraordinary, princess-cut diamond ring being slid on her finger.

She knew just by looking at it that it was exorbitantly expensive.

And she didn't care one bit.

"Oh my goddess!" This was said (more like screeched) from behind

them, coming from Mags.

Sibyl finally found her voice.

"Does this mean you think you can boss me around for the rest of my natural-born days?"

He tugged sharply at her hand, Sibyl fell into him and his arms closed around her.

"And through eternity," he promised against her lips, this said in his low, effective, deep, rich voice.

She was powerless against it and therefore instantly agreed.

"Okay."

WHILE SIBYL AND Colin ate vegetables on sticks and were given pats on the backs, hugs, kisses, handshakes and many congratulations through smiles and tears . . .

Nearly five hundred years earlier, at the same precise time, Royce helped Beatrice onto Mallory's sleek, dark, back.

They were going home to Lacybourne.

He swung into the saddle behind her and the moment he settled, he felt her tremble against him.

"Nerves, my sweet?" His voice rumbled deliciously in her ear.

She shook her head and looked back at him, pressing her chin endearingly against her shoulder. "I just can't wait to be home."

Then she smiled, a lovely, inviting, slightly anxious smile.

And at the sight, his guard lowered.

And Royce Morgan, for the first time in his life, became vulnerable.

Chapter TWENTY-NINE

The Real Consummation

"What are you doing?"

Sibyl whirled then, with an obviously guilty movement, shoved behind her back the small, pink box with glossy, intricate writing embossed on top.

They'd just finished their vegetable shish kebabs and she'd ducked upstairs to begin planning her first night with her new fiancé, who also just happened to be in love with her.

In love with her.

It was, maybe, the most important night of her life.

And it was, definitely, the happiest.

That fiancé was now standing in the door to their bedroom but he didn't look happy. His face was like the thunder beginning to threaten outside.

"What are you doing up here?" she asked, her voice just as guilty as her posture.

"I asked you a question, you disappeared."

No, he was definitely *not* happy.

"I told Mags *and* Phoebe where I was," Sibyl explained.

"You still haven't answered my question." Colin was a dog with a bone.

"*And* Jemma," Sibyl continued, for good measure, as he clearly still was not happy.

"Sibyl," he growled.

She finally gave him an answer, though not enough of one for his liking.

"I needed to check something."

"What?" he asked instantly.

She hesitated.

"Some . . . thing," she stalled, drawing out the word for as long as she could.

Slowly he moved into the room and slowly he closed the door.

And also, very slowly, he turned the key which now sat in the lock on a permanent basis.

And then, still slowly, he turned back and put the key in his pocket.

"Explain," he said curtly when he again caught her eye.

"I . . . can't," she whispered.

"And why is that?" He didn't allow her to answer but kept interrogating. "Do I have to repeat that I very much *do not* like it when you disappear?"

She was silent. She felt this was the best course of action until she actually *could* explain or think of a credible lie she might be able to impart without getting caught in it.

She thought, rather hysterically, that the happy, euphoric tone of the evening that followed his vow of love and marriage proposal was sadly brief.

"Explain," he repeated.

She decided she couldn't keep her silence (because, obviously, he wasn't going to let her) and he'd never believe a lie, so she gave in.

"I can't explain . . ." she rushed on when he opened his mouth to what she was sure would be bark at her, "I have to show you. I was just getting ready for later."

He was silent but his silence was not hesitant or anxious. It was expectant.

Impatiently expectant.

"Just . . . hold on," she said and then she ran to the bathroom and shut the door, praying he wouldn't follow.

Luckily, he didn't.

And she loved him a little bit more at that show of trust.

And if she loved him much more, she'd explode with it.

What was in the box was Mags's present that she'd brought Sibyl from America. Not any of Sibyl's favorite treats that she couldn't get in England, like spiced, black corn chips or grape jelly. But instead, a nightgown so racy that when Sibyl had opened it, Bertie had stood abruptly and left the room on an expletive.

Now Sibyl folded back the pale pink tissue, looked at the contents of the box and wondered if she had the guts to do this. She wondered also if Colin was right and maybe she was a tad bit prissy (but only a *tad*).

She heard a soft noise from in the bedroom and she immediately rushed to take off her clothes.

This was because she really didn't want to keep Colin waiting.

She donned the nightie, which was made of stretchy, lavender-colored lace, hugged her body everywhere it touched, hit her just below where her thighs met her bottom in a lovely scalloped hem and had underwire that pushed her breasts up rather suggestively. It also had a pair of lavender satin string-bikini bottoms.

She stared at herself in the mirror in the bathroom and thought, perhaps, she couldn't do this. That perhaps, she *was* a bit of a priss (and maybe more than a tad) and she ran her hands through her hair in anxious frustration.

In doing that, she caught sight of the ring on her finger. She dropped her hands but also dropped her head to gaze in wonder for a moment at the sparkling diamond on her left ring finger.

That was when decided she could, most definitely, do this.

She opened the door and entered the bedroom and Colin, who was impatiently snapping the drapes shut on the windows, whirled around when he heard her.

He froze at the sight of her.

"It's from Mags," Sibyl whispered.

Colin didn't say a word.

"I . . . um, thought it would be a nice celebratory gesture, you know, get into the swing of things while we're breaking the curse."

"Get over here," Colin snarled in a tone so savage, she didn't know if he was angry or . . . something else.

"I'll take it off," she offered, "we have guests . . ."

Colin's response, "They can wait a couple of hours. Get over here."

Sibyl's body jerked and her eyes grew wide.

"A couple of hours?" she breathed.

The room was huge. It would take a normal person twelve, maybe thirteen strides to get across it.

Colin made it in five.

MALLORY PULLED OUT of his early evening nap, got to his feet far more gracefully than he had ever done in his whole doggie life, and he walked into the house, following the last person of the party to enter as they all went in to escape the oncoming storm.

He walked directly to his master and mistress's bedroom and sat properly, not lounged, at the door.

And thus he stood sentry.

IT WASN'T JUST people who were reincarnated, you know.

AFTER MRS. GRIFFITH had risen to hug Sibyl and Colin upon their engagement, Bran leapt from her comfy lap to the ground and stayed in the shadows most of the evening.

The air smelled funny and he didn't like it. Most of it was good, very good, but there was a hint that was very, *very* bad.

He followed the dark-haired man who'd come into their lives some time ago.

He liked this man. This man was arrogant and assertive and autocratic and a lot of other things that Bran respected.

Bran had long since approved of this new human in his life.

Without being noticed, Bran slid into the bedroom when the dark-haired man (quite rightly in Bran's opinion) confronted Bran's human about her latest reckless endeavor.

While she was in the cold, white, shiny room, Bran silently jumped to a chair, and then after his new human closed a set of drapes, Bran deftly leaped to the curtain rod and crouched low, his dark body hidden by the top of the drapes and the shadows.

And he stood guard.

CATS, HOWEVER, WERE never reincarnated. They already had nine lives.

Bran was on his third.

Bran thought it should be noted, however, that the loss of the first two was not his fault.

MEANWHILE, IN ANOTHER time . . .

"ROYCE, STOP."

At Beatrice's words, Royce pulled back Mallory's reins and the horse dutifully halted.

His beautiful new bride twisted to look at him and he caught her eyes, hiding his impatience. He was keen to get to Lacybourne, the weather had turned and the sky was threatening rain and worse.

But with one look at his beautiful new wife Royce thought that imminent rain was the less important of the two reasons there were to get home, as quickly as possible, to Lacybourne.

"Is something amiss?" Royce asked, staring down into her eyes, noting they'd softened to a mellow brown with only the barest inflections of green at the pupils.

"This morning . . ." She pulled her lips between her teeth in a gesture he had become used to over the last several months, a habit he found quite endearing. Then she released them and whispered, "I should have told you before we wed, you may have decided . . ."

Royce sighed his impatience. "Beatrice, rain is coming, do you not feel it?"

"Royce, I think I've gone quite mad," she burst out.

Before he could comment on this, her latest bizarre utterance to add to the wealth of bizarre utterances she had amassed since he met her, she went on.

"I . . . sometimes I . . ." she paused, looking for the right words then she found them, "drift away. These past months, with you, always with you, I just go away, somewhere nice, somewhere peaceful and then I come back and I find time is lost to me. You do not seem to notice I've been gone and we have . . . done things while I'm not here . . . and . . . I just do not remember." She pulled in a broken breath and watched him closely before she whispered, "My love, I think I am mad."

He did not speak because his entire body stilled.

She dropped her gaze to her lap. "What's worse, sometimes I think you do it as well." Her head lifted with a snap and her eyes caught his again. "Sometimes you are simply . . ." she hesitated again then finished, "not you."

Royce regarded her for a moment and then swiftly alighted from Mallory's back. He put his strong hands on Beatrice's waist to pull her down and he set her before him. Very close before him.

She tilted her head up and he stared at her, her beautiful, dark, glossy hair shining on her shoulders (she'd worn it down, just for him). It was threaded liberally with flowers and he thought, with pleasure and unusual whimsy, that she looked somewhat like a nymph.

But now, her eyes were frightened and wary and she was waiting for him to react to her words.

"I feel it as well," he admitted, "in me and in you."

Her eyes warmed and she breathed, "Truly?"

Royce nodded.

Beatrice sagged against him.

"Oh, thank goodness," she said with extreme relief. "I thought it was only me."

"You are pleased we are both mad?"

Her eyes were shining when she looked at him. "No . . . yes . . . no, but I think . . . yes."

He grinned at her with every intention of keeping from her, for her own protection (of course) that he felt he knew the woman she became when she was no longer Beatrice. That he had a vague feeling they had been together, somewhere, not there. That she was good and kind, just like Beatrice. That there was nothing to fear because, in some way, she *was* Beatrice.

It was a fanciful notion and a man like Royce did not waste time on fanciful notions.

He lifted his hand to her neck, setting his thumb on the soft skin under her chin.

"Do you fear this night? Our night?" he asked gently.

Her eyes rounded. "Yes . . . no . . . yes, but I think . . . no."

He shook his head but still grinned at her.

"You have nothing to fear, beloved."

Her eyes melted to liquid.

And, at that familiar sight, Royce had no choice.

He bent his head to kiss her.

ESMERALDA CRANE RUSHED out of her cottage on her way to Lacybourne and was nearly so attuned to her task of saving the doomed lovers that she missed the change in the atmosphere.

Then she saw it.

It was not just golden but thick as stew.

She felt a timid hope spring into her heart and she quickened her step, clutching the potion to her.

IN THE PRESENT time, in the library, at Lacybourne . . .

IDLY, MARIAN PULLED the volume out of the shelf as she heard Phoebe ask distractedly, "What *could* have happened to them?"

Marian thought about what she hoped had happened to Colin and Sibyl—that they were breaking the curse. Which, considering Colin's reputation, might take a while.

She turned the pages, leafing through the book as the guests chattered and the children played.

"I *cannot* imagine," Mags answered Phoebe, enunciating every word playfully.

Marian's eyes skimmed down the book. She hadn't seen it in years and she had no idea what drew her to pulling it from the shelf. She had mostly memorized it, of course, but . . .

Her eyes stopped dead on some words on the page and her body got tight.

A date.

A date nearly five hundred years before.

How *could* she have forgotten?

And then her eyes widened when she saw all the words after the date had become misty and unreadable.

As if, even though they were meant to tell the story of long dead lovers, they had not yet been written.

As if they were waiting to form, waiting for the story to unfold, a story that should have been forged with time.

A story that clearly was not.

A thrill ran up her spine, her head jerked up and she asked a question to which she already knew the answer.

"What's today's date?"

She said it too loudly and with too much alarm. Several pairs of eyes swiveled to her and several mouths gave her the information she sought.

Marian snapped the book shut and strode purposefully toward Mags.

And when she made it to the other woman, she announced gravely, "Marguerite. It's time."

IN THE WOOD, the man shifted through the leaves, trying to be quiet and definitely being watchful.

No matter how quiet or watchful he was, he would never have heard or seen the specter drifting behind him.

However, he did *feel*, for a brief, painful moment, the blow that struck him on the head.

The man collapsed, unconscious, to the ground.

The specter drifted away.

Light work, it thought.

Resurrected by the dark soul mere moments previously, the specter had only one gruesome mission this night. His reviver had tried to use beings in this time but they had failed. Thus, it had been called forward to do again what it had done many years before.

Once the task was complete, it could drift back to its oblivion, a dark oblivion it had occupied for nearly five hundred years.

A dark, wicked oblivion.

The specter was happy for its task.

It needed a break from that place.

IN THE BEDROOM, Colin lifted Sibyl up in his arms and he kissed her as he walked toward the bed. Her arms slid around his shoulders, one hand drifting into the hair at the back of his head as she kissed him back.

He stopped at the side of the bed and dropped her legs, allowing her feet to fall slowly toward the floor, all the while her body skimming against his.

"I take it you like the nightie," she breathed, her eyes liquid.

In answer, his hands glided down her sides and he felt her delicious shiver.

"I'll count that as a yes," she whispered.

His hands came forward and he watched them as they moved across her ribcage, up under her breasts where they stopped.

Oh yes, Colin most definitely liked the nightie.

"Someone told me once," Sibyl was saying.

Although he wasn't listening to her, he was pleasantly contemplating where to put his hands next. Thinking maybe he'd tug the hem up to get a better look at the satin panties of which he could now only see a tantalizing glimpse. Or, perhaps, he'd run his palms against her nipples to see how they looked hardened under that exquisite lace.

She kept talking.

"That you should never commit to a man unless you've been with him through all four seasons."

"Mm?" he mumbled as he decided on her nipples.

Then he heard her breath catch as he carried out his plan.

Her voice continued doggedly (although it was now quivering a little). "We've only been through one season and we're not even through that."

He decided that, as God saw fit to grant him *two* hands, he could use them for *two* splendidly different purposes. He ran one down her side, shifting it to slide down the small of her back to her ass. The other, he kept at her breast and again lightly ran his thumb over her nipple.

That earned him another catch of her breath.

But she kept speaking.

"Colin? Are you listening to me? Maybe we're being a bit hasty."

With great reluctance, he lifted his eyes from his fascinated study of what his thumb was doing to her breast. He looked at her face just as his thumb, joined by his finger, became a little more relentless. As she was talking, indeed carrying on what seemed a weighty conversation, he decided he wasn't doing his job very well.

As his fingers tugged at her, his hand cupped her bottom and pressed it to his rigid groin.

Her eyes grew dazed, her mouth parted and a soft breath escaped.

"Sibyl?" he called.

She nodded, "Unh hunh?"

"Shut up."

IN THE GATEHOUSE, another specter dispatched the watchful guard at the same time the last was felled at the edge of the third terrace of the back garden.

The plan was coming together.

ROBERT FITZWILLIAM LOOKED at the clock on the dashboard of his car and then out at the rolling hills. He deduced he was, at most, fifteen minutes from Lacybourne Manor.

He did not like the look in the eye of his employer that morning and he never wanted that look directed at him again.

He was just going to make a quick stop to check on his team.

AT THE SAME time, but many years earlier, in the wood a fifteen minute horseback ride away from Lacybourne . . .

ROYCE LIFTED HIS head. His body was, as usual after he kissed Beatrice, on fire for her.

He yanked at the chain that held his cloak together at his neck, pulled it from his shoulders and whirled it out to lay it on the ground beside them.

"What . . . what are you doing?" Beatrice gasped, her eyes dazed, her lips swollen from his kiss.

"I cannot wait." His voice was gruff.

He no sooner wanted to bed her their first time on the forest floor in the threatening rain than he wanted the world to come to an abrupt end.

But he told no lie. He simply couldn't wait. Something was driving him and at that moment, with his new bride's eyes hazy with passion, her cheeks flushed, his body burning, he had no desire to question it.

She gulped and turned her beautiful eyes to his before she admitted quietly, "Nor I."

At her words, he snatched her to him and he was not in any mood for romance and gentleness. His mouth devoured hers and she moaned against his lips, against his tongue in her mouth and he swept her up and dropped to one knee, laying her on his cloak.

The horse (neither of them noticed) shifted slightly closer, its ears up and alert.

Royce stretched out beside his Beatrice, his hands roving her body, his groin pressed demandingly against her hip.

Lightning streaked the sky as his mouth took possession of hers and he roughly pulled up her skirts, his hand finding the smooth skin of her thigh and gliding across it, touching it for the first time, and the silken feel of it made him wild.

"God's teeth," he cursed, burying his face in her neck as thunder rent the air.

If he didn't have her soon, he'd spend himself before they were skin against skin.

"What do I do?" she whispered, her voice half timid, half filled with desire.

"Touch me," he replied without hesitation.

"But . . . where?"

"Anywhere."

And she did.

THE DARK SOUL stood, hidden behind the copse of the trees.

The air had gone golden even as the clouds rolled in and lightning lit the sky. It made no sense and, further, strangely, it was hard to breath.

"They should be here now," an accomplice hissed.

The others shifted, uncomfortable, uneasy with the golden air, the delayed carnage.

Something was wrong. The dark soul felt that it should have been done by now.

That somehow, it *had* been done by now.

And yet, it wasn't.

JUMPING FORWARD IN time, at Lacybourne . . .

RICK STRODE INTO the library.

He motioned to Kyle with a quick jerk of his head.

Kyle read the gesture and without word or delay he followed him into the Great Hall.

They had words.

Rick went out the front.

Kyle went out the back.

THE (OTHER) PLAN was in motion.

Phoebe wheeled Meg into the lounge with the children.

Meg had her orders, she had a key to the door and she had the cordless phone.

The children had their DVD.

Annie joined them.

The children decided to take turns shouting to Annie about what was on the screen.

Phoebe carefully locked them in.

And just as carefully, Marian sprinkled a protection charm on the threshold.

MAGS RAN TO the kitchen. She found the huge pot hidden in the butler's pantry, and with an unladylike grunt, she tugged it out, brought it to the kitchen proper and hefted it onto the burner. She lit the gas underneath it to the highest heat and pulled the lid off the pot.

She peeled the aluminum foil off the top.

Then she removed the plastic wrap that had been underneath the foil.

It *did* have a very foul odor, one that needed to be hidden for a variety of reasons.

Marian bustled in sprinkling something from a glass vial onto the floor and whispering under her breath. This she had done all through the house where Colin and Sibyl's guests would be.

Jemma and Tina bustled in and Phoebe followed them.

Mrs. Griffith (a little slow anyway) brought up the rear.

"Mrs. Griffith," Jemma said, trying to sound stern, "you should be in the lounge."

"If you think I'm going to miss this, you're mad," Mrs. Griffith returned, a highly unusual smile cracking her face.

Before anyone could say anything else, Marian seemed to come to herself and noticed the pot.

"That will not do at all," she said to no one and then snapped her fingers.

The flames flew up on all sides of the pot, licking it and crackling in the air.

Everyone jumped back a step.

"Let's go, ladies. We have work to do," Marian commanded.

Without hesitation, as they had been instructed earlier at the barbeque, they formed a semi-circle around the pot, trying not to breathe the putrid fumes.

And they started to chant the words Marian had taught them over vegetable shish kebabs.

SIBYL WAS ON her back on the bed, Colin on top of her, Colin all *over* her. His mouth was at one breast and he'd pulled down the other cup of the nightie, and there his fingers were teasing her.

Unlike normally, when the spirals of hot desire went from her breasts, her stomach, tingling up from her toes and zooming *toward* the space between her legs, instead, the spirals were zooming out from between her legs and going *everywhere*.

She'd torn his sweater off, nearly ripped it off over his head before he pushed her back on the bed. Now he was only in jeans, she in her nightie and she could stand it no more. She wanted his skin against her skin, she wanted him inside her.

She put her hands in his hair, tugged his head up to hers and kissed him with every bit of love (which was a lot) and every bit of arousal (which was *a lot*, a lot) she felt.

He tore his mouth away and gazed at her with eyes blazing so intensely, she was sure she'd melt.

She whispered, "Now."

Without hesitation, he left her. As she absently heard thunder fill the air, she watched with fascination as he removed his jeans and then leaned forward and in one, quick, luscious jerk, he pulled her panties down her legs.

He smoothed the lace up over her hips as she reached for him to bring him to her.

He spread her thighs and surged over her and with one, fierce, beautiful, fluid movement Colin filled her.

"Yes," she breathed.

"YES," BEATRICE BREATHED.

They were finally naked on the cloak, skin against skin. Royce had taken pains to make her ready for him, he'd tasted her, tempted her, teased her. He could not believe the beauty of her body, could not believe she was all his, to touch with his hands, his lips, his mouth.

He was certainly going to enjoy a lifetime of this. Very, *very* much.

Now with his head bent to her breast, he pulled her nipple sharply in his mouth, rolling his tongue around it and listening to her soft, exquisite moans.

His fingers had found resistance earlier but he had loosened it using her unwavering trust in him against her instincts, as well as his talented fingers, and they were now, finally inside her.

And she was dripping wet.

She was ready for him.

He spread her legs and rolled between them while his mouth took hers in a sweet kiss, his hands moving to frame her face.

"This will hurt, my love," he murmured against her lips as he found her with the tip of his shaft, and controlling his hips with an immense effort of will, he slid inside her just an inch.

Her eyes grew wide as she felt his invasion.

"Royce," she whispered.

He slid in more, mere centimeters, and gritted his teeth. He had avoided death in countless gory battles on countless blood-drenched battlefields but the exquisite torture of her lush tightness was finally going to kill him.

"I can't stop the pain, but I shall try and make it . . ." He had to stop speaking and again grit his teeth so he wouldn't drive into her with the wild abandon his body was demanding but only press in less than an inch more.

"I can't . . ." she whispered.

"You can, my sweet." He slid in further. "Trust me."

"I can't . . ." It was softer this time and her head moved to the side as he slowly inched in and let her adjust to his further intrusion.

"Trust me," he repeated.

"I can't . . ." she said.

And then with a glorious jerk, she slammed her hips down towards his. She emitted a soft cry of pain that was drowned out with his low growl as she embedded him fully inside her.

Her eyes opened and they were clear and trusting when she finished, "*Wait.*"

IN BOTH TIMES, the golden air sparkled brightly with white-hot flashes, some of them nearly blue.

They tingled skin, they glittered through hair, they brightened the air and they flashed everywhere like fireworks close to the ground.

IN THE KITCHEN at Lacybourne . . .

"Oh my . . ." Mags muttered, staring at the air.

"Don't stop chanting," Marian ordered, staring in the pot.

CLOSE TO A copse of trees outside Lacybourne . . .

"Dear goddess . . ." Esmeralda breathed as the sparks tingled her skin.

The dark soul cursed under its breath.

ROYCE DROVE IN further, deeper, hearing her soft panting and feeling it throughout his body as Beatrice's hands moved, restless and demanding, all over him.

"Royce, something . . . is happening . . . to me." She couldn't control her voice.

"Let go, my sweet, let it happen," he urged.

Trusting him, her head tilted back, her neck arched, she lifted her knees and he drove into her deeper as he buried his face in her neck and listened with profound satisfaction to the glorious sound of the pleasure overwhelming his sweet, beautiful new bride.

COLIN FELT SIBYL lift her knees and he buried his face in her neck, her movements allowing him to thrust his cock even deeper inside her and she quietly panted.

"Colin, I think I'm going to . . ."

And then he listened with profound satisfaction to the glorious sound of his sweet, beautiful new fiancée's orgasm.

ROYCE MORGAN FOUND his own release moments later and after he did, the rain came.

COLIN MORGAN CAME back to himself after his intense climax and vaguely heard the rain against the windows.

THEN, MAGIC SHAFTING through time, the two worlds collided.

And for a brief moment, all time stopped.

Chapter THIRTY

History Shifts

Royce lifted his head.

With great reluctance he had slid out of Beatrice, but he did this with utmost care, not wishing to cause her pain after her pleasure. At the same time he lifted his head, he moved his hand to smooth her lustrous, dark hair.

But his hand arrested for her hair was not dark.

It was the same color as his own.

"You." He watched the dazed pleasure fade slowly from her familiarly unfamiliar eyes as she focused on him.

He knew her.

"Oh my goddess!" She jerked beneath him but he kept his weight firmly on top of her.

He wanted answers and, this time, he was going to get them.

And what Royce Morgan wanted, he found a way to get.

"Where is Beatrice?" he demanded, his hand, instead of smoothing, gently but firmly fisted in her silky, golden locks.

Her eyes turned panicked.

"I don't know," she answered, blinked, her body shifted slightly under his and then she rapped out a string of quick questions, "What are you doing? What are *we* doing? What were you doing with Beatrice?"

His voice held an edge. "Bring her back, I want her back."

"Colin is going to *kill* me," she muttered, what he considered absurdly, and she did this as if to herself as she tried to wriggle out from beneath him.

Considering he'd just consummated his union with his beloved bride, he'd done this soundly and with great pleasure for the both of them and now, mere moments later, another being was lying naked beneath him, Royce lost patience.

Therefore he did not check himself and roared, *"I want her back!"*

She shook her head, "I can't . . . I don't know how to bring her back." Then she stated urgently, "Royce, please, you must listen to me, did you just make love to Beatrice?"

"You are a witch," he declared and started to pull away, to bring them up. He couldn't have this conversation lying naked atop her.

But she wrapped her soft limbs around him and something in her eyes, her familiar, beloved eyes, halted him.

"Listen to me," she begged, her words both urgent and panicked. "Did you just make love to Beatrice?"

"Yes," he snarled.

And to his surprise, her face cleared immediately and she sang, "Hallelujah!" just as tears sprung in her eyes. She tilted her head back and she shouted it again. *"Hallelujah!"*

He stared at her, everything about her was so familiar, even her sweet touch of lunacy.

"Are you mad?" he asked softly, finding his angry confusion had melted away and he was suddenly concerned.

She pulled her arms from his body, put both her hands to his cheeks and gave him a quick kiss.

When she pulled away, he noted she was crying freely but she still went on, "No, I'm not mad."

She looked at him with love shining in her eyes. Somehow, even though he did not know her, she loved him and he felt that knowledge sear straight through his soul.

His hand loosened from her hair and almost against his will, he found himself wrapping a tendril around his finger.

"You have my hair," he murmured, staring at it.

"And you, in my time, have Beatrice's hair," she whispered and his eyes moved to hers at this bizarre pronouncement. "I'm from another time, years from now. Royce, your and Beatrice's love is so great, you and she come back and become Colin and me. We fall in love all over again." Her voice lowered in pitch but heightened in intensity. "And you are *so* like him. And today, he asked me to marry him."

She said this last while a funny, adorable smile played on her lips.

He felt something inside him shift as he listened to her words.

She was *so* like Beatrice.

She blinked and he knew something was happening. Her face changed, disappointment filled it and then urgency replaced that.

"Before I go, you must listen. In the copse of trees . . ."

He saw her hair darken slowly and he couldn't help himself, he watched in fascination.

"Royce! Listen!" She was beyond urgent. Now frantic, her hands tightened on his face and his eyes went from her changing hair to her. "They're waiting for you, in the copse of trees, outside Lacybourne. They're going to slit your throat, Beatrice's too. You must stop them."

His body tensed at her words and she felt it. Her arms wrapped around him again, protectively, lovingly, in a way the warrior had never felt before, not even with Beatrice (although Beatrice had no way of knowing her life, or his, was in imminent danger or she would have done the same, *exact* thing).

She held him tightly against her. "I tried to tell you this morning . . . or . . . some morning. That morning when I was there . . . here. I know you think I'm mad but you must believe me and you *must* stop them."

Her hair was almost, but not quite, nearly to black.

"I do not think you are mad," he told her but she wasn't listening.

"Promise me!" she cried.

He nodded.

He would not die this night nor would his Beatrice. And he wanted this woman to know that. He wanted her to trust him, to believe, and he wanted that fear out of her eyes.

He nor his bride were going to die this night, he would be sure of it.

At his nod her entire body relaxed.

She trusted him.

Completely.

"I'm Sibyl, by the way," she told him. "And don't worry, I don't think I'm coming back."

And then she smiled magnificently, one finger tenderly touching his cheek. Royce had seen a great number of heart-stopping smiles from his wife but this smile was all Sibyl's own.

She continued speaking.

"And if you've been granted the gift of a longer life, try not to boss Beatrice around too much. She'll find it *immensely* irritating."

He knew in that instant, she *was* Beatrice even though she was not.

And therefore he grinned down at her.

Then she lifted her head, pressed her lips against his and she was gone.

AND TIME STARTED again.

"YOU'RE CRYING."

Colin stared at her face, something was right yet something was wrong, something profound had changed even though not a second had passed. He knew it, he felt it.

They'd just shared the most extraordinarily passionate, intense, intimate moment together in a long line of such extraordinary moments, making it hard to believe it had even happened.

But Sibyl was crying.

He could hear the rain hitting the windows.

Then he heard thunder rend the air and seconds later, lightning flashed through the room.

He turned his head, for some reason, to look at the storm.

And saw the warning light next to the panic button blinking.

AS THE WOMEN chanted around the pot, Marian felt the darkness enter the house and a shiver went up her spine.

She'd done what she could do, for now. It was all (or mostly, as she did have *a few* more tricks up her sleeve) now up to true love.

She looked into the history book, the book that told the tragic story of Beatrice and Royce Morgan.

She saw some of the words after the date change, shift then settle—just a sentence, then two, then a paragraph.

Then it stopped.

And she stared in disbelief at what she read.

ESMERALDA CRANE, BEING a witch, was attuned to things other people would not sense.

Now she was attuned to time, history, shifting and reforming itself.

She was becoming confused, muddled, she saw shapes moving before her in the copse of trees but she was supposed to be doing something else at this moment, something she was not doing and this feeling made her restless, guarded.

She quickly hid herself, conjuring a glamor to make herself invisible. All the while she could see, as if it was a memory, the dead, entwined bodies of Royce and Beatrice Morgan under the trees.

But they were not there. There was nothing there except the impatiently shifting forms that lay in wait for ambush.

Someone was playing with time, Esmeralda knew.

And that was a very dangerous game.

COLIN LEAPED OUT of bed, leaned forward and grabbed Sibyl's wrist, dragging her up behind him.

"Get dressed," he hissed then he let her go, bent to his jeans on the floor and shoved his feet into the legs.

"Colin, what is it?"

"Dress!" he clipped and she stared at him, not liking what she saw, and in less than a second, she ran to the bathroom.

He pulled his sweater over his head and pressed the panic button that would alert both the alarm company and the police.

She ran out of the bathroom still struggling into her clothes.

"Is something wrong?" she whispered, rushing toward him.

"Someone's in the house."

Her body jerked and her eyes flew to the door.

"The kids are down there." Her voice was rising and panicked.

"Sibyl, get into the sanctuary, lock the door and do not come out, no matter what you hear," he ordered as she buttoned her jeans.

Mallory started barking just outside the room, his barks angry and loud with warning. Then the barking turned to fierce, consistent growls.

Sibyl was still staring at the door and started toward it.

"Sibyl!" Colin flew toward her, hooking her around the waist with his arm as she started to bolt toward the sound of her beloved dog.

Then they both froze when they heard the blood-chilling, obscene noise of a high-pitched, canine cry of agony.

ROBERT FITZWILLIAM STOPPED at the gatehouse.

One of his men was supposed to be inside but did not come out at the approaching car.

Robert stopped and got out, looking around him. The rain was beating down and yet not twenty minutes before it had been sunny and clear. Now the sky was dark, thunder and lightning were rolling over each other in waves and the wind was whipping at his body.

He walked into the gatehouse not liking what he felt.

Something was wrong.

He saw his man lying on the floor, unconscious.

Robert swore under his breath and rushed straight to the prone body.

ROYCE TOLD BEATRICE everything as they rode to Lacybourne, Royce driving Mallory quickly through the pouring rain as he held Beatrice firmly to his body, the ten-minute ride cut down to five.

She believed him, to his astonishment. But then again, Beatrice was not like other women.

He stopped well outside the copse of trees that was meant to be the place of their demise, if the woman named Sibyl (a witch's name if he ever heard one) could be believed.

But he felt . . . nay, he *knew* he could believe her.

He alighted from Mallory's back and again pulled Beatrice down.

"Run, just as I told you, straight to the witch's cottage. Explain and she will keep you safe."

He had no way of knowing this but he felt it to be true.

She nodded, got up on tiptoe to press her lips against his and without hesitation, she ran.

He watched her go, watched her out of sight then mounted his trusted steed.

He made a clicking sound with his teeth and the horse moved forward.

Unbeknownst to Royce, once out of sight, Beatrice changed directions.

Something sinister was afoot and Royce might need her, after all, and she was Beatrice Godwin, now Morgan, and Beatrice Morgan was certainly not the kind of woman who would desert her beloved new husband when there was a possibility her strong warrior might need her.

Not a chance.

THE LOCKED DOOR to Sibyl and Colin's bedroom flew open with such violence, it crashed against the wall.

With a strong jerk, Sibyl was yanked straight off her feet by Colin's arm at her waist and nearly thrown behind his back as the figures drifted through the door.

The dark, faceless, shifting figures from their dream.

She felt a scream surge up her throat.

"Run to the sanctuary. *Now!*" Colin thundered.

She couldn't move. She couldn't leave Colin alone to face those *things*.

"*Now!*" Colin roared.

And then the figures attacked.

MARIAN WATCHED THE words in the next paragraph forming, read them quickly and gasped.

"What is it?" Phoebe broke the chant.

Marian slapped the book shut again and threw it on the counter.

Without answering Phoebe, she rushed from the room.

THERE WERE FOUR of them, five with the figure standing outside the trees watching.

The rain was driving down and the wind was whipping through the branches. Royce had more than enough experience to battle four opponents; he had done it in the past. But these seemed to be filled with otherworldly strength and he didn't have his sword. It was his wedding day, he didn't think he'd need his sword. If he'd had his sword, he'd have mowed them down like just as much wheat in a field.

He only had the dagger he carried at his belt.

And his strength.

It served him well but it was the battle of his life.

With a fierce roar, he surged up from the crouch they'd forced him into and he threw two off his back, exposing his belly.

A third came in for the kill.

At that moment, Mallory drove forward, head bent low, scattering the others, knocking Royce aside and taking the dagger that was meant for Royce through his own throatlatch.

The warhorse went down with a mighty crash.

THERE WERE FOUR of them and three of them were on Colin while one of them dragged Sibyl away.

She struggled, hissed, spat and kicked.

She saw through her battle that Colin had managed to get a hold of one, and with a fierce roar he threw it flying through the air.

He shrugged off the other two as if they were merely annoying gnats and surged toward Sibyl.

But the wraiths quickly recovered and pounced yet again, stalling his progress and beating him down.

It was then that Sibyl felt the blade at her throat.

EVEN WITH MALLORY'S sacrifice, Royce was losing.

He felt it.

He knew it.

The strength was leaving him, draining out of him. His attackers seemed without limits, relentless. It was almost as if they were sucking his own power and using it against him.

And still the figure watched from the trees.

He knew with a certainty that he was going to die.

But he would do it like a warrior and go down fighting.

This he vowed.

And it was then the strangest thing happened.

COLIN VAGUELY NOTED the figure standing in the door watching the scene. He could not take the time to process it. He was too busy fighting his way to Sibyl. And the beings, whatever the hell they were, were unnaturally strong.

The blade was at her throat and any second it would tear across it and he would lose her.

He knew it.

He felt it.

The agony of the thought shot through him, searing to his very soul.

He opened his mouth, just like he did in the dream, to roar his denial.

Then, in that moment, the strangest thing happened.

OLD LADY GRIFFIN dashed into the clearing, wielding her cane like a battle axe and screaming like a banshee.

Everyone, even the figure standing and watching, even Royce

himself, stopped what they were doing and turned to stare at her in stupefaction.

With an almighty swoop of her arms that was borne half out of fury, half out of terror, she crashed the cane against the face of one of Royce's attackers.

Instantly smashing his jaw and his cheekbone, sending shards of bone into his brain.

Instantly breaking the dark soul's dark spell.

From the other side of the clearing, the town's midwife and resident witch, Esmeralda Crane bounded forward and moved her arm before her in a downward slash. With a flash of green-white light, the watching figure flew across the clearing and slammed against the trunk of a tree. There it stayed frozen, invisibly pinned.

Royce broke out of his stunned freeze and dispatched two more attackers, one with a blade to the heart then he whirled expertly and took out the other one with a slice across the throat.

That was when Beatrice surged into the clearing with what could have been credited as a pretty decent war cry (if Royce hadn't been so infuriated by her very presence) and she jumped on the back of the last of the attackers. She pulled at his hair as he blundered about in vicious circles, trying to dislodge her.

Royce, with immense patience and controlled anger, strolled up behind them. He grasped Beatrice by hooking an arm about her waist and pulled her from the man, calmly setting her down behind him.

He then buried his blade in the man's gut and yanked it savagely upward.

Before the attacker had fully fallen to the ground, Royce whipped around to Beatrice.

"I thought I told you to go to the witch's cottage!" he barked.

"I couldn't leave you out here by yourself!" she flashed back, her eyes, even in the darkened, rainy evening, he could see were emerald green.

He looked to the heavens, praying to the good Lord above for patience.

THE WRAITH SLASHED the blade against Sibyl's throat and Colin let out a ferocious roar as Sibyl emitted a blood-chilling scream.

But instead of penetrating, the blade glanced off her throat in a magical shower of green-white sparks, leaving Sibyl untouched and alive.

At that point Bran flew from the curtain rod, a low, frightening, continuous growl rolling from his feline throat. He landed on the specter that held Sibyl. The phantom gave a start at this turn of events, its hold loosened on Sibyl and she tore free.

Hissing and spitting, Bran tore at the specter with his claws and the ghost struggled to fight back against this strange, unexpected aggressor.

The figure that Sibyl had seen watching from the doorway all of a sudden, with a flash of green-white light, flew across the room. It slammed against the opposite wall and was pinned there, frozen and held captive by invisible shackles.

Marian, her arm lifted and pointing at the figure, calmly walked in the room.

And suddenly, the bedroom was flooded with people.

First came Rick, roaring in like a bull, and without even noticing he was battling a corporeal ghost he simply started to beat the living (or not-so-living) daylights out of it.

Then came Kyle, who jogged in and took a look around. His brows lifting momentarily, he swooped down on one of the two wraiths with whom Colin was still struggling and pulled him away.

And another man, who Sibyl had never seen before, came tearing into the room and stopped dead, immobile at what he saw. With nothing for it, he surged forward and spelled Bran who dropped from his ghost and ran from the room.

With a strange, eerie, final-sounding pop, Rick's specter just disappeared with Rick in mid-swing.

Not a few seconds later, Kyle's did the same.

With another pop, the other one went, leaving the unknown man literally spinning on his feet.

And finally, Colin threw off the last, and as it flew through the air of the room there was a final crack, and one moment they all saw it flying and less than a second later, it was gone.

Without hesitation, Colin whirled on Sibyl.

"I thought I told you to go to the sanctuary!" he barked.

"I couldn't leave you here to fight them alone!" she snapped.

He stared at her angrily for a moment and then lifted his eyes toward the ceiling.

Sybil was relatively certain he was praying for patience.

WITH A MENACING stride, Royce walked toward the figure pinned to the trunk of the tree.

The witch still had her arm lifted. Royce knew, even though he didn't want to believe, that the woman was holding the figure captive using something Royce had refused to believe existed.

Magic.

Royce approached the tree and he felt Beatrice close behind him, and when he stopped, he made sure she stayed well behind him by roughly pushing her there with his arm.

The figure was cloaked, the hood hiding his face.

"Who are you?" Royce demanded.

With a flick of her hand, Esmeralda Crane unmasked the creature.

Royce drew in his breath as he heard Beatrice gasp behind him.

COLIN STALKED WITH menacing strides toward the figure pinned to the wall.

Marian was clearly holding it there with her arm still aloft.

Colin didn't even want to think what *that* meant.

He felt Sibyl close behind him, and when he stopped, he made sure she stayed behind him by pushing her there with his arm.

The being was hooded somehow, its face masked.

"Who the fuck are you?" Colin demanded.

With a flick of her hand, Marian tore the glamor away from the thing.

Colin drew in his breath as he heard Sibyl ask from behind him, "Who the heck is that?"

In a low voice, Colin answered, "Mrs. Manning."

"Mrs. Man . . . *the invisible housekeeper*?" Sibyl burst out.

"You killed my son!" the woman screamed.

Her voice, Colin realized, used to sound old, damaged and scratchy. Now it was just old.

He should have thought of that earlier when Robert told him about the voice their attackers from the Centre had described. But he didn't. He would have never suspected his efficient, mostly unseen housekeeper of plotting his murder.

Now he stared at the woman who had not only kept his house but kept his aunt and uncle's house before him.

"You killed her son?" Sibyl breathed.

Colin whirled with disbelief on his fiancée. "I didn't kill her son!" he exploded.

"You killed my son!" Mrs. Manning shouted.

"*She* says you killed her son," Sibyl stated and turned her eyes to Mrs. Manning. "You are a crazy lady," she noted angrily, sidestepped Colin and started to approach the housekeeper, would have done if Colin hadn't again hooked his arm at her waist and yanked her back hard against his body. Even though he did so, he could actually *feel* Sibyl's fury boiling inside her. "You nearly killed us!" Sibyl yelled.

"He killed my son," Mrs. Manning spat.

"He didn't kill your son, you silly cow," Sibyl spat right back and Colin would have grinned at Sibyl's defense of him if it all wasn't so bizarre, and, of course, he wasn't so *fucking* angry.

Mrs. Manning turned her malevolent eyes to Colin.

"He was your squire. You took him into battle. He died at your side." She was talking, glaring, hatred oozing from every pore and not making a lick of sense. "He was so *honored* to be your squire. To be the squire of the great knight, Royce Morgan. And then he died. And his blood will *forever* be on your hands."

Colin felt Sibyl's body freeze.

At the same time, Marian whispered, "You're an eternal."

"What?" Colin, Sibyl, and Colin could swear at least two, possibly three, other male voices said at the same time.

"An eternal, she's used dark magic to live for centuries, to stay alive throughout time to exact vengeance, knowing Esmeralda had set her spell to restore true love," Marian explained to her audience and then turned back to Mrs. Manning. "You killed Royce and Beatrice nearly five hundred years ago, it was you."

"I did but now *she* saved them, the filthy witch whore," Mrs. Manning spat, her eyes moving to Sibyl.

It was Colin's turn to freeze and then he poised to strike.

"No, Colin," Marian warned, and at her tone Colin's eyes shifted to the older lady. To his surprise she smiled smugly at him. Then she said something even more bizarre than any of the events of this night. "Let Royce take care of this."

"Royce!" Mrs. Manning screamed, her voice hysterical and utterly, completely mad. "He nearly killed me before but he didn't do it," she crowed. "He cut my throat but he didn't sever it."

"There is no scar," Marian informed her, the smile never leaving her face. "Not yet, at least."

Mrs. Manning's eyes widened.

"Royce didn't kill your son," Sibyl, still seething with rage, butted in. "You shouldn't have blamed him. I'm certain your son died with honor. He wouldn't have thanked you for killing Royce and Beatrice."

"You don't know," Mrs. Manning snapped.

"I *do* know. My dad's a professor of Medieval History, *of course* I know! A squire would be honored to train under a knight of Royce Morgan's reputation, his strength, his character. It would be learning from a master."

"You don't know!" Mrs. Manning screamed. "He was stupid. Royce felt such guilt at Henry's death, he let me into his home. He gave me food, clothing. He took care of me. Miss Beatrice told me he cared for my son, in his way, he loved him." She shook her head, her eyes narrowing malevolently and she spat out, "Bah! He didn't love him. He *murdered* him. It wasn't his blade that brought Henry down but it might just as well have been. All the while I was at Lacybourne, I plotted their deaths. All the while I waited for the perfect moment when his guard would be down. When I came out of those trees on the night of their wedding, Royce smiled at me and bade me good eve right before he

watched his bride snatched from his arms and her throat slit." Her face split in a hideous grin. "It was the most beautiful moment of my life."

At these words, Sibyl reared, tore from Colin's arms and rushed forward.

"SHE WILL NOT stop."

Royce was holding Beatrice back as the venom poured out of Mistress Manning's mouth.

His new bride was furious, he could feel it emanating from her body.

Contrarily, regardless of her bloody-minded temper, Beatrice was the most gentle of creatures, had a heart so full of love, he worried it would burst. It definitely got her in a serious number of even more serious muddles.

But now, he knew, she could commit murder.

"She will not stop," Esmeralda repeated. "She will hunt you for eternity. She will haunt your line. She will never stop."

Royce thought of Sibyl, the woman from another time and just as he did, Esmeralda continued.

"You were supposed to die this night. There is powerful magic in the air. I don't know how it happened but you have been saved. Someone, somewhere, saved you both. You may live a peaceful life but this woman will be avenged. It might not be you and Miss Beatrice but it will be someone in your line somewhere along time. She will stop at nothing. She will have her vengeance."

Royce's mind filled with the golden-haired vision of Beatrice. He heard her words about her lover named Colin, a lover that was *him* in her time. He saw her passion-filled eyes realizing belatedly that somewhere else, they were experiencing the profound beauty of the union he shared earlier with Beatrice. Her Colin had asked her to marry him that very day.

Then he remembered her beautiful smile.

And wherever she was, she was in danger.

"If you don't do it, I will," Old Lady Griffin threatened, standing amongst their group and holding her cane menacingly.

He ignored the old woman and realized Sibyl had saved his life and Beatrice's by warning him. He didn't wish to believe it but he did.

For that, Royce didn't hesitate.

He moved forward with deadly intent.

Beatrice didn't utter a single word in protest.

BEFORE SIBYL COULD arrive at Mrs. Manning, the vengeful old woman threw back her head in surprise and pain, let out a shrill scream.

And suddenly she simply just disappeared.

Chapter THIRTY-ONE

Safe

"What is that *smell*?" Rick asked, sniffing the air with a comical expression of distaste on his face.

In his line of work, he'd seen a lot of crazy things.

This, of course, took the cake. He'd never seen anything quite like *this*. However, he long since learned not to ask questions. He would tuck this experience safely away and never think of it again. It was just another day at the office to him.

"Where'd she go?" Robert Fitzwilliam asked, staring at the place Mrs. Manning had been.

"She's been dispatched, nearly five hundred years ago," Marian explained to Robert even though he thought her words didn't explain anything at all, and then she turned to Rick. "And that smell is one of my personal concoctions. It made the specters, when they were in this house, incarnate, so they could be fought, so they would be vulnerable."

Sibyl was listening to all this and staring at the wall where Mrs. Manning had disappeared and as she did so she felt the anger drain out of her.

She felt like she'd just finished a marathon. She felt like laughing and crying and screaming, all at the same time. She wondered what it all meant. She wondered about Royce and Beatrice and what it meant for them.

Then she remembered Mallory and her eyes flew to Colin.

But he was already striding with purpose to the door.

She ran after him and skidded to a halt outside in the hall, her heart tearing apart at what she saw.

"Mallory," she whispered, tears clogging her throat.

Colin was already in a crouch by Mallory's head. Mrs. Griffith was on her knees behind the prone body of the dog.

Mallory was lying in a pool of his own blood.

The older woman was stroking the animal like he was still alive and whispering soothing words to him. Bran was curled up in the area between Mallory's still belly and motionless hind legs.

When Colin reached out to touch the dog, the cat agilely gained his feet and hissed. Colin's hand froze then changed directions and without fear of the hissing cat, he stroked its head. At his touch, the cat stopped hissing and then rubbed its body lovingly against Mallory's belly.

Sibyl felt the tears drop from her eyes and slide down her face as she stood frozen, watching as Colin felt the dog's chest then he turned and looked up at Sibyl.

At the queer expression on his face and the muscle leaping in his jaw, all her hope died.

She dropped to her knees beside her fiancé and burst into uncontrollable tears.

She vaguely realized that people were coming from the bedroom and others were coming down the hall. Sibyl put her shaking hands out and gently rested one on her dog's still warm flank, the other on his ribcage where his big doggie heart was no longer beating.

She bent her head and whispered to the floor, "He died trying to save us."

She barely finished the last word when she found herself moving toward Colin as he pulled her into his arms and surged to his feet. He brought her up with him and tucked her close to his warm body. She buried her face in his chest, wrapped her arms around him and gave in completely to the anguish ripping agonizingly through her heart.

There was movement and muttering around her and she lifted her head and saw Colin's throat working spasmodically. She couldn't bear the sight of him trying to control his emotion because she was in no state to soothe him.

She turned her head and pressed her cheek against his chest as she watched and listened. She did everything but look at the body of her dog. She couldn't see Mallory like that again. From now on—she swallowed against the pain the thought caused—she had to remember him as he used to be, goofy, sweet, loyal and loving.

Colin stroked her hair with one hand and held her firmly against him with his other arm.

"Let's get you up, Mrs. Griffith," Kyle said softly, his voice kind.

"I'm not leaving him," Mrs. Griffith returned fiercely.

"I've got him." Rick was walking toward the scene, carrying a sheet from some bed.

Gently, more gently than Sibyl would have imagined he was capable, he crouched and carefully tucked the sheet around the dog. He then, utilizing the utmost care, lifted the dead, awkward weight of the enormous dog and settled Mallory in his arms.

"Where are you taking him?" Sibyl asked as she tried to break free from Colin but both his arms tightened around her.

"Don't worry." Rick smiled at his charge for the first time of their acquaintance. It was not a happy smile, it was a sad, trust-me smile. "I'll take care of him, I promise."

At his smile, Sibyl let her weight sag against Colin and he took it on without sound or movement. Then she nodded at her bodyguard.

Rick walked down the hall, carrying his burden.

New tears sprang to Sibyl's eyes and clogged her throat.

"Colin, get her to the library. Get her a relaxing drink, you both could use one." Phoebe was next to her son, her thoughtful eyes on Sibyl.

Colin did as his mother told him, pausing only to scoop up the cat, which he handed to Sibyl and she tucked the feline protectively in her arms. For the first time, Bran seemed quite content to be where he was.

Colin guided her down to the library and Sibyl heard behind her . . .

"I'll get this cleaned up." That was Mags.

"I'll help." That was Jemma.

"No, my dear, you get the kids home. We'll take care of this." That was Phoebe.

She stopped listening when Colin turned her toward the stairs and they went to the library. All the while, Sibyl realized absently, unable to process it completely, that she was very lucky to have such wonderful people in her life.

Colin took her to the couch and pushed her gently into it. She didn't resist. She'd started her journey on this couch, it seemed fitting to sit there now. The minute she sat, Bran settled in a curl on her lap.

She heard noises coming from other areas of the house. Their friends and family were all trying to be quiet but their tasks of tidying up and leaving and cleaning a pool of dog blood would not allow them to shield their noise from Colin and Sibyl.

Listening to the noise, Sibyl's face was frozen in a constant wince.

Colin took one look at her and walked to the door to close it but the unknown man filled its frame.

"The police are here," he told Colin, glanced at Sibyl, tried (and failed) to smile at her reassuringly and then looked back at Colin.

"I pressed the panic button," Colin told him then sighed. "Can you deal with them?" His hand went to his hair and he pulled his fingers through it in a frustrated gesture.

"Of course," the man assured then left and Colin closed the door behind him.

"Who is that man?" Sibyl asked as Colin walked to the drinks cabinet.

"A security specialist and an investigator, he and his team have been watching over you for weeks. They've also been trying to discover who was behind all this."

Sibyl nodded, allowing the pleasant thought that Colin had hired a team to protect her to penetrate the numbness that had enveloped her.

He poured two drinks and brought them both to the couch. He

handed her one and she automatically took it. He settled down beside her, stretching his long legs in front of him, crossing them at the ankles and wrapping his arm around her shoulder before he pulled her into him and she rested her head in the curve of his neck.

"What's this?" she asked, lifting the tumbler filled with a fluid that matched his eyes.

"Whisky. Drink it," he ordered.

She sighed. "You are *so* bossy," she told him, her voice weary but filled with affection.

As an answer, his hand went to her hair and lifted its heavy weight.

She sipped her drink and felt the pleasant warmth slide down her throat and into her belly.

"Are we safe now?" she whispered.

"Yes," he answered so definitively she believed him and she finally felt the tenseness flow from her body. "Until you get us into another disaster by taking Parliament to task for their defense spending and becoming public enemy number one," he noted in a mock-beleaguered tone.

Despite all that had happened, she felt a giggle rise up her throat and let it loose as she looked up at his handsome face.

"I love you," she told him, her voice strong with emotion, tears coming back to her eyes.

He looked down on her and his face shifted.

She would understand that shift when he vowed in a low, even, fierce tone, "After tonight, I swear to God, you're never going to have a reason to cry or be frightened again."

"I'll take it from that comment that you love me back." She grinned shakily at him.

He bent his head and brushed his lips against hers.

"Yes, darling, I love you back," he said softly against her mouth.

This feeling shined in his eyes and he looked at her as if she was the sun and the moon, as if the world revolved around her, as if she was his entire universe.

She settled against him again, far more contentedly, and they sat there for some time before she whispered so quietly, her words barely made a noise, "Mallory was a good dog."

"Mallory was a walking, barking calamity," Colin returned but the fondness in his tone caused Sibyl no distress. "There will never be another Mallory," he finished gently.

She nodded her head against his shoulder in agreement and infinite sadness.

There came a soft knock on the door and Colin called his permission for entry.

Mags, Marian and Phoebe walked in, their faces carrying identical expressions of concern.

Marian was also carrying a book.

"It's all sorted, darling," Phoebe murmured, her eyes avoiding Sibyl's and looking directly at Colin.

She felt rather than saw him lift his chin to acknowledge his mother's words.

"Everyone's away. They all say their goodbyes and they'll talk to you later, Sibyl," Marian informed her.

Sibyl smiled weakly at her friend.

Mags came to her daughter and sat heavily down beside her, making both Colin and Sibyl's bodies lift momentarily.

"What a night," she noted in an understatement, her body sliding sideways, leaning against Sibyl with her head on her daughter's shoulder.

"You okay, Mom?" Sibyl asked, handing her glass with a grateful look to Phoebe as she put her arm around Mags just as Colin had his arm around her.

"If you're okay, I'm okay," Mags replied then went on, "I don't think I'm going to tell Bertie about this though. He'll have a coronary."

"Good idea," Phoebe agreed. "I'm not telling Mike either, or Claire and Tony for that matter. Tony wouldn't begin to believe me but Claire will be furious she missed it." She walked to the drinks cabinet, asking for the other women's orders.

They all settled into chairs, Mags coming upright as Phoebe gave her a drink. Colin handed Sibyl his and ordered her to finish it. Not having enough strength to defy him, she did as she was told.

Sibyl sat with her family and friend, stroked her cat and sipped her whisky. They all seemed content to be together but alone with their thoughts.

After a while, Colin broke the silence and called, "Marian."

The older woman started. "Yes, Colin, dear?"

Sibyl peered up at his gorgeous face, wondering at his thoughts and saw his jaw clench and that familiar muscle dance there.

Then he inquired, "What happened tonight?"

Sibyl wanted to smile but she bit it back. He didn't want to ask, he didn't want to know. But he clearly couldn't stop himself.

Marian watched them both carefully before taking a sip from her gin.

Finally, she spoke.

"I don't exactly know." She put her drink down on a table beside her and opened the book, sifting through the pages. "I think . . ." she started to say and then stopped, finding her place. She scanned, her eyes racing left to right then back again, over and over. Finally, a smile tugged at her lips. "It appears that the legend has changed somewhat."

"How's that?" Mags asked, her body coming to attention.

Sibyl lifted her head and stared.

"Well . . ." Marian continued to read while she spoke, "Apparently, there was a vicious plot to kill the mighty warrior, Royce Morgan, and his new bride Beatrice on their wedding night. A plot conceived by a trusted member of the household. This, Royce foiled because, well . . . he was a mighty warrior." Her eyes lifted and she looked at Colin then back down to her book.

Sibyl gasped before she asked, "They didn't die?"

Marian shook her head.

At the news, a burst of energy flowed throw Sibyl. She surged off the couch and Bran flew from her lap with an angry mew.

Sibyl, unable to contain her delight, did a happy jig and sang, "Hallelujah!"

Everyone, including Colin, watched her with a grin on their face.

Sibyl stopped just as abruptly and turned back to Marian. "What happened?"

Marian looked down at the book.

"Let me see. Well, this writer is far more into history, the facts, as it were. It says Royce foiled the plot as he was a seasoned warrior and could easily fend off his five attackers. The author does hint that there was a great deal of talk that lasted through the centuries about magic and . . ." she narrowed her eyes on some words, "it says here, some old woman from the village, a friend of both the Morgans and Godwins, was riding home from their wedding feast, came upon the struggle and dashed in, dispatching one of the villains with her cane."

A burst of laughter erupted from Sibyl before she cried with glee, "What?"

"That's what it says here," Marian tapped the book, her lips forming a smile.

"How delightful," Phoebe murmured.

"Well, I'll be," Mags muttered.

Colin leaned forward apparently not ready to have Sibyl out of touching distance for more than a few moments. He pulled her down to the couch and settled her into his side again.

"I wonder if Japan has fallen into the sea," Sibyl whispered under her breath.

Marian shook her head. "I don't think so." And then she smiled and stared intently at Sibyl. "The book says more, my dear."

"What does it say?" Mags leaned forward eagerly.

Marian closed the book and continued to watch Sibyl. "There is more to this new legend. Apparently, a witch from another time watched over the doomed pair, coming to Royce before the terrible event happened, informing him of the plot and helping him to thwart the evil plan."

Colin's body stiffened and Sibyl immediately thought, *uh-oh*.

"What?" Colin uttered that one word in a low and even voice.

"I think, and I'll have to check the Book of Shadows because I'm sure Esmeralda will tell me more, but I think that Sibyl was destined to save Royce and Beatrice and this is why history has shifted without calamity for what was actually meant to be has now happened. They simply had to wait for her to be born so she could go back to Royce and warn him. Then they could live their lives together. Which, by the way, they both lived to be a ripe old age and Royce sired four children by his Beatrice."

Colin, clearly not listening to these additional words, patiently repeated himself, "What?"

Sibyl felt the stirring of unease.

Marian turned her eyes to Colin. "What I mean to say is, they weren't actually supposed to die but they had to wait for Sibyl to be born, for you two to meet and your love to bloom, so she could save them. I don't think Japan has fallen into the ocean because *that* was not the way it was supposed to be. *This* is!" she finished triumphantly.

Colin was not getting the answers he desired.

"I understand that but what I'd like to know, Marian, is more about the part where Sibyl goes to Royce to warn him. When did that happen?"

Sibyl tensed and Colin's arm around her tightened significantly, pinning her in place by his side.

"The book doesn't spend much time on specifics of the legend, just facts as they were known. The Book of Shadows will tell me more but the legend does say, rather romantically, the witch from another time came to Royce, inhabiting Beatrice's body directly after Beatrice and Royce consummated their marriage."

Colin's arm became a steel band.

"Oh my," Mags uttered, her voice filled with humor.

Sibyl shot off the couch and whirled and looked down at Colin. The muscle in his jaw was back to jumping spasmodically.

"Colin," she said soothingly.

He slowly rose.

"Did you go back to him?" he growled.

She took a step back.

Colin took a step forward.

Then she admitted, "Kind of."

He took another step forward.

She took another step back.

"Exactly what do you mean by 'kind of?'"

His voice was more than a little peeved.

She tried to smile at him.

He ignored her smile and took another step forward.

"When did this happen? Did it happen tonight? Did it happen after we'd—?"

She took another step back.

"Um . . . kind of." She drew out the words as long as she could.

His eyes flashed.

He took another step forward.

She turned and ran from the room, thinking this was her best course of action.

Colin strode quickly from the room, following Sibyl and muttering distractedly to the assemblage, "If you'll excuse us."

"Not at all," Phoebe told the space where his tall departing frame was only moments before.

The three women who were left in the room looked at each other and then they burst out laughing.

Colin came back into the room and their laughter died.

He strode to Marian's chair and looked down at her.

She looked up.

And quietly he told her, "You should know, that thing had its blade at her throat, it glanced off, didn't even come near it."

Marian's mouth parted in surprise.

Even *she* didn't know she was that good.

"Thank you," Colin went on softly, his eyes on the woman warm and shining with gratitude.

And without another word, he strode back out of the room.

"You're welcome," Marian whispered to the space where his body was only moments before.

ROYCE MORGAN DESCENDED the stairs in the dead of night, leaving Beatrice exhausted and sleeping peacefully in their bed.

As he moved down the steps, he saw Esmeralda Crane stood in one of the semi-circular windows, staring thoughtfully out into the night.

Instead of her making the trip back to her cottage in the dark after the events of that eve, Beatrice had insisted the witch stay at Lacybourne with them. Also at Beatrice's stubborn demand, Old Lady Griffin was there, Royce had heard her loud snores as he'd walked by her chamber moments before.

He quietly strode across the Great Hall and stopped to stand beside the witch, looking out into the dark night and joining her for a moment in her silent reverie.

After some time, he spoke.

"Is she safe?" he asked softly, his deep voice rumbling low.

Esmeralda knew exactly to whom he was referring.

"Yes, I believe she is."

She was watching him and she could swear to the goddess that she could actually see the tension leave his powerful frame.

"And her betrothed?" he inquired.

"Yes," she answered quietly.

Royce Morgan nodded.

Then he turned and walked back across the room with wide, ground-eating strides and ascended the stairs, two at a time, to rejoin his bride.

It was then Esmeralda Crane turned back to regard the night.

When she did she allowed herself to smile.

EPILOGUE

Mallory had been caught by a sunbeam, of which there were a great deal in doggie heaven.

Being thus, he immediately deposited his big body on a soft bed of grass and took a snooze.

This was rather irritatingly interrupted by a Chihuahua.

"The Big Dog wants to see you."

Mallory lumbered up and headed to the enormous tree where the Big Dog liked to hang out. Although he much preferred to stick with his nap, one didn't really keep the Big Dog waiting.

"Mallory," the Big Dog woofed when Mallory arrived.

"Big Dog," Mallory woofed back.

"It appears you're going back down."

Mallory groaned and slid into a lying position.

He hadn't been in doggie heaven very long.

The Big Dog continued, "As you died valiantly, you get to pick what you want to go back as. You could even return as a human."

Mallory lifted his head at this news.

Any animal that was given this choice went back as a human (just to see what it was like). They also chose tiger (not enough food, Mallory thought, or sometimes they made you do silly tricks at circuses), lion (still not enough food and you had to run to catch it and it was usually too hot where you lived or you were caged), a wolf (people were scared of wolves and Mallory liked people) or a horse (Mallory had been there and done that, although he'd done it well, *very* well, it was a lot of lugging his big warrior around and then there was the blood on those battlefields).

Mallory shivered at the memory.

"I'll pick dog again," he told the Big Dog and vowed to himself not to do anything brave and fearless this time.

He missed his mistress, she was very nice and she always found the right spots to scratch behind his ears. And Mallory also missed his new master, he liked him a lot. He would have liked to have lived a few more years with them.

"As you wish," the Big Dog stated.

Then instantly, Mallory was reborn, the last (of course, always lagging behind) of a litter of Newfoundland pups.

Mallory thought it was fun being a puppy but somewhat exhausting.

Then, one day, six weeks later, he was lying contentedly in another sunbeam when he heard the woman who watched over them say, "They're over here."

His brothers and sisters all exuberantly ran to whoever it was that had entered the room.

Mallory lifted his head to have a lazy look at what was transpiring.

Then he saw his tall, strong, dark-haired master.

He jumped to his big, puppy feet and ran to the man who was now crouching low over the litter of puppies, examining them closely.

Mallory pushed his brothers and sisters aside, surged toward his master's hand and gave it a sloppy lick.

Colin's gaze immediately shifted to Mallory.

"I'll take this one," he stated.

"Are you sure? He was the last one out. He's a bit of the runt."

Colin chuckled as his big hand closed around Mallory and lifted him into his arms.

"That figures," he mumbled.

Mallory was beside himself with glee.

The pretty dark-haired lady that came with his master held Mallory while Colin drove them back home to Lacybourne.

Then he was put in a room for several hours. He was happy there. The room had food, water, treats, and kids and people came in every once in a while to coo over him, play with him or take him outside.

And, of course, the sun was shining brightly and there were some mighty sunbeams.

Eventually he had several hours to himself. He used them wisely and took a long puppy nap.

Suddenly the door opened and the dark-haired woman walked in with a red-haired one. He knew both of them and he ran to them and gave them as many puppy kisses as they'd allow, which Mallory thought with delight was a lot even though they were both all dressed up in pretty frocks.

They tied a silly pink and cream ribbon around his neck but he didn't mind as it was rather fun to try and reach it so he could chew through it.

"Take off that ridiculous ribbon," Colin ordered upon entering the room.

"But Colin, he's a gift!" the dark-haired lady said.

"Claire, take off the ribbon," Colin repeated.

"The ribbon has to stay, Sibyl will *love* it," the red-haired woman declared.

Mallory could swear he heard his master growl.

Then Mallory jumped from the redhead's arms and into Colin's. His tail was wagging and his body was wriggling and he tried to reach his master's face to give it a big, wet kiss.

Colin deftly avoided his tongue as he followed the two women out of the room, into the hall and toward the stairs.

He was still trying to lick his master's face when he heard the loving, familiar laugh.

Mallory froze, looked across the Great Hall, his floppy ears flying, and saw her standing under the two big portraits.

There were tons of people milling all over the place, drinking golden liquid from fragile glasses and eating food (some of which, Mallory fervently hoped, would drop to the floor). They were talking, laughing, joking, smiling and having the times of their lives.

Most of them Mallory knew, some of them he didn't.

But Mallory didn't care.

He only had eyes for one of them and he had to get to his mistress *now*.

Everyone was slowly stopping their chatter and turning to look as Mallory and Colin descended the stairs. And then *she* looked and she saw and Mallory was delighted as her face, already glowing, brightened to magnificent.

She looked so pretty in that cream dress with the pink flowers in her long, golden hair.

And she looked so happy, happier than he'd ever seen her, and she was normally quite happy.

When they reached the bottom of the stairs, she swept forward and the crowd parted as she ran toward them.

And for the second time in his life, Colin Morgan was upstaged by a dog.

"Oh my goddess!" she breathed, snatching the puppy out of Colin's hands.

She brought Mallory straight up to her face and she looked beyond him at Colin with love shining in her eyes.

"Oh, Colin, thank you!" she cried gleefully.

She didn't care if he licked her, she never did, so Mallory gave her a big, sloppy kiss right up the side of her face.

Her body stilled before she pushed Mallory away from her and held his squirming puppy body up to her radiant face, looking directly into his eyes.

Hers were startled.

Colin's arm came around her and he kissed the top of her head.

Her eyes melted from hazel to sherry as she brought Mallory forward and tucked him lovingly under her chin then she wrapped her arms fiercely around his puppy body.

She lifted her head and kissed her husband on the mouth before she whispered, "Oh, Colin . . . *thank you.*"

He muttered, "You're welcome," and then *he* kissed *her* (this one took a bit longer).

When the kiss was done she dropped her chin and looked at Mallory again.

And she said, in a voice only Colin and Mallory could hear.

"Welcome home, my darling Mallory."

THE END

The next tale in the Ghosts and Reincarnation Series, Penmort Castle, is available now.

Author's Note

LACYBOURNE MANOR, COLIN and Sibyl's home in the book, is loosely based on Clevedon Court, a property owned by the Elton Family who open and manage it for The National Trust. Clevedon Court, located in Clevedon, North Somerset, UK is a beautiful home with a core that has survived from medieval times.

The National Trust is a UK charity dedicated to conserving and opening to visitors historic houses, gardens and large parts of the countryside and coastline.

I highly recommend, if you live in the UK or are just visiting, that you plan a trip to Clevedon Court or the many National Trust properties open to the public: *www.nationaltrust.org.uk*.

Connect with KRISTEN Online:

Official Website: *www.kristeashley.net*

Kristen's Facebook Page: *www.facebook.com/kristenashleybooks*

Follow Kristen on Twitter: @KristenAshley68

Discover Kristen's Pins on Pinterest: *www.pinterest.com/kashley0155*

Follow Kristen on Instagram: KristenAshleyBooks

Need support for your Kit Crack Addiction?

Join the *Kristen Ashley Addict's Support Group on Goodreads*

59410585R00300

Made in the USA
Lexington, KY
04 January 2017